WINTER SUN

WARRIORS OF THE FIVE REALMS

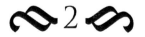

2

HOLLEE MANDS

WINTER SUN

Warriors of the Five Realms

HOLLEE MANDS

Winter Sun

Copyright © 2021 by Hollee Mands.

Editing and proofreading by Kelley Luna

Proofreading by Spell Bound

Cover design by Covers by Christian

To Denali Day, who lit the path for me

CONTENTS

A CAUTIONARY TALE FROM THE
BARD'S COMPENDIUM

Once, long ago, a goddess bled her wrist into a well,
Her powers overflowed, soaking the ground in a spell,
Of all who brave her Heart,
None can ever depart,
Either to be torn asunder or made anew,
Power in blood, and might in sinew,
A mage will die, an archmage to take his place,
Such is the rule of Railea's grace.

PROLOGUE

"They're so beautiful, Mama!" Freya buried her nose in the petals of a white bloom.

Ildara smiled at the glee in her daughter's voice and willed more seedlings to spring from the soil. "Now you try, darling."

Freya shut her eyes eagerly and laid her palms flat over the grass. Magic rippled the air like a soft, murmuring breeze as Freya channeled her innocent powers into the ground, coaxing life from the seeds of Ozenn's energy buried deep in the earth.

"Grow," Freya whispered, and the ground obeyed. Life blossomed, tiny blooms unfurling velvety faces to smile at the sun.

Ildara beamed. Pride surged in her chest. Unlike Ildara's singular rose bush, Freya's creation covered an entire swatch of ground. "Well done, sweeting."

Freya's shoulders sagged in time with her downturned lips. "But I was trying to grow roses . . . to match yours."

"These reflect who you are, my little one, and they are perfect."

It was truth. The ground was freckled with a rainbow of

wildflowers—tiny white freesia, pink poppies, yellow canola, and delicate daisies.

"But Felicity can grow roses, just like you—"

Bells tolled in the distance, deep and ominous.

Freya glanced up with a frown, and Ildara's chest constricted. The bell tower only rang when there was death in the estate.

Or an attack.

Vidar had told them to stay here. Her husband had argued that Freya would be safe within Jilintree Castle. Freya didn't understand it yet, but she could be in danger even from her allies—the magic she'd inherited from Vidar was all too tempting for even loving relatives to exploit. The next Jilintree. Seeliekind's most formidable weapon.

Footsteps pounded the courtyard, her guardsmen stirred by the bells. Indiscernible shouts rose into a clamor.

"Come, Freya." Ildara had gathered her skirts, intending to seek out the source of the matter, when her handmaiden rushed to her side.

"Princess Ildara, Princess . . . ," the rotund maid sputtered with eyes wide and face flushed.

"Kilminnie, what happened? Why are the bells ringing?"

Boom! A shudder quaked the ground.

"We are surrounded by soldiers! Some are attempting to scale our outer walls with grappling hooks."

Ildara didn't wait for the maid to continue. She hauled Freya up into her arms and raced into the bailey, searching for her head guard.

Kilminnie hurried alongside, panting as she strove to keep up with Ildara's rapid pace. "Guards say they appeared out of nowhere, Princess." A shallow inhale. "They must have come through portals."

Ildara had barely reached the threshold of the bailey when

another boom shook the earth, dusting the air with a cloud of debris. Freya coughed, and her little arms curled around Ildara's shoulders, tightening with fright.

"Ballista!" yelled one of her guardsmen from the ramparts. "They have a ballista!"

Stunned, Ildara backed away from the castle walls. The enemy was firing projectiles with a catapult. How could Unseelie portals transport such a large siege weapon?

This was no paltry attack.

It was a planned invasion.

"Fire!" someone shouted.

Her guardsmen, though caught unaware, now surged up the battlements and the defense towers, rapidly firing crossbows from the arrow slits. Lightcasters filed in, fortifying the wards that kept out enemy magic.

If the wards fell, it didn't matter if the walls stood.

"Quentin!" Ildara spotted one of her most trusted lieutenants amid the commotion.

"Princess Ildara! Lady Freya!" Relief colored Quentin's wholesome features. "This way! Quickly! Captain Herryion is in the battle room, but he will take you and Lady Freya off the premises immediately."

With her husband away, the captain was the only Seelie with enough strength to cast portals.

"I can't leave while the castle is under siege," Ildara said. But the sickening sound of metal violently penetrating flesh and bone stymied her protest. A gurgling scream.

Freya's shriek punctuated Ildara's own horror.

She shifted so Freya, still clutched against her chest, faced away from the sight. But she knew the image of the lightcaster nailed to the wall by a spear-sized arrow was already etched into her daughter's memory.

Another loud boom echoed, scattering a hail of gravel into

the wind. A tremor shook the ground, and another scream rent the air. A projectile the length of a polearm struck another lightcaster in the face, rendering the man's head a pulpy mass.

"Princess!" Quentin bellowed. "You must leave!"

Ildara did not argue again. Wrapping her arms tighter around Freya's trembling form, she broke into a sprint toward the battle room.

Magic crackled in the air, laced with the tang of darkness. Unseelie.

Fear spiked her pulse.

The wards were breached.

A dark portal unfurled nearby, emitting a surge of horse-back riders who whooped war cries and screamed for submission.

"Surrender, and we will spare your life!"

Caught in the frenzy, Quentin fired bolts of light. They sizzled as they clashed against Unseelie darkfire. He unsheathed his sword as the riders closed in. His blade glinted as he sought to dismount the enemy through magic and steel. It was a near-futile effort as Unseelie riders kept swarming through the portal while most of Ildara's guards were on the ramparts defending the walls.

A rider galloped in her direction.

"Run, Princess!" Kilminnie darted forward, buying Ildara precious seconds. Kilminnie, her faithful servant for over two centuries, barely released a scream when the rider slashed her throat. Her blood fell in a dark smatter on the ground.

In a scream of outrage, Ildara earthed her magic.

Prickly vines, thick and dense, erupted from the ground to surround her and Freya in a moat of thorns. The horse whin-nied and reared, throwing off its rider.

"Seelie *rutta*!" He snarled. Seelie *whore*.

Darkfire burst through the thorns, a torrent of shadow and

death. Instinctively, Ildara spun, using her body like a shield to cover her daughter.

"Mama!" Freya's cry was followed by the unmistakable pulse of Jilintree magic, nullifying the darkfire that would have otherwise seared Ildara's skin. But Freya was only a child. One who had yet to fully master her abilities.

The thorny vines Ildara had summoned shrank and receded into the earth. Freya had inadvertently suppressed *all* magic in the vicinity. Including Quentin's lightbolts.

"Freya, stop!" Ildara shouted.

Freya shuddered in her arms, and the magic halted. The Unseelie soldier staggered, seemingly confounded by the sudden loss of his powers.

"*Mordida sipa!*" cursed an authoritative voice. Captain Herryion fought his way through the mania, slashing his sword and firing lightbolts. "Princess Ildara, this way!"

The captain summoned a portal, pale light coalescing into an oval doorway.

"Go, Princess! Go!"

Ildara leapt into the shimmering portal with Freya still bundled in her arms, but the Unseelie soldier lunged, too—and managed to fist a hand into Ildara's hair.

Freya screamed again.

"No, Freya!" Ildara cried.

Another pulse of nullifying magic burst from her daughter's tiny form. Herryion's portal dissolved and imploded before it was complete.

When the light faded, Ildara collapsed to the ground with Freya trembling against her. She glanced around frantically. Trees. They were in a forest, the sky covered by thick yews and pines . . . and the man who came through the fractured portal with them was *not* Herryion.

Ildara dragged Freya to her feet and dashed through the

trees. They fled through a twisting pathway of underbrush and pine needles until Ildara heard nothing but her own pounding footsteps and Freya's scampering ones.

She slowed to a stop beneath a heavy oak.

"Never," she stuttered through gasps of breath. "*Never* use your magic in fear, Freya."

Freya nodded as her little chest breathed hard.

"Promise me," Ildara demanded. They were lucky to be unscathed despite the splintered portal. She shuddered to think of what *could* have occurred.

"I'm sorry, Mama," Freya whimpered with round eyes. "I promise."

Ildara let out a shuddering sigh and drew Freya into a fierce hug.

A snap of a nearby branch alerted Ildara that they were still in danger.

The Unseelie stepped into view, a sneer on his lips. "Did you think you could escape me that easily?"

Left with nothing but the farce of intimidation, Ildara lifted her own lips in a snarl, allowing her canines to punch through her gums.

"Fool! I am Princess Ildara of the Summer Court, wife of General Vidar Jilintree. Touch me or my daughter, and you will incite a war."

The Unseelie only laughed. "Stupid woman, the war has already begun." He pointed at Freya, who cowered behind her skirts. "*She* is what we want. Give her to me, and I will spare your life."

Despite her thundering heart, a wave of calm flooded through her.

"Enhance my magic, Freya," Ildara murmured, praying to Ozenn that she could do what needed to be done.

"So be it," said the Unseelie. Darkfire erupted in the palm of his hand.

Freya's magic surged again, amplifying Ildara's own with a rush that made her feel stronger than she'd ever been. Instead of attacking, Ildara cast a portal and shoved her daughter into it.

"Stay in the portal!" she commanded.

A jolt slammed into her, pain searing her senses as darkfire scorched through her dress to lap at her skin.

Freya's shouts muted her cry of pain. "Mama!"

Her knees buckled.

Not yet.

A few more seconds to complete the portal and ensure Freya's safety. Ildara threw herself against the Unseelie, fingers clawed, fangs reared.

He batted her off easily, slamming her to the ground. Ildara slumped, and relief curved her lips as she saw her portal enclose her daughter fully and fade away. Freya's agonized screams echoed through the forest.

Safe. The thought was a balm to her languishing consciousness. *Freya was safe.*

"*Rutta!*" The Unseelie rounded on her, fists clenched.

She didn't even feel pain when fangs sank into her throat.

ONE

LEAVE IF YOU VALUE YOUR LIFE.
AN ARCHMAGE HAS NO NEED FOR FAE WHORES.

E vangeline stared at the note. Disbelief dried her mouth. The handwriting was the same bold script, printed on the same stock of pristine parchment.

Her hands trembled. This was the third of its kind she'd received. She clenched her fist, crumpling the parchment. Her anger rose at the thought of the perpetrator sneaking into the bedroom, rummaging through her things to leave the note where *she* would find it.

"What is it, little fire?" Her archmage emerged from the bath chamber wearing nothing but loose breeches that rode tantalizingly low on his hips. Dark brows slashed together as he ran a towel through short strands of raven-black hair.

Evangeline hastily stuffed the crumpled note into her pocket. "Nothing." She forced a smile. "Just a letter from my mother. She misses me." That wasn't a complete lie. Agnes *had* written, seeking her company.

His scrutiny lifted, and his brows smoothened. "Shall I send Killian to warp her to the castle?"

"You know she doesn't like leaving Arns." Evangeline brushed a hand through her hair and swallowed the bitter taste of deception. "I should return for a visit."

"Then I will go with you."

The firmness in his tone pursed her lips. Half a year had passed since the battle with Zephyr, yet Declan remained adamant in keeping her within his sights whenever she ventured from the castle, which wasn't often at all. She didn't enjoy distance from him either.

Yet there were times a girl simply craved her mother's company.

Evangeline folded her arms, only to sigh when their gazes met.

The uncertainty in the depths of his brilliant green eyes was so at odds with his dictatorial response that it snuffed out her vexation.

With the rest of the world, her archmage remained a master at hiding his emotions behind a wall of impassivity. He was equally proficient in wearing authority like a crown. But with her, he allowed his vulnerabilities to surface—even if only through his gaze.

"I love your company," she said. "But this time, I would prefer to visit Mother on my own." She added a smile that usually brought softness to his eyes.

It didn't work this time.

"You are not to leave the castle unprotected, little fire." His words were flat and his tone resolute.

A huff escaped her lips. She padded across the carpet, went to the tips of her toes, and curled her hand around the nape of his neck to haul him down for a kiss. A thrill ran through her as he obliged readily, and the stern set of his mouth softened as he met her lips. His towel dropped to her feet as his arms coiled around her, holding her close as though she were liable to run from him.

She licked into his lips with a hum and caroused in his mouth with her tongue as her fingers ran down the hard planes of his ridged abdomen. Even after all these months together, she still could hardly believe he was hers, this perfectly sculpted man who radiated a godlike beauty.

His scent alone caused heat to bloom between her legs. Musky and male, tinged with spice and the barest hint of cedar soap, he smelled of deepest comfort. And carnal sin. Evangeline melted into the kiss, and for that one blissful moment she almost forgot the note in her pocket.

When she finally pulled back, she panted in silence and stroked the crown of his head, toying with the damp strands as she stared into his intense jewel-green gaze.

You should not seek to leave the castle. His psychic voice flowed into her mind like a river of ice ablaze with silken fire. *Not with Zephyr's whereabouts still unknown.*

Evangeline narrowed her eyes and planted another kiss on his lips. Encased in her arms and given enough time—and kisses—Declan often spoke his true mind.

He sighed. *Every time you leave my side, I worry. Let me come with you, little fire . . . please?*

There he was. The boy who had once sat beside her at the pond had not gone. He was simply buried deep.

She smiled and administered another kiss to loosen the knot between his brows. "Your mating bond has strengthened my ability to project my thoughts at a distance. I can reach you easily from Arns."

The slope of his jaw tensed. Then he resumed their mouth play, his tongue delving deep, drawing a mewl from her throat before he telepathed, *All right. But I will have Killian scope out the village before your arrival and have men stationed around your mother's home.*

Evangeline groaned into the kiss, but she projected her acquiescence. It was about as much of a concession as she would get. At least her archmage hadn't proposed to station his men *inside* her mother's cottage.

He frowned, lips still slick from hers. "What else worries you, little fire? Are you unwell again?"

He wasn't reading her mind. He had long ago promised not to, yet he remained uncannily sensitive to her emotions. Perhaps it was their half-formed mating bond. Or perhaps he was worried. Railea knew she'd given him sufficient cause.

Since her phenomenal recovery from the otherwise fatal injuries Zephyr had caused, Evangeline had been plagued by seemingly innocuous . . . *afflictions.* Headaches. Dizziness. Lethargy. Over time, the afflictions grew more aberrant, showcasing her fae traits: sudden bursts of Seelie magic that caused the flora within her vicinity to either wilt or grow abruptly. Sometimes the rim of violet around her irises thickened until it threatened to swallow the amber in her eyes; sometimes her ears lengthened and sharpened of their own accord.

Evangeline shook her head and avoided Declan's penetrating gaze. "I'm just . . . restless, that's all." That wasn't a complete lie either. She looked up and wrapped her arms around him to splay her fingers over his sinewy back muscles.

"It's been days . . ." She pressed herself against him.

His eyes darkened, and his hands worked through her hair, ruining the updo Tessa had so meticulously crafted that morning. He trailed kisses down her neck toward a spot that had become one of his favorites—the modest swell of her breast now etched with the starburst pattern of his mating mark. As he nuzzled her, grazing the golden lines with his lips and teeth, a deep rumble escaped his throat, akin to a panther's purr.

Evangeline shut her eyes with a sigh. A delicious shiver ran down her spine to curl her toes. "Declan," she whispered into his ear. "I want you."

He ground against her belly in an almost absent fashion. He was *hard*, yet the distance he kept between them made his resistance obvious. Denying himself even though he was ramrod stiff.

Paradoxical.

Her archmage had always teetered on the edge of extremes. Wild but gentle. Indomitable yet vulnerable. Fire and ice. That was who he was, and she loved him with such ferocity it threatened to subsume her.

Slowly, she scrubbed her knuckles down the soft, short bristles at the back of his head, skimmed her fingers along the span of his shoulders, and trailed down the satiny plane of his back. Then she cupped the spectacular curve of his bottom, and with another hand, cupped him from the front.

He sprang away from her, as though her hands were hot brands and he unsuspecting cattle flesh.

"Evangeline," he protested. "Don't do that. You know how insatiable that makes me."

She lifted a sultry brow. "That was *clearly* my intention." His need was as palpable as the hard length of him. Perhaps with a little more encouragement . . .

She locked her arms around him and backed him into the wall. He gave her a look that was a frustrating, contradictory blend of need and denial.

"I want you, Archmage. I want us together."

He let out a low moan, then licked his lips.

In a smooth motion, he flipped their positions, pinning her to the wall. He lifted her high, and with a small burst of telekinesis, she found her knees hooked over his shoulders, her legs spread and aligned for his face. The mechanics that would have hampered normal men had never stopped him—an arch-mage who wielded his mind like a second set of hands.

Her skirt slid up her thighs as though of its own accord to reveal her undergarments, which were quickly ripped at the seams. He was about to burrow his face into the heat of her core when she barred him with a hand over his lips.

His gaze, lit by a wicked glint, slid up to meet hers. She glared at him. Undaunted, he licked her palm, slow and sensu-ous, leisurely wrenching a gasp from her lips. More heat slicked between her legs.

"No," she said, trying to keep her voice even. "Not unless you'll allow me to pleasure you in return."

The glint in his eyes took on a playful edge. "Your pleasure *is* mine, little fire."

Frustration almost had her bucking her hips, but she was determined to draw the line. "I will give you the same pleasure. I want to give you release."

The playfulness in his eyes dimmed.

"Not when *my* release sends you into unconsciousness."

"Hogwash." She pursed her lips. "That has nothing to do with it. You know it can happen anytime, anywhere."

Her *afflictions* had recently included fainting spells. And they presented in the most embarrassing and public moments. She'd collapsed in hallways, during work, and in the middle of conversations. Just last week, she'd been traversing a stairwell with Alexander and several other councilors when her body had decided to shut down. If it hadn't been for Lex's dexterity, she'd have hurtled headlong down the narrow stairwell and probably ended up with a few broken bones.

But the most mortifying time had been during her first attempt to complete the mating bond with her archmage. Granted, Declan had been particularly vigorous, but he hadn't been overtly rough. No matter how aroused he became, he was always careful with her, yet she'd literally swooned in the throes of passion—only to wake in the infirmary under the bemused scrutiny of Mailin and several nurses.

Declan hadn't touched her in any remotely sexual way for two full weeks after that. Then they'd tried again. And she fainted. Again. Since then, he'd refused to join their bodies until it became more than he could bear—doling out his own releases like starvation rations.

It made her want to snarl and hiss, except her vocal cords remained human, and she couldn't quite achieve the tenor she intended.

"It almost *always* happens after I take my own pleasure." He firmed his jaw, and when their gazes locked, she didn't see the eyes of a man who loved her. They were of a man who ruled supreme, and one who had just run out of concessions.

"I will not risk it again, not until we find a way to circumvent your fainting spells."

She flattened her lips. "Then let me down."

A muscle in his jaw ticced, and she swore she almost saw him pout. "You are mine." His hands tightened around her hips possessively. "Mine to taste. Mine to pleasure." He gazed up at her with such want that she squirmed with need.

"Will you deny me even that, little fire?"

She swallowed. She would deny him nothing, but she would not encourage the madness of his abstinence.

"*Release me,* Declan."

He released her reluctantly, but not without planting a quick kiss upon her needy flesh.

She scowled as she scrounged the dresser for fresh undergarments and straightened her skirts. With her back as stiff as a fire poker, she marched to the door.

"Where are you going?"

She shot him a sidelong glance. "I'm taking a walk. Enjoy your evening, Archmage."

"*nother* one?" The councilor's gaze could have melted stone to wax as he stared at her from across the lacquered desk of his office. Alexander Alvah waved the little note in the air. "And still, you've kept this from him?"

Evangeline winced and sank deeper into her seat. The guilt of lying to her archmage was gnawing at her from the inside out. "What else would you have me do? I don't want to cause more conflict for Declan and his council."

Amereen Castle had gone into an uproar when the people had realized their archmage had not only mated, but he had mated himself to a *fae* who couldn't even control her own magic. Apart from the fact that she was Seelie, they knew nothing of her true identity as Freya Katerina Jilintree, surviving princess of the Summer Court—a secret Declan was eager to keep for the sake of her safety.

And the council had been particularly vocal about their censure. They had gone as far as to issue a memorandum on the subject, declaring her an unsuitable mate due to her "lack of magical abilities" and her "questionable immortality," which made her a "weak match." The memorandum included a recommendation for their archmage to disown his claims of mating. To denounce the news and render it a rumor. As though Evangeline were a dirty secret to be hidden away. In fact, one brazen councilor had petitioned for Declan to claim her publicly—as an ayari. A trained consort.

Declan had frozen the councilor's lips together. Literally. A brutal punishment, for when the councilor's lips finally thawed, his flesh was a necrotic mess. Even as a mage, it would take him agonizing months to fully heal. No one had dared raise the subject again, but that didn't mean they accepted her.

Their disdain had only grown.

"But this has gone too far." Alexander hissed out a breath. "The first two notes were derogatory, but this?" He slammed the parchment onto the desk with enough force that the papers shifted and his quill jumped. "My brother needs to know someone in his court is *threatening* his would-be elorin de ana."

Only to those in the castle. To those who'd seen the starburst mark etched into her skin from the day he'd recklessly bound himself to her, willing to negate his own immortality just to keep her alive—she *was* Declan Thorne's elorin de ana. His mate. Ironically, the fact that *she* had yet to bind herself, to etch her own mark into his skin . . . seemed to go unnoticed.

"And what then?" Evangeline lifted her gaze from the clutter of the desk to meet tawny eyes. "Should I watch him tear his court apart to find the perpetrator?"

"This cannot be allowed to escalate." He glared at the note as though it were a rattlesnake. "We need to put an end to it."

"Yes, and no one is more eager than I. But can we not attempt to settle this . . . peacefully?"

Alexander heaved a sigh and ran his fingers through his flaxen hair. "Evie . . . you're asking me to continually lie to my own brother. Lie to my archmage."

"Lex, I'm sure I can settle this without causing more discord in his court." Evangeline shook her head with more determination than she felt. "And really, does he need to deal with this now?" Her archmage hadn't only been facing disgruntled council members or worry over her afflictions. He'd also been working ceaselessly with his Unseelie allies in search of Zephyr—with little success.

The grimness in Alexander's eyes receded to mirror the

bleakness in hers as he drummed his fingers over the table. "Well, the council has been . . . agitated. Declan has never completely disregarded their wishes in the past. They think you have their archmage under some magic spell." More drumming of his fingers, then a ruminative nod. "If they are indeed behind these notes, perhaps it would earn you some respect if you did not run to Declan at the very first opportunity." He shook his head. "But no amount of respect is worth risking your life, Evie."

Her shoulders stiffened. "That's why I'm here." She laced her fingers together. "Won't you help me find out who the author is? There is no one else I can trust in Declan's council." Alexander alone championed her relationship with Declan.

He eyed her warily. "What would you have me do?"

"I do suspect someone from the council is behind these notes." The quality of the parchment suggested the perpetrator was a high-ranking official. "I just need more proof."

Alexander huffed. "Oh, for the love of Railea, don't look at me like that with your baby-deer eyes! Of course I'll help you." He threw his gaze up to the ceiling, as though seeking divine intervention. "If Declan finds out, he'll probably have my hide . . . but I've committed worse sins against him and survived." Then Lex pinned her with a glare. "But promise me this, little sister. You'll tell my brother the moment you feel true threat to your safety."

Despite the gravity in Lex's tone, laughter bubbled up her throat. "*Little* sister?" Evangeline gave an indelicate snort. "If I do my math right, I have at least one century on *you*, little brother."

Lex gave a frivolous wave. "Semantics. You've been stuck in the Abyss for over four centuries while I actually lived it." His lips tilted in a lopsided smile that had likely won him countless favors. "So? Do we have a deal?"

Evangeline nodded. "Fae's promise." She drew a little X on her chest, causing the councilor to chuckle.

Lex leaned back in his chair, seemingly satisfied. "So, while we hunt down this bastard who dares threaten my little sister, what else will you do?"

Evangeline's smile was faint. "Find a way to regain the entirety of my memories. Maybe then I'll find a way to . . . stabilize my immortality."

If she could do that, perhaps her afflictions would cease and her archmage would have no cause to treat her like a figurine of spun glass. And maybe then Declan's people would eventually come to accept her as their archmage's elorin.

Maybe then she could come to accept it, too.

TWO

Declan eyed the bed with disdain. Logic told him he needed sleep. Ever since the battle with Zephyr, he'd been prone to fatigue, and now weariness weighed like a brick at the back of his head. But since he'd grown accustomed to sleeping with Evangeline snuggled close, the prospect of sliding into bed alone made him scowl into the fireplace.

The flames crackled with heightened intensity. Where *was* she?

He stifled the urge to track her down with his mind and haul her back to their bedchamber. He would not further stoke her displeasure. Besides, *she'd* walked away from him. He couldn't remember the last time a woman had spurned his advances. It stung more than he cared to admit.

Did she think *he* enjoyed abstinence? It had driven him close to the edge, sleeping beside her each night, wanting desperately to bury himself in her, yet knowing he would likely bring her more harm than pleasure.

Declan exhaled. He shucked off his trousers and crawled

into bed. He was a grown man. An archmage, one of the Echelon, for Railea's sake. He'd been sleeping on his own for centuries.

The bed felt barren. An involuntary shiver ran down his spine as yearning yawned wide in his chest. Ever since Evangeline, he had grown susceptible to shifts in temperature. As though she'd ignited a literal spark in his bloodstream, destroying the part of him that had once been immune to the cold. And isolation. Now he experienced both as keenly as he sensed her absence.

He shut his eyes, seeking sleep. He breathed deep, only to draw in the scent of woman and wildflowers with a hint of cream. Declan shifted away from the side that had become hers. Then he shifted back to burrow his face into her pillow.

Despite the lulling lethargy, his body hardened, seeking a release that could only come with her, but one he would not permit. Declan threw off the covers and pulled on his clothes.

She wasn't the only one entitled to wander.

Declan found himself meandering down the marbled hallway toward the infirmary. He had wanted to walk off his unrest, but his feet had taken him here. The infirmary was where Evangeline spent most of her time without him, and deep down, he hoped to find her here now.

The main ward was dimmed, but light flickered from the doorway of the office. He hastened his steps but hesitated just shy of the door. Surely she didn't mean to spend the night in there?

He pushed the door wide and peered in.

A woman sat behind one of the heavily cluttered desks, poring over a report. Disappointment coiled in his chest. She didn't have glossy hair of chestnut brown or skin the color of rich cream.

"Sire?" Mailin leaned back in her chair to reveal the rounded bump of her growing belly. "Was there something you wanted?"

"Why are you still here at this hour?" Before Evangeline, it would never have occurred to him to pose such a question. But the halfbreed healer had become so dear to his little fire that Declan was well aware the woman was down to her final summer of gestation.

Mailin stifled a dainty yawn and rubbed absently at her bump. "Since Killian is still away, I thought I might as well get more work done."

Declan nodded, noting not to send his commander on tasks that took him away from his pregnant mate. He turned his gaze toward the desk that now belonged to Evangeline. Just like Mailin's, it was messy, scattered with papers and reports, little trinkets and feathered quills. A jar of dried and scented flowers stood tall amid the clutter, draped with a handwoven band of black and white beads. An identical band sat on his own desk in his office.

Declan wandered over to finger the beads. The sides of his lips lifted as he recalled the words of the child who had gifted them.

"Surin is now teaching other girls to weave," Mailin said with a smile. "Her craftsmanship is much improved."

Declan nodded again. He knew that. He also knew the child was now speaking the mage tongue as fluently as her mother was adept at baking in the kitchens. Evangeline regaled him with the developments of every survivor in the infirmary.

He turned to leave.

"Sire?" Mailin said, stopping him in his tracks. "Is everything . . . all right?"

He heard the concern in her tone. He wasn't interested in conversation, but he'd always respected the healer. And if anyone could help his little fire's condition, it was Mailin.

"Have you found more information on Evangeline's ailments?"

The healer's shoulders sagged, and lines of frustration bracketed her lips. She shook her head and gestured to the books and reports on the desk. "I've been reviewing old texts, but so far I've not found much to explain Evie's symptoms."

Declan surveyed the scattered books on the healer's desk with renewed gratitude. "You needn't do this in your personal time."

Mailin's brows winged up as though in affront. "It is not just my duty to help her. Evie is my friend."

Declan almost smiled. It heartened him that there were still some in his court who regarded his little fire as a friend even though she was fae.

"But her condition isn't the only thing that worries me." Mailin's gaze fell to the texts, and her head bowed. Declan frowned. The healer had never been one to hold her tongue.

"Speak freely, Mailin."

Mailin nodded, but she kept her gaze averted as she considered her next words.

"Sire," she began in a measured tone that heralded bad news. "I have found little record of the effects of *incomplete* mating bonds." The woman shifted in her chair and fidgeted with the edge of the page. "From the few accounts I've read, incomplete bonds often disintegrate with time."

Declan stiffened. His throat suddenly dried. "What do you mean?"

"An incomplete bond wears down the one who initiated it.

They are . . . weakened until they can no longer sustain the one-sided bond." Mailin continued to fiddle with the papers on her desk. "It is nature's way of ensuring no mated pair is borne of coercion."

Declan swallowed the knot in his throat and shifted his gaze to the burning sconce on the wall. Was that what his people thought? That he'd forced his mark onto Evangeline's skin? The darkest part of him sneered. Hadn't he?

"Sire." Mailin sighed. "I know why you initiated the bond. Even the blind can see what she means to you . . . and I know what *she* feels for you. But the bond needs to be completed as soon as possible."

Declan dragged his gaze back to meet Mailin's. "You know we've tried."

But whenever Evangeline tried to entwine her psychic presence with his, the final step in completing their mating bond, her mark failed to manifest on his skin. And in more recent months, he could no longer bring himself to try. Every time he did, Evangeline would grow limp, her mind and body shutting down as though indicating their incompatibility.

Mailin's gaze turned woeful. "If you can't complete the bond . . . Forgive me, my liege. But if you can't complete the bond, you must find a way to sever it."

A growl left his throat. "Know your *place*, Mailin."

Mailin winced, but it didn't stop her from saying, "Sire, Evie isn't the only one I consider a friend."

Declan stared at the healer, a woman who had served his court for over a hundred summers. In his own way, he had always regarded her as a friend, too. For that, she would suffer no further reprimand for her audacious suggestion.

"The council's memorandum isn't completely baseless, sire," Mailin added, seemingly eager to test the strength of their friendship. "In her current state, Evie is a liability as a mate."

"Evangeline's condition may not be something we've encountered before," Declan admitted. "But it doesn't make her weak." On the contrary. His little fire was a surviving *Jilintree*. If the Summer Court still existed, Evangeline could be *queen*.

"Sire, that was not what I meant." Mailin blew out a frustrated sigh. "The rate at which her body fluctuates between mortal and immortal states causes her fae magic to rise and ebb at unpredictable levels. And even at the height of her immortal state, Evie displays magical abilities of a fae *child*."

"That is understandable. Her immortal state is slowly reawakening after centuries of stasis."

"That may be so, but I worry that even if she regains her immortality, it will pick up where it was before she was trapped in the Abyss."

Uneasiness roiled in his gut. "You believe her magical abilities will not grow to match her age?"

"I can't say. I can only say this could be the reason she is not able to complete the mating bond." Mailin gave him a meaningful look. "And she might be unable to do so for as long as she remains immature in her immortality."

Declan drew in a ragged breath.

Freya had been a child when she'd been trapped in the Abyss. Evangeline had escaped the Abyss four centuries later, a child stripped of her immortality. And in thirteen short years, she'd grown at the rate of a human. Into a mortal woman.

Now that her immortality was rekindling, it made sense that her body was too mature for what it should be. Immortals grew at a much slower rate than mortals.

An immortal child trapped in a woman's body.

Declan rubbed at the strain pulsing between his brows.

"The records," he snapped without meaning to. "Did they mention how long it took for the incomplete bonds to disintegrate?"

How long did he have to complete the bond with Evangeline?

"It depends on the strength of the one who imposed it. A one-sided bond could break in a matter of days. For some, it took weeks. The longest incomplete bond in recorded history stretched for a full sun cycle."

A full year.

His mating mark had been etched into Evangeline's skin for over six months now. But he was an archmage. Surely he had strength enough to sustain an incomplete bond far longer than an average mage?

Mailin stirred in her seat, as though reading his thoughts. "Sire, it was the lord archmage Castano who initiated and held the longest incomplete bond."

"What?" Declan blinked at the healer. Alejandro Castano, the archmage of Salindras who lived with a harem of ayari was the last person Declan would expect to initiate a mating bond.

Mailin twisted her lips in a wry smile. "It is what the records say." And Mailin was part of the Healer's Order, a union of healers who shared records necessary for healing, regardless of their allegiance.

"Apparently, the archmage Castano once etched his mark onto a woman . . . but the bond broke before the year was over. The woman was not willing to reciprocate."

Suddenly Declan was unable to meet the healer's gaze. Evangeline had not been conscious when he'd tied himself to her on the psychic plane. She hadn't given him consent when he'd poured his powers into her body in a desperate attempt to claim her before death did. In fact, she'd woken up mortified when she'd realized he'd bound himself to her.

"It's not the same for Evie, sire," Mailin said, her voice gentling. "If it were not for her current . . . condition, I'm certain she would have completed the bond with you."

Declan swallowed again, wanting to take solace from the healer's words. But the darkest part of him continued to sneer. If Evangeline had known who she was from the start, would she really have chosen a man like him?

Mailin sighed. "But you must guard yourself against the possibility that she may *never* fully recover her immortality."

THREE

Evangeline woke to warmth streaming through the balcony doors, and her lips curved despite the sleepy fog still clouding her mind. Her archmage lay sprawled on his chest, still entrenched in slumber. She edged closer, enjoying the view of him in unfettered rest.

She had returned to the bedchamber last night to find Declan brooding over a glass of wine. He hadn't asked where she'd gone. He had simply swooped her up into his arms and carried her to bed. After a few heady kisses, he had pushed from her arms and rolled away, leaving her breathless and bereft. It was only when his ragged breaths evened that he returned to her side and eventually drifted to sleep with a knee wedged between her legs and an arm locked around her waist.

Evangeline curled her fingers, resisting the urge to stroke his chiseled cheekbones. Gently, she dislodged his arm that was still wrapped possessively around her hips, half expecting him to wake. He didn't.

With a grunt, he turned and snuggled closer, his chest rising and falling in the steady tempo of sleep. Worry wormed into her own chest. Declan was usually easy to rouse, but ever since he'd initiated their mating bond, he'd been sleeping far more deeply than usual. And even though he wouldn't admit it, she'd noticed the fatigue shadowing his eyes.

Evangeline slid from the bed before leaning close to press a soft kiss against his temple.

He didn't even stir.

She sighed. She loathed to leave him. She wanted nothing more than to lie abed, to run her fingers over the tantalizing ridges of his body and trace the swirling symbols on his skin with her lips. But indulging herself would not bring her any closer to the answers she needed.

A bracing gust of air greeted her in the main courtyard, heralding the onset of autumn as surely as the turning leaves. Having forgotten her cloak, she hastened her steps until she came to a set of heavy wooden doors. She pushed through them and strode into the scent of fresh lacquer, dust, and time-weathered pages.

With its polished shelves and ornate, curving staircases, the library had become one of Evangeline's favorite places in the castle. She veered into the culture section and began selecting everything she could about the fae.

Though Mailin and the rest of the healers seemed to be convinced her case was unique, Evangeline harbored hopes. Surely she couldn't be the *only* fae to have been trapped in the Abyss who had escaped?

Carrying as many books as her arms allowed, Evangeline made her way to the reading area. Her steps faltered when she realized she wasn't alone. Occupying one of the cherry wood tables were the senior councilman, Lord Councilor Reyas, and a younger councilor she recognized as Lord Councilor Joram, books and official documents strewn between them. Though she had no mind to interrupt, both men stood stiffly upon noticing her presence.

"Lady Evangeline," they droned unanimously, greeting her the way school children might a despised teacher.

Ever since the council had discovered she meant more to their archmage than simple amusement, polite respect had been displaced by curled lips and thinly veiled contempt. All in her archmage's absence, of course, and she'd been careful not to mention it to him. Yet she sensed the council's disapproval as clearly as Declan's mark stamped over her skin.

Evangeline could hardly blame them.

She did not believe herself fit as an archmage's mate, either.

"Lord Councilors." Evangeline curtsied and dipped her head low to show deference. "Please do not stop on my account."

Reyas's gaze flitted down, taking in the work dress she'd donned. Declan had gifted her a far more elaborate wardrobe, but wearing those dresses required Tessa's help, and she hadn't wanted to disturb her lover's slumber.

"My lady," Reyas murmured, his dark eyes narrowed. "You really ought to take more care with your choice of attire."

Joram smirked his agreement. "Reyas is right, my lady. It is rather unseemly for the sire's elorin de ana to be seen in . . . commoner's garb."

Evangeline's cheeks warmed. They had never been so outwardly censorious before. "I . . . I only seek to read."

"Read," Reyas repeated, as though the activity were far less prosaic than it sounded. "But what does the sire's elorin need to read about, hmm? Do those slaves no longer amuse you?"

Joram laughed as though Reyas had made a particularly fine joke.

An odd tingle formed at Evangeline's gums. "There is nothing amusing about slavery, Lord Councilors."

"Of course not." Reyas nodded, although the tilt of his lips insinuated otherwise. "Those poor humans, captured and sold into the shadow realm." Reyas's tongue rolled over the word *humans* as though it were synonymous with *vermin*. "And how very commendable you are, my lady, spending a fortune of Amereen gold, rescuing the lives of the inconsequential. In fact, thanks to your noble efforts, our infirmary is now overrun."

Evangeline ran her tongue over her lengthening canines and bit down on her lower lip. Councilor Reyas's words weren't completely groundless.

True to his promise, Declan *had* created a task force dedicated to slave rescue. A task force involving peace negotiators, soldiers, and Unseelie operators to create interdimensional portals. It was a costly affair.

The infirmary *had* grown in its occupants, to the point that the entire top floor of the eastern wing had become a home for convalescent slave-trade survivors. Soon, she would have to find a way to house them without overwhelming the castle staff.

Evangeline lifted her chin with as much dignity as she could muster despite her flaming cheeks. "Declan and I are working on a solution to reinstate the survivors into society. It will be a sustainable operation. You'll see."

Joram shook his head, while Reyas snorted. "Of course, my lady, of course. Whatever you do, I'm sure you'll have the sire's unwavering support."

The sire's support. But not his council's.

Evangeline managed a wooden smile and a curt nod before retreating to an unoccupied table. She would not be cowed into leaving the library.

Until they discovered the culprit behind the notes, Lex had warned her to stand her ground with the council members. *You are the woman my brother has chosen. They need to accept you, not the other way around.*

Ignoring the weight of the councilors' contemptuous gazes, Evangeline concentrated on her books. A brick-heavy tome, ambiguously titled *A Study of The Five Realms* seemed rather promising, until she reached a section titled *Mating Practices: Bacchanalian Orgies.* The text read:

Being inordinately susceptible to the change of seasons, the fae folk perform religious practices at the turn of each season. The Spring Fever *celebration involves rites where the fae petition the god of chaos and order, Ozenn, for general fertility, livestock fecundity, and a rich harvest.*

The rites include the consumption of a potent narcotic that heightens lust and relaxes inhibitions. The females then perform carnal dances stimulating the males into an ecstatic frenzy (refer to glossary on enthusiasmosis).

Evangeline scowled.

The females further encourage the mating fervor through public masturbation, which results in copious sexual activity between multiple partners, driving birth rates for the next season.

"Oh, for the love of Railea, how can this possibly be true?" she muttered.

A loud snort of disdain sounded from the councilors' table, and Evangeline realized she'd inadvertently read a part of the text *aloud*. Her cheeks flamed anew.

She gathered the books. She should probably read the rest in the infirmary office. Given her halfbreed nature, Mailin could likely shed some light on her research.

"Leaving so soon, my lady?" whispered a low voice at her back.

Evangeline jolted, only to find a pair of amused violet eyes peering down at her.

"Gabriel!" She clutched at her chest. "You startled me. What are you doing here?"

Her exclamation earned her more discriminatory gazes from the other table. The councilors narrowed their eyes at Gabriel, expressions darkening as they clearly identified him as Unseelie. Gabriel hadn't bothered veiling his appearance— violet eyes and pointed ears on full display.

The council did not hold faekind in high regard.

Gabriel ignored them with ease. Resting his hips at the edge of her table, he replied, "Checking in on you." Ever since he'd discovered she was a Jilintree, Gabriel had treated her like an animal at the brink of extinction. Which, Evangeline mused, was not far from the truth.

"What are *you* doing here?" Gabriel shot back, peering over her shoulder to read the text.

"Researching," Evangeline said defensively, ignoring the heightening warmth at the tips of her ears.

"Ah, the mating frenzy," he said with a salacious wag of his brows. "Scandalous, compared to the ways of these uptight mages. Don't you think?"

"It's not true, is it?" She recalled nothing of the sort from her childhood. Then again, some of her memories remained sketchy.

At her wide-eyed expression, Gabriel guffawed.

Councilor Reyas muttered something inarticulate.

"Not entirely." Gabriel flipped the book to glimpse the author's name. "Lord Barnaby appears to be describing the fae Choosing and Binding Ceremonies . . . albeit in exaggeration."

Evangeline grinned her relief. "So we don't hold orgies every spring?"

Gabriel gave an indiscreet chuckle. "No. Though our

Choosing Ceremonies do include the consumption of crushed *vitalis* while the women dance around their chosen men before the Binding."

"Vitalis?" Evangeline raised a brow. "That is no lust-inducing narcotic. It is a common herb. A mild aphrodisiac, at best."

"Hmm, one wonders how Lord Barnaby came to his observations."

Evangeline snickered.

"That's quite enough!" Reyas jumped from his seat so abruptly his chair nearly toppled.

Evangeline blinked, dumbfounded by the councilor's outburst.

"Reyas," Joram interjected with a nervous tug at his colleague's shirtsleeve. "That's no way to speak to the sire's elorin."

Reyas shrugged off Joram's hold. "Precisely so! She *is* the woman the sire calls elorin, which is why I will not stand idly by and watch her dally shamelessly with another man behind his back!"

Evangeline's jaw fell slack. *"Dally?"*

Gabriel chortled. "I told you these mages were uptight!" He turned to Reyas with a smirk. "Loosen up, Councilor. When was the last time you visited the lounge beside the kitchens, eh?" The taphouse where courtesans gathered, seeking pleasure.

"Ludicrous." Reyas folded his arms. "I have no need for the lounge."

"Can't find a willing woman there, huh?" Gabriel gave a sympathetic nod. "I know several discreet brothels. The women aren't as fine but . . . "

Reyas sputtered, and his cheeks turned puce.

Joram tittered, but the older councilor's glower quickly silenced him.

"You reprehensible creature . . . how utterly disgraceful!" Reyas whirled to Evangeline. "My lady, you need to remove yourself from his polluting presence at once."

"Councilor Reyas," Evangeline pushed up from the table, her patience frayed. "Calm yourself. You have completely misunderstood the context of our conversation. Declan would have taken no offense. Gabriel and I are—"

At the mention of Declan's name, Reyas curled his lips. "Of course, the sire wouldn't find fault with *you*. You've all but robbed him of his senses!"

"Reyas," Joram squeaked, eyes wide. "Remember what happened with Brandor!"

The councilor who suggested Declan claim Evangeline as an ayari was still recovering from his injuries.

"Brandor was the boldest of us all!" Reyas squared his shoulders before turning back to Evangeline. "You may have the sire bewitched, my lady, but you can't fool his council. We see right through your antics."

Beside her, Gabriel stiffened, the muscles on his forearms bunching as his fists balled. "Do you know *whom* you're speaking to?"

"Gabriel," Evangeline said in warning. Apart from those present at the battle with Zephyr, no one knew of her Jilintree heritage. Or the status of her birth. It was a secret she wanted to keep.

Gabriel's posture slackened the way a snake's might before it struck prey. "Rein in that blasphemous tongue of yours, Councilor, before I rip it from its cavity." He gave a fanged grin. "That is, if your archmage doesn't flay you first for your impudence."

Reyas jumped to the balls of his feet to gain height enough

to match Gabriel's gaze. "The sire values my service! I have been by his side since his ascension and served him far longer than any other council member. He knows I have his best interests at heart."

"Slandering his woman isn't going to win you any favors," Gabriel said with a roll of his eyes.

"Slander? I merely state the facts!" Reyas puffed out his chest. "I see through manipulation, even if it is wrapped in the guise of innocence!" A sneer. "Brandor was right. I can no longer keep my silence, watching this"—he aimed a trembling finger at Evangeline—"she-devil bewitch the sire with her wiles. She has done nothing but weaken him. She will be his *ruin!*"

Stunned by Reyas's bitter vehemence, Evangeline gaped.

A guttural hiss came from her side. In a blur of movement, Gabriel lunged and lifted Reyas off his feet. The senior councilor coughed and clawed wildly at his neck as Gabriel constricted his windpipe. Joram scuttled back with a yelp, knocking over chairs to distance himself.

"Stop," Evangeline snapped when she finally found her tongue. "Release him!"

Gabriel withdrew his grip, dropping the gasping councilor like a sack of coal. Violet eyes narrowed at her. "How can you allow him to speak to you in this manner?"

Her lengthened incisors dug into the bottom of her lip, and the taste of iron coated the tip of her tongue. "Declan can deal with him."

Eyes prickling, she turned on her heel and stormed out of the library.

"Reyas is nothing but a braying mule. I will recount every one of his blasphemous words to Declan," Gabriel grumbled when he finally found her in the dim hallway tucked beside a display case filled with artefacts.

"To what purpose?" she muttered, staring listlessly at the swirling motes illuminated by the light filtering through arched windows. "So Declan can exact some kind of brutal punishment? It would be a sure way of silencing them, but punishment won't change their views. It will only further condemn Declan before his council."

Gabriel released a long and weary exhale. To her surprise, he lowered to his haunches and settled beside her, leaning his back against the wall. "Evie, your lover is an archmage. He doesn't need his council's approval."

"Which is why his court is in discord," she said scornfully. "Because his councilors resent me."

"Only because they do not know who you really are."

Gabriel's faith in her heritage was laughable.

"They see me as a weakness." Evangeline folded her arms around herself. "Declan's weakness. Tell me, are they wrong?"

Gabriel seemed to be at a loss for words. When he finally spoke, his tone was oddly gentle. "Evie, I'm not going to lie; you *are* his weakness."

Her shoulders sagged.

"But you are so much more than that. You are also the last heir of the Summer Court, the only Jilintree in existence."

Evangeline released a caustic laugh. "I know you're trying to make me feel better, but I haven't been Freya Jilintree for an eon. I don't even know if I'm truly fae or if my body remains mortal." She shook her head with disdain. "I can't even summon magic to veil my eyes." They remained an odd blend of violet and amber, a physical taunt at her own ineptitude every time she looked into the mirror.

"Listen to me." Gabriel waited until she met his gaze. "I've known Declan for almost two centuries now, and I can't remember the last time I saw him crack a smile. Since you came into his life, I've caught him laughing. More than once."

Evangeline bit her lower lip. "Making him happy doesn't mean I'm right to be the elorin of Amereen."

"Would you be content to share him, then? Warm his bed while he crowns another woman with stronger abilities and better connections?"

At the glower on her face, Gabriel chuckled. "I thought not."

A wavering smile played on her lips to match the wryness in his gaze.

"His people view him as the symbol of their strength," Gabriel said after a moment's silence. "And now they see him soften in ways they've never witnessed. That scares them. Because they see it as weakness."

Gabriel leaned closer so their gazes aligned. "But you should ignore them. Those who do not approve, they merely see Declan as an archmage. More god than man. They do not see him as a real person. But those who regard him as *vinaro*, they want to see him happy."

Evangeline blinked. In the fae tongue, *vinaro* meant brother. Or, more accurately, a brother of different blood.

"And the truth is, *you* make him happy," Gabriel added gently. "Ridiculously so."

Tears welled in her eyes.

"*Vinaro*, huh?" Evangeline managed through a little sniffle. "I thought you found him uptight . . . "

Gabriel mock grimaced. "Don't ever repeat that. I'll deny it till my fangs grow dull."

An unladylike snort escaped her lips. On impulse, she threw her arms around the Unseelie. "Thank you, Gabriel."

Declan woke to empty sheets and a pounding headache.

Mailin's theory haunted him. Terrified him. Dreams of Evangeline leaving him for the fae realm plagued his sleep. The nightmares were so vivid he could still hear her gut-wrenching words. *"I don't belong here. I don't belong with you, Declan."*

A shudder ran through him.

Without a completed mating bond, Evangeline would never be truly *his*.

Declan slid out of bed and trudged into the bath chamber, weary as though he hadn't slept through the night. He splashed water onto his face and stared into his own bloodshot eyes in the mirror.

Evangeline loves you, he reminded himself. Freya had returned for *him*. The thought gave him a measure of calm, yet a seed of doubt niggled at the back of his mind. A notion borne from his years in the enclave, honed by Corvina's repeated abuse, until he'd learned to encase his emotions in ice. Now the notion crept to the fore, sly and insidious.

What woman would want a man unwanted by his own mother?

Declan shut his eyes and exhaled.

She was still very much Evangeline right now, his little fire with a mortal heart. A woman who held him in awe and needed him for protection. But as the years passed, she would grow into Freya's memories. She would *be* Freya.

Freya, who had once been his everything.

The niece of the Seelie queen. A Jilintree who had powers

to make or break kingdoms. What need would Freya have of him then?

Declan turned on the faucet and cursed.

The water had turned to ice.

"Control yourself," he commanded his reflection.

Evangeline was *his*. She bore his mark on her skin. She slept in his bed. She kissed him, whispered words of love to him . . . especially when he pushed her over the brink.

He hardened at the thought.

He would give her so much pleasure she would scream the words over and over and never want another.

With that in mind, he traced her presence on the mental plane and warped.

Declan materialized in the corner of a secluded hallway, momentarily confused. This was not a part of the castle he'd expected Evangeline to be in. The rays of sunlight backlit the couple tucked together between glass displays of relics and gilded weapons.

They spoke in hushed tones. Gabriel leaned closer, whispering secrets into her ear. Ice trickled down Declan's fingertips. Then Evangeline laughed, throwing her arms around Gabriel's neck in a way that had Declan swallowing hard.

Declan gave himself a mental shake. Gabriel was his ally. One he trusted with his life. Gabriel would not encroach on his woman. And Evangeline . . . he noted the friendly way she patted Gabriel's back when they drew apart.

Yet a bitter taste rose in the back of his throat. What were they discussing, hidden in the recesses of a dim hallway, tucked away from the world?

Declan stepped into the corridor, needing to make his presence known. Evangeline lurched up when she saw him. The distress in her expression made his heart pound faster. But she hurried into his arms, burrowing into him far more intimately than she had just embraced Gabriel.

Gabriel sauntered over, lips set in a dour line.

"Archmage, you ought to have some words with your council." The guildmaster proceeded to give Declan a detailed account of what had transpired in the library.

Feeling the fool, Declan buried his face into Evangeline's hair and breathed in her scent.

How could he have ever doubted her?

FOUR

Declan warped into the kingdom of Flen, jaw tense and fists clenched. Killian materialized beside him, but the grim set of the commander's mouth slackened as he surveyed their surroundings.

Mirrors lined the ceiling and the walls, reflecting light from the burning sconces in a dazzling array of kaleidoscopic color, creating the illusion of endless space.

"My son," drawled the archmage upon a glittering throne of swords rooted in a mass of black crystal snakes. "I was wondering when you'd come."

Dressed in a royal-blue tunic and a jeweled girdle, his kingly attire complete with a fur mantle, Nathaniel Strom appeared every bit the god he fancied himself to be. As Declan and Killian approached the lofty dais, Nathaniel acknowledged their presence with the barest flick of his gaze.

"Archmage Strom," Killian said as he bent one knee. The row of soldiers lining the wall did the same in synchrony, genuflecting at Declan's arrival. Soldiers who served as much

42

purpose as the mirrored walls. No archmage needed any more arsenal than the power flowing in his veins.

"I apologize for the inconvenience, Nathaniel," Declan said, not bothering with pleasantries. "Where is he?"

"Hardly an inconvenience." Nathaniel chuckled, rising from his seat. "Reyas's predicament proved an entertainment." He signaled for his steward. "Prepare the revelry, Kyson. Archmage Thorne and his commander have arrived. I will dine with my son tonight."

"Thank you for the generous hospitality," Declan interjected. "But I will not further intrude on your time. We will retrieve Councilor Reyas and be on our way."

Nathaniel's emerald eyes, a mirror of Declan's own, glittered with displeasure.

"It has been many summers since we shared company."

Impatience churned in Declan's gut. He was not here to indulge Nathaniel's delusion of a healthy father-son relationship. He was here to retrieve a deserter of his court.

"Where *is* he?" Declan repeated.

"Patience," Nathaniel intoned with an infuriating flick of his wrist, dismissing his steward. "Mulled wine?" he asked, and a buxom maid scurried up with a tray of glasses, eyes darting between Declan and Killian like a wary fieldmouse's.

"You would harbor a renegade?" Declan waved the servant aside.

"Reyas warped into *my* lands, seeking *my* help. I am no more interested in harboring him than harboring the damned birds that flock from Sebastian's mountains to mine, squawking and defecating where they land." Nathaniel released an imperious huff as he picked up a glass from the servant's tray. "What sort of court are you running, my son, that a seasoned councilman would flee from it, fearing for his life?"

"That is none of your concern."

The moment Gabriel had recounted Reyas's diatribe, the councilor had been a man on the cusp of a bloody punishment. But Evangeline had pleaded for Declan to reconsider.

"Such severe punishment of a senior councilor would do nothing but heighten discontent among your council," she had argued. His little fire loathed violence in any form or fashion and would seek to avoid it even on behalf of a man who preferred she stayed out of existence.

Declan had concurred. He might not share Evangeline's benevolence, but he agreed with the wisdom. A council that worked under malcontent and fear would not serve him well.

But Reyas had chosen to flee. The blackguard had chosen Flen in hopes of receiving impunity from Declan's father. And from the sound of it, the councilor had disclosed Declan's affairs to Nathaniel in hopes of intervention. That was an offense on its own, one that would incur a punishment far worse than a simple lashing.

Nathaniel's sigh was both disturbing and disconcerting in its somberness. He commanded his soldiers from the receiving chamber before turning to Killian. "Commander, would you join my soldiers and wait outside?"

At Declan's nod, Killian filed from the room.

The moment the chamber was devoid of listening ears, Nathaniel warped from the dais so they stood toe to toe.

"My son." Words edged with reprimand. "As a fellow arch-mage, I should not have given your councilor an audience. As one of the Echelon, I should not seek to interfere, but as a father . . . " Nathaniel shook his head warily. "As a father, I *can't* refrain from either. If only you could see the paradox, then you would understand my dilemma."

Declan considered the other archmage with narrowed eyes. Nathaniel had always been eager to remind him of their familial ties, but never had the other man been so forthright in his displays of *fatherly* affectation.

"Councilor Reyas's concerns are not baseless," Nathaniel added. "An archmage has no cause to bind himself to a woman who brings no economic or political gain. If you want a companion, surely the Keep is not short of ayaris?"

The notion of Evangeline as a replaceable fixture caused heat to simmer beneath Declan's skin. "You have neither cause nor need to care." A man who had sired him through rape had no right to dictate his life.

"I am your father." Nathaniel fumed, the symbols on his skin illuminating in a flash of quicksilver, gleaming against his pale skin. The temperature of the chamber dipped, and frost crept over the mirrors in a latticework of ice. "I have every cause for concern, especially when it's clear you're being led around by your cock!"

Declan allowed his own symbols to flare in response. Heat rose. The mirrors misted, casting the room in a blurry haze as fog descended around them.

Nathaniel stood stiff, uncharacteristically fractious. Then he asked, "Has it ever occurred to you that I may have once loved your mother?"

An acerbic bark of laughter rose in Declan's throat. Nathaniel was no more capable of love than Declan of innocence.

Nathaniel lifted a hand. Ice licked up his forearm to coagulate in his palm and form an intricate sphere of knitted ice.

"Your mother called them ice gems," he murmured as he studied his creation. "She loved them; did you know that? Fancied them more than any jewel, and I would fashion hundreds . . . just to please her."

Dumbfounded, Declan stared. He didn't know what was

more shocking, Nathaniel's words or the wistfulness in his expression.

"We were never suited for each other. Corvina was always needy and possessive. A spitfire, in both ability and personality." A facetious quirk of Nathaniel's lips. "And I was never one for fidelity."

"You were lovers," Declan stated, utterly confounded by the revelation.

"She never minded the whores in my court. How was I to know she would be so incensed by my involvement with Zephyr's queen?" Nathaniel sighed. "Seraphina meant nothing to me, but what hot-blooded man never dreamed of fucking a fae? Those beguiling violet eyes staring up at you . . . "

When Declan didn't respond, Nathaniel sighed again and clenched his fist. The ice sphere splintered. Jagged edges caused blood to trickle down his forearm, staining his sleeve even as the wounds healed.

"Like a fool, I filled the seas with these *ice gems* just to appease her. But your mother, she wouldn't have any of it. She set the waters on fire to spite my apology." Nathaniel laughed, wry and wistful. "What a woman."

Declan swallowed, suddenly wishing he'd accepted the glass of wine.

"But she did more than set the seas afire. She went as far as to mate with one of her battlemages." Nathaniel flung the shards of crimson-coated ice to the ground. "I wouldn't have cared if she'd sought an affair with another. But she mated— just to rile me."

More ice filmed over the mirrors as the symbols on Nathaniel's markings simmered flame-white. "She said I'd never touch her again." He shrugged. "So I showed her exactly what she'd given up."

"You raped her," Declan gritted out.

"I wasn't gentle"—Nathaniel sneered—"but she didn't mind."

Declan shook his head, trying to shake off the disgust and disbelief roiling in his gut. "She said . . ."

"Do you really believe a woman like your mother would have allowed a man, even an archmage, to plow her if she wasn't spread and willing?" A roll of his eyes. "Yes, she detested it after. Detested the fact that I managed to leave my seed in her. She knew how much I wished for an heir. She allowed your life to gall me. Every day you drew breath without my knowledge, she kept me from my heir. *My* legacy. By keeping you in the enclave, she was punishing me for my sins."

Although he tried to appear unaffected, the world around Declan tilted. He had always believed his existence to be a blot of shame. An abomination bred of violence and coercion. But if Nathaniel was to be believed, he had been nothing but a pawn caught in the spite and squabble of two lovers.

He forced himself to meet Nathaniel's gaze, searching for signs of falsehood. But all he saw was grim sincerity.

"Why have you never disclosed your account?" Declan demanded. History books were filled with the version he'd been raised to believe. None had mentioned his parents ever having been lovers.

Nathaniel thinned his lips. "So I can go down in history as the besotted archmage who once filled the seas with ice? A spurned fool tossed aside for a simple battlemage?" Nathaniel huffed. "It does nothing for my reputation."

"Why tell me now?"

"Because I see *you* making the same mistake I once did, giving your heart to a woman who doesn't deserve it."

Normally, Declan wouldn't take offense, but this time, affront surged up his throat. Nathaniel thought Evangeline undeserving of him, when it was *Declan* who was undeserving of *her*.

"You don't *know* her."

There must have been something in his tone, for whatever else the other archmage had intended to say went unvoiced. Instead, Nathaniel scoured him with a contemplative gaze as he rubbed his beard.

The doors of the chamber opened to emit the steward, followed by a stiff-necked Councilor Reyas and a glowering Killian.

"Sire." Reyas bowed low before straightening his back with his head held high, appearing regretful but not the least fearful. "I humbly ask for your forgiveness."

Declan gave the councilor a look devoid of emotion. "I believe you are familiar with the sentence reserved for traitors, Reyas?"

The councilor had the gall to appear wounded. "Sire, you must understand. I only came here because I thought your father could help you see reason—"

Nathaniel's snort interrupted the man midsentence. "Did you not flee in fear for your life?"

Reyas swallowed, and seeming to muster more gumption, he added, "Lord Archmage Strom, I am a loyal subject of Amereen. I came seeking your counsel for perspective on my liege's . . . choices."

"And by choices, you mean Lady Evangeline," Killian said with a sneer.

Reyas's lips flattened. "After witnessing Brandor's fate, I was left with little choice but to seek intervention from Lord Archmage Strom. This is the only way I can hope to make the sire see sense where that woman is concerned!"

Declan reached out with one hand to wrap his fingers around the councilor's throat. "I'll have you know that despite your insolence, it was she who pleaded to lighten your sentence."

Reyas struggled to free himself. When he failed, he cried, "A sham! She is manipulating you, sire! I have seen her perfidiousness in your absence. I have witnessed her discussing vulgarities with the Unseelie male you have so wrongly placed your trust—"

Declan only tightened his grip, and true fear crept into Reyas's eyes.

"You c-cannot e-execute someone in the lands of a-another archmage," Reyas said between gasps.

Declan would argue otherwise, considering Reyas had just declared himself a loyal Amereenian. However, despite the cold wash of his rage, Evangeline's disapproving frown flitted across his mind. His little fire's compassion appealed to him even in her absence.

Declan loosened his hold, and Reyas stumbled back.

Then a scream escaped the councilor's lips. A sheen of ice flowed from the ground to lap at his ankles and course up his knees at a leisurely pace like a vine creeping toward the sun.

Reyas's eyes widened, and a wheezing sound escaped his throat.

"You're right, Councilor." Nathaniel's markings on his skin flared frost white like a glacier glimmering beneath the moon. "An archmage can only execute those within *his* domain."

Reyas released an inarticulate whimper as he stared at Declan in panic.

Ice crept higher, up his thighs.

Nathaniel chuckled, and the ice faltered. He strode up so he filled the councilor's line of sight. "I applaud you for your boldness and thank you for bringing my son's . . . erroneous choices to my attention. However, it is rather ill-advised to betray the trust of an archmage, even if it is done with good intentions."

"Sire," Reyas pleaded, his voice hoarse as he strained his neck to pin Declan with an imploring gaze. "H-help . . . "

Declan stared at the man who'd dared insult his little fire. A man who had served him without compunction since the day he'd ascended. A man who had taken him through the intricacies of archmagedom and contributed to his reign for over two centuries.

Declan emitted a burst of heat to counteract the frost climbing up Reyas's legs, drawing a frown from the other archmage.

Son, you have grown too soft for my liking.

"Reyas is a citizen of Amereen," Declan said. "I reserve the right to decide his punishment."

Nathaniel considered him for another moment, then gave a resigned shake of his head.

"Very well." Ice retracted, and Reyas slumped to the ground.

Wordlessly, Killian lifted the prostrate and barely lucid councilor by his arms and warped.

Declan gave the other archmage a stiff nod, signaling his own departure. Nathaniel reached out swiftly to clasp Declan's shoulder.

"I would meet this woman who has caused such ruckus in your court."

FIVE

The aroma of cinnamon and oven-fresh buns elicited a sigh of pleasure from Evangeline's lips. This was exactly what she needed. The familiarity and comfort of home.

She drizzled a generous heap of honey across the steaming buns, creating a mouthwatering glaze.

Her smile dampened as she caught her mother's gaze from across the scarred and pitted kitchen table dusted with flour and eggshells. As she kneaded fresh dough, Agnes Barre's usually placid gray eyes were dark and troubled. Coupled with the knot between her brows and the pinch of her lips, it was an expression Evangeline knew well.

A lecture was forthcoming.

Evangeline busied herself with the glaze, coating each bun with industrious intent. "I think we need at least three more trays," she said, manufacturing a jovial tone. "Last year we baked far more, if you recall, and they were all gobbled up as soon as they were laid out."

As far as her memory served, there hadn't been a single Reckoning feast without Agnes's honey-glazed cinnamon buns.

"Do not change the subject, Evie." Agnes smeared flour against her cheek as she tucked a stray strand of auburn hair behind her ear. "I know what you're doing."

Evangeline conjured a cheeky grin. "I promise I won't lick the honey from the spoon this year . . . at least not until the buns are done."

Mother made a noise of irritation in her throat.

"I can help you with the dough if you like," Evangeline offered.

Mother responded with a dismissive snort.

Evangeline pursed her lips and dropped her merry facade. "Isn't this why you wanted me home? To spend the day together like we always do before the village feast?"

"What I want is for you to face your fears," Agnes said, blunt as always. "Hiding away in my kitchen will do you no favors."

"I came back to spend time with you."

"And you did. You've been here for days now. It's time you went back."

Evangeline's mouth parted like a trout's, and a dollop of honey dripped on the kitchen table. "You're throwing me out? Just before the feast?"

Her mother sighed and gave an absent wave. The kitchen rag slipped from the tack on the wall and floated its way into Agnes's hand. "Of course not. You know you're always welcome here. I think you should be with your archmage this year. That's all." She dipped the cloth into a wash bucket and wrung it before wiping up the spill.

Evangeline didn't respond, returning to her task with far more focus than necessary.

Agnes sniffed. "The Reckoning marks the ascension of the first archmage . . . don't you think your archmage will want you by his side?"

"Yes, but I love celebrating it with you." It was the truth. This was their tradition. She couldn't remember a single year as Evangeline Barre that she hadn't spent the day of the Reckoning feast in this tidy little kitchen, covered in flour and laughter with the woman who had become her mother.

A faint smile crested upon Agnes's lips. "As do I, but Evie, my dearest child"—she wiped her hands on the frilly floral apron to lean against the table beside Evangeline—"I know you dislike confrontation, but you can't shy away from it anymore. I would demand an apology from that cow-headed, lily-livered councilor. He had no right speaking to you in that manner."

Evangeline had kept no secrets from her mother. Not even her recovered memories as Freya Jilintree. She trusted Agnes Barre implicitly, so she had regaled the woman with her life at the castle—including her misadventures.

"He couldn't apologize even if he wanted to." Evangeline grimaced. "He hasn't been able to utter a coherent word since he arrived at the infirmary. Mailin said his nerves were deadened from the legs up and part of his spinal cord was damaged enough that he'll be incapacitated for months."

Utterly unmoved, Agnes said, "I hope his recovery is a slow and painful one—I'm surprised your archmage allowed him to live at all."

"He's already in a great deal of pain, Mother," Evangeline said quietly. She had witnessed Reyas's half-withered state when Killian carried him into the infirmary. The councilor's expression was twisted in abject pain, and the lower half of his body appeared shriveled, somehow. His skin was parched and paper-thin, as though his nerves had been liquefied and his bones were brittle enough to snap at the lightest pressure. Evangeline hadn't the slightest idea what her archmage had done to the councilor.

She couldn't bring herself to ask. Declan had warped home soon after, his expression unreadable as always. But his eyes had been glacial, as removed and distant as when she'd first laid eyes on him in the shadow realm.

A silence descended over them, and Mother returned to her kneading while Evangeline continued her glazing, unwilling to entertain further thoughts of Reyas and the council.

A small smile tugged at her lips as her thoughts wandered to Declan. He would be horrified by the amount of honey she was using. The man didn't possess a single sweet tooth—unless he was tasting her. Heat kissed her cheeks even as a pang formed in her chest. She wanted her lover here. She wanted to spend their first Reckoning together.

"You should really reconsider your plans for this evening," Agnes murmured. Her mother could well be reading her thoughts.

"Do you truly wish for me to meet the Echelon?"

"What I wish is for you to take your rightful place beside your archmage."

Evangeline dunked the honey dipper back into its jar and folded her arms and regarded her mother with narrowed eyes. "How have you changed your tune so quickly? I distinctly recall the time you warned me against Declan."

"Oh, Evie, that was before I knew who and *what* you were." Her mother batted the air with a negligent wave of her hand. "Now that I do, what better suitor could I possibly want for you? Who can keep you safer than an archmage?" An approving glint lit her eyes, and her lips twitched. "Besides, the way the man looks at you . . . "

Evangeline's cheeks warmed, and she squirmed in place as she sought to change the subject. "Well, I am not going to the banquet tonight." She lifted her arms helplessly. "I have no idea how to behave around an archmage."

Mother merely quirked a brow.

Evangeline flushed and fidgeted with the brush in her hands. "I mean other archmages. The entire Echelon will be there."

If her mother possessed telementation, her gaze certainly would have bored a hole through Evangeline's person. "Yet the archmage of Flen has requested your presence. Has he not?"

"It doesn't matter. Declan has no intention of bringing me along," Evangeline said with a touch more bitterness than she intended.

Whatever had happened in the frosty lands of Flen had cast a layer of frigidity over her archmage, as though he'd returned encased in a glacier. He had disclosed his father's wish that she attend the annual banquet in honor of the Reckoning. But before she could properly digest the implications of Nathaniel's invitation, Declan had sneered his contempt.

"Customs be damned," he had said dismissively. *"Nathaniel can issue as many invitations as he likes, but you won't be attending. I will not allow it."*

It had chafed that he hadn't thought to seek her consideration in the matter.

Though she had conceded.

She wasn't ready to meet Nathaniel, much less the Echelon. She didn't want to meet them. Beings so lethal they could each crush her with an errant sneeze. Yet . . .

"Is that what you want?" Agnes asked. "To be isolated for the rest of your life?"

Evangeline twisted her head away so her mother wouldn't see her crestfallen expression. Declan's dictatorial decision had chafed, for she heard beyond the words to what he did not say —that she was too weak to meet his peers, much less his father.

"Who am I to attend a banquet hosted by the Echelon when I can't even keep my own magic in check?" The words came out so quiet Evangeline wasn't sure if her mother heard them.

Agnes stared as though her daughter were daft.

"You are Freya Jilintree, daughter of a princess," she said with ostentatious pride, as though she were announcing the presence of the Seelie queen. "You are Evangeline Barre, a woman I've raised myself. Most of all, you are a survivor." Agnes reached out to tip up her chin. "When I first found you in the ravine, I thought it was only a matter of days before you wasted away . . . yet you survived. You are far stronger than you think, dearest."

Agnes gave her a gentle smile before returning to the kitchen bench. She fashioned circular mounds on the baking tray, leaving Evangeline staring down into the jar of viscous amber that was almost the shade of her eyes. Before the rim of violet had threatened to eclipse them and change her identity.

She stared for a long time, until her thoughts cleared and clarity descended. She stood, and the creak of her wooden chair drew Agnes's attention from the baking tray.

"Will you save me some buns leftover from the feast?" Evangeline asked softly.

Agnes's smile stretched wide, and her eyes shone with pride.

"The next time you come, I'll bake you fresh ones."

Evangeline strode through the halls, her slippered steps near soundless over the marbled ground. It hadn't been hard to return. All she'd had to do was command one of the battlemages stationed outside Agnes's cottage to warp her back.

She threw open the doors leading to Declan's—their—bedchamber to find her archmage staring at her expectantly. He stood shirtless and magnificent beside the wardrobe that spanned the length of their bedchamber.

"Back so soon?" he asked, without a hint of surprise.

Of course he knew of her return. His battlemages had probably informed him the moment she'd requested to be warped home.

She didn't bother explaining. She strode over to greet him. He bent to meet her lips in a sweet but annoyingly chaste kiss. Before he could pull away, she cradled his face, holding him in place as she kissed him to her satisfaction. When she was done, he blinked at her between uneven breaths with his hair a little tousled, his eyes a little glazed.

She grinned.

After patting his cheek, she turned to the wardrobe, selected one of his more formal shirts, and held it out to him. He donned it obediently and allowed her to do up his buttons. His gaze lingered on her lips. Her fingers skimmed his firmly ridged abs, and the ripple of his muscles caused an involuntary clench between her thighs.

A slow smile played upon his lips. Her muscles clenched harder, and she felt the subtle reversal of power between them. She knew what her kisses did to him, and the devil knew what his smiles did to her.

Before she completely lost her confidence, she blurted, "I wish to go with you."

He raised a questioning brow while his lips still toyed with that wicked smile.

"The banquet," she clarified. "I wish to accept your father's invitation."

The curve of his mouth flattened.

"Little fire, being my elorin does not mean you're to be made a spectacle to anyone wishing to assuage their curiosity. You will meet them on your own terms, when you are ready."

"I am ready."

Brackets framed his lips. "You're in no position to meet any one of the Echelon right now. Especially not Nathaniel."

Evangeline kept her eyes on the buttons, completing the final one at his collar before meeting his gaze.

"Are you ashamed of me, Archmage?"

His head snapped up as if he were startled. "No."

The incredulity in his tone soothed her hackles, and instantly she regretted her choice of words. Declan had bound his own life to hers just to keep her alive.

"*Never* think that." His vehemence lifted the edges of her lips. "I want nothing more than to show the world you are mine"—he ran a knuckle along the mating mark etched over the soft swell of her breast—"and to one day wear your mark on my skin."

"Show the world, then. Bring me to the banquet with you tonight."

With his brow still furrowed, Declan leaned close so their foreheads touched. "Little fire, as far as we know, Zephyr is still alive."

Evangeline bit her tongue. That was the reason she tolerated his guards in the first place. "But Zephyr isn't likely to show up at the banquet hosted by your father, is he?"

"No," Declan agreed. "But I am not eager to parade my heart before those who would have no qualms in crushing it."

Evangeline bit back a curse when he pulled away. If she was to be his elorin de ana, she would stand beside him, not cower behind him. Agnes had been right. She couldn't hide forever. Shying away from the banquet would only serve to fuel public perception that she was too weak to be an archmage's mate. And instinctively, she knew it would continue to feed Declan's overprotective tendencies . . . which of late had become almost overbearing. She wanted to be his mate. His equal. Not a lover cosseted and wrapped in cotton wool, too fragile to be presented to the world.

"I know you're concerned about my safety, Archmage. But I haven't suffered any headaches or lost consciousness for days now, and I feel perfectly fine. Having dinner with archmages will not worsen my condition, nor will any harm befall me." She pressed an entreating kiss against the strong column of his throat. "Not with you right there with me."

The masculine bump on his neck bobbed, but her attempts to charm did not sway him.

"Evangeline, this banquet is no mere social call. The Echelon already knows you are Seelie." Declan had been no more successful in quelling news of her race within the castle walls than he had been in keeping it from spreading like wildfire across the realm. By now everyone knew her as Seelie. "But if they knew who you truly are . . . " Declan shut his eyes, and a shudder ran through him. "No, I will not allow it."

Evangeline sputtered, shoving out of his hold as indignance choked her. "Do you intend to hide me away for the rest of my days . . . because of my birthright?"

"You're a Jilintree. Do you know how valuable a weapon that makes you? And until we know for certain what is happening to your body, to your immortality, I will not risk you."

"What if I never regain my immortality? What if this

state"—she gestured down at her body—"is what I have to live with for the rest of my life, however long that may be?"

Declan flinched, and his voice no longer held the confidence of a man who ruled supreme over the ground beneath her bare feet. "We'll find a way to complete the mating bond." He encircled her from behind as though to placate her, but he sounded as though he was placating himself. "Then we'll have more time to treat your afflictions."

A hysterical bark of laughter leapt from her throat. More time for her while she drew upon her archmage's life force and dwindled his lifespan. Evangeline twisted out of his grasp and turned to face him. "Declan, it has been months. I cannot live in constant fear of Zephyr or at the mercy of my own mortality."

His eyes hardened into glimmering shards of green. He remained silent for a long moment as a dark intensity clouded his expression. She stiffened in response, readying for another bout of dispute.

"I will not have you hurt again." His words were barely a whisper, but they melted the steel in her spine. "Do you understand?" He swallowed as if the next words were stuck in his throat. Maybe they were, for his mental voice crashed into her head like a tidal wave.

I cannot bear it.

Suddenly overwhelmed by weariness, Evangeline sighed. Running her fingers into the short strands at his nape, she cupped his cheek with her other hand.

"If I am to be your mate, your elorin de ana, then . . . I need you to treat me like one."

He stood rigid in her embrace, and a muscle at the side of his neck grew taut. But Evangeline knew she'd won when he lowered his forehead to meet hers in a gesture that had become more intimate than a kiss.

"You'll need your cloak," he muttered. "The lands of Flen are icier than Draedyn's realm."

SIX

The warmth of Declan's bedchamber faded away to be replaced by frost-licked mist.

Evangeline gasped, filling her lungs with the scent of snowflakes and fresh spring water. With Declan's arms still wrapped around her, she stood on the edge of a heavy wooden drawbridge leading into the fabled kingdom of Flen. It had been day in Declan's land, but here the skies were painted a forbidding gray. The mist was so dense that it appeared a lover cradling the castle in its nebulous embrace.

Despite the gray and gloom, the castle glistened. Evangeline's lips parted. The gleaming stone walls were hewn of . . . black *crystal*? A series of slim towers edged every visible corner, spearing the dismal skies with sleek, spiraling turrets. Winds whistled a lighthearted tune, shifting through the amorphous fog. The castle appeared a breathtaking centerpiece amid the ring of glacial peaks that surrounded it like solemn sentinels.

A shiver racked Evangeline's spine despite the thick woolen cloak shrouding her shoulders. She glanced up at her archmage, glad for the steady warmth of his embrace, until she noticed his strained expression.

"What's wrong?" Her voice came out a little too loud in the silence.

A little shake of his head.

"What—"

I've been warping far distances too frequently of late. His telepathic voice sounded weary. Declan rubbed a finger between his brows, an action that reminded her far too much of the young, vulnerable boy he'd once been. *I'm a little tired. That's all.*

Despite the lightness of his tone, alarm enfolded her heart like the icy fog hugging them. Her fingers ran to stroke the side of his coat she knew the vicious drakghi gouge marks lay beneath, faded scars on his skin.

I'm all right, little fire. He repeated, as though sensing her anxiety. Then he straightened and linked their hands before nudging her forward. The drawbridge creaked beneath their feet.

The portcullis was raised in welcome, but the sharp ends lining the bottom made Evangeline feel like she was trotting into the maw of a dragon. As they passed the threshold, soldiers standing guard behind the palisades bowed in perfect, silent synchrony.

"Everything looks so . . . " Evangeline struggled for the right word to describe the perfectly polished armor of every soldier, who all appeared to be of the *exact* same height and build. She wet her lips. "Orderly."

"Nathaniel enjoys precision and uniformity," Declan said, as though there was nothing unusual about the stone slabs lining the ground—every piece cut in identical shape and size. Declan switched back to telepathy as they entered the court-yard. *He prides himself in perfection. So he makes it a point to dictate everything. From the curating of his guards down to the materials that go into his castle.*

The perfectly square courtyard was paved with dark, gray-veined marble, and arching trellises filled with white blooms marked pathways that wound from sight. Beautiful. Immaculate. Just like the glacial peaks surrounding them. And every bit as cold.

Up close, Evangeline realized the walls were *not* crystal. They were a kind of black rock, but covered by a glistening layer of . . . What was it?

She ran a finger against it.

Ice.

Evangeline widened her eyes at her archmage.

Declan shot her an exceedingly wry smile. "Nathaniel makes a habit of enveloping his outer walls in ice—it acts as his shield. Also, volcanic glass is otherwise too brittle to hold against an attack."

Evangeline raised her brows and cast her gaze around in shock. "The entire castle is made from volcanic *glass?*"

"Otherwise known as obsidian, my lady," interjected an austere voice. "Sourced from the volatile lands of Teti Unas." In contrast to his somber tone, the man wore a blithe smile as he hurried across the courtyard toward them, his footsteps muted against the marble walkway that was thankfully free from ice.

With an illustrious bow, the man introduced himself as Nathaniel's squire, tasked with ushering guests to the site of revelry known as the Hanging Dome. As the squire led them down a path flanked by neatly trimmed hedges, Evangeline had a distinct impression the route had been chosen with the sole purpose of showing off the castle.

Crabapple trees, flowering in deep pinks, gave the obsidian splashes of color. Charming quartz baubles hung from their low branches and lit the walkway with an uncanny glow. Utterly fascinated, Evangeline slowed to better study the flickering ornaments. Upon noticing her interest, the squire halted his stride and, to her surprise, unhooked an orb and offered it to her for examination.

Evangeline drew in a breath. The orbs were not quartz.

Again, it was pure ice, shaped in a porous sphere, holding a burning flame within.

"How is this even possible?" Evangeline turned the ornament in her fingers. The flame flickered, but the ice remained pristine even though fire lapped against it.

The squire smirked, clearly pleased by her reaction. "Burning ice crystals, my lady. A little beeswax, salt . . . and some ingenuity. My liege is, after all, the realm's greatest cryokinetic, and he happens to appreciate simple beauty. It takes negligible effort for him to sustain the ice."

Evangeline blinked and studied the path with fresh, dumbfounded eyes. There had to be *hundreds* of such ice baubles hanging from the trees, lighting the entire length of the walkway. What sort of man enveloped his walls in and decorated his castle with ice crystals?

Declan ran a gentle knuckle over her cheek. He did not seem the least impressed.

They are parlor tricks, little fire.

Evangeline swallowed. Parlor tricks designed to remind his guests of the amount of power he wielded. When they rounded the bend, she knew they'd arrived at the Hanging Dome.

The clearing was nestled beside a lake so still it reflected the snowy glaciers like pristine glass. More crabapple trees cordoned the area, and the abundant baubles of burning ice crystals cast a dazzling luminosity around the clearing and the people milling in it. True to its name, the Hanging Dome glistened fifty paces over the ground—an intricate latticework of *ice* hovering over guests and cocktail tables.

"The archmage of Amereen, Declan Thorne, and his elorin de ana, Lady Evangeline Barre," the squire boomed, drawing the attention of every guest in the clearing.

The weight of gazes fell upon her, and suddenly Evangeline felt like a lost fawn who had just wandered into a wolf's den.

Are *you all right, little fire?* Declan's mental voice brimmed with concern.

Evangeline tightened her grip over the crook of Declan's arm and reminded herself she'd insisted on coming here.

Yes. She sucked in a deep breath, filling her lungs with crisp, misty air laced with crabapple blooms. *I can do this.* An assurance to him as much as it was to herself.

A servant dressed in livery sidled up, offering to take her cloak. Evangeline slid a hesitant hand over the clasp that pinned the garment at the base of her neck. Shedding the heavy woolen coat which kept his mating mark from sight would be the final step in baring herself to Declan's world—officially announcing herself as his elorin de ana.

Despite her affirmation, Declan must sense her lingering apprehension, for he leaned close and surprised her by undoing the clasp himself. His gaze was warm. Reassuring. And . . . transfixed.

Even though apprehension brewed in her gut, tension melted off her shoulders. With as much poise as she could muster, she shed her cloak and relinquished it to the servant without taking her eyes off her archmage.

When Tessa had first presented her with the garment,

declaring it the height of fashion, Evangeline had been doubtful. The style was a touch too bold, the color too rich, and the fabric too fine. It had felt far too ostentatious a gown.

But now, under Declan's ravenous gaze and his slightly openmouthed expression, Evangeline decided she would be happy for Tessa to dictate all her future wardrobe choices.

Her shoulders were daringly bare, displaying enough décolletage so that Declan's mating mark peeked through to tease the eye. Embroidered lace encased her arms, the only embellishment to the fall of lush ivory that was styled to enhance every curve.

With a devilish glint in his eye, Declan dipped his head to whisper words that roused heat on her cheeks . . . and between her legs.

The interlude had been enough to bolster her confidence, so when a rather stunning couple swept up to meet them, Evangeline managed an unwavering smile.

Alejandro Castano, archmage of Salindras, and his favorite ayari, Lady Sariel. The congeniality in Declan's telepathic tone further set Evangeline at ease, telling her she was in the presence of those he regarded as friends.

Garbed far more elaborately than her own archmage, Alejandro wore a coat of rich blue damask with silver embroidered edges. The brocade of a silver-blue dragon lay stark over his shoulder, a serpentine body that wound down his knee-length coat. His boots were so polished Evangeline could almost see her reflection shining in them, though the silver rings on his fingers glittered as though vying for attention. Evangeline drew her gaze away, trying hard not to stare. She had never seen a man dressed with such extravagance. His raiment reminded her of the blue feathers of a parading peacock.

Alejandro regarded her with equal curiosity, eyes widening

at the start of the starburst pattern peeking above her neckline. He released an incredulous laugh as his gaze darted from the mating mark to Declan and back.

"Railea's tears, the rumors are true! I was just telling Sariel that a coldhearted bastard like you couldn't possibly have taken a de ana."

There was not a twitch in Declan's expression, but Evangeline knew from his stance that he took no offense.

"I may be cold, but I am no fool. I know my mate when I see her."

Evangeline flushed, from both pleasure and mortification, as Declan guided her forward, holding one hand at the small of her back as he introduced her with enough pride in his voice to widen Alejandro's grin.

Then Declan applied some pressure to his hold.

Taking the cue, Evangeline swept down in a curtsy that had her knees almost kissing the ground, but not before plastering a hand over her chest to prevent exposing an overgenerous view down her neckline.

She knew little of the intricate customs of the Echelon and the subtle nuances critical to court life. But she took comfort that her archmage would remain by her side, giving her subtle guidance.

Without prompting, Evangeline turned to the ayari and made another curtsy, deep enough for nobility. Sariel's eyes widened, and the arch of her brows ripped into Evangeline's faltering confidence. Had her curtsy been too shallow and perceived as disrespectful?

In turn, the ayari dipped low enough that the brilliant shimmer of her silver dress pooled on the ground like melted moonwax as she addressed Declan. And much to Evangeline's surprise, Sariel dealt her an equally deep genuflection—one afforded *only* to archmages.

"What an honor to finally meet you, Lady Evangeline," Sariel said.

Sensing Evangeline's confusion, Declan spoke into her mind. *You are my elorin, little fire. My equal. Sariel is wise to acknowledge you as such.*

"The honor is mine," Evangeline replied, then bit her lower lip. *Should I have extended the same respect toward her?*

Though he appeared wholly focused on Alejandro, who had launched into lighthearted chatter, Declan's telepathic voice held amusement. *No. An archmage's ayari is merely his companion. You've shown Sariel inordinate respect with such a curtsy, little fire. An archmage's elorin does not genuflect to ayaris. In fact, apart from to members of the Echelon, you are not expected to bend your knee. All social graces you extend will reflect your esteem, not deference.*

Before further conversation could unfold, another couple swept up to meet them—a portly human man and a woman Evangeline had assumed to be his *granddaughter*, until she'd caught his intimate hold on the young woman's hips.

The vicegerent of Nathaniel's southern lands and the woman who will one day kill him in his sleep to wed his son.

Evangeline tried to keep her expression straight as verbal introductions were made.

Declan's telepathic voice turned flippant. *Nothing the old lecher doesn't deserve—insisted on marrying the girl even though he knew she was his son's lover to begin with.*

They had barely exchanged niceties before more guests approached them, people who were all clearly eager to meet for themselves a woman who was not only an archmage's mate but rumored to be one of the lost Seelie race.

Declan continued to make private introductions with stoic wryness. To her amusement and contrary to public belief, her archmage *did* possess a sense of humor—a rather dark and raunchy one.

General Vikoff and his wife. The man has the gall of a pigeon and is the last person you'd want at your back in battle . . .

Emissary LaSalle. The woman has a tongue of silk she uses to twist her way through any political debate. She is also known to employ a dagger where her tongue fails . . .

Councilor Yosef and his latest mistress. If mages could develop syphilis, he would likely be the first to contract it . . .

As a servant bearing a polished silver tray of refreshments approached, Declan beckoned him closer and turned his back to the milling crowd still waiting to greet them, affording them a moment's peace.

How do you even know half these things, Archmage? Evangeline projected her thoughts as she gave the servant a polite smile. Drinks of varying shades in crystalline flutes of every shape and size lined the tray.

Declan gave her a lopsided grin, as rare as it was utterly devastating, and it distracted her enough to settle her jittery nerves. *I served in Nathaniel's court as a soldier for over eighty-three summers before I ascended, little fire.*

Of course he had. He'd told her before, but amid the whirlwind of introductions, she'd momentarily forgotten her archmage had once lived here, in this fortress of rime and splendor. Issuing a cognizant hum, Evangeline selected a glass of liquid that sparkled like stars. And nearly dropped it.

The flute was not made of crystal.

"Is *everything* made of ice in this place?" she demanded, unable to hide her disbelief.

At her incredulous expression, Declan actually threw his head back and laughed. "Nathaniel expects his guests to have the ability to withstand frost, or . . . " He nodded at one of the nearby guests who appeared engrossed in conversation while a chalice levitated in the air beside him. "For them to be telekinetic."

She stared as the man took an absent sip from the hovering ice chalice. Declan chuckled. He took both her hands and closed them over the flute underneath his. Warmth flowed into her hands until the flute was no longer icy to the touch.

Evangeline cocked her head. "He expects everyone to wield fire or be telekinetic?" If so, their host was proving inconsiderate.

Only archmages had control of the elements, although there were known exceptions. But even so, not all archmages mastered the element of fire. And not every mage mastered telekinesis.

"No," interjected a lofty feminine voice from behind. "But the ones who don't, usually stay away from drinks meant for . . . their betters."

Declan stiffened, wholly imperceptible to the eye, but Evangeline sensed the sudden tension in his muscles. She followed his line of sight.

A woman with gold-spun hair and skin of burnished umber eyed Declan with such blatant covetousness that Evangeline's gums prickled.

She met Evangeline's gaze with a blithe smile as she stroked the fur mantle draped over her shoulder. The accessory did nothing to distract from her plunging neckline and enviable cleavage—a sight outshined only by the liberal slit at her hip.

How was she not swarmed by suitors?

The man who accompanied her appeared muted in her presence. His brackish brown hair was braided into a thick coil that hung like a rope. Silver threaded his temples, and along with the feathering lines at the corners of his eyes, indicated he was well past the first two thousand years of life.

Sebastian Khan, the archmage of Batuhan, and his daughter, Vera.

Declan provided no further commentary.

"Ah, finally we meet the mysterious woman who won Nathaniel's son," Sebastian said in the quiet voice of a man who knew he commanded enough power without the need to raise it.

As introductions were exchanged, uneasiness grew in Evangeline's gut. Vera's lingering gazes at her archmage suggested they were more than acquaintances, while Sebastian, like every other guest, studied Evangeline with unconcealed curiosity. "Never thought I would again encounter one of the lost Seelie race," he said with a musing smile. "You must tell us how you survived the Winter War."

Declan shifted closer to her side. "A tale for another time, Sebastian. It is hardly appropriate for my elorin to be recounting war tales on a festive night such as this."

"Indeed, *dadyia*," Vera interjected with a silky smile. "No one cares about old war stories." Up close, Vera was tall enough she regarded Declan eye to eye. She slunk close enough that she loomed over Evangeline's line of sight. The fur mantle upon her shoulders *shuddered* abruptly to reveal two beady eyes. It snarled and flashed tiny, sharp teeth.

Evangeline startled, sloshing the wine in her glass. Declan gave her a reassuring squeeze of his hand.

Vera released a haughty titter. "There now, it is only Simon." She ran an affectionate hand along the ferret's head and glanced down at Evangeline with a smirk. "He didn't frighten you, did he?"

"No," Evangeline said with a stiff smile. "It . . . surprised me, that's all."

"So tell me, Lady Evangeline. What do you make of the revelry so far, hmm?" Vera asked, her voice nearly a purr as she stroked her furry companion. The ferret continued to glare at Evangeline.

"The Kingdom of Flen is breathtaking," she said truthfully.

"And I've never before seen the Reckoning from such a high vantage point . . . " Her archmage reached out to slink his arm around her waist, distracting her midsentence to draw her nearer to his side. "But Declan tells me Flen is the best place to view it."

Vera's jaw hardened ever so slightly as Declan's hand rested over Evangeline's hip. She arched her brows. "Lord Archmage Thorne is right. You're in for a treat. There is nothing like seeing the Reckoning from these glaciers."

Sebastian chuckled, seemingly oblivious to the brewing tension. "Yes. It is no secret I maintained such close friendship with Nathaniel just so I can make use of his lands to view the Reckoning every Winter Solstice. Speaking of which, where is our ungracious host?"

"Undoubtedly waiting for all his guests to arrive to make the final entrance," quipped a stout official who had been hovering nearby, waiting to slip into the conversation. "Lord Archmage Strom does have a flair for theatrics. While we're waiting for his entrance, have you had the pleasure of meeting Councilor Gruon, my lords archmage?"

The official beckoned an elderly man into the circle.

With Declan's attention occupied, Evangeline was left under Vera's scrutiny. Eager for something to do with herself, she took a sip of her drink and grimaced. The flute might no longer be cold to the touch, but the wine remained frigid.

Vera chuckled at Evangeline's expression and shot Declan a disapproving shake of her head. "Archmages can sometimes forget the rest of us feel temperatures far more keenly than they do." She extended a hand. "Here, allow me."

Evangeline hesitated.

Her archmage was still engaged in conversation. It would be ridiculous to interrupt him just to have him reheat her glass. And Vera didn't give her a chance to refuse. The other woman sidled near and laid her free hand over Evangeline's just as Declan had done.

"Just a touch warmer, and you'll find the wine absolutely divine."

Gentle warmth flowed through her hands, heating the liquid within the ice-fashioned glass that remained impervious to the rise in temperature.

Evangeline was smiling her appreciation when a sudden, scorching pain assailed her. With a yelp, she wrenched her hands from Vera's grip. The glass splintered as it hit the ground.

Declan started and clutched her shoulders. "What's wrong?"

Evangeline clutched her trembling hand to her chest, keenly aware of the scene she'd just caused. A silence had descended upon the Hanging Dome as the weight of everyone's attention settled upon her.

Vera's eyes were laughing when they met hers. Her hand stroked the ferret's tail the way one might a lover's cheek. "Oh, I'm terribly sorry, my lady. I did not expect you to be quite so . . . fragile."

"Evangeline." Declan pried her hand from her chest. "*Show* me."

All laughter left Vera's expression when Declan stared at Evangeline's hand with his jaw hanging. A miasma of scalded flesh, peeling skin, and rising blisters. Seared in the distinct shape of Vera's handprint.

SEVEN

A wave of violence superseded Declan's shock, threatening to tear from his chest and unleash itself over the gaping crowd. How could this have happened, right under his nose? Evangeline trembled like a leaf in the wind. Her violet-rimmed irises dilated with shock as she stared at her mutilated flesh, her skin beginning to purl as blisters boiled.

On the psychic plane, Declan delved into the half-formed mating bond between them, channeling power through it. It was a nascent thread, frail and almost insubstantial due to its incompletion, but it served to reverse the effects of Vera's burn. The sores on her skin subsided, her flesh knitting together with preternatural speed—and the scars on his flank began to ache. A subtle reminder of how he'd once come so close to losing her. It wasn't until Evangeline's skin was smooth and unblemished that Declan allowed himself to loosen his grip on her arm.

And glare at the perpetrator.

Vera appeared a vision of bewilderment, as though *she'd* been the one who had just suffered a burn deep enough to have lost a limb had he not intervened.

"How dare you?" Declan clenched and unclenched his fist, trying to rein in the outrage insistent on lashing out and wreaking havoc. But a small semblance of rationality held him back—any violence on his part would likely incite a civil war.

Vera's gaze snapped up to meet his, wide and filled with dismay. "I-I didn't know." The termagant shook her head with a hand at the base of her neck as she staggered back. "I was just . . . playing with her."

Barely three hundred years of age, Vera was even younger than Declan's half brother, Alexander, who was still occasionally prone to callowness. But Vera's claim was preposterous, even for one as young as she.

Declan snarled through the arsonist haze descending upon his senses. "Playing?"

The ridiculous ferret draped over Vera's shoulder reared up on two front legs to release a malicious hiss, as though warning him back.

"Oh, for Railea's sake! She is your mate, is she not?" Vera flourished a defensive hand. She glanced around the gathering crowd as if to seek support. "She warms the bed of an archmage who wields *both* ice and fire. One would assume she's strong enough to withstand a little heat! How was I to know she's as weak as a human?"

Vera's final question, punctuated by a petulant pout, snapped the final thread of civility in Declan's chest. He took one menacing step forward, and Vera shrank back against her father, who took on a protective stance.

"Calm down, Thorne. Vera may have—"

At Declan's glower, Sebastian cleared his throat and

amended his statement. "Vera *has* crossed the line. But your elorin is fine, isn't she? No harm done."

No harm done? Evangeline stood silent, a quivering rabbit nearly mauled by a fox.

Still clutching her newly recovered arm, she stared at no one in particular, eyes glazed, lips flattened to a seam.

"Yes." Vera sniffed delicately beside her father, clearly unrepentant. Her words grated against Declan like flint sparking fire. "If she'd trained at the Keep, she would have been taught to endure minor injuries without causing such a scene."

At the thought of Evangeline subjected to more burns, the markings on Declan's skin came alive of their own volition, shimmering gold beneath his clothes. Gasps of alarm rolled through the crowd. Whenever the glyphs on an archmage's skin came alive, death was never far behind.

Sebastian narrowed his eyes and shoved his daughter back, then took a combative stance. In silent response, his own markings illuminated beneath his bearskin pelt, flashing bright in clear warning.

"Perhaps an apology is in order," drawled Alejandro from a cocktail table.

"Yes," chimed Sonja Tuath, the archmage of Yarveric, who had moved forward to join the growing crowd around them. "She *is* an archmage's elorin, after all."

The entire Echelon, save Nathaniel, had gathered to witness the dispute, likely the reason for Evangeline's continued silence.

At the not-so-subtle murmurings of the crowd, Sebastian nudged his daughter forward. "Apologize, Vera."

Vera twisted her lips. "But *dadyia*, I was only trying to help—"

"Now, Vera Anastasia Khan." Sebastian's voice rose like a whip, and his daughter obeyed with impressive alacrity. Vera

went swiftly down on her knees, yet her contrition sounded unconvincing to Declan's ears.

"I apologize, Lady Evangeline. I meant you no harm."

Before Declan could repudiate her insincerity, Evangeline offered a weak nod, indicating her acceptance. Sebastian grunted in satisfaction.

"Vera is merely a child, Thorne. I trust you understand her impetuous nature and forgive her transgression."

Evangeline might have offered clemency, but it did not mean Declan did. When he didn't back down, the crowd rippled with nervousness. But no one came between bristling archmages. Intervention usually resulted in more bloodshed.

That fact was clearly lost on his little fire as she moved into his line of vision, inserting herself into the precarious space still crackling with tension between him and Sebastian.

"Declan," she whispered.

When he didn't move, his gaze still locked with Sebastian's in a war of dominance, she tugged at his lapels.

"Declan," she repeated, this time with enough command in her voice to tear his gaze from Sebastian to her. Her apprehension had cleared only to be replaced by alarm. *Archmage, I am no longer hurt.*

Declan resisted the urge to snarl. *You could have lost your hand.*

Her eyes were bleak. *Vera has already apologized. Let it go.*

Declan narrowed his own eyes. He had always adored her big heart, but this time, her compassionate nature only frustrated him. He was not, and never would be, benevolent. Not like her. And it was best the world knew it.

"You have every right to accept her apology, Evangeline, but do not think to dictate my actions. I will not tolerate such a transgression against my mate." He ground the words through his teeth, loud enough to be heard by all in the vicinity.

She flinched. An instant wash of shame flooded his chest, but his outrage still churned like a maelstrom without an outlet.

I was foolish to allow Vera close enough to touch me in the first place. Her mental tone was measured and insistent. *It is a mistake I won't repeat. Please, Declan, that woman is not worth a war.*

Her final words acted as a leash over the darkness rioting in his gut. Declan swallowed the blistering words in his throat. The thought of Vera sauntering off unscathed chafed his skin and scalded his pride. But Evangeline was right.

Retribution would assuage his outrage, but at what cost?

He took a step back and pinned Vera with an acrimonious glare. "Let this be known, Vera. If you so much as come near my mate again, regardless of the consequences, I will burn you alive."

E vangeline blanched at Declan's verbal diatribe but sighed in relief when the flare of gold on his skin ebbed. In response, Sebastian stepped back with a disgruntled huff.

Friction waned from the air, but the weight of the gazes of all six archmages continued to rest heavy upon her.

A sudden wave of nausea overwhelmed her, and bile rose to the back of her throat. Vera's words—labeling her as fragile and weak—had hurt more than the pain of the burn.

Her weakness had nearly led her archmage into a war. Desperate to be free from public observation, Evangeline tried to pry herself from Declan's grasp.

He frowned down at her, not releasing his hold, but Evangeline pulled away with more urgency. "I need the restroom."

His lips firmed. "We'll go home." *I should never have brought you here.*

Evangeline stiffened. His telepathic words felt like a slap after Vera's vicious stunt.

She shook her head in silent refusal. She would not flee like a little mouse seeking cover. She would not allow Vera to cow her.

Declan only tightened his grasp over her forearm. "We are going home," he repeated in a mellow voice that was not to be mistaken for a suggestion.

Evangeline jerked her hand from his, surprising them both.

"No," she said, more sharply than intended.

Declan's brow furrowed. "Evangeline . . . "

Cognizant of the gazes around them, she fashioned a weak smile. "I need to remove the stains." She indicated the dribble of drink that had caught her hem when she'd dropped her glass.

Please, Archmage. Allow me a few moments to compose myself.

A flash of silver in her periphery interrupted them. A woman with ebony hair and skin as pale as moonlight.

"I'm just on my way to the powder room to freshen up, my lady. Perhaps you would like to join me?" Sariel bobbed a little curtsy and offered a smile, hesitant but not unkind.

Evangeline nodded, glad for the woman's timely intervention. Declan said nothing, but his reluctance was as palpable as the prying eyes of the crowd, which might have dispersed, but still studied them without reserve.

As Sariel led her away from Declan's hawklike gaze, a wave of light-headedness suffused her senses. Slowing her stride but not stopping, Evangeline prayed she wouldn't lose consciousness. *Not here. Railea, goddess of light, Ozenn, god of chaos, please, please don't let me faint here.*

She made it to the powder room without event.

It was spacious and warm, with a stately fireplace embedded in the pristine black wall. Polished oak panels and luxurious chairs upholstered in red velvet lined the other side of the room, and ornamental mirrors with gilded frames hung over the glossy walls. Evangeline studied herself in a mirror. She was a disheveled mess. A sickly pallor had leached into her skin, and stray hairs escaped the elegant chignon that Tessa had created.

Half tempted to ring one of the heavy tassels for a maid to deliver some fresh water so she could wash her face, Evangeline resigned herself to fixing her hair instead. Water would only ruin the kohl Tessa had carefully applied to accent her eyes.

"Will you allow me to help you, my lady?"

Evangeline whipped around. The other woman had been so silent that Evangeline had nearly forgotten her presence. Mustering a faint smile, she shook her head. "I am quite all right, Lady Sariel. You are most kind."

Sariel regarded her with what appeared to be amusement, but not the mocking kind. "Sariel," she said. "There is no need for formalities." She slipped a slim silver case from the satchel she carried. "I have rouge for your cheeks if you like."

Evangeline regarded the woman's reflection in the mirror. Tension eased from her shoulders as she responded to Sariel's genuine smile.

"I could use some color, couldn't I?"

Sariel dusted rouge onto her fingers and reached for Evangeline's cheekbones.

"It's all right. I can do it myself," Evangeline said, mortified at the thought of having an archmage's ayari play her maid.

Sariel's smile turned wry. "You know, I was once a queen's maid before I became an ayari. I used to serve Queen Seraphina herself."

At the name of the long dead Unseelie queen, Evangeline's jaw hung.

Sariel laughed and took the opportunity to brush the rouge over her cheeks. "I am Unseelie. Were you unaware?"

Evangeline shook her head, staring at the woman's rounded ears and hazel eyes. She shouldn't feel surprised—Declan had told her of Alejandro's penchant for *collecting* women of different cultures and races.

Sariel wore a mischievous smile as her ears sharpened and her irises took on a flash of violet for a split second before morphing back into their previous appearance.

Evangeline couldn't stop her own grin. "I wish I could do that." Veiling her eyes would draw less curiosity to her.

Sariel tilted her head. "You truly can't wield magic, then?"

Evangeline tucked stray hairs back into her coiffure. "If I could, I would have changed my eyes to a less distinct shade."

"I thought you'd deliberately left them half rimmed to make a statement."

Evangeline paused. "Why would I do that?"

Sariel shrugged. "Some women like attention." She stepped back to study their reflection in the mirror and beamed. "There, nobody would guess you'd just had a nasty encounter with one of the biggest shrews of magekind."

A chuckle eased from Evangeline's lips.

With deft hands, Sariel proceeded to fix her own hair. Evangeline cocked her head to regard the other woman. "How did you become ayari to an archmage?"

"When Queen Seraphina passed, her husband became crazed . . . and started the Winter War."

Despite the warmth from the crackling hearth, a chill

trickled down Evangeline's spine. "King Zephyr," she murmured.

Sariel nodded, and her gaze took on a distant quality. "He loved the queen a great deal. Most say her death was the catalyst for the war."

Evangeline couldn't help the stiffening of her spine and the tightening of her jaw. She'd always thought the Winter War was a result of Zephyr's thirst for power. "Zephyr massacred my people because of his wife's death?"

Not seeming to mind her reaction in the least, Sariel gave a listless smile as her fingers continued to tuck in stray hairs. "He didn't just decimate your kind, you know. Zephyr sacrificed many of his own."

Hearing the sorrow in the other woman's voice, Evangeline gentled her own tone. "Did you lose someone?"

"I lost . . . everything. My father and brother were the only family I had left, but King Zephyr insisted every able-bodied man enlist in the war . . . " Her lips pinched. "They perished. And I became destitute. I couldn't stay in the realm that had become a wasteland of blood and screams . . . so I fled. I wanted to live in a place free from Zephyr's grasp, so I came to Railea's realm. It was only by chance I trespassed on Alejandro's lands."

The set of her lips softened and a light danced in her eyes. "But instead of killing me, he took me to his table and fed me." A slow smirk. "Then he took me to his bed."

At the rising color on Evangeline's cheeks, Sariel laughed throatily. "My liege has always had an eye for women, and he knows what he wants when he sees it." Her eyes twinkled. "I'm sure you'll agree that this is true for *all* archmages, my lady. They do rule supreme, after all."

Evangeline issued an oblique hum, and said, "Do call me Evie."

Sariel's lips parted with a slow blink.

"You did say no formalities," Evangeline reminded her with a smile.

Sariel's beam was dazzling. "Evie. You are not what I expected."

"What were you expecting?"

"Another self-absorbed woman. I met plenty in my time at the Keep."

Evangeline turned away from the mirror to face the woman directly. "You trained at the Keep?"

"Of course. I was nothing more than a peasant, and after the first night"—a salacious wink—"my liege decided to keep me, so he had me enrolled in the Keep."

Evangeline stared at the other woman. "Why did you need to train at the Keep if Lord Archmage Castano had already decided to . . . keep you?"

Sariel rolled her eyes. "The Keep equips every acolyte with the deportment expected of an archmage's ayari. And the necessary skills to *please* an archmage without getting hurt during intercourse."

Declan's destructive tendencies rose in her mind, and Evangeline's cheeks warmed. Before her fainting spells, her archmage had warped them to the tip of Torgerson Falls frequently enough that Evangeline wondered if the constant erosion of the opposing rock face would eventually cause it to crumble.

At her mute expression, Sariel tilted her head in a quizzical fashion.

"Lord Archmage Thorne . . . does he not hurt you by accident when he gets . . . excited?"

Evangeline shook her head, appalled by the idea that an ayari expected to be hurt.

Sariel opened her mouth but said nothing. She blinked.

"Well." The ayari smoothed down her skirts. "Lord Thorne must be remarkably self-possessed, then. Although it is hardly a surprise. I don't think I'd ever seen him laugh. Until today, that is."

"He does"—Evangeline swallowed her embarrassment —"destroy things."

Sariel's brows shot up. "He diverts his powers during sex?"

Evangeline's cheeks burned, and she allowed the woman to draw a conclusion from the silence. Sariel bit her lower lip as though suppressing a laugh.

"That is incredibly considerate of him. But Evie, if that is the case, you know he isn't fully . . . enjoying himself, don't you?"

"What do you mean?"

"The overflow of an archmage's powers when they are . . . ah, overstimulated, is to be expected. In fact, it indicates their enjoyment. But for an archmage to be consciously diverting his powers during intercourse, well . . . it's a little like . . . " Sariel wrinkled her nose and tapped a finger to her chin. "A little like putting food in front of a starving man and telling him to wait until it goes cold before he is allowed to eat."

Evangeline frowned as she considered her archmage's bedroom behaviors. Declan's markings did flare brighter, and his actions were less measured whenever they were out on Torgerson Peak. Evangeline had always thought he'd thoroughly satisfied himself with her . . . but she had never been with another man. Had he always been holding himself back, somehow?

Then she swallowed, sudden sickness rising in her gut. She'd always known ayaris were trained for the personal use of the Echelon, but . . . "Every ayari is expected to be *hurt* for an archmage's enjoyment?"

Sariel chuckled. "Certain discomforts and abrasions are

inevitable during intimacy with a being who wields so much power. Lord Alejandro is always gentle with his women. Even so, he may *unwittingly* bruise us, but"—she shuddered—"the same cannot be said for the *other archmage*s."

At the incredulity of Evangeline's expression, Sariel sighed and shifted to lean a hip against the polished counter. "At the Keep, they would submerge us in water so we'd learn to hold our breath and keep our pulse steady. They burned us, too, with hot coals until we learned not to scream."

Evangeline stared down at her singed hand. She'd nearly blacked out from the pain. And Vera had claimed it was a joke?

Blood drained from her cheeks, and Sariel clucked. "There now. It isn't as bad as you think. Immortals do heal quickly."

Evangeline exhaled her outrage. "That is hardly an excuse."

Sariel only shrugged. "That's why Vera assumed you would be able to handle her little trick. Railea knows she was dealt worse while training at the Keep."

Evangeline's throat knotted. "Vera *trained* at the Keep?"

Why would an archmage's daughter, clearly doted upon, and one powerful enough to wield fire, choose to train at the Keep?

"I served alongside her." Sariel snickered. "But merely three seasons passed before my liege came to collect me. Vera, however, served the full *decade* before she entered the Court of Amereen."

Evangeline blinked.

Sariel cocked her head. "You didn't know?"

Evangeline fidgeted in her seat. The room suddenly felt stifling and her throat unbearably tight. Sariel swallowed and turned back to the mirror to fuss with her skirts.

"I thought you knew. But it is hardly a secret Vera served in Lord Thorne's court for almost four seasons before . . . "

"Before?" Evangeline prompted, her voice coming out hoarse.

Sariel wet her lips. "Before Lord Thorne warped through an imploding fae portal and returned with a human woman. Then he sent Vera packing, back to her father's court."

"Vera was Declan's ayari." The words dropped like stones from Evangeline's mouth.

Sariel winced. "Well, not *officially*. As far as anyone knows, Lord Thorne has never held a formal claiming. But everyone knows what Vera feels for him. As a mageling, Vera used to follow on his heels like a devoted lamb. When he ascended, Vera's father even proposed they mate . . . but"—Sariel pursed her lips—"your archmage refused. Then, Vera subjected herself to ten years at the Keep with the sole purpose of serving his court."

Tension coiled in her chest, colder than ice.

Declan hadn't breathed a word of this to her. Why hadn't he? He'd claimed he'd never had an ayari, yet Vera had served his court only to be sent away after he'd met Evangeline.

No wonder Vera had acted the way she had.

Why hadn't Declan told her?

Sariel folded her arms, propping her sleek figure against the gilded frame of the mirror where her shimmering dress glinted like a constellation of stars. "It must be hard for Vera's pride, being spurned after years of devotion to a single man. And for that man to be seen so enamored of another woman . . . " Sariel shook her head. "There was another acolyte who had proposed to serve as ayari in the Court of Amereen. Not long after, she was found at the bottom of a ravine with her spine irreparably broken."

Evangeline's lips parted in shock.

Sariel shrugged. "To be fair, no one knows what truly happened. But Vera did wield enough telekinesis to shove a woman off a ravine, and she'd always made her intentions clear where your archmage was concerned."

The ayari's gaze turned solemn to match the grimness of her tone. "I suggest you keep your distance, Evie. And watch your back when she is close."

EIGHT

Though Declan kept his mind trained on Evangeline's psyche, he couldn't keep himself from staring in the direction she'd disappeared with Sariel. What was taking them so long? He resisted the urge to rub up against her on the mental plane and demand she return, resisted the urge to warp toward the sunlit shimmer of her psyche that beckoned him like a seafarer's beacon.

She needed time to regain her composure.

Declan clenched his jaw. He simply needed to take her home.

Spying a servant hovering nearby with a silver tray, he stalked up, snatched a crystal tumbler, and eyed the amber contents. Mujarin. Perfect. He swilled the whiskey, welcoming the burn down his throat. No longer in a mood to socialize, Declan wore an intentional glower to ward off conversationalists—but he didn't brood for too long before Evangeline's voice met his ears.

His little fire finally emerged from the alcove, exchanging an easy laugh with Sariel as they strolled down the pathway back to the pavilion. Evangeline seemed to have her spirits restored. Her head was held high, and color had returned to her cheeks as though the ugly scene with Vera had never occurred. But when her gaze met his, the flicker of doubt in its depths drew a frisson of uneasiness down his spine.

While Sariel made her way back to Alejandro's side, Evangeline came to a halt a thumb's length before Declan—a miniscule gap to the public eye, but to him, it might well be a gulf separating continents.

"Evangeline . . . " He reached out to pull her into his arms. She didn't resist his touch, yet she didn't lean into him as she usually did. She looked up at him, her expression pensive.

A knot formed at the base of his throat.

Declan bridged the displeasing gap and brushed up against her mind on the mental plane for good measure. *What's wrong, little fire? Are you still feeling unwell?*

She hesitated briefly before wetting her lips, then a furrow marred the spot between her brows. He leaned in to brush his lips over the offending crease, but she tilted her head to the side, refusing his kiss.

"Declan, I—"

Light flickered around them. The mass of burning ice crystals festooning the trees blazed bright, muting the words on her lips. An anticipatory silence descended across the crowd while the squire's voice boomed through the pavilion.

"Your host, Nathaniel Strom, the archmage of Flen, and his ayari, Lady Galinka."

Nathaniel Strom's love for theatrics often overshadowed the depth of his powers, belying his true nature—that of a connoisseur of cruelty, a collector of carnal pleasures, and a cyrokinetic capable of freezing the world over if he wished.

Instinctively, Declan tightened his grip around Evangeline as Nathaniel's assessing gaze swept the crowd to land on her.

Galinka, dressed in a sparkling gown and jewels, hung onto the crook of his arm like an accessory as Nathaniel made his way across the pavilion, pausing intermittently to shake hands and exchange pleasantries. As they approached, Declan felt a sudden irrational urge to warp his little fire away from his father's rapacious appraisal. He didn't want to introduce the one bright spark in his life to a man who tended to efface all things pure and innocent.

But fleeing was not an option.

So when Nathaniel and Galinka came within proximity, Declan betrayed no emotion while he made the necessary introductions.

"How delightful to finally meet you," Nathaniel murmured, and from the way his eyes narrowed, it was clear he meant none of those words.

"Yes," Galinka said in a gushing tone, "we've all heard of how you pursued her into the fae realm to rescue her from the clutches of King Zephyr."

Evangeline, clearly discomfited by the subject, gave the ayari a strained smile. But Galinka prattled on without waiting for a response. "How utterly romantic! And why have we received no invitation to a Promise Ceremony, Lord Archmage Thorne?"

Had the question been posed by any other, Declan might have taken offense. But from his years of service to Nathaniel, he knew Galinka's interest to be genuine. The woman, while vapid, was never malicious—a surprise, considering the archmage she served.

Declan indulged her. "An oversight on my part." He turned to Evangeline and stroked the length of her arm in silent apology. "But we will hold a ceremony one day." In truth, Declan had wanted nothing more than to bind Evangeline to him in a public setting. But he couldn't—not until their mating bond was complete, and his skin properly marked by her.

A derisive scoff escaped Nathaniel's throat. "A ceremony is hardly necessary given you've already"—the archmage's gaze roved to the symbol peeking above Evangeline's neckline, and his lips curled as though he smelled something foul—"branded the girl's flesh."

Despite his rising hackles, Declan kept his voice even. "Evangeline *will* be properly presented to the gods, and officially introduced to my people as my elorin."

Galinka, clearly sensing the tension, hijacked the conversation with idle chatter while Nathaniel's telepathic voice slashed into Declan's mind like an ice-wrought rapier.

I had thought to give her a chance, but now I understand Reyas's rebellion . . . The wench can't even veil herself properly. My son, you have committed a true folly.

Nathaniel was wise not to air his thoughts aloud, but as it was, Declan barely tolerated his father's disapproving comments.

My decisions are not yours to judge.

Nathaniel pressed his lips into a censorious line. *If you wanted something exotic for your bed, I have a number of animati who would gladly spread their legs for you.* Nathaniel's gaze roved over Evangeline's form, evaluating her the way a farmer might livestock before purchasing. *Save those large fawn eyes, I see nothing about her that warrants such devotion.* Nathaniel curled his lips. *In fact, she looks almost too delicate for proper use.*

Nathaniel's blunt assessment did not shock him. The other archmage frequently took it upon himself to dole out unsolicited advice that Declan ignored with flippant ease. But not this time.

The Hanging Dome levitating above their head issued a weighted groan before a sharp cracking resounded. The intricate construct of hovering ice splintered and snapped into pieces as if it were corrugated glass.

Evangeline and Galinka both jumped in concert with the alarmed buzz of the unsettled crowd. Guests darted out of the way as though expecting the pieces of ice to crash over their heads. But not a single shard fell; the fragments continued to drift tranquilly in the air.

Declan cast an idle glance overhead. "You may want to consider a proper trellis in the future, Nathaniel," he mused, "and perhaps some real silverware. I find some of your current amenities . . . too delicate for proper use."

The glare Nathaniel shot him was one he might use on a recalcitrant child.

Playing the part, Declan lifted a haughty chin.

Evangeline leaned into him as though seeking reassurance. Taking the opportunity to pull her closer, Declan gave Nathaniel a curt nod. "We thank you for your hospitality, Nathaniel. Lady Galinka. It's been a pleasure, but I think it is best Evangeline and I take our leave now."

Galinka's eyes widened with what appeared to be genuine stupefaction. "Oh, but we are just about to begin dinner, and the Reckoning is sure to commence soon. It would be such a shame for Lady Evangeline to miss it."

Declan hesitated. Indeed, the Reckoning was best viewed from the glaciers of Flen . . . but then again, they would have

a decent view from Torgerson Peak. It might not be as spectacular, but they would be away from prying eyes—where he
could peel away the layers of tension that had somehow come
between them. Not to mention he'd developed the devil's itch
to peel the dress from her body. It would be torturous for
him, of course, as he had no intention of allowing himself
release lest it trigger another bout of unconsciousness. Still,
he craved her pleasure. At the very least, he wanted to hold
her close, to assure himself that she was still his. He
needed it.

Evangeline must have changed her mind about staying, or
maybe she'd simply sensed his impatience, for she dipped into
another deep curtsy that was entirely unnecessary. "It is a
shame, Ayari Galinka," Evangeline said with a wan smile, "but
do accept our apology. I am feeling rather . . . weary."

Galinka pouted, the mannerism incongruent with a woman
old enough to have birthed Declan twice over. "But we barely
got a chance to speak, Lady Evangeline. I've been looking
forward to making your acquaintance."

"Yes," Nathaniel interjected smoothly. "I was keeping it a
surprise, but I'll admit I have planned something that requires
the presence of the Echelon"—a meaningful arch of his brows
—"so I insist that you and your elorin join us for dinner."

A formal request involving the Echelon could not be
slighted. Left with no other choice, Declan dipped his head
grudgingly. "Very well."

Nathaniel's lips curved in a satisfied smile. He stepped
back to address the crowd. A seasoned showman, he didn't
speak until he'd garnered the attention of every guest in the
pavilion. With exaggerated grandeur, he gestured to the air,
and the shattered ice dome still hovering above erupted in a
dazzling show of disintegrating ice crystals. Only when every
piece of ice had decomposed to its base form did Nathaniel

allow it to fall from the air, dusting his guests in a flurry of powdered snow.

Murmurings of delight swept over the crowd. Evangeline's eyes widened as she glanced overhead. *I know your father is a master of ice, Archmage, but this is . . . incredible.*

Declan's little fire, like the rest of the crowd, appeared mesmerized by the drifting snow that was nothing but an overt display of power. Declan found nothing impressive in the gesture.

For Nathaniel, everything was an opportunity for exhibition.

Declan was, however, mesmerized by the naked wonderment on his mate's face. Her lips parted as she threaded her fingers through the air, sifting through swirling snowflakes. Declan wanted to thread *his* fingers into her hair and kiss the specks of white peppering her nose.

With another flourish, Nathaniel raised a hand more for effect than by necessity, and the spheres of ice crystals around them blazed again—a symphony of flickering lights illuminating the lake that cradled the edge of the pavilion. In the middle of inky waters, where night had dimmed the glaciers into muted shades of black and gray, an echoing spark flared to life.

Gasps of awe rolled through the guests, while Declan's lips twitched in wryness.

Nathaniel was clearly trying hard to impress.

A myriad of other sparks simmered to life in accompaniment, outlining the shimmering platform he must have created —an island of ice, large enough to be a ballroom, floating in the middle of the lake.

Servants were already stationed on the island, their figures growing more distinct as intricate treelike candelabras of burning ice crystals sparked ablaze. The space had been prepared for the banquet, complete with long, ornate tables and upholstered chairs.

At the dumbfounded reaction of the crowd, Nathaniel's smile stretched wide. "Esteemed members of the Echelon and honored guests, it is with great pleasure I share with you my lands and my table as we anticipate the Reckoning of Railea for the last hundred seasons."

The people released a chorus of cheers.

"However"—Nathaniel held up a hand for silence as revelers continued to chatter with excitement—"this season I have received a rather unorthodox . . . request."

He paused for effect.

"I assure you it is a request I did not take lightly. As one of the Echelon, I take it upon myself to watch over the safety of the realm. Over the last century it has become increasingly evident our realm has been steadily imposed upon . . . by the Unseelie monarch."

Evangeline stiffened. Declan clenched his jaw, suddenly wary of Nathaniel's *surprise*.

"From espionage to the unscrupulous slave-trade cartel, the Winter Court has tainted our realm with its darkness and impinged upon the safety of our people." Nathaniel's emerald eyes cast a cursory gaze over the crowd. "So I have decided to grant the request with the hopes of freeing our realm from the Unseelie's corrupt dealings. My people, I assure you of your safety. No harm will befall you, not in the confines of my castle and especially not in my presence."

Another weighted pause.

With a pointed glance at Declan, Nathaniel continued, "And to my fellow members of the Echelon, I request nothing but your attention . . . and an open mind."

As though on cue, a dark sphere materialized upon the now brightly lit island.

Gasps resounded, but bolstered by Nathaniel's speech, people moved closer to the edge of the lake for a better look as the stygian portal unfurled, a stark contrast against pristine white ice, spreading like a ball of festering rot.

Evangeline's breath hitched, and her fingers dug into Declan's skin.

"Declan," she whispered in a strangled voice.

Despite his need to ferry her home to the safety of his own lands, he could no longer do so. Fleeing from this would not only raise animosity; it would signify weakness. He could not afford to appear weak before the Echelon. Not if he was to keep her safe.

The Winter Court will not have you, little fire. Not as long as I draw breath.

Despite his reassurance, his little fire radiated tension.

A dark figure emerged from the portal. Nothing more than a silhouette across the distance—but the glint of silver-white hair was unmistakable.

"Fellow members of the Echelon," Nathaniel said with a devious grin, "there is someone I wish for you to meet."

NINE

Evangeline straightened her spine and drew strength from her archmage, who stood beside her like a pillar of fortitude. He gave her arm a reassuring squeeze before he warped them onto the island of frost and frivolity.

Evangeline felt utterly out of place.

The other archmages had left their ayaris behind at the pavilion with the rest of the crowd, but Declan insisted on keeping her by his side. Members of the Echelon—archmages she had yet to meet—made no mention of her presence, a silent acknowledgement of her current standing, while Alejandro openly grinned in her direction. Declan's father, however, was an entirely different creature.

Nathaniel made his disapproval known with the pervasive curl of his lips whenever his gaze landed upon her. But Evangeline was far too bewildered by the Unseelie presence in their midst to pay heed to his open censure.

Piercing eyes, the color of purest violet, swept over her.

Her skin prickled as an involuntary tremor worked down her spine. She was aware of his presence the way a mouse might be a snake's. Felt the need to flee the way a fox might from a hound.

He was eerily arresting. Up close, his hair shone under the moonlit sky with a quicksilver luster. If the slim crown encircling his head wasn't telling enough, he wore the traditional black and silver coat of Unseelie royalty. The brocaded fabric hugged his lithe frame, falling to his knees where it parted into two broad lapels. Floral motifs were intricately stitched into one end, while forest animals and birds adorned the other—a tribute to the two races that had once made up the fae realm. Seelie and Unseelie.

"Welcome to my kingdom, Prince Zion," Nathaniel said as he strode with the easy confidence of a man used to walking on solid ice.

Despite the prince's exceptional build, he held himself with an air of grace and a calm indifference as he greeted the members of the Echelon with a sweeping bow. "It is my honor, Archmage Strom. I am grateful to be granted an audience with the legendary Echelon of Railea's realm." He straightened, fixing his gaze on Evangeline. "And the woman rumored to be the last of Seeliekind."

The prince took a step forward, and Declan's voice cut through the murmuring lap of the lake like a whiplash of frigid air. "Keep your distance if you value your life."

The prince held up both hands in a gesture of peace. "I am merely curious to meet someone from a race long thought extinct, Archmage Thorne. I bear her no ill will."

"Yes, Prince Zion is no threat to anyone here," Nathaniel interjected with a chuckle, as though he found the awkward situation highly entertaining. "He joins us today as my *guest*."

Nathaniel's assurance fell like a leaf in the wind. Declan's markings only flared in silent challenge. The prince wisely dipped his head in a gracious bow without taking another step forward. "And how may I address you, my lady?"

Before she could answer, Declan's response came swift. "You may call her Lady Barre."

The Unseelie prince raised a critical brow. "That is not a Seelie House I am familiar with, Lady Barre." Clearly, Zion was asking for her *fae* title.

"I hail from no noble house, Prince," Evangeline said, the lie forming easily on her lips. Prince Zion could not know she was the daughter of a house so powerful it was no less venerated than the Summer Court queen herself.

And if she wished to live out her life as Declan's elorin de ana in this realm, she would have to ensure her identity as Freya Katerina Jilintree remained unknown. "I am the daughter of humble tenders of the land, from the plains of Rivven," she added with a little bow of her head, hoping to show meekness.

That was not totally a lie. Her family *owned* the lands of Rivven.

"A daughter of farmers." Zion's eyes sharpened with a flash of shrewdness. "How extraordinary that *you*, of all Seeliekind, would have survived the Winter War."

Declan remained as stone by her side. To the public eye, her archmage appeared unflappable as always, his expression a flawless canvas. But she knew better. Tension thrummed off him in silent waves, as palpable as her own fear.

"Did you come here simply to gawk at *my* elorin, then?" Though Declan's tone remained even, his threat of reprisal rang clear.

Nathaniel cut off whatever the Unseelie prince would have said with a disgruntled sigh. "You're wise to explain your purpose, Prince, before Archmage Thorne decides to boil you in the water. He's more than capable, you know, of setting the lake on fire."

The wry exasperation in Nathaniel's voice, coupled with the hint of unmistakable pride as he spoke, disconcerted Evangeline. The older archmage did not speak of Declan as another member of the Echelon, one of equal standing. Instead, Nathaniel spoke of him the way a father might a precocious son.

And though Declan gave his father no response, Nathaniel shot him a mild smile as though to placate. "Prince Zion has a proposal to make, one that will be of interest to us all." To the rest of the Echelon, Nathaniel gestured to the grand banquet table on the other end of the icy terrain. "Let's take a seat, shall we?" Nathaniel smiled wide, displaying a row of perfect teeth, and Evangeline had to tear her gaze away.

The physical resemblance between her archmage and his father was uncanny.

They shared the same sensual mouth, the cutting cheekbones, and the fathomless green eyes, guarded by thick, slashing brows. Only Nathaniel seemed far more conscious of his own physical appeal, while Declan appeared a younger, more austere version, who possessed not a single narcissistic bone in his body.

The upholstered seat at the head of the table slid out of its own accord, and Nathaniel lowered himself into it like a king taking his throne. As the Echelon seated themselves, Declan led Evangeline to the table and held out a chair for her.

"Well then," Nathaniel murmured to the still-standing Unseelie prince, "the Echelon is waiting, Prince Zion."

Declan kept an arm wrapped firmly around Evangeline's shoulders, but he didn't take his eyes off the prince. He knew the prince by reputation alone—the second heir to the Winter Court throne, commander of the southern region of the fae realm, had a reputation distinct from the other Unseelie princes.

Zion was neither indolent nor cruel. No, he was an exacting prince, lauded for his leadership and loved by his people. Even Gabriel, who continued to act as one of Declan's spies in the fae realm, had found nothing to tarnish the prince's sterling reputation.

It only made Declan all the more wary.

"My father, King Zephyr of the Winter Court, has been missing for over six months now," Zion said as he remained standing, his hands clasped loosely behind his back as though he were a clergyman delivering a reading. "While most believe him still alive, I do not share the hopeful sentiment. The heir to the throne, Prince Zenaidus, my eldest brother, is soon to be crowned on the Eve of the Waning Moon. I am—"

A soft, feminine chuckle drew everyone's attention from the prince.

Sonja Tuath was the only other woman seated at the table, and unlike Evangeline, who watched the prince with rapt, wary eyes, the archmage of Yarveric was wholly at ease. "While I find this utterly fascinating, I fail to see how the loss of your king affects the Echelon, young prince."

Sonja drummed jewel-tipped nails over the polished surface of the table. "Unless, of course, you seek vengeance on your father's behalf. If that is the case, you can stop wasting our time and take your battle to Archmage Thorne directly."

She threw Declan a sly smile. "Although I'd advise against it. I'm sure the Winter Court wouldn't want to lose another member of its royal family so quickly after Zephyr's untimely . . . disappearance."

Zion stiffened perceptibly, the first fissure in his unruffled composure. "Lady Archmage Tuath, my purpose here is not revenge or retribution. I am here to ask for help."

Sonja tilted her head in question, her fingers tapping an incessant click, click, click while Alejandro leaned forward in his seat. "What manner of help?"

"Your endorsement." Zion squared his shoulders and lifted his chin. "I am here to request your attendance at the coronation, where you will pledge your support to *me*. Your collective presence will sway the Winter Court nobles. The gods know, most already believe I am more fit to wear the crown."

Declan shook his head with disgust. He should have known this was just another power play. Despite Zion's seemingly placid demeanor, Zephyr's spawn behaved more like rabid dogs than fae royalty. Alejandro snorted and leaned back in his seat, as though he, too, found the prince's sentiments distasteful.

"If you wish for the crown, why bother with such fanfare?" Declan asked. "Would it not be simpler to kill Zenaidus?"

Zion's eyes widened as though in alarm. "I have no wish to do my brother harm. I want to claim the throne—*without* bloodshed."

"Preposterous." Dakari Chikere, ruler of the lands abutting Declan's own, slammed a meaty fist over the table with a huff. "How dare you make such demands of us? Do you think we have nothing better to do with our time?"

"Precisely so. What makes you think we care about fae politics?" Arjun Jai demanded.

Zion opened his mouth as though to speak, but the rising murmurings of the other archmages drowned him out. Nathaniel waved a hand as though to broker peace. "Come now, my friends. Can we not allow the prince to say his piece?"

"Nathaniel," Orus said, breaking his silent observation with a raspy voice that echoed the dry sand dunes of Teti Unas. "Surely you of all people wouldn't agree to go as far as entering the fae realm, where we would be *weakened* by the gods, just so Prince Zion can usurp his brother's throne?"

Nathaniel's chuckle caused Declan to shift closer to his little fire, who remained a stiff spectator. It was not like his father to be interested in fae statecraft, especially in the midst of revelry.

"I know how unorthodox this all sounds, old friend." Nathaniel nodded encouragingly in Zion's direction. "Go on. Tell the Echelon what you've explained to me."

The Echelon quieted as curiosity thickened in the air. Zion cleared his throat and steepled his fingers upon the table as though considering his next words with care. "My lords and lady archmage, forgive my insolence, but you do not understand what is at stake."

"My father had centuries to nurture alliances with the animati and glider clans—augmenting our own forces with drakghis and all manner of demons. A legion. All sheltered under the magic of animati shieldmakers."

A weighted silence fell. Zion paused, knowing he now held his audience's full attention. Archmages might rule supreme in Railea's realm, but the combined forces of three separate realms posed a significant threat.

"My brother, Zenaidus, is eager to perpetuate my father's reign, but I am not. If I wear the crown, I will not only act to circumvent an invasion against your realm. I will also see to it that all Unseelie involvement in the slave-trade cartel that plagues your lands be curtailed."

The prince shifted in his chair. "And all I ask is a few minutes of your time. Yes, you will be weakened upon entering my lands, but the realm's equalizing effect on beings as powerful as yourselves takes hours, if not days, for completion. Your accumulated presence would be enough to render the Winter Court ashes if you so wished. And there will be no shortage of Unseelie from which you can wrench portals at any point should you wish to depart." Zion smiled mildly. "It is *I* who bear the risk by inviting your presence."

While the rest of the Echelon seemed to consider Zion's words, Declan narrowed his eyes. He'd fought Zephyr himself. He knew of the Unseelie king's motivations.

"We all know why Zephyr intends to invade our lands." Declan kept his tone even as he studied Zion's expression. Earnestness was all he saw. Either Zion genuinely believed in his agenda, or the prince was an excellent thespian. "Your father wanted vengeance against a man"—Declan nodded openly at Nathaniel; now was no time for subtlety—"who cost him his wife. Queen Seraphina, your mother."

Declan paused, allowing the fact to simmer before continuing. "I find it implausible that you would appear before us now, eager to cast aside old grievances to work with a man who robbed you of a mother, and"—Declan ran a hand down Evangeline's side in a slow, possessive display lest anyone need the reminder—"another who would kill your father on sight should he prove to still be alive."

The prince bared his teeth, flashing sharp canines. A low hiss escaped his throat, which caused Evangeline to lean closer to Declan's side. "My father was a fool to abduct Lady Barre from your castle, Archmage Thorne." Zion's eyes darted to Evangeline, and Declan fought the urge to set the man aflame for his incisive gaze. "The last Seelie or otherwise . . . my father had no right to an archmage's woman."

If Zion meant to appease him with the open capitulation, he'd failed. Trust wasn't something Declan gave easily.

"And as for what happened with my mother—" Zion

seemed to falter. He swallowed before continuing. "What happened in the past is no concern of mine. I wish only to end the cycle of deceit and hatred festering between our realms. I want nothing more than peace for my people."

Despite the apparent veracity of Zion's speech, Declan couldn't halt the tide of cynicism cresting in his chest. But Prince Zion didn't allow him another chance to speak. "Archmage Thorne, have I not shown my sincerity by appearing before you without a single guard? Where you could crush me with a blink of an eye if you wanted?"

Zion regarded the rest of the Echelon with an earnest gaze. "My lords and lady archmage, my father is dead. I have held my silence for the years under his rule, but it is now time for a new era. A new reign. It is time for the fae realm to be rebuilt to its former glory. It is time for peace. That is why my brother cannot inherit the crown."

"Make a promise."

Evangeline's words were quiet and soft, but they halted Zion in the middle of his impassioned speech, drawing the attention of everyone around the table. Nathaniel huffed in open rebuke at her audacity to speak. But Evangeline merely held the prince's gaze, her lips fashioned in a firm line.

Pride and amusement swelled in Declan's chest. His little fire was ignoring a man commonly regarded as the strongest member of the Echelon, at his own table.

"If you truly mean it, then make a promise, Prince Zion," Evangeline repeated, her chin lifted as though in challenge. "Promise you will not wage a war or cause any harm to those living in Railea's realm for as long as you live, should the Echelon endorse your claim to the crown."

Declan smiled. Seelie or Unseelie, the fae could never break a promise. Not even if they wanted to.

Without hesitation, Zion surprised them all by pressing a

fisted hand to his heart with his head bowed and repeating Evangeline's words in a sealing covenant. Only the prince added a caveat at the end. " . . . should the Echelon and Lady Barre help me wear the crown."

Declan couldn't stop the growl in his throat. *"What?"*

Zion swiftly dropped his gaze from Evangeline's paling face. "In the past, a monarch's coronation has not been complete without a vote of faith from both Seelie and Unseelie."

"Evangeline comes from no noble blood. She is of no use in the coronation," Declan said even as he despised himself for the disparaging comment. Evangeline could challenge to reinstate the Summer Court if she chose to return to the fae realm as Freya Katerina Jilintree. There were plenty in the fae realm who would welcome a Seelie reign. Gabriel and the Red Guild, for instance, would wholeheartedly support her.

Evangeline could be queen.

Only she chose to remain in his realm, by his side.

"She would be." Zion took a step forward, placing his palms over the table as he gazed at Evangeline with a near-rapturous interest. "She could well be Lady Felicity Jilintree herself. Anyone who knew Felicity would not refute the likeness."

Zion's wondering smile unnerved Declan more than an impending war with a thousand drakghis under the cloak of a hundred shieldmakers.

"If I hadn't seen Lady Felicity's Soul Tree for myself," Zion murmured, "I would have thought you to be her, Lady Barre . . . for you bear her image."

Evangeline's lips parted in shock. "Felicie's . . . " She bit her lower lip, catching herself. "You know of Lady Felicity's Soul Tree?"

Every fae who passed was buried in a Soul Tree, where their body returned to the sands of Ozenn through the roots and their soul to the ether through the branches. Evangeline had thought Felicity's soul long lost, as her sister had passed in the mortal realm while escaping the decrepit cabin where Zephyr's henchmen had held them captive.

Beside Evangeline, animosity crackled from her archmage, the muscles of his arms stiffening. Evangeline clenched and unclenched her own fist. Zephyr must have brought Felicity's body back into the fae realm and buried her sister within the Winter Court. Even in death, her sister remained Zephyr's captive.

Zion raised a curious brow. "Yes, Lady Felicity's Soul Tree resides outside the Winter Court Palace. Do you know of her, Lady Barre?"

"Yes, of course," Evangeline murmured, inwardly berating herself for the slip of tongue. Peasants did not refer to her sister with such familiarity. "She was the lady of the great House Jilintree that owns the lands of Rivven."

Zion's eyes glinted with interest. "Lady Barre, if you're inclined to pay your respects, I would be honored to show you Lady Jilintree's final resting place on coronation day. All you have to do, of course, is declare your Seelie heritage before the Winter Court and pledge your support to me."

TEN

Evangeline picked at the food on her plate, trying to settle her riotous nerves.

The moment Prince Zion took his leave, the crowd had warped onto the floating island, materializing like a gaggle of geese, squawking their excitement as they appraised their archmage's ingenious creation. Most regarded her with renewed vigor, lauding her as the first civilian to have sat in on a private gathering of the Echelon, while some eyed her with a mixture of incredulity and contempt. As she was the first elorin de ana to be claimed by one of the Echelon in the last thousand years, Declan had warned her to expect a varying reception. Only Evangeline hadn't realized how difficult it was to present an air of unaffected serenity despite the turmoil raging beneath her skin.

A skill her archmage had perfected down to an art. Beside her, Declan appeared utterly implacable as he sipped wine from an ice chalice. The only glitch in his composure to reveal that the Unseelie prince had affected him was his unyielding hold on her hand beneath the table. He hadn't released it throughout the first course of the meal, which they'd both eaten with one hand. Now, servants moved obsequiously around the ostentatious table serving small tureens of soup. Despite the nauseating waft of braised pheasant, Evangeline forced herself to sample the dish. The stew went down her throat like sludge.

Her senses prickled with annoyance when she felt the scrutiny of a woman from the far end of the table. Vera's stare was hard enough to wear a hole in her temple. Frustration swarmed like gnats beneath her skin, biting at the edges of her already raw nerves.

Evangeline forced herself to ignore the other woman's vulturelike gaze and focus on the incessant chatter of the ayari, Lady Galinka, who was seated to her left.

"I made sure the cooks strung the pheasants over a low fire before they were stewed. The slow roast brings out such a rich flavor . . . "

Visions of Felicity presented themselves in obscure flashes of memory—pinned on the dingy cabin floor while Evangeline's own hands were bound like a trussed pheasant, body tethered like a leashed dog beside the fireplace. The blistering heat of the fire had not been half as traumatizing as witnessing her sister's torture.

Sickness roiled in her belly as bile coated the back of her throat.

Evangeline clutched her spoon, her knuckles turning white as Felicity's screams mingled with her own echoed in her ears. The spoon dropped from her hands and clattered to the table, calling even more attention to her.

She had a sudden urge to peel her lips back and hiss her agitation.

Declan leaned into her. "Little fire?"

His scent was a soothing balm of cedarwood and cool

breeze, mingled with the hint of spirits on his breath. She wanted to bury her face in the curve of his neck, draw in his scent where it was strongest, lose herself in his arms, and lay out her burdens at his feet. But even the enormity of an archmage's powers couldn't erase the scars seared into her soul.

"What's wrong?"

She glanced up at him, the sole reason she endured this entire facade. Concern marred the dark slashes of his brows, distorting his mask of reserve, and an overwhelming wash of tenderness flowed through her. She would endure a thousand more nights like these just to sit here beside him.

Yet she did not respond. Her hands remained stiff by her side. Her lips clamped tight even as her mind ruminated on concerns that continued to assail her since her interlude with Sariel.

Had he lied to her about Vera?

Her heart rebelled. She knew of his time in Nathaniel's court—of the countless women he'd had. He hadn't lied to her about his past, had no reason to lie about Vera. Then again, Declan was also the only archmage without an ayari.

But how could he have allowed such a stunning woman to serve in his court for half a decade without *touching* her? And why would he cast Vera from his court at the very moment Evangeline had entered his life?

"Is everything all right?" He applied gentle pressure on her hand as servants cleared away their soups, replacing them with a carvery course.

Evangeline swallowed the lump of pheasant still lodged in her throat.

"No," she whispered.

Declan mistook her response for fear.

I won't let anything happen to you. Regardless of what the Echelon decides for the Eve of the Waning Moon, you'll remain in the castle. I'll have Killian increase your guard.

Once again, dictating her actions.

She would snap if she spoke aloud. But keenly aware of watchful eyes around them, she projected her ire instead.

Has it occurred to you that I'd want *to attend Zion's coronation?*

The creases between his brows deepened. She pulled her hand out of his grip with the excuse of operating a fork and knife. *I want to see my sister's Soul Tree.*

Declan's lips firmed. *Visiting your sister's grave is hardly worth your safety.*

The note of finality in his tone told her he welcomed no further discussion on the matter. Unquestionably dictating her actions.

Her gums prickled as her canines lengthened. The tips of her ears tingled. She had long since learned that emotion affected her appearance, and anger was proving to be a strong one. At the sudden intake of breath from the minister seated opposite her and Galinka's unblinking stare, Evangeline rubbed her ears to relieve the sharpened tips. She kept her head dipped, mortified by her own lack of control. Under the weight of stares, she felt like an exotic animal on display.

Declan cast a whittling glare around the table, and people swiftly dropped their gazes. Evangeline kept her head down and feigned concentration on the food. She couldn't wait for dinner to be over. Unfortunately, the meal turned out to be a degustation. Spiced meats. Seared scallops. Stuffed mushrooms. Rounded beef tenderloins. Evangeline had never been served such dainty portions on such enormous plates. She did her best to eat, or she would earn the scrutiny of Lady Galinka, who seemed to take a personal interest in Evangeline's enjoyment of each dish.

When servants cleared what must be the *third* round of

desserts from the table, Declan reached out for her hand. His fingers enveloped her wrist easily. Only his grip no longer felt like that of a lover, but that of an iron manacle.

"We should go," he said, despotic as ever.

"So soon?" Lady Galinka glanced up, dabbing a napkin delicately at the corner of her full lips. "But you haven't tried our spiced plum wine yet. It is served hot and a Flen delicacy."

Evangeline mustered a smile. "We'll stay," she said the same time Declan declared, "We've had enough."

Galinka blinked, looking between the both of them. "But . . . the Reckoning is soon to begin. It would really be such a shame . . ."

Evangeline glanced up at her archmage. *Leaving now will only draw more attention to us.*

Little fire, I don't care what others think. We are leaving.

She was saved from the petty impulse to hiss when a masculine voice sounded behind her. "Leaving so soon? But we haven't even been properly introduced."

From the man's swarthy complexion, the arcane symbols swirling over his skin, and the insignia of a bronze dragon stamped onto his leather bracers, Evangeline guessed him to be Orus Jin, the archmage dubbed the Hand of Benevolence, who ruled the peaceful lands of undulating sand dunes. Orus was bare-chested despite their frigid surroundings, wearing nothing but a pleated drape of ivory cambric thrown over one broad shoulder. Instead of trousers, he wore a wraparound fabric that extended to his knees, fastened at the waist with a thick leather belt. Sandals lined his feet. Clearly, Declan wasn't the only one impervious to the cold.

"My friend." Orus's voice sounded hoarse but warm. "I've waited all night to meet your lovely elorin."

The creases between Declan's brows smoothened as the mask slid flawlessly over his face. "I apologize, Orus. It was most ungracious of me not to introduce you." Declan rose from his seat to make a proper introduction. Following a brief exchange of insipid conversation, Evangeline found herself on the receiving end of a striking smile and the crook of Orus's arm. "May I have a dance, Lady Barre?"

Declan's mask cracked, creases re-forming between his eyes.

Before he could interject and possibly risk antagonizing another one of the Echelon, Evangeline placed her free hand on Orus's bare skin and forced a weak smile. "I would be honored."

Declan swallowed the acid in his throat as Evangeline relinquished his hold to follow Orus. Nathaniel had even thought to supply a dance floor of sanded marble—one suitable for guests who did not wield enough telekinesis to keep themselves steady on textured ice.

Evangeline seemed to test the viability of the ground under her feet, tapping lightly with her heeled boots before venturing farther onto the marble slabs. Orus grinned down at her, his face brightening with gentle amusement at her wariness. He wouldn't let her slip. Not only would it reflect poorly upon his ability to buffer his dance partner with telekinesis, but he would have Declan to answer to.

The thought of Orus's telekinetic shield—or his hands—wrapped over his little fire made his jaw grind.

Prior to his ascension, Declan had acted in the form of Nathaniel's emissary and had spent considerable time traveling between the various kingdoms of the realm. Of all seven rulers, Declan had always looked up to Orus, quietly admired the archmage's exacting yet generous rule. Declan's regard for the archmage had held long after his own ascension.

But now, it took every dab of self-control to tamp down the irrational urge to plow his fist into Orus's face and wipe off that damned pearlescent smile, haul Evangeline off the dance floor, and warp her home. Declan clenched his fist, appalled by the barbarity of his emotions. He'd known Evangeline's presence tonight would pose a challenge, but he didn't expect it to reduce him to such base instincts.

Declan drained his glass.

The events of the evening had spiraled so frenetically that it had threatened his sense of gravity. Vera's antagonistic attack had not only emphasized Evangeline's frailty. It had highlighted his ineptitude as her elorin de han. Zion's unexpected appearance had not only echoed the growing dissent in the fae realm. It had reminded him that his claim on Evangeline was not absolute, their mating bond incomplete. More, the Unseelie prince's proposal had somehow widened the rift between them. And now, all he could do was watch her dance in another man's arms.

Declan beckoned a servant and selected another chalice of hefty spirits.

Orus's hand curved around the small of Evangeline's back, drawing her closer than Declan would have approved, but not close enough to warrant intervention. Orus leaned into her ear and said something. It had to be witty, for it caused her lips to curve into a genuine smile and lit a light in her eyes.

A light Declan wanted only for himself.

His throat felt dry, his collar suddenly constricting. He yearned for a soft caress on the mental plane, which Evangeline often did when she sensed his agitation, but this time she gave him none. There were no placating psychic kisses, no telepathic murmurs to soothe him as Orus spun her in circles in time with the lilting melody.

Declan cursed under his breath.

When exactly had he turned into a man who needed coddling? Disgusted with himself, Declan tried to wrench his gaze away, knowing full well he presented the very image of a jealous lover, glowering from the fringes. Only he couldn't seem to help himself.

To his relief, the song finally ended. Before Evangeline could step off the dance floor, Arjun Jai sidled up to her with a courtly bow, signaling his open regard and request. Evangeline appeared flustered. Quickly setting his chalice aside, Declan rose and took a step forward, only to be intercepted by Vera.

"Lord Thorne, will you grant me a few minutes of your time?" She appeared wan. Almost meek. A farce she was more than capable of.

"No." Ignoring Vera's crestfallen expression, he sidestepped her in time to view Evangeline hesitantly accept Arjun, who pulled her into his arms.

Declan reached out to her telepathically. *Do you wish to stop, little fire?* Offense or not, he would carry her off if she wished.

There was a moment's pause before she replied. *I am quite all right.*

"Women can never resist Arjun. The devil looks like Ozenn himself," drawled another presence by his side. Declan wiped the scowl from his face but gave Alejandro no response. Unfortunately, his silence only served to amuse the archmage of Salindras, who smirked. "Try not to crack the ice prematurely, Thorne. My Sariel is excited by the prospect of viewing the Reckoning from the heart of the glacier."

Declan ignored the other archmage, as well as Vera, who skulked nearby, seemingly determined to catch his attention. But his gaze was trained solely on Arjun—the archmage of Kalizmet had a gleam in his eye that annoyed Declan to no end. The man grinned his pleasure, gradually dancing Evangeline closer to the edge of the platform. He slowed to make an exaggerated flourish with his hand. Rivulets broke the tranquil surface of the inky lake in graceful, undulating spires shooting into the air in staggered bursts, each stream timed to match the percussion of the band. The liquid display drew an enthusiastic cheer from the crowd, most of whom clapped and clamored to the edge for a better view.

Declan nearly rolled his eyes.

Clearly, his father was not the only one predisposed to exhibitionism.

Alejandro chuckled. "If you wanted a woman under your thumb, you should never have made her your elorin. It gives them far too much power, being an archmage's equal."

"I do not want her subservience," Declan said without taking his eyes from the marvel on Evangeline's face as she took in the water spectacle. "Surely you, of all people, would understand."

Declan's subtle query seemed to have taken the other archmage by surprise, for Alejandro went uncharacteristically silent.

"Been digging through the healer archives, have you?" Alejandro finally mused, idly twirling the wine in his glass.

"If it were something you hadn't wanted known, you wouldn't have allowed your healers to pen their observations." Healer's Order or not, Alejandro could have ensured his people's silence.

Alejandro heaved a sigh. "It was a long time ago. When I was far younger and a great deal more gullible. I fancied myself in love." He surprised Declan by adding, "Kalinna was a great deal older and wiser. She rejected my bond, and I am thankful.

Now I cannot fathom an immortal lifetime bound to a single woman."

Declan kept his voice steady, trying to conceal his curiosity even as he asked, "And your bond disintegrated with time?"

"No," Alejandro said with a shadow of a smile. "She died."

Declan's breath caught as he struggled to quiet the myriad of questions spiraling through his mind. He could not probe further into Alejandro's past without rousing further suspicion on the nature of his own mating bond. There were other ways to determine the manner of Kalinna's death.

"In any case," Alejandro said, his tone resuming its usual edge of hubris, "your lady is certainly a . . . refreshing choice."

Declan turned his attention back to the dance floor, noted the increasingly familiar way Arjun swayed Evangeline to the music and the widening smile on the man's face. Alejandro chuckled. "Even Arjun seems quite taken with her."

As though on cue, Arjun's hand slid further down the arch of Evangeline's back, like a spider creeping into a baby's cradle.

Declan's wine evaporated, misting the air with a cloud of spirits. He relegated the wine glass to the tray of a nearby servant and excused himself.

He was done watching her in another man's arms.

"I can also manipulate the weather to a certain extent," Arjun said with another grandstanding grin, his teeth perfectly white against his tanned skin. "Even the clouds are subject to my influence."

Evangeline answered him with an easy smile.

Arjun was not what she'd expected of an archmage fabled to be so outrageously handsome that the goddess Railea herself had once graced his bed. Evangeline had always thought the claim preposterous, but now she could appreciate how such rumors had come to be. With Arjun's striking features and powerful build, he could likely persuade a celibate monk to sin. Charming a goddess into his bed was not a stretch.

Only his prepossessing gaze appealed to her the way oil slid against water—smooth, but without blend.

The back of her neck prickled with awareness.

Evangeline's eyes widened when she caught Declan stalking across the dance floor in her periphery, dark intent etched into his every stride. His gaze caught hers, and her mouth went dry. Arjun might be stunning enough to tempt a goddess, but to her, Declan *was* a god. A god whose very proximity turned her blood to paraffin and whose gaze alone was enough to set her veins afire.

Arjun, too, noticed Declan's approach, and the two men must have exchanged telepathic words, for Arjun's hand lifted from the small of her back and he stepped back with a slight nod. "It was a true pleasure making your acquaintance, Lady Barre. Thorne is a lucky man." He strode away just as Declan came to a halt before her.

Evangeline expected him to insist on going home, and a part of her was prepared to concede. Dancing had cooled her frustrations; she was now ready to face the answers to the questions weighing on her chest like a block of ice. More, Vera's continued gaze on her archmage's every move from across the platform did not escape her.

But he only gazed at her with eyes of unfathomable green, silent as always. Wordlessly, he bowed, lowering his head in a wholly unprecedented manner for one of the Echelon. Evangeline's lips parted at the unexpected public gesture, then curved when she realized what her indomitable lover wanted.

A dance.

ELEVEN

E vangeline's palm was cool in his, her skin chilled from
their glacial surrounds. A new song began, filling the
air with the poignant notes of a haunting melody that
matched the emotions coursing through him.

Declan placed his hands on Evangeline's hips and drew her
close. Her nearness eased the tautness in his chest. Her heeled
boots added to her height, so the top of her head nearly
reached his chin. Craving the scent of his mate, he dipped to
rub his nose to her temple and caught a whiff of another man.
Arjun's pomade of spice lingered faintly around her.

He scowled. Nudged her temple with his chin. "Arms
around my neck."

Indignance lifted her brows, and her sunset eyes flashed.

Declan wisely dropped the note of command, allowing her
to hear the yearning in his voice instead. "Closer," he
murmured. "I want you closer."

She could never be close enough.

Her eyes softened, and she acquiesced. But she didn't just

wrap her arms around his neck. Her hands curled at the back of his head, fingers weaving into his hair and scrubbing the short strands at his nape in a way that never failed to alleviate the tension from his shoulders.

Finally pacified, he sighed. "Tell me what I've done to displease you, little fire."

Her luscious lips pursed slightly, painted red as raspberries. She gazed at him, likely building a campaign to attend the Unseelie coronation, but Declan already had his counterargument ready. There was nothing she could say that would sway his need to keep her safe. Only her words were wholly unexpected, throwing him off course.

"Have you lied to me about Vera?"

Declan blinked.

"Apparently she once served your court as your *ayari*."

Understanding finally dawning, Declan gave a vigorous shake of his head. "Vera served my court, but I never claimed her." For clarity, he added, "I never bedded her."

Evangeline had never displayed possessive tendencies, but she was clearly jealous now.

"Why? Vera is a beautiful woman"—her eyes narrowed across the dance floor—"and she obviously wants you."

"I had no need of an ayari. I had plenty of courtesans to choose from." Beauty was cheap. Women were always more than willing with him.

A scowl that would have been unflattering on any other woman only made Evangeline more alluring. "Then why did you allow her to serve your court for five years?"

"She refused to leave. And my council had petitioned for me to claim her. While I was not above claiming her to strengthen my ties to Sebastian, I was not eager for the commitment involved. Vera would expect much of me." She'd made that obvious, and Declan didn't have much to give. "After I returned from the shadow realm, I ordered her from my court because I knew my chances of taking an ayari had dwindled down to nothing . . . " Declan pressed his forehead to hers before brushing his lips lightly across hers. "My heart already belonged to someone else."

Her limbs relaxed against his like melted wax, her body molding against his like living flame. A tenderness stole into her eyes and unraveled the knot in his chest.

"Is that all that bothers you, little fire?" A niggling feeling in his chest told him that Vera wasn't the sole cause of the sudden divide between them.

"Whenever you . . . " A flush crept over her cheeks as she swayed against him. "Whenever we come together . . . are you truly satisfied?" She colored further, the wave of rose dipping down her neck while her hands trailed down to fidget with the lapels of his coat. "I'm not a trained ayari . . . " Her voice dropped to the barest whisper he had to strain to catch. "And Sariel says a conscious diversion of your powers means you're depriving yourself in some way."

Declan's eyes widened. "You discussed our lovemaking with Sariel?"

Evangeline turned scarlet. "I . . . The topic just came up."

At her mortified expression, Declan couldn't suppress the huff of laughter crowding his throat.

"I'm sorry, Archmage, I-I . . . " She cringed and stuttered so adorably that he couldn't resist. He halted abruptly to cup her cheeks and hold her still among the other dancing couples. He leaned down and plundered her mouth. He had never been prone to public displays of affection, but there was something intensely gratifying about kissing her in full view of the crowd. It was marking his territory in the basest way, and where Evangeline was concerned, he would never tire of staking his claim.

"You're the *only* woman who has ever made me feel replete," he said when he finally allowed her air.

Declan had accepted that he would never again have a woman with complete abandon after he'd risen from the pit of Arksana. The first woman he'd taken after he'd ascended had been a seasoned courtesan, whom he'd enjoyed with his usual fervor . . . until she'd screamed out not in passion but in pain, her skin blistered as though with a hot brand.

The thought of hurting a woman, trained ayari or courtesan, to assuage his personal urges had sickened him enough that he'd learned to control his needs. Since then, he'd never allowed himself to go completely over the edge with a woman. It hadn't been much hardship. Sex had always been little more than an act of release—until Evangeline. But the conscious diversion of his unruly powers had been a small price to pay for the chance to drown himself in her warmth.

"You're the only woman I continue to crave no matter how many times I've had you." He pressed a gentle kiss on her slightly swollen lips. "The only woman I'll ever need."

"Truly?"

"I've never lied to you, little fire, and I never will."

She beamed up at him then, so bright it was like the break of dawn, and his world righted once more.

Absently, Declan realized the song had ended and a light-hearted tune played. Servants bearing trays appeared, signaling the time for refreshments. The Reckoning would likely descend soon, and other couples around them had already dissolved from the dance floor.

But he wasn't done yet. He arrowed a telepathic command to the band of minstrels and requested a song of old, one a little girl had once hummed while she sat with her feet in a duck pond.

Evangeline's eyes widened as she recognized the whimsical

melody. Declan resumed their dance, this time feeling much lighter on his feet. They moved as one, their movements so well matched it was as though they'd had centuries of practice together. He set her twirling, close enough that the fabric of her dress sashayed against his legs like a sensual whisper. She giggled when he dipped her low, and her giddy laugh roused something deep within him. A sudden urge to play. Only with her did he ever feel like a boy.

Declan picked up speed and danced her to the edge of the platform the way Arjun had. Only he didn't stop. He spun them both off the ledge, right onto the open lake. At her open-mouthed shock, he laughed.

Perhaps he wasn't above showing off after all.

They were dancing on water.

Not precisely. She'd come to an abrupt halt, dumbstruck by the radius of ice blooming beneath their feet, a growing slab solidifying with faint crackling sounds as water thickened and coagulated. The longer they stayed put, the wider the ice grew.

Evangeline gazed up at Declan, eyes wide with utter amazement.

She didn't doubt his ability to create ice. He could freeze the lake twice over if he wished. What amazed her was the playful glint in his eyes and the roguish grin on his lips that rendered him heart-achingly beautiful. For a moment, the rest of the world melted away and he was the only thing she could see.

Without warning, he swayed them both, rocking the slab of ice beneath their feet so precariously, yet she felt no danger of falling. A cushion of air seemed to form around her—invisible to sight but tense enough she felt the pressure around her skin—keeping her balanced no matter how far she swayed.

"Dance with me, little fire." A remarkable friskiness in his tone. "I won't let you fall."

Wholly enthralled, she went to the tip of her toes to brush a teasing kiss against his lips. "Only if you catch me," she whispered as her inhibitions diminished like the gradually solidifying water around them. Emboldened by the unnatural yet unyielding balance around her, she toed off her shoes and stepped away from her archmage. Where her feet touched, ice formed—thick, solid. Unnatural, but comfortably cool beneath her skin.

His look of bafflement as he viewed her discarded shoes only enhanced her delight. She shot him a coquettish smile. "And no warping."

Without another word, she spun on her heel and fled.

Ice sparked to life beneath her feet, glowing white beneath the moonlight. His shout of laughter quickened her pulse. With a whoop, she bunched up her skirts and picked up the pace. No matter how quickly she ran, the ice never failed beneath her feet. She was flying on water.

She whirled around, enough to see the ice behind her thickened into a spiral. She'd run so far she was almost halfway across the lake. Declan remained where she'd left him, a solitary figure backlit by the glow of Nathaniel's island. Evangeline faltered at his unmoving stance. But with a sudden burst of speed, he *moved*.

A little shriek of excitement escaped her throat. She spun and sped. She ran along the lake's bight into a narrow icefield framed by sloping glaciers so tall she couldn't see their tops. She ran farther, until the mountains closed in around her in steep, ice-encrusted walls.

She slowed, her breaths coming out in puffs of white.

As she turned back, her pounding heart gave a frenzied thump. The island of festivity was now a little speck in the distance. Amid the darkness of the glaciers, with only the moon and stars to bear witness, her archmage was an otherworldly apparition, stalking her across swirling ice with feline grace and predatory intent. A sheen of gold emanated from the swirling marks on his skin, and the mere sight of him stole her breath away. No man could be more beautiful. No man more devastating.

He would have caught her if he'd really wanted to, but he was clearly enjoying her game, his eyes lit with exhilaration . . . and desire.

An answering ache formed between her legs, a wash of damp heat.

He warped abruptly, materializing just shy of her lips. Her breath hitched. With a knavish grin, he hefted her up by the waist to draw her flush against his chest as though she weighed less than a child.

"You cheated." Her accusation came out unsteady as he cupped her bottom in a bold, intimate hold.

"You gave me little choice." His voice was a little raspy; his breath was hot against the side of her neck as he nuzzled lusty kisses along her throat. "And gods, it . . . chafes." He rubbed his straining arousal against her. Hard as rock.

She strove for sternness, but her giggles between breathless pants betrayed her. "You ought to be punished for cheating."

"Me?" He pressed kisses on her lips. "*You*"—his tongue licked deep into her mouth—"ought to be punished for running from me."

Her skin prickled with excitement when she realized he'd shoved her up against the closest rock face. The jagged surface didn't touch her skin. A thin layer of air cushioned her back, like a tensile mattress against the wall.

"Wha . . . what do you have in mind?" She dug her nails into his skin, trying to pull herself higher, eager for her *punishment*.

His hands roved down to her hips. A single rip and the seams of her skirt gave way.

She yelped. "I like this dress!"

His response was a soft grunt—he nudged her legs apart and pulled her up so they wrapped over his hips. He ripped her dress higher. She was half laughing and half batting at him. But her archmage was seemingly lost in his exploration. His hand slipped beneath her gaping skirt, groping up her thighs with unerring intent. Evangeline squirmed against his touch, looping her arms over his shoulders, attempting to hold on tighter as he rained openmouthed kisses over the swell of her chest.

He pulled back abruptly and swallowed hard, staring at her with wild, dilated irises. Staring at her as though willing self-restraint, trying to stop himself from devouring her whole. His fingers tunneled higher between her thighs to sneak beneath her underwear, and the noise he emitted sounded like a cross between a whine and a growl. It fueled her excitement, but she didn't want his fingers.

She wanted *him*, and it wasn't a battle she cared to lose this time.

She shoved his fingers away. With one arm clinging to the broad expanse of his shoulder, she nibbled on his lower lip to distract him and used her other hand to undo the fastenings of his trousers.

He seemed transfixed by her lips, frozen as the ice continued to thicken beneath his feet to merge with the edge of the glacier wall. His breaths came out harsh, and he shuddered as she slipped her fingers around him. Hard as ice, and hot as fire.

"Love me, Archmage," she whispered into his ear. "I need you."

The markings on his neck flared to life, illuminating the muscles quivering beneath her touch.

"Evangeline," he groaned. In passion or resignation, she wasn't sure, but she welcomed his lips readily. She smiled against his ravenous mouth. His tongue was hard and demanding while his body crowded her firmly in place.

She'd most definitely won.

Little fire. His telepathic voice swarmed her mind, filled with so much raw need and longing that it drew out ancient parts of her. Her canines lengthened for the second time in the night, and the taste of iron laced her tongue.

Iron? Evangeline jerked back.

She'd bitten him.

But he didn't seem to mind.

His eyes held naked wonder as crimson welled from her bite on his lower lip. The wound was quickly resealed, but his eyes darkened with desire.

"Little fire." A deliciously husky whisper echoing his telepathic voice. His fingers lifted to caress the sensitive parts of her ears that had sharpened to their true form. She hissed in excitement. He nibbled one of the tips, causing her to whimper and clench her fists over his coat. She clawed at the fabric. How was he still wearing all his clothes?

But he couldn't seem to wait.

He plunged into her in time to the sudden scorch of light that overtook the inky sky. She gave a gasping cry and threw her head back. The army of stars streaking across the heavens emblazoned her eyes while Declan emblazoned her flesh with his, grinding her into the rock face cushioned by air. She held him tight, sinking her nails into his skin as her body bowed with irrepressible ecstasy. But soon he faltered, as though belatedly trying to rein in his own release. A groan. A strangled oath. With one hand supporting her and the other braced against the rock wall, he tried to slow and pull out of her.

Impossible, silly man.

"Don't stop." Evangeline tightened her legs around his hips in a possessive demand. He shook his head, muttering something unintelligible.

"Come inside me," she commanded. She rocked her hips, tiny jerks that wrenched a litany of inarticulate groans from his throat.

"Evangeline," he pleaded. "Stop. I can't . . . I can't . . . "

She only rocked harder, until he finally lost the battle and spilled deep, his body shuddering and his breaths ragged. With their bodies still tightly fused, Declan garbled words with the eloquence of a drunken man. "I love you," he whispered, over and over.

Once, he hadn't been able to utter those words. Now, he couldn't seem to stop.

With the skies still ablaze with celestial fire, she caressed his cheek and returned those three affirming words into his ear.

He pulled out of her, contrition on his face. "I lost control." His hand roamed south and found the cove of her sex, still wet and throbbing from his use. "Little fire, my love, let me give you pleasure. Let me . . . "

Evangeline chuckled. She was so pleased with his release that she barely missed her own, but she allowed him to move his fingers between her legs. She wanted everything he had to give.

"Declan," she whispered with a happy sigh. Her muscles felt strangely lax, as though she'd already found her own pleasure.

Lethargy lulled as he strummed and stroked. He was

crooning his love into her ear when her fingers grew numb and her grip around his shoulders loosened. The brilliance of the Reckoning dimmed from her sight, and the last thing she heard was his startled shout. "Evangeline!"

TWELVE

The bite of the icefield and the erotic warmth of her archmage's body pressed against hers melted into scorching, dry heat. She was no longer pressed against a glacier but on a weathered stone bridge. A frothy mist rose from the rush of a wide waterway, a cooling respite from the sun searing down her back.

Evangeline's breath came in short spurts, and her heart pounded, but it wasn't from the aftermath of psychedelic sex. Fear taunted her. An insidious presence that crowded her mind, constricted her throat, and clawed in her chest.

She glanced up, and air whooshed from her lungs, her fear momentarily forgotten.

The bridge led to an uncanny wall of white brick and gnarled trees. Bark and branches jutted from the haphazardly laid bricks, while heavy roots trundled beneath the rampart to create uneven ground. There was not a gust of wind, but the branches rustled and the leaves murmured. Strange, yet familiar. She *knew* this place.

The Wall of Whispers.

And far beyond the wall, perched upon the rolling hills, was a majestic citadel of gleaming red domes and fluttering white banderols. Even from such a distance, she could make out the beautiful metropolis, a wink of color against pale skies.

Evangeline stood and brushed grass from her skirts. Her limbs were fleshier and shorter. She glanced down. Instead of her ripped ivory gown, she now wore a sky-blue muslin frock trimmed with white lace. Her feet were bare and battered, and her toes caked with dirt and grime. She took a hesitant step forward, relishing the feel of warm stone despite the stinging lacerations on her soles. A glimmer of memory danced just out of reach.

Why was she here?

The echo of a scream. A man growling "*Seelie rutta!*" before he sank his fangs into a woman's neck. Evangeline's knees buckled from the weight of the recollection, vivid and vicious in her mind. The memory kindled into a bonfire. One that razed all knowledge of Evangeline Barre, replacing it with one all-consuming thought: *Mama.*

A choked sob escaped her throat. Mama!

Freya broke into a run and fled down the stone bridge.

Mama had sent her here. The wall was the closest anyone could get to the palace. It warded the palace against portals and unwelcome visitors. She reached the trees, evenly spaced between bricks. Wooden sentinels guarding against anyone without an invitation from the Summer Queen. The branches would come alive to whip and lash; gnarled roots would spear from the soil to drag intruders into the earth. But not her.

"Help me!" she cried as she ran up to the wall. "Please!"

Her foot caught on an uneven root. She went sprawling to the ground, but roots unfurled with startling dexterity to catch and break her fall. She had been born within these walls, played with these trees. First as a crawling babe, then a tumbling toddler.

They were her friends.

"Thank you," she whispered, stroking at the unearthed root as she would a well-loved pet. "I need to see the queen."

The roots helped steady her feet, then relinquished their hold, rasping as they returned to the ground and submerged themselves in the earth. Branches moaned and leaves murmured. Bark creaked against brick, shifting to create an entryway just wide enough for her to pass.

Welcome, a rustling echoed in the wind, *Freya, daughter of Princess Ildara.*

As she dashed through, vines reached down to brush her hair.

Welcome home.

Declan stroked her cheek with the tip of his finger, almost not daring to touch. She appeared so small, nestled in their bed beneath the blankets. So beautiful, like a sleeping princess from a fairy tale. Only he was no prince charming. His kisses did nothing to wake her. In fact, he'd all but broken her.

Her breathing remained steady, but her eyes moved rapidly beneath her lids.

What was she dreaming of?

He delved into the psychic plane and brushed against her mind. She remained bright. Effervescent. But unconsciousness coiled around her mind like an impenetrable fog, barring his reach. He felt like a bird desperately trying to fly toward the sun, but no matter how high he flew, he could never seem to reach her.

Wake up, little fire.

She remained inert. Three days had passed since the Reckoning, and still she had not stirred. Three *days*. She had never been unconscious for more than a few hours. His healers were at a complete loss. They had tried every possible therapy, from human remedies to Mailin's halfbreed magic. Nothing worked.

Declan resorted to channeling power through their half bond that resulted in nothing more than the occasional twitch of a fingertip.

"Sire?" squeaked a small voice. Wide brown eyes peeked from the doorway. Evangeline's handmaid, Tessa. The girl had slipped in and out of the room like a shadow in the last few days, bringing his meals and occasionally opening the windows to let in fresh air.

At his nod, she scurried into the room. "I'm sorry to interrupt, sire, but the fae"—her lips pinched—"Mister Blacksage? He said he needs to see you urgently."

Declan's brow furrowed. "Gabriel is in the castle?"

"Yes, sire." Her hands plucked at her skirts in a nervous tic.

"What has you so uneasy, girl?"

Tessa was the forthright sort, and she'd encountered him often, serving as Evangeline's handmaid. She'd never cowered at the sight of him. But now she lowered her lashes and clasped her hands together with a fidgety air.

"I . . . Mister Blacksage appeared from the shadows in the middle of the hallway." She smoothed her skirts again. "Startled me, that's all."

Declan pulled himself from the edge of the bed, scrubbing at his eyes with the back of his hand. He didn't want to leave Evangeline, but reason told him he should. Gabriel wouldn't have requested an audience with him if it weren't important.

"I'll stay with my lady, sire," said the tiny maid. Her gaze brimmed with sadness as she viewed Evangeline on the bed.

"Send word if she stirs." Declan ran a hand through his hair and shrugged on his coat. With one last lingering gaze at his sleeping heart, he exited the room.

It wasn't Gabriel who waited for him in the hallway.

"Brother." Leaning against the wall with his arms folded, garbed in the official robes of white and gold, Alexander appeared every bit the councilman. An irate one.

"More envoys from the Kingdom of Flen," he said without preamble. "Enquiring about your swift departure from Nathaniel's lands."

Annoyance flared deep in Declan's chest. "Again?"

Since their leave, Nathaniel had sent envoys warping into his lands every day.

"I've sent them on their way, though they were none too pleased to be shown the door without an audience with you."

"Good," Declan muttered. If they were still about, he might just have sent them back to Nathaniel with a few bones broken. The archmage of Flen, it seemed, needed a reminder that Declan was no child.

"The council," Alexander added, "has been grousing about the number of assemblies you've missed. Many are unnerved by Reyas's state. I fear . . . "

Alexander's words faded out of focus. Declan rubbed his temple.

"Respect for Evangeline is *not* optional. Everyone knows I have no tolerance for disloyalty," he interjected. His disgruntled council would have to smooth their own ruffled feathers. "Where is Gabriel?"

Alexander sighed and crossed his arms. "Waiting for you in the atrium, I believe." He shook his head. "The way he swans in and out of this castle, it's like he owns the place. You shouldn't have given him free access through the wards, if only to assure the women."

Annoyance flickered again. Alexander skirted the edge of a reprimand. But Alexander was the only kin Declan regarded with affection. The only kin he trusted.

"The last time I checked, Gabriel was very much welcome in the taphouse," Declan said. The Unseelie male was popular with the ladies.

Alexander snorted. "Courtesans revel in novelty as much as they do pleasure. Unfortunately, the women you have on your staff do not share the same predilections. Gabriel's portals unnerve them." A wry smile. "That goes for some of the men, too. Once, the bastard appeared in the middle of the gardens on a whim, and the sudden flare of shadows nearly gave Jorge a heart attack."

Remembering Tessa's earlier remark, Declan gave a weary nod. The castle did house people who were not used to the fae and their portals.

"I will speak with him."

Alexander was not quite satisfied. "While you're at it, perhaps you should consider having him veil his appearance." He bared his teeth in a mock grin. Gestured to his canines. "Those fangs are particularly disturbing."

"Duly noted," Declan replied, impatience edging his tone.

Alexander shuffled his feet, but Declan gave him no opportunity to voice further complaints. He warped to the atrium. He was in no mood for his brother's grumbling and grievances. It wasn't until Gabriel stood to acknowledge him, his chair scraping against the marble, that Declan wondered what Alexander had been doing, lingering in the hallway outside his bedchamber.

"Archmage." Gabriel let out a low whistle. "You look like you just came back from another stint in Draedyn's realm."

Declan hadn't eaten or slept much since returning with

Evangeline limp in his arms. He certainly hadn't shaved. He canted his head. "You're one to talk."

Claw marks savaged the other man's left cheek as though he'd had a run-in with a bear, the wounds raw enough to suggest a recent scuffle. His lips were split; his nose was crooked and bruised. When Gabriel wasn't working for Declan, he was master of a guild of assassins, and likely the most cutthroat of them all. His recent mark must have given him a good run for his coin.

"Something happened to Evie?" Gabriel asked, wariness replacing the usual insouciance in his demeanor.

I let myself touch her when I shouldn't. I allowed my lust to outweigh my judgment and handled her like a courtesan when she remains as breakable as a mortal. But all Declan could bring himself to say was "She's fallen unconscious again."

Gabriel wandered close to mirror Declan's stance, standing with his arms crossed. Though his worry was evident, Gabriel radiated a subtle eagerness akin to a hound's on a scent. "I may have a way to help her."

Declan jerked his head up, suddenly alert.

"Have you considered shamans?"

"Animati?" Declan waved a dismissive hand. "Their healing knowledge cannot possibly surpass the skills of my healers, or those of Unseelie physicians."

"While that is true, animati have a predisposition for magic." Gabriel patted at his split lip absently. "Just like the fae."

"Animati *generate* magic, while you fae *harness* it," Declan responded in a flat tone. Comparing animati to fae based on their affinity to magic was akin to calling a duck a fish because it lived around water. "The species are markedly different in form and function."

"Praise Ozenn." Gabriel curled his lips with obvious

distaste, causing a drop of blood to well up. "Animati are nothing more than beasts, the lot of them."

"So what would shamans know of fae physiology?" Declan asked, his impatience settling in. "How can a shaman be of any help to Evangeline?"

Gabriel arched one annoying brow and gestured for Declan to take a seat. When Declan remained still, Gabriel shrugged and slouched against the heavy oak table, seemingly incapable of upright posture.

"While facilitating one of your rescue squadrons across the fae realm, I came across an animati fighter for sale on the black market." A gleam lit Gabriel's eyes, making him look like an excited child on the morning of Harvest Day. "When he takes his animal form, he becomes"—Gabriel frowned—"I don't know *what* he is. A malformed beast. But he hails from the pantherai clan, so he must be a shapeshifting feline of some sort." The gleam in his gaze heightened. "Sonofabitch is one of the best fighters I've ever encountered."

Declan eyed the claw marks on Gabriel's face with renewed interest. "I ordered you to rescue the slaves, not fight them."

"Byrne was fresh off an auction fight. Easy to goad." Gabriel cracked his knuckles, and Declan realized they were bruised and scraped. "Besides, I'd never gone barehanded against one of his kind."

Declan shook his head in disapproval. Though Gabriel was physically fit, the fae were not built for combat like the statuesque animati. In fact, the fae's regenerative abilities were only one step ahead of humankind's. Gabriel could have gotten himself critically injured. And Declan still didn't see how an animati slave had anything to do with Evangeline's recovery.

Gabriel smirked. "You used to be much better at hiding your emotions, Archmage."

When Declan's expression turned stony, Gabriel held up

his hands in a placating gesture. "All right, all right. I'll cut to it, but the least you can do is offer me some water. I came straight here without giving myself a chance to recover."

Declan stymied the urge to roll his eyes, but he indulged the fae in favor of accelerating his tale. He strode to the sideboard and poured himself a glass of Mujarin and Gabriel a glass of water. He would have offered the other man Mujarin, but Declan knew he had an aversion to alcohol.

"I learned Byrne's inability to fully transform into his animal was because his magic was somehow *knotted* inside."

At Declan's frown, Gabriel shrugged again. "His words, not mine."

Gabriel sniffed at the contents of his glass as though to ensure Declan hadn't mistakenly offered him a glass of spirits before taking a sip.

Declan dragged out a chair and sank into it, nursing his own drink with frayed patience. "I believe you were about to tell me how this concerns Evangeline?"

The fae drained his glass and licked his lips. "Byrne believes his clan's shaman is his only hope if he ever wants to recover his true animal. Shamans are trained to unravel magical knots. But unfortunately for the bastard, he was exiled and sold into the slave trade."

Declan sipped his drink with a considering frown, beginning to see Gabriel's theory. Mages were a wholly *psychic* race. They had no true magical abilities; even his command of fire and ice was a result of psychic manifestation. And magerian healers, like Mailin, were trained to address physiological wounds—not magical hiccups.

Gabriel shrugged. "Animati generate magic that enables them to shift, but really, how different is that from my ability to possess an animal? Or the Seelie equivalent, coaxing life?

Perhaps Evie's abilities are simply *knotted* and they just need to be straightened."

Frowning down at the glossy grain of the hardwood table, Declan ruminated on Gabriel's supposition. Radical. Not entirely illogical. But . . .

"Wouldn't your Unseelie physicians have realized this?"

"As far as we know, no fae has ever returned from the Abyss. No fae has ever lost their ability to wield magic. Not only is she the first Seelie they've seen in centuries, but none of our physicians have ever encountered her condition. Malformed shapeshifters, though?" Gabriel waggled his brows. "Apparently not such a rare occurrence for animati."

Declan would drain the Torgerson Falls if it meant a chance to help his little fire.

But he had little contact with the elusive shapeshifting race. His only link to the animati realm was Noto, a man he'd come to trust enough to make him a battlemage. Only, Noto had long ago renounced all ties to his home realm. With good reason. Declan would never approach the griffi clan with anything but decimation in mind.

The clan had chosen its side on the chessboard when they supplied Zephyr with shieldmakers in exchange for human slaves abducted from Declan's realm.

Declan glanced up. "Where is this Byrne now?"

"Currently in my residence, at the guild." Gabriel gestured to the still-bloody marks on his cheek as though they were badges of honor. Like all immortals, fae healed at expedited rates, but their regenerative abilities were slow compared to those of an archmage.

"I'm hoping to convince him that he'll enjoy killing for coin far more than he enjoyed killing under the lash of a whip."

Declan met Gabriel's gaze, mildly surprised. He'd never heard of Gabriel recruiting.

"What did he do to cause his exile?"

"Murdered his uncle, apparently," Gabriel said with a flash of his canines. "All but turned the man to mince."

Not a crime to deter Declan's interest. "If he is willing to lead me to his clan, I will get him access to a shaman—or whatever it is he desires most."

Animati were an allegiant lot, and most would rather slit their throat than betray their own.

"I'm one step ahead of you this time, my friend." Gabriel smirked wide, then grimaced as his wounds stretched. "Byrne has already agreed to help, no recompense necessary. As repayment for his freedom." Gabriel rolled his eyes. "But it's obvious he's hoping you'll rain ice, fire, and death over the man who sanctioned his sale."

Absently pouring Gabriel another glass of water, Declan released a soft breath. A small seed of anticipation bloomed in his chest, and his spirits lifted precariously close to hope.

"How soon can you arrange for us to arrive in the animati realm?"

"How large an army do you intend to bring?"

Declan shook his head. "I'm not bringing an army."

Shock showed in Gabriel's eyes, his irises dark amethysts. "Even as powerful as you are, I don't think they'll willingly surrender a clan shaman."

"No," Declan agreed. "But they might be willing to do a trade."

THIRTEEN

Declan strode out of swirling shadows into humid heat, narrowly sidestepping a large patch of sludge. His unwary companions, however, exited the portal to step right into muck.

"Ah, fuck," Gabriel muttered, grimacing at his mud-splattered boots. "You could have warned us we'd be trekking into a bloody jungle." Unlike a mage's teleportation, the fae's portals were not limited to places they had been. Fae could cast them anywhere across the five realms, even to places they'd never seen, so long as they had a willing guide.

"Rainforest," said the animati male in his thickly accented voice. When his sandals stuck in the slurry of dirt and peat, Byrne waded to dry land, seemingly content to abandon his footwear.

"Jungle, rainforest . . . what's the damned difference? Wretched dirt-infested places." Gabriel pressed one hand against a fallen tree decorated by curling ferns and fastidiously stamped his boots against the ground of interlacing roots.

Ancient trees soared to the skies to form an umbrella of

green that blocked out most of the sun. A black bird tipped with startling red feathers flitted across the branches, as though attempting to dodge stray wisps of sunlight. Declan drew in a deep breath. There was a wistful quality to the air, an ethereal presence whispering solitude and secrets.

"The crocodilae clan governs the Pohutu Jungle. It is a far more perilous place, filled with predators. But my people . . . " Byrne cleared his throat and shook his head, his movements reminiscent of a wet dog's. "The pantherai rule here. Jijunga Rainforest. The great canopy protects us from the winged ones. Gives us peace."

A band of howler monkeys darted overhead, disturbing the *peaceful* air with hoots and rustling branches. The rainforest seemed to startle. A macaw shrieked, then wings flurried in boisterous unison.

"Oh, yes," Gabriel said. Now his wounds had healed, the fae's lips curled with abandon. "Such peace. Serenity is practically screaming in my ears."

Byrne shoved overlong hair from his forehead. Scowled.

Unperturbed, Gabriel rolled up his shirtsleeves. Moisture clung to the air, compounding the stifling heat. Declan was already regretting his choice of attire. Following Gabriel's lead, Declan shrugged out of his coat and tossed it to the forest floor.

Byrne raised his brows at the discarded coat.

Declan gestured around. "The air is respiring as we speak."

He was tempted to go shirtless, like Byrne, but resisted because he wore a dagger sheathed and strapped over his chest. Besides, it was folly to reveal the markings on his skin unnecessarily.

"You can't *litter* Thurin's lands with your clothes," Byrne said as though Declan had committed sacrilege.

"He's a bloody archmage." Gabriel snorted. "He can litter when and wherever he wants."

Byrne only sputtered.

Declan exhaled, flicked his finger, and his coat burst into flames. Within seconds the flare ebbed and extinguished.

Wide-eyed, Byrne swallowed whatever retort was poised at his lips.

The incendiary show was a small act on Declan's part. He needed the animati male to believe him indomitable despite the equalizing effects of the five realms.

The moment Declan had stepped from Gabriel's portal, a familiar pressure had weighed upon him, as patent as the moisture in the air. The gods draining his powers with every breath he took.

"Lead the way," Declan commanded the animati.

Experience told him he would soon lose his ability to call on fire and ice. He needed to meet and convince the pantherai clan primus to barter a shaman well before that happened.

"Reiken will probably kill me on sight," Byrne mumbled.

Declan didn't bother reassuring the man. So long as Byrne fulfilled his end of the bargain, Declan would not only ensure he walked away with his life intact, but as a man free to live his life in Amereen, if he chose to abscond from Gabriel's guild.

Byrne veered determinedly south. Declan followed without question. Like wild salmon swimming against the tide, animati were born with an instinctive sense of home. Of course, with Gabriel around, the group could travel by portal, but every clan was kept safe under shieldmakers' bloodspells. Even its own residents couldn't lead foreign forces into the clan without passing through the barrier.

They trekked in silence but for the occasional shrill of birds, hoot of curious monkeys, and the incessant symphony of buzzing insects.

But the farther they went, the quieter it became.

No more monkeys darted through the branches, no more critters rustled in the undergrowth, and the birds released nary a sound. The trees grew taller, wielding thicker branches encased in darker bark. Straight and imposing, they gave off an air of warning. Declan's neck prickled. It was almost as though the trees watched them. Silent guards standing vigil.

Byrne only prowled deeper, a sense of urgency in his movements.

Declan and Gabriel trailed after him, ducking and shoving against broad fronds and hanging tendrils. Strangler figs grew in abundance, parasitic lianas climbing up bark in crisscrossing layers, suffocating their hosts to form a curtain of aerial roots dangling halfway to the forest floor. Gabriel's harsh intake of breath as he parted the mass of live roots accompanied Declan's own amazement.

A colossal tree dominated his view, wrapped in scores of vertical vines that hung so high the tree appeared a cathedral of roots. The girth of each individual vine spanned the width of Declan's shoulders.

Byrne halted, his body tense with an anticipation that spurred adrenaline in Declan's veins. "We are *here*," was all he said, words so guttural they were barely comprehensible.

Black fur sprouted from tanned skin, spreading in straggly patches over a hunched back. His jaw extended to form a grotesque snout that was neither canine nor feline in form, crowded with jagged teeth. His arms retracted to form bestial limbs; hands became paws. Fingers thickened to short stubs— neither human nor beast—adorned by wickedly curved claws.

Declan widened his eyes, having never witnessed such a sight despite all his years. Gabriel was right. Byrne was a deformity, his shifted form a confused mangle of man and monster.

A blur of black burst from between corded roots, stealthy

and sleek, plowing into Byrne with the ferocity of a gale. The two tumbled and tousled in a frenzy of bristling fur and slicing claws. Declan sent the attacking creature sailing back. It crashed into a nearby tree with a heavy thud and a piteous whine.

Growls reverberated, rising into a crescendo of primal fury. Panthers slunk from between heavy roots and stalked the branches high above. They crowded closer to form a circle of growling muscle and sharp teeth.

A panther lunged from the closest branch.

Gabriel hissed a warning as his sword sung from its sheath. Before fae steel could spill blood, Declan sent the creature crashing back.

Bloodshed would not make a good first impression.

"Behind you!" Gabriel snarled. Declan swiveled just in time to escape rending fangs. Byrne bellowed and charged headfirst like a battering ram. Clearly his deformity did nothing to reduce his speed or his ferocity. A panther snarled, jaws snapping and claws slashing, while another pounced onto Byrne's back. A whip of its paw left bloody furrows on Byrne's hunched shoulder.

Yet another panther snapped at Gabriel, precariously close to experiencing the lethal tip of the fae's blade. More circled overhead, paws silent against branches, preparing to pounce where Declan stood.

Too many to fend off without a slaughter.

Declan earthed his powers. Fire licked the ground, burning around him in an unholy ring, startling the panthers enough to scatter them.

One prowled forward, but not close enough for fire to singe fur. It was the largest Declan had ever seen. The beast could well be the size of a small bear. With a menacing growl, it reared onto its hind legs. Rippling fur receded seamlessly into smooth skin. Bones cracked and reformed, lengthening and straightening into those of a human. A large, barrel-chested man wearing nothing but his skin bared his teeth in a sneer.

"What is a *krai ji* archmage doing in *my* lands?"

Declan kept his expression unreadable when the air stirred as the primus moved through an unseen barrier. Walking past a shieldmaker's magic caused every hair on his skin to rise, but he entered without question.

A small army of animati—in human and animal form—crouched before a labyrinth of aerial vines. The men glowered, and panthers growled, their claws barely sheathed and tails flicking with distrust. They had been completely imperceptible beneath the shield, made by the same bloodspell Declan had tested and thwarted firsthand at the Dwyer Farm in Arns.

The barrel-chested man—Primus Reiken—did not bother with pleasantries. Nor did he lead them any deeper into the clan's lair.

"You ally yourself with a traitor of the clan, barge into my lands, injure my men, and expect me to gift you one of our most treasured daughters?" The primus asked after Declan explained the reason for his presence.

"I have asked for no gift," Declan corrected, "but offered a deal."

Reiken, still utterly nude and unperturbed, folded his arms and sneered. "Why should I believe you? The talisman has been lost for centuries."

Declan removed the dagger from the leather sheath over his chest. The same dagger he'd once loaned Evangeline in the shadow realm.

When the primus caught sight of the inscription on the blade, he drew in a sharp breath and took an unwitting step forward, his gaze transfixed.

"The *draga sul*," he whispered, reverence in every word. "How is the soul catcher in *your* possession?"

Declan did not disclose that a former heir of the griffi clan served him as battlemage. Nor did he clarify his guardianship of the dagger. He owed the primus no explanations. Precious as the weapon might be, Declan had no qualms in trading it for the chance to help Evangeline.

"Should your shaman succeed in healing my mate where others have failed, the dagger is yours."

The primus narrowed his eyes and folded his arms. "And I am to believe you will keep your word? Archmages have been known to void deals on a whim."

"I will leave the talisman in your keeping while your shaman tends to my mate."

The primus's brows arched. "You would leave the *draga sul* behind? For the simple services of a shaman?"

Declan could easily summon the dagger through the realms whenever he wanted. The talisman was blooded to him the moment he was appointed its guardian. But there was no need to tell the primus that, either. Instead, he said what he knew the primus wanted to hear.

"The *draga sul* on its own is useless without its counterpart, the *draga morli*. And even if I had both talismans, I would have no way of utilizing them without the blood of a seer." The last seer was fabled to have perished in the Winter War. "Without both, the *draga sul* is nothing more than an ornamental dagger. Should your shaman succeed where my healers have failed, I will cede it as payment." And it was truth. Declan would willingly trade his soul, much less a sacred talisman, if it meant Evangeline could recover.

Reiken snorted his disbelief. "And why would a man with your means make no attempt to seek out the *draga morli*? Or a seer?"

Declan shrugged. "I have no need for them."

The *draga sul* and the *draga morli* were necromancer talismans said to preserve souls. For *true* immortality. Declan had never wanted to be a god. He could not fathom anything more damning than eternal life.

The primus began to pace as his warriors watched. Byrne, who had since returned to his human form, stood taut, as though he expected to feel the sharp edge of a spear or be caught in the jaws of another pantherai at any moment. Gabriel stood with his arms crossed, his distaste for animati obvious from the terse line of his jaw.

"And what if my shaman fails?" the primus demanded.

"Then I will return for the *draga sul*."

A sharp nod. "Fair enough. And what if she inadvertently causes your mate harm?"

The only reaction Declan allowed on his face was a slow blink, even though his heart thudded at the thought. "She will not attempt anything without extreme caution. If she damages Evangeline in any way, there *will* be consequences."

Primus Reiken bared his teeth in a sneer. "And if I choose not to accept your deal?"

Declan turned his gaze to the vines and roots that made the labyrinthian entrance of the clan's lair. "Your lands are lush," he murmured, softly but loud enough to be picked up by sensitive animati hearing. "I would hate to see them burn."

A farce.

Since his last display at the clearing, he doubted he could dredge up enough power to conjure that much fire. But he needed this deal. He was desperate, even.

The primus's body went rigid, and low, angry snarls

resounded from the warriors around them. For a moment, Declan wondered if he'd made a tactical error, if he'd pushed where he shouldn't have, but after a lengthy beat, the primus gave a terse nod.

"Wait here," he ordered before disappearing through the darkened tunnel. He returned far quicker than expected, clad in a leather loincloth and dragging a woman behind him.

"Here," Reiken said with a brusqueness that belied the turmoil in his gaze. "Behold the most gifted shaman the pantherai clan has to offer."

Declan frowned as he surveyed the woman. She was tall, as were all animati women, but she appeared disturbingly young. Not at all what he'd expected of *the most gifted shaman*. Clad in a sarong tied around her neck as a formless dress, she clutched at the primus's forearms, her nails scoring skin, her eyes wide with fright. She uttered not a single word, but she shook her head in evident refusal when Declan took a step forward.

Reiken growled low and shook off the woman's grasp, snarling for submission. She gestured wildly with her hands, her motions clearly a manner of communication.

"She is mute?" Declan asked, seeming to startle the woman to stillness.

Reiken thinned his lips. "Do you want to help your mate or not?"

"She appears unwilling to leave your side."

"She has never left the clan in her whole life."

Declan narrowed his eyes.

"She is my twin," Reiken admitted. "But if anyone can help your mate, it is my sister. Shyaree is *mahalwei*."

Declan clamped his mouth shut, understanding he was being given a boon without need for further explanation. *Mahalwei* never changed their shape, which meant their magic was pristine for secondary uses, be it casting bloodspells or, in a shaman's case, healing. Yet the patent fear in her eyes lined his gut in unease. He wasn't here to take a woman captive.

"You are welcome to send a guard to ease her fright, or accompany her yourself," Declan offered after a moment's thought.

"My place is here with my people," the primus said. "Besides, if you meant to do her harm, no number of guards could thwart you."

An ugly truth he could not refute. Declan raised a different concern. "Can she project her thoughts?"

Reiken stared at him warily. "We are not a psychic race. Shyaree speaks with her hands."

Sign language? Declan might speak the animati tongue, but he did not know hand signals. In his realm, muteness was very rarely a barrier to communication. Most learned to communicate telepathically. But Shyaree's inability to do so could prove a problem . . .

Gabriel cleared his throat. "I can help."

Declan furrowed his brow at the guildmaster. "You understand sign language?"

My sister was born mute, Archmage.

Sister? He'd never known Gabriel had a sister. But before Declan could question the fae, the shaman made a series of hand signals. Her motions were fluid and vehement.

Gabriel's lips twitched, and to Declan's surprise, he signed back.

The shaman's eyes widened, and she shrank against her brother, the fear in her eyes flashing to animosity.

What did you just say to her? Declan telepathed with a glare in Gabriel's direction.

Gabriel smirked. *Don't worry, Archmage. Just trying to put her at ease.*

At ease? The woman looked more wary than ever. *Gabriel—*

Reiken shifted to face Declan squarely. "Know this. If a single hair is hurt on Shyaree's head, I *will* find a way to make you pay."

Declan nodded. He expected nothing less.

Reiken swallowed and blinked, emotion thick in his gaze as he tugged the shaman by her wrist, forcing her forward. "Hand over the *draga sul*, Archmage, and we have a deal."

FOURTEEN

Awareness jolted through her body. Evangeline tried to pry open her lids, but they remained heavy, and her limbs, leaden weights.

Someone inhaled sharply. "Sire, she's coming to."

Mailin. Evangeline recognized the voice of the healer who had become one of her closest friends. Evangeline tried to move her lips, but she couldn't even lift a finger.

Her heart began to race.

Why couldn't she *move*?

Footsteps approached. Gentle hands stroked the crown of her head.

"Evangeline?" A man whispered close to her ear, his breath warm against her nape. Declan. He nuzzled her, brushing his lips along her throat. "Little fire, can you hear me?"

The waver in his voice made her heart ache. But she couldn't respond, couldn't reassure him, her mind locked in a void that could well be a glass case. It was as though she were back in Dwyer Farm, hidden beneath the shieldmaker's spell.

Only this time, she was locked in a prison that was her own body—Declan's psychic presence nothing but a shadow she couldn't touch.

I'm here, she cried. *Declan, I'm here.*

Declan shifted away. "She hasn't moved at all since I left?"

Left? Where had he gone? How long exactly had she been unconscious?

A quiet rustling of fabric sounded like a nervous shuffle.

"Not a twitch, sire," another voice murmured, one Evangeline identified easily as Tessa's.

Foreign words tumbled from Declan's lips, but his speech lacked its usual fluidity. His words were choppy and curt. The cadence, clipped. Not the common tongue. Declan was speaking in an entirely different language. And seemingly to himself.

No one responded, as far as Evangeline could hear. Padding footsteps indicated people moving about in the room. Evangeline's ears perked when Declan reverted to the mage language.

"Mailin, would you care to explain what you've attempted so far?"

"Of course," Mailin said, sounding uncertain. "But can she understand me?"

"I will translate," Declan said.

Translate? To whom?

Mailin began reciting the herbal concoctions and medication Evangeline had been given, followed by the healing therapies they'd attempted since they discovered she was Seelie. Declan repeated words in the choppy language. Who were they talking to?

A pause filled with silence. Then Declan resumed speaking in the foreign tongue, pausing every so often. Conversing with someone whose responses she could not hear.

Gentle hands touched her forehead. Feminine hands. Mailin's?

Sudden warmth seeped through her skin. A strange, new sensation. Not Mailin's usual healing magic. There was no honeyed warmth, no soothing ripples running through her blood. Instead, this sensation was prickly and abrasive, almost like stroking fur in the wrong direction. It wasn't her archmage, either. She would recognize the jolt of Declan's powers. He had channeled through their half bond often, a steady current of lightning that filled her veins with raw power.

This energy was less contained, less measured. Tart and tangy, it tasted . . . savage. Primal. Like a wild animal, running through her bloodstream, clawing at her veins. Returning sensation in her limbs.

Railea's tears. It *hurt*.

Evangeline wanted to voice her protest, but her tongue felt too thick in her mouth. In wave after wave, the energy assailed her, intensifying with every surge. Little knives tearing at her innards. A small whimper escaped her throat.

"Little fire?"

Please, stop. She managed a small flutter of her fingers.

The woman's hands lifted, and the pain halted abruptly.

Comforting warmth shrouded Evangeline as Mailin's unmistakable healing energy pulsed through her skin. The fog began to lift, and she could see Declan stalking the edges of her mind, his psyche a brilliant thing of sharp angles and shadowed light.

Wake up, Evangeline. The desperation in his voice was painful to hear. *Wake up.*

A lick of frost and fire penetrated the fog, and suddenly she was steeped in him. Wrapped in the possessive cocoon of his embrace. Evangeline's lids flew open and immediately snapped shut against the sudden glare of the room. A disgruntled moan escaped her lips. Declan's sharp inhale was drowned out by Mailin's cry of relief.

"Thank Railea! Evie, can you hear us?"

Evangeline managed an inarticulate mumble. Her tongue remained heavy, as though she'd imbibed too much spirits. Declan drew her into his arms and squeezed her close.

Evangeline reached up with a sluggish hand to reassure him, but when she cracked her eyes open, she caught sight of a stranger looming at the side of her bed.

Stormy gray eyes studied her.

The stranger reeked of magic and obvious hostility. Evangeline blinked against her blurry vision. When her sight steadied, the woman had retreated to the foot of the bed, a shadow eclipsed by Declan's need for her attention.

With one hand cupping her cheek and the other curled over her back, he pressed furious kisses over her temple, her cheek, her lips. Shadows lined his eyes; strain bracketed his mouth.

"I'm sorry, little fire," he whispered. "Never will I lose control with you again."

"Thank you, Tessa," Evangeline murmured as she accepted the mug of steaming tea from the maid. She breathed deep the herbal notes of kovi leaves before taking a sip. "You make the finest teas."

Tessa's smile was tremulous. "I'm glad you're finally awake, Evie. How are you feeling now?"

Evangeline had long since insisted on the lack of formality between them, though Tessa had only acquiesced to using her name when they were alone.

Before she could reassure the maid, Declan's voice floated from the bedchamber, muted by the sound of running water. "Bath's ready."

Tessa bobbed a quick curtsy and receded from the room just as Declan materialized to scoop Evangeline from the bed, cradling her as though she were a babe fresh from the womb.

"I'm able to walk," she protested even as she looped arms over his broad shoulders, reveling in the strength of his hold. Her voice, still hoarse, earned her a dark look.

"Mailin said you require plenty of rest."

Evangeline wrinkled her nose. The prospect of being further confined to bed was not a palatable one. "Any more rest and I might just slip back into a coma," she said with a chuckle, aiming for levity, only her laugh came out croaky.

He shot her a serious frown. "I am not amused."

Evangeline wisely clamped her lips shut. She understood the panic she must have caused. Understood his need to fuss. And fuss he *had*.

He'd all but spoon-fed her the rich broth Tessa had delivered, insistent on attending to her every whim without allowing her one foot from the bed.

"You've grown even lighter than usual."

"I feel fine." To wipe the scowl from his face, she nuzzled at the warm hollow of his throat, drawing in the scent of cedar and something deliciously masculine. His response was a reverent kiss to her temple as he carried her into the bath chamber.

Steam coiled from glistening water, beckoning her with misty fingers. Evangeline sighed in happy anticipation. Declan's *bath* was in fact a miniature pool, reminiscent of the ones in public bathing houses. Only his was wrought from slabs of marble and had spigots of gold.

He set her down by the edge, careful as though she were

157

spun glass, and helped remove her nightdress. As her skin met the damp warmth, his eyes widened.

Not with lust but alarm.

He ran gentle hands down the sides of her body, pausing at the narrow dip of her waist. She had always been slender, but now she probably resembled a reed.

"I can almost see your ribs," he muttered, seemingly to himself.

Four days spent unconscious *had* hollowed her out.

"Well," Evangeline said, attempting a nonchalant tone even as she squirmed under his scrutiny. "I'll just have to glut myself over the coming days and pray to all that's divine that Mailin's brews are quick acting." She patted her near-concave abdomen nervously, self-conscious of her skin and bones. "Otherwise, you'll just have to put up with this for a while."

He crushed his lips against hers without warning.

A startled gasp escaped her. Unlike his hands, his kiss was neither gentle nor careful. It was fierce and demanding, full of tongue and teeth. When he finally freed her lips, he left the most feminine part of her aching with need and her heart threatening to break free from her chest. Fully clothed, he thrust against her naked body, the length of his desire hard against her belly.

"*This* is what you do to me," he rasped, giving her another gentle buck as his hands roamed to cup and caress the small mounds of her breasts. "I'm *not* putting up with anything."

"Well," she managed with a breathless laugh. "You sure know how to stroke a woman's ego, Archmage."

"Your ego isn't the only thing I wish to stroke," he murmured, solemn as a priest.

The heat between her legs intensified. "Perhaps you'd like to demonstrate?"

He clenched his jaw, hard enough she heard his teeth grind.

"No," he said flatly. "I'm not risking you again." He nudged her into the bath. "Get in before the water gets cold."

With a sigh of resignation, she waded reluctantly down the curved steps and sank into heated bliss, perfectly aware of Declan's ravenous gaze latched onto her every movement. She slid into a curved nook and shivered with delight. He had even thought to scent the water with her favorite poppyseed oil.

She shot him an inviting smile. "Don't you need a bath, too?"

"I will, after you." Not budging one bit.

She flicked a handful of water at him. He glared. She flicked more.

A tiny wave splashed into her face.

"Not fair!" she sputtered. He hadn't even raised a finger. But the resulting smirk on his face made her too happy to keep up the farce of indignation. Finally, he seemed to relax.

"Tell me about the animati realm," she said, when it was clear he would remain fixed to the edge of the pool. "And the shaman."

She shifted close to where he sat.

She reached for a bar of soap, slicked it between her palms, and began scrubbing it over her skin. The column of his throat worked. After a pause, he folded up his shirtsleeves and lathered soap into her hair as he spoke, kneading at her scalp. Her eyes rolled back in pleasure.

When he completed his recount, she twisted her head to frown at him. "And the primus allowed the trade? For a talisman that doesn't even work?"

Declan had once told her the dagger was no ordinary blade. But at the time she'd been too distraught in the shadow realm to see it as anything other than a means to protect herself.

"Animati have coveted the *draga sul* for centuries. Primus Reiken is no different." He gave her head a gentle nudge, seeking to rinse the soap from her hair. Evangeline shut her eyes and leaned back to allow him better access.

"But to want it enough to trade his sister?" Evangeline said, now feeling nothing but sympathy for the poor woman. "While knowing it was possible she could be burned to a crisp if she unwittingly caused me harm?"

She intended the latter as a jest, but when Declan said nothing to defend himself, sickness churned in her stomach. No wonder the shaman had stared at Evangeline with such derision. She decided then that her archmage could *never* know of the pain she'd felt from the shaman's magic.

"Should she succeed," he said instead, "she would earn her people a great prize and an archmage's unending gratitude."

Evangeline's throat grew dry despite the humidity in the air. Declan's tone implied the shaman had been bestowed a great honor, not snared in the dealings of two powerful men.

"You have all but ripped her from her home. She must be terrified."

"I did not coerce her."

Evangeline couldn't help the roll of her eyes. "You've set up a deal in which she is required to fix a broken fae or suffer the repercussions. No choices. No alternatives. That sounds suspiciously like coercion to me."

"You are not broken." His words were all but a growl. "And I only said that to ensure her motivation. Fear, Evangeline, makes for a very strong incentive."

Evangeline shot him an incredulous look.

"Her own brother agreed to the deal," he said defensively.

She firmed her lips. "Yes, clearly *he's* given her much choice in the affair."

"What another man does with his own matters naught to

me. I would do anything, trade anything, for the chance to see you better."

"Tell me," Evangeline murmured. "What *would* you have done had the primus refused you?"

"I would have found another clan, sought another shaman."

"Indulge me, Archmage. Say there were no other clans. No other shamans available to you. What would you have done?" She wasn't trying to be difficult, but it *mattered* to her, the lines he would cross in her name.

There was a pause. His jaw tensed at a hard angle.

"I would have taken her," he said finally, a challenge in his gaze. "I said I would do everything within my power to help you, and I meant it."

Evangeline averted her gaze to focus on the glistening suds running over her skin. Swallowed the bitterness rising in her throat.

"Seeing you like that was enough to break me again." The words were a whisper at her back, so soft she wondered if he meant her to hear them.

Evangeline angled her head back to meet his gaze, torn between love and frustration.

She saw the exhaustion in his gaze, the worry. She was not the only one who had lost weight. His cheekbones appeared more like cut glass than ever.

Guilt scoured her gut.

He edged closer until water seeped into the fabric of his pants.

"I'm sorry if I have disappointed you." He swallowed. "But I would do it again, and without compunction. My effort has already paid off. Shyaree woke you when no one else could."

Her guilt turned to exasperation. What would she have done if their roles were reversed? What *wouldn't* she do? Evangeline reached up to rub her thumb over the shadow beneath his eyes. Her touch left a trail of moisture on his skin.

His eyes grew hooded.

"She will suffer no repercussions if she fails," Evangeline insisted.

No one should pay for her weaknesses.

"Promise me," she added when he did no more than stare, his lids growing heavier with every stroke of her thumb.

Declan sighed. "I promise, little fire."

Appeased, Evangeline beamed up at him, and the tension between them dissolved into the steam. With a faint smile, he intercepted a levitating towel with one hand. She slid from the bath, rivulets of water running down her skin. He dragged a hard and heavy gaze over her body before wrapping her in the towel, then warped.

Evangeline blinked for several seconds when they reappeared by the vast armoire that spanned the entire length of the wall. Warping was still disconcerting. With the towel wrapped under her arms, she rummaged through a drawer for a nightdress.

Evangeline stiffened, every hair on her skin standing to attention.

"What's wrong, little fire?"

She managed a weak smile. "Cold," she said as she quickly traded her towel for a woolen robe. "Why don't you go take a bath? I would like for us to take a walk in the gardens before it gets too dark."

His brows gathered, but he conceded with a nod. The fireplace flared to life, crackling heartily as he strode past. Only when she heard the quiet splash of him treading into the bath did Evangeline release her breath. She opened the drawer again, searching for the stiff parchment, artfully snuck between layers of silk.

Her entire body trembled with fury as she read the boldly written script.

THERE IS NO GREATER SORE,
THAN AN OBSTINATE WHORE,
WHO REFUSES TO FLEE,
EVEN FOR HER OWN SAFETY.

FIFTEEN

"Alexander?" Evangeline gave a hesitant rap on glossy oak.

She pressed her ear against the door and chewed on her bottom lip. Silence.

Dawn had barely broken, the sky still smudged with sleepy clouds and the hallway lit by yawning sunlight. The quiet melody of daybreak filled the castle, a tune that would soon give way to humming maids, harried footsteps, and hushed conversations. But Evangeline had risen hours ago, her body fatigued but sleepless.

"Lex?" she whispered and rapped again, more boldly this time.

Could Alexander have already arisen and left for the day? Evangeline had left her archmage fast asleep when she snuck from their bed, eager to implement her plans. Guilt had gnawed at her throughout the night for keeping secrets from the man who slept clinging to her like a child hugging his favorite blanket.

Evangeline raised her hand to knock again when the door

flung open to frame an irate and bedraggled Alexander. Wearing nothing but a pair of faded pants and a scowl, he muttered, "Who in Railea's bosom—"

Tawny eyes widened at the sight of her.

Alexander stuck his head out to do an inconspicuous check of the hallway before he all but dragged her into his bedchamber. "I'm glad to see you well and awake, Evie, but by all the gods, what are you doing here?"

"I have a plan, Lex," Evangeline began, only to falter and frown. "Are those . . . feathers? In your hair?"

Alexander's lips tipped into a lopsided grin.

She blinked. Feathers were scattered everywhere, as though Alexander had a roost of pigeons secreted away in the room. Strewn on the carpets, clinging to the settee . . . and the pair of smooth legs stirring beneath silken bedsheets.

Heat crawled up Evangeline's cheeks like a rash.

"I'll come back later." She swiveled on her heel for escape.

A strong hand gripped her forearm. "Don't be ridiculous, Evie," Alexander said with a wry smile. "I'll warp you out. Have you any idea how inappropriate it is for you to be seen exiting my chambers at this time of day?"

Evangeline grimaced. She'd been so consumed by her plans she hadn't been thinking straight. *Inappropriate* was an understatement if she were caught exiting a councilor's private quarters—no matter the hour.

Alexander ran fingers through tousled hair, dislodging several white tufts as he served her an expectant stare.

"I've thought of a way to ensure the sustainability of the slave-rescue operation," Evangeline mumbled with her eyes firmly averted from the bed.

"And you couldn't wait for a more decent hour?" Alexander folded arms over his wide chest.

Evangeline opened her lips to protest but promptly shut

them. She was meant to meet the shaman today. She had no idea what to expect, or what it would lead to, but she needed to see Alexander before she accumulated more threats.

"I shouldn't have come here. I'm sorry . . . " She flailed for the right words but couldn't come up with any. So she settled with "Can you get dressed?" Evangeline mustered a strained smile. "Please?"

Alexander smirked at her obvious discomfort but moved to the woman still sprawled on his bed. Keeping her sight fixed on the damask curtains on the far side of the room, Evangeline settled on the arm of the settee—the only part of the furniture not covered in feathers—cursing her own naivety. She should have known Alexander wouldn't be alone.

Shuffling sheets, soft murmurs, and a sultry giggle. Then Alexander disappeared through the doorway into the connecting bath chamber.

Languid and lovely, wearing only freckled skin and flame-colored hair, the courtesan rose from the bed to give Evangeline a deep curtsy, seemingly unfazed by her nudity. And why wouldn't she be? The woman had lush curves in all the right places.

"My lady, I am honored to make your acquaintance."

Embarrassment a gag over her mouth, Evangeline only nodded.

Sauntering close, the redhead gestured to the scrap of lace Evangeline perched upon. "May I, my lady?"

Evangeline sprang up. What she had assumed to be an elaborate armrest cover turned out to be a slip of lace and ribbons.

The most intriguing piece of underwear she had ever seen.

Face scorching but unable to resist, Evangeline swallowed her shyness. "Did you procure this from Madam Rossa?" The castle seamstress now made everything Evangeline wore.

The courtesan snickered as she donned the garment, clearly pleased by Evangeline's interest. "Oh, my lady, Madam Rossa may make the most beautiful gowns, but I fear these pieces are far too salacious for her spinsterly mind."

She spun to show off the intricate laces and the tiny stays. "One of the girls in the lounge is a milliner's daughter." A saucy wink. "Her little creations have been known to drive men a little . . . " She picked up a nearby feather and blew it from her palm.

By the time Alexander emerged from the bath chamber, Evangeline had exchanged first names with the courtesan and was waving Ilana out the door with a cheery smile.

Dressed and decent, Alexander blinked. "Did Ilana just blow you a kiss?"

Evangeline grinned. "She's lovely."

"Yes. Yes, she is." Alexander scowled, sinking into the settee with his arms crossed. "So tell me the reason you've chased her prematurely from my bed?"

Evangeline fiddled with her fingers. There was a reason she approached him and no one else. Alexander was the closest thing she had to an unbiased opinion. He was also her perfect mouthpiece—a councilor revered by his peers, and one who had her archmage's ear.

"Would you be willing to present my proposal to Declan and the council in the next assembly?" As the elorin of Amereen, she could very well present it herself, yet she knew her presence in the atrium would automatically raise the hackles of every councilor loyal to Reyas.

At Alexander's questioning brow, Evangeline explained her proposal where each councilor would be given the right to vote on her proposed initiative. It was an unorthodox idea, given Declan held final say in all matters. But because he was predisposed to champion her causes, he would, very likely, sanction her proposal without conferring with his council.

Evangeline had no wish to bring him yet another point of contention with his court.

A court already biased against her.

She wanted a solution to appease the council. An initiative to make them see she could be more than their archmage's weakness. But Evangeline was also no fool. Given the incident with Reyas, most councilors would reject her proposal on loyalty alone.

Hence she had also made it mandatory for every veto to be accompanied by reasons. Handwritten reasons.

Discerning as always, Alexander scowled. "Have you received another threat?"

"Yes," she admitted.

An angry chuff worked its way up his throat. He held out a palm. "Show me."

"I don't carry it around, Lex, but it's definitely written by the same person." Her lips firmed at the recollection of the note. Every dip and curve, every bold stroke was etched into her memory.

Alexander snorted. "Is that why you're giving the councilors a chance to veto your plans? To get a sample of their handwriting?"

She had opted for a more democratic approach, but she had no intention of disbanding the slave-rescue operation. Nor would she have her archmage turn a deaf ear to the council's harangues over Amereen's dwindling coffers. Her primary intent was to understand the rationale behind each rejection, assuming the decisions were made based on legitimate objections and not driven by pack mentality.

But, of course, the feedback would serve her secondary purpose.

What better way to gain access to the penmanship of each councilor?

"Evie, the author of those threats may not be someone from the council. It could be a squire, a courtier, a spouse, or even a scullery maid!"

Anyone who believed Evangeline an unfit mate for their revered archmage.

Evangeline offered the councilor a calm nod and an even smile. "I've already considered that. Which is why I've also made it a point to convene with the castle scribes."

At Alexander's blank look, she leaned forward with a grin. "Apparently all parchment used in the castle is procured from papermakers in the capital."

Alexander stared at her as though she'd sprouted two heads. "Are you trying to tell me that you would soon be visiting paper mills, bent on comparing all the parchment they have in stock?"

"How many papermakers can there possibly be in the capital?"

The notes were of pristine quality. White as chalk and smooth as silk. She doubted many papermakers could produce such fine stock.

Alexander rubbed his temple as though Evangeline had just roused a headache. "I have a far easier plan," he muttered after a moment's silence, drumming the edge of the settee with measured taps of his fingers.

Evangeline stared at him expectantly.

"It is not too late to tell my brother. Let him resolve it."

At the thought of Declan, her lips quivered. "You know better. If Declan even caught a whiff of dissension among his people . . . " She shuddered.

Then chagrin had her biting into her bottom lip.

If she were honest, fear of her archmage's wrath was not

the reason behind her need for secrecy. Evangeline wanted to resolve this conundrum without his help. She wanted to prove to him that she could hold her own with his people. More, she needed to prove to herself that she was more than a fugue fae with forgotten abilities. To prove she was worth the weight of her titles—Lady Evangeline Barre, elorin of Amereen, and Princess Freya Katerina Jilintree, last daughter of the House Jilintree.

"I'll tell him," she said with a stubborn nod. "When I find the culprit."

Wariness cut lines across Alexander's handsome face.

"I can handle this, Lex," she said, imploring him with her gaze.

With a weary groan, he sighed. "Have it your way, then. But I'll be damned if the elorin of Amereen is to visit the paper mills on her own."

Alexander had just warped her into the infirmary office when she felt the brush of warm silk against her mind. Her archmage had awoken.

My little fire . . . A drowsy pause. *Where have you gone?*

Evangeline curved her lips, knowing he could perceive her yearning in the mental plane. She rubbed back against his mind. Fae were not psychic beings, and her ability to interact with him on a telepathic level remained minimal. But as the moon knew the stars better than the sun, immortals were more attuned to the mental plane than humans.

She could now see his psyche as plainly as the stars in the sky.

I wanted to catch up with work. You were still sound asleep, and I didn't want to wake you.

Another slow stroke against her psyche sent sensual shivers down her spine.

I miss you, he telepathed, as though he hadn't just spent the whole night in her embrace. But her heart swelled just the same, growing almost too large for her body.

Will I see you this morning? She asked a little ruefully. Her archmage would likely be sequestered in the Receiving Hall for the day. Prior to working in the castle, Evangeline'd had no clue of an archmage's responsibilities beyond the simple fact that they ruled supreme. Now, she understood the enormity of his duties.

Declan oversaw everything within his lands—through the lens of his delegates, with whom he regularly convened. Village governors through to the vicegerents of state made regular reports to the council, who escalated matters requiring higher judgment or consideration.

Alexander had relayed that Declan hadn't tended to his duties for as long as she had been unconscious. Evangeline could only imagine the scores of councilors frothing for his attention.

I'll see you this evening. His words carried a longing she reciprocated wholeheartedly.

She rubbed her mind against his in a telepathic kiss.

A flare of warmth limned glacial planes. *I have instructed Gabriel to come to you. He will assist your communication with the shaman.*

Evangeline frowned. *How is it that Gabriel understands hand signals?*

Apparently Gabriel has a sister who was born mute. A pause. *Or had. I can't be sure. I have never heard him speak of her until now.*

As though summoned, the Unseelie sauntered into Evangeline's office, a glint in his eyes and a glide to his steps.

"There she is," he said as he leaned against the edge of her desk. "Amereen's very own sleeping beauty. Did you have a good nap, my lady?"

Evangeline narrowed her eyes at the smirking fae, even though her lips curved at the sight of him. "I heard you lost a fight while I was asleep."

Gabriel straightened. Scowled. "Who said that?"

"Oh, half the castle saw you with your face ripped open," she said with her sweetest smile. The fae's visage darkened. Not a shadow of injury marred his cheeks.

"It was Lex, wasn't it? I saw him strolling out on my way in. Bastard's always out to tarnish my reputation."

Evangeline's shoulders shook. She'd heard it from a solemn-faced archmage but didn't think Gabriel would appreciate the clarification.

"Byrne got close enough to sink his claws into me," Gabriel added. "But just to be clear, I most certainly did not lose the fight."

"Of course," Evangeline said with as much seriousness as she could muster, but facetiousness must have shone through her smirk, for Gabriel mock snarled.

Laughing aloud, Evangeline asked, "Isn't it still a touch too early to meet the shaman?" She moved to the windows. Peered out. "The sun's only just risen."

"That woman was poking about the castle grounds while the owls were still flying." The fae rolled his eyes. "I don't think she actually slept."

Evangeline's brows knitted. "And how would you know that?"

Gabriel folded his arms, a touch defensive. "Though your archmage thinks her harmless, I believe otherwise. There's too much magic in that woman to allow unmonitored."

Evangeline opened her mouth to chide, only to clamp her lips. She recalled the wild taste of the shaman's magic, the sensation of knives cutting into her veins. Regardless of his powers, Declan remained a mage who could not *sense* magic. Gabriel, on the other hand . . .

"Do you believe her dangerous?"

The Unseelie shrugged. "All I know is she doesn't want to be here. And a caged animal will use its claws if given the chance."

The shaman was a stunning creature. Even the drab cloak couldn't hide exotic eyes of copper and a complexion of sun-drenched wheat. Like all animati Evangeline had encountered, she was long-limbed and limber. But only when they approached did Evangeline realize the shaman was so tall that she was close to Gabriel's considerable height.

Catching sight of Gabriel, the shaman glared. But when her gaze landed on Evangeline, wariness bled into brass eyes. She took a hesitant step back, watching Evangeline the way a maltreated circus lion would its ringmaster.

Evangeline didn't blame her.

Declan might not be present to facilitate her introduction, but he had never been one for subtlety. Guards filled the courtyard and trailed her skirts like bees after their queen, a silent hive of eyes tracking the shaman's every movement.

"Shyaree?" Evangeline wore a cordial smile and pointed at herself. "Evangeline."

"Lady Barre to the likes of you," Gabriel muttered, under his breath but loud enough for the shaman's ears. Even if she didn't understand the common tongue, she was still able to hear the derision in Gabriel's tone.

Evangeline shot the fae a warning glare before saying, "I

hope you found your quarters to your liking. I heard you've been out and about since before dawn."

Dutifully, Gabriel translated. But unlike Declan, who seemed to speak Animatish fluently, Gabriel's grasp of the shaman's language seemed subpar. He spoke a few halting words, then utilized hand motions to complete his translation.

The shaman responded with grace in her gestures and scorn in her expression.

"Yeah?" Gabriel scoffed. "Well, if you'd prefer sleeping in the gardens, I'm sure that can be arranged." He made a few hand signals that caused the shaman's motions to grow more agitated and her expression more affronted.

Evangeline sucked in an exasperated breath, wishing she had thought to corral Mailin and bring her along for moral support. "*What* are you saying to her?"

"I told her that her only task here is to heal you." Gabriel did not take his gaze from the shaman while he spoke, his tone lofty. "And the sooner she gets to it, the sooner she gets to go home."

"Oh, for the love of Railea, Gabriel!" Evangeline pinned him with a hard stare. Glancing over to Shyaree, she mustered a strained smile. "Shyaree, I apologize. Gabriel is usually far more charming than this."

Whether Gabriel translated her exact sentiment Evangeline would never know, but a little sneer twisted the shaman's mouth after he was done.

"It must be really hard for you to be so far from home. Perhaps you can tell me what I can do to make you more comfortable?" Evangeline said.

It only earned her a slight hardening of the shaman's jaw as the woman openly assessed her—and Evangeline didn't think she liked what she saw.

"I understand you don't want to be here," she said, willing

the other woman to hear her sincerity in the tone of her voice. "I am sorry you're caught up in this, but I promise no one will hurt you."

Upon Gabriel's translation, the shaman shot her an incredulous look and made a rude-looking gesture that had Gabriel baring his fangs. Evangeline decided it was just as well she didn't understand sign language.

"Shyaree, please be assured that all you need to do is try your best to help me recover my abilities. And if you fail, there will be no consequences, despite what you've been led to believe."

Seconds crawled like a caterpillar as Shyaree stared, slow and prickly. Just when Evangeline began to question if Gabriel had translated her words properly, the woman stretched out an open palm.

Hesitantly, Evangeline met Shyaree's hand. Long, slender fingers enveloped hers.

Warmth emanated from the shaman's touch, magic suffusing the air around Evangeline, rising within her. She gasped, her breath growing ragged. If she was caught in a maelstrom of magic, then Shyaree was the eye. Calm and focused, the shaman simply stared.

Evangeline jerked back and dry heaved.

Dimly, she was aware of Gabriel's concerned hand on her back and the guards' alarmed footsteps. She quickly waved her hand and shook her head. "I'm fine. I'm fine," she mumbled, lest anyone panic prematurely and flag the attention of an overprotective archmage.

When she glanced up, the shaman seemed to have shrunk in place, arms wrapped around herself as though she were liable to be apprehended at any moment.

Evangeline sighed. "Guards, I need you to step back."

Her guardsmen shifted with a nervous air. But unable to

ignore her direct order, they retreated a single step. Evangeline frowned and waved a hand at the stoic-faced men, shooing them like geese. "Can you perhaps go a little farther?"

"The sire commanded us not to let you from our sight," protested the lead guard.

Evangeline huffed, but her still-roiling gut caused her to cough instead. "Well, you'll still be able to see me if you move back there, into those corridors, won't you?"

The guards reluctantly retreated.

"Thank you," Evangeline called after them.

Gabriel regarded her with open amusement. "I don't think an archmage's queen thanks her guards for following orders," he whispered, words meant only for her ears.

Evangeline pursed her lips.

Command did not come naturally, but she was learning, wasn't she?

Appearing far less tense, Shyaree motioned with her hands. Gabriel gave the shaman a grudging nod before turning to Evangeline.

"She is willing to help, if you are willing to try."

Evangeline managed a weak smile. "A little pain won't deter me."

Shyaree's hands cleaved the air with terse motions.

Gabriel stiffened, then translated in an equally grim tone. "If you thought that hurt, then you don't know what real pain is."

SIXTEEN

Declan paced the edge of Torgerson Falls, trying to walk off the agitation pinching his chest. There was a certain peace to be had watching the gushing river wrestle its way into the tide. But today, even the brine-laced mist and gull song failed to soothe.

This place no longer belonged to him alone. It had become theirs through all the times he'd warped Evangeline here whenever he wanted release without the worry of destroying his castle.

He sighed in frustration.

Every day, Evangeline would have a session with the shaman, which she *insisted* he stay away from. Every evening, she would greet him with a smile and a kiss and tell him everything had gone well.

Declan didn't believe her.

During each session, he sensed a strange sort of *strain* rippling through their half bond in small jolts. Sometimes in alarming waves. But Evangeline was always quick to assure him she was fine. Gabriel and his men had also reported nothing extraordinary, vouching for the shaman, who was apparently fast becoming friends with his little fire.

So Declan had stayed away.

The gods knew keeping his distance had served him, too.

Each night had become a torment.

Once, when Evangeline had shied from his touch and shunned intimacy, Declan had resigned to never bedding her. He had been ready to live with that. He would never dream of asking his little fire for things she couldn't afford to give.

But to know her taste and not touch her? To lie beside her each night, wrapped in her intoxicating warmth and her beguiling scent, and *not* bury himself between her thighs? It was a form of torture he'd never experienced before, one that bordered on agony.

Like an addict suffering from withdrawal, Declan had spent each night restraining his urges. To make matters worse, she thought his attempts egregious. She would wriggle close, rub up against his flesh, and make it physically impossible for him to sleep.

Cold baths did little to temper his needs, nor would he allow her to ease him in any form or fashion. He would not risk her again. His only relief came from the solitude of his own palm, but that only added to his frustration. He resented the act. It felt unfaithful somehow, even though she featured in every fantasy.

But today, fresh from the morning assembly with his council, Declan's frustration had grown to surpass his ability to function.

Alexander had just presented a proposal on an initiative to fund the slave-rescue operation currently in place.

Dubbed the Survivor Rescue and Rehabilitation Scheme, it proposed all rescued slaves be trained in a skill and reinstated in society with a trade. To encourage societal support, every tradesman who hired a woman or man under the SRRS would enjoy reduced tithe and tax rates. A percentage of wages earned by SRRS individuals in the first three years would then be siphoned to *fund* the scheme.

An initiative that would not only reduce the burden on Amereen's coffers, but one that would, in turn, instill a sense of societal contribution in SRRS individuals.

Alexander had delivered the entire speech with his usual panache, gaining steady traction of nodding heads in the audience. By the end of his proposal, Lex had given full credit to the Lady Evangeline Barre, surprising more than the sea of baffled councilors.

Declan had been aware Evangeline was intent on finding a solution to quell his council's nattering of financial drain. But considering her daily training sessions with Shyaree interspersed with the regular work in the infirmary, he had assumed she'd put her efforts on hold.

"Why haven't I heard of this before?" he had demanded of his brother, who had simply shrugged. "Evie told me not to worry you with the details."

The statement had stung more than just his ego.

Did Evangeline not trust him enough to come to him first?

But when he had reviewed the proposal, pride had been a glowing brand on his chest. Her initiative was detailed, complete with meticulously calculated tax-reduction rates. With some refinement, Declan would have heartily sanctioned her proposal. Instead, she had decided on *ballots*.

Did she not trust him to ratify her plans?

Declan drew in a deep breath of moisture laced with salt. The river crashed headlong into the sea, the roiling waves mirroring his frustration.

He had spent his whole life licking his own wounds and

shrugging off hurts. But now, a small part of him, perhaps the most vulnerable part, felt bruised.

A bruise that could only be soothed by one woman.

He sifted through the mental plane, soaring past countless minds of varying shapes and sizes until he found a distinct one shimmering in amber flames. Her mind was poised, thoughts coiled in concentration. Another session with the shaman.

He had promised to stay away, but he needed to see her.

Declan warped and reappeared in one of the watchtowers overlooking the sparring compound. His little fire was below in the large courtyard framed by battlemented walls. Beside her, Gabriel sprawled on the ground like a lazy cat sunning itself. Evangeline sat tranquil and cross-legged, hands connected with the shaman's while the animati mirrored her prim posture.

A faint smile played over Declan's lips. The very sight of her eased the ache in his heart. She was his personal vision of home. Of love. And he was so *proud* of her he wanted to—

Evangeline pitched forward as though shoved by an unseen force. A sharp cry leaked from her throat, barely audible from the distance. Strain flowed through their bond, punching him with alarm.

Declan warped into the courtyard on his next breath. "What happened?"

Shyaree jumped to her feet and skittered back. Gabriel, who had hunched over Evangeline like a protective shield, released her shoulder as though he were a child caught with his hand in the cookie jar.

"Declan?" Evangeline blinked at him. "Everything is fine." She quickly scrubbed at her nose with the back of her hand, but he didn't miss the scarlet staining her sleeves.

Declan warped the three steps that would have taken him too long, reappearing to cradle her face in his hands. Her irises were wildly dilated, her pallor the shade of whey. Blood, so dark it was almost ink, trickled down her nose. Sickness churned in his gut. He turned to the shaman, who seemed to shrivel before his glare.

"What have you done?" he demanded, dimly aware the symbols of his ascension had flared.

Evangeline's palm cupped his cheek, her gentle touch commanding his attention.

"Shyaree is doing exactly what you brought her here to do." Her voice sounded hoarse, but the serenity in it calmed him.

"To help you." Declan ground his teeth. "Not to hurt you."

"I am not hurt." She wiped at her nose again and gave a little shrug. "I'm fine."

Declan shook his head. He knew her well enough to recognize true pain on her face. "Until I'm sure this isn't causing you further damage, these sessions will cease."

Her eyes widened, challenge and annoyance flaring simultaneously.

"It most certainly will *not*. I can feel the threads of magic more keenly than ever before. Shyaree is really helping."

A muscle ticced at the side of Declan's jaw. "Whatever she's doing is causing you to bleed." For all he knew, the shaman's magic wreaked more havoc on her body, causing internal injuries.

Evangeline's lips twitched. "A *nosebleed*."

"How many nosebleeds have you had? What other ill effects have you suffered?"

Why hadn't she *told* him these things?

She answered him with a sigh. "I did not want to worry you unnecessarily. I did consult Mailin. She found nothing alarming in a nosebleed or two."

Declan raised his brows.

"Mailin has likened me to a paralytic regaining use of her

muscles. Minor symptoms are to be expected. But with time and practice, I will get stronger."

"If you stop them now, Archmage, Evie will only lose the progress she's made so far," Gabriel interjected.

Declan shot him a warning glare, but the Unseelie only shrugged.

"Honestly, Evie is getting stronger. I've felt her abilities flaring up once or twice. It's as though Shyaree's magic is stoking an ember, and I've witnessed the sparks," Gabriel said, with what sounded disturbingly like *awe* in his voice.

Evangeline smiled up at the damned fae, her expression filled with such affection that an acrid tang rose to the back of Declan's throat.

Declan, please, trust me. Her psychic voice was an imploring force in his mind. *I want to do this. I need to. I feel so close . . .*

For all his powers, he was powerless to resist her will.

If it gets any worse, will you promise to tell me?

The curve of her lips grew brighter than the sun. She rewarded his capitulation with a kiss to his cheek while Shyaree remained staring at him like a petrified rabbit.

Evangeline gave his cheek a gentle pat. "Perhaps you ought to return to your work? I'll come to you when we're done here."

Declan flattened his lips. Now she wanted him *gone?*

"Archmage, I am bound to feel a measure of . . . discomfort. I really think it's best you're not here to witness it." She dropped her voice. "You're also scaring Shyaree."

She wrapped her arms around his neck and placated him with another kiss before ushering him off the compound. Reluctantly, Declan warped. Instead of in his office, he rematerialized by the window of the watchtower, belatedly realizing he hadn't told her the reason behind his interruption. She hadn't asked.

Evangeline had resumed her position at the center of the compound with Gabriel hovering around her like a cloud. Declan dragged his gaze away. Jealousy was infantile, and it certainly would not help matters.

Yet he had the most juvenile urge to push his way between them, shove Gabriel into the closest sinkhole, and pull her into his arms. Be the one who soothed her pain.

But she didn't want him there. Didn't trust him to be.

Just like she hadn't trusted him enough to divulge her plans with the SRRS.

Somewhere in his chest, the bruising deepened. He took a hasty step back, retreating into the shadows. Shut his eyes with a calming breath. When the pounding of his heart regulated, Declan risked another peek through the window.

Gabriel gazed down at Evangeline with something in his expression that caused Declan's fist to clench. Evangeline didn't pull away. She leaned into him.

Declan woke with a groan in his throat and an ache in his groin.

"Shhh," a sultry voice whispered in the dark.

He blinked, trying to shake off the dredges of his lusty dreams before he realized he *was* awake. And a nymph was in his bed, naughty intent in her eyes.

Even the moon peeking through the balcony doors seemed to revere her, glinting off her hair like an ethereal crown, caressing her bare skin with luminous fingers.

She crawled over him, lips a seductive curve, legs straddling his hips. His breath hitched. None of his dreams could ever compare because he never really knew what she would *do*. Still inexperienced by his standards, she was artless in bed. But by the gods, she was eager. Demure yet deviant, she was an erotic combination he was happy to spend the rest of his days enslaved to.

She drew his arms up either side of his head, as though to pin them down with her slender hands. Then she leaned forward to kiss the hollow of his neck, her breath hot as she grazed him lightly with her teeth. A pink tongue flicked over his skin as she made her way down to his chest. Tiny licks traced the symbols of his ascension, wrenching moans from his throat.

With whatever rationality he had left, he managed a half-hearted, *"No."*

He pulled from her grip and reached up to stop her, but his fingers somehow tangled in her hair. Glorious silk in his hands. Her tongue glided down the ridges of his abs, every lick holding him in thrall.

Then she reared down to lap at the hardest part of him while her hands cupped the softest. He bolted upright with a curse, displacing her from his person as he warped. In his haste for escape, he misjudged the width of the mattress, rematerializing so close to the edge that he nearly tumbled from the bed.

"Now you're just being ridiculous." She huffed, but her annoyance was short-lived. Playful determination flashed in her eyes. She lunged at him with surprising dexterity and pushed him down, pinning him on the bed. With an impish grin, she ran fingers down his abs. Her frisky tickling soon became a sensual taunt.

"Evangeline . . . stop." He intended to command, but his words came out a plea. He was aroused to the point of pain. He seized her arms and donned his iciest glower. One he wore solely to intimidate.

He received an exaggerated pout that only made him ache to kiss.

"I know what you want, what you need," she murmured, her voice a sexy little purr. "Come now, Archmage. You've been churlish lately, and I don't enjoy it, even from you."

Did she think sex the only thing he needed from her?

"Do you enjoy unconsciousness?" he snapped. The fact that he *did* sound churlish only increased his annoyance. "Because I do not find that titillating in the least."

"Oh, Railea's tears, you don't know for certain that is the true cause!"

Still too stubborn to admit that his releases triggered her fainting spells.

She crossed her arms, challenge flaring in her eyes. "Or are you so wound up that you're afraid you won't last long enough to bring me pleasure?"

There was only so much a man could take.

Declan had her flat on her back before she could gasp. "I'll show you pleasure, you little minx."

He lashed her with his tongue, punishing her in a way that would make even the most seasoned courtesan scream. She found ecstasy easily, his name chanted like a carnal prayer on her lips. Before her breaths evened, she reached for him, a wanton fae with pointed ears he wanted to lick and parted thighs he throbbed to plunder with more than just his mouth.

Her eyes narrowed at the look on his face.

"Don't even think about it," she warned. "Don't you *dare* wa—"

Silencing her with one final, angry kiss, he warped.

SEVENTEEN

"What did the book do to offend you?"

Evangeline dragged her gaze from the page. "I am *reading*."

Gabriel regarded her with raised brows, hands clasped behind his head, booted feet resting indolently on the table. "You look like you're trying to rip through the page with your eyes."

Evangeline deepened her scowl, which seemed to amuse the shaman, who smirked. Shyaree had taken to following her around each day, wherever she went. If Evangeline worked in the infirmary, Shyaree would observe with unconcealed interest. If she worked in her office, the shaman would sit in an obscure corner. And whenever she did research in the library, Shyaree would pore through any illustrated book she could find.

Gabriel's violet gaze grew speculative. "Have the winds been fair with your archmage?"

"Yes," Evangeline mumbled. "Why would you even ask that?"

"If not him, who could have upset you this much?" Gabriel asked. The rare gentleness in his voice caused a sudden surge of warmth in her eyes.

She hung her head. "I'm tired. That's all."

Exchanging a quiet glance with the shaman, Gabriel leaned back in his seat, an unusual chariness in his expression.

It wasn't a complete lie. Evangeline did feel worn. A small tug of a loose thread and she would unravel into a tangled mess.

Her daily sessions with Shyaree were physically exhausting and often, excruciating. And so far, she had managed nothing salient.

The council had decided to cast their votes on her proposal in a fortnight, which meant she was no closer to deciphering the identity of the author of the threats.

Declan had been obscure at best with his thoughts on her initiative. When she'd broached the topic, eager for his appraisal, he'd regarded her with a cool, near callous, impassiveness.

"The projections are far too optimistic," he had said without a hint of a smile. *"Further refinement is necessary for a more realistic estimate. I will adjust your calculations, should the council vote in favor."*

Evangeline hadn't been seeking praise. She'd suspected her projections too idealistic, her calculations crude. She was no learned scholar, nor was she a trained councilor. But she had worked so hard to surprise him with this proposal she'd hoped would help ease his burden in some small way. She'd expected some form of acknowledgment, at the very least.

Though his increased frostiness did not seem directed at her alone.

"The sire has been highly irritable lately, if anyone knows to look beneath the ice," Killian had muttered one morning, looking at *her* with hope, as though she were able to deter his liege's surliness.

But Agnes had told her men grew churlish whenever they went too long without. And Declan hadn't touched her since the glacier. So Evangeline had done what any sensible, self-serving woman would have done.

She had attempted seduction.

But her efforts had backfired. Declan had all but reduced her to a mewling puddle, demonstrating clear disparity in their sexual prowess. Then he'd left her to lie alone, loose-limbed and languid, yet hollow with the knowledge she'd brought him no pleasure.

She was gutted. Embarrassed. Furious. So incensed she had avoided him the whole of the following day. When he had come to bed that night, she had feigned sleep. To her outrage, the man had warped from the room—*again!*—completely eschewing their bed for the night. So spurned, Evangeline had perpetuated their suffocating dance yet again this morning, childishly avoiding any part of the castle where their paths might cross.

Shyaree's chair creaked as she motioned, her gaze on Evangeline.

Gabriel dutifully relayed the shaman's intent. "She wonders if her sessions have taken a toll on you."

"Nothing I can't handle," Evangeline said. Touched by the concern in the shaman's copper gaze, Evangeline reached out to clasp her hand. "Thank you, Shyaree. If there's anything I can offer to repay your efforts, please let me know."

Gabriel translated even though Shyaree had already learned some basic words such as *thank you* and *please*.

The shaman shook her head dismissively and lowered her gaze back to the illustrated book on the various regions of the realm she had been perusing with abject fascination.

"Are there any places you wish to see?" Evangeline asked hesitantly. "Anywhere you would like to visit?"

Shyaree seemed to consider her offer, and after a long pause, she flipped the pages of her book until she came to a specific illustration. She held the book up so Gabriel was unable to see the pages and pointed shyly to it.

Evangeline frowned.

In a display of utter juvenility, Gabriel snatched the book from Shyaree's hands. He snickered. "The sea?" His lips twisted into a sneer. "Of all the things you could ask for, you want a trip to the *beach*?"

Though Shyaree glowered, a faint blush rose to the shaman's cheeks.

Gabriel was relentless. "Aren't cats supposed to be afraid of water?"

The sound of striding boots saved Gabriel from the scathing rebuke on Evangeline's lips.

Her pulse sped.

Declan strode into view, as though conjured by her yearning alone, his expression inscrutable as always. He was so disarmingly beautiful, so painfully distant that her heart twisted.

Shyaree rose to acknowledge Declan's presence with a stiff bow. Gabriel, on the other hand, drawled, "Haven't seen you in a while, Archmage," without removing his boots from the table. Irritation cracked the impassivity of Declan's expression, and Evangeline wondered dimly if the fae lived for the thrill of recklessness.

Waltzing into a den of lykosa was likely a less dangerous endeavor.

"What brings you here?" Evangeline said, disrupting Declan's glare, but her attempt at nonchalance sounded brittle to her ears.

Before she could protest, he caught her chin with one hand, his grip rougher than usual, and took her mouth in a blatantly proprietary fashion. It wasn't a conciliatory kiss, but a stamp of possession.

Evangeline broke his hold with a jerk of her head. Her traitorous body was molten from the brief contact. He was utterly glacial, and his tone, deceptively soft.

"Do I now need a reason to see you?"

Her glower only incited further impassiveness. A mask he donned whenever he wanted to hide, or when he *hurt*.

"Of course not," she murmured with a sigh.

He blinked, seemingly thrown by the gentleness in her voice. Then he reached for her again, this time caressing her chin with the pad of his thumb. A silent apology in his touch.

She didn't pull away.

"Are you finished with work for the day?" She gave a hesitant smile, placing a palm over his chest. "Mailin said a traveling circus is performing in the capital and . . . " She swallowed when he averted his gaze.

"I'll be leaving for Flen this eve."

Evangeline's lips parted. "Whatever for?"

"The Echelon is gathering for a decision on Zion's coronation."

Her throat tightened. "You're going to this gathering without me?"

"You are not bound to honor the Echelon with your presence."

A familiar tightness coiled in her chest even as she choked out a shaky laugh. "Not even when I've been personally invited by the prince to attend the coronation?"

"A coronation we will *not* be attending." The surety of his statement told her he'd already made up his mind, and the finality in his voice brooked no further discussion.

"But I wanted to"—she hissed in exasperation, trying unsuccessfully to articulate the innate need that had been growing in her—"*see* my sister's Soul Tree."

The possibility that Felicity had been entombed in the Winter Court all this time caused a sickness in her soul.

Declan's jaw tensed. Whatever softness her brief capitulation had conjured in him chilled to form domineering shards.

"Do not be absurd. Visiting a grave won't bring your sister back." Spoken as an archmage who tolerated no disobedience.

Evangeline flinched as though he'd physically struck her.

"You call me elorin de ana, yet you make these decisions without conferring with me," she cried, unable to rein in the outburst. She swallowed and balled her fists, belatedly realizing a bewildered Shyaree and an equally stunned Gabriel were witnessing their exchange.

I am trying to protect you. Quiet words of ice in her mind.

I am not a child, Declan, she replied, struggling for composure. *I am your mate. Start treating me like it.*

Coldness shrouded him like armor, and his retaliation was a crushing silence as he warped, once again, from her sight.

Declan reappeared in the hallway outside the library, nearly frosting the walls. So undone by the exchange that he'd had to remove himself from the situation lest he inadvertently wreak more damage. Declan clenched his fists, furious with himself.

He had intended to make peace with Evangeline before he left for Flen, but the sight of Gabriel in her company had incited another surge of jealousy. His self-control was paper thin.

Footsteps chased him down.

"What devil has you possessed lately?"

"Be *careful*, Gabriel," Declan said, barely grinding out the words. The fae was one step away from having his skin charred.

Gabriel bared his teeth to reveal his fangs in a jeer. "Is that what you want? For people to be so careful around you that no one dares mention the shiv shoved up your ass?"

Declan ground his own teeth till his jaw hurt. He had always found Gabriel's honesty refreshing and his blatant disregard for respect faintly entertaining. None in his court dared address him as though he were not an archmage, but an equal. A *friend*.

Now he just wanted to wring the man's neck.

"Have you any idea how hard Evie's been working lately?" Gabriel asked, undeterred by the warning flare of his symbols.

Declan had discovered the strain ebbing through their bond equated to pain. Evangeline's pain. Ever since, he had counted the length of every session, agonized the extent of each one. So much so it had distracted him from his responsibilities. How could he rule his lands when he couldn't rule his own emotions?

"Do you know she continues to practice long after Shyaree has declared their session done?"

Declan picked up his pace and reminded himself that Gabriel was an irreplaceable asset. He could easily procure another Unseelie spymaster, but none he trusted the way he trusted Gabriel.

"Have you even read her proposal for the slave-trade rescue fund? Do you know how much time she spent in the library learning to write an official proposal?"

Declan halted abruptly. Had *everyone* been privy to her efforts but him? He grabbed Gabriel by his lapels and slammed him against the wall.

"Unless you want to wear your entrails around your neck," Declan growled, "do not presume to lecture me."

Gabriel didn't even flinch. Instead, he snarled, fangs and ears lengthened to antagonistic points. "Do not forget I am a free man who has *chosen* to serve you."

Declan narrowed his eyes. "As long as you serve me, you will not question me. You will not challenge me. You will do exactly as I bid, or I *will* show you your place."

Gabriel stopped struggling, and an expression that looked strangely like disappointment colored his face. "Yes, I serve you," he agreed. "That's why I'm trying to get your damned head out of the ditch!"

The fae kneed Declan in the stomach, knocking the wind out of him.

"You stupid, insolent—"

"If you paid her more attention, you'd realize she likely cried herself to sleep last night, you bastard!"

Startled, Declan loosened his hold on Gabriel's crumpled jacket. Evangeline? Crying? Then something else occurred to him that had him sucking in a breath.

"How the"—Declan slammed Gabriel into the wall again with such ferocity the fae wheezed—"fuck do you know that?"

Had the bloody fae been *in* his chambers last night?

"Anyone who bothers looking can see it in her eyes!" Gabriel curled his lips with distaste as he struggled to remove Declan's unyielding grip. "Where in Ozenn's asshole are you hiding, Archmage?" Another infuriating jeer. "Or have you grown bored of her already?"

"Fuck you, Blacksage!" Declan roared, fire and ice surging simultaneously through his arms in an uncontrollable burst of fury.

Gabriel's curse and the scent of burnt flesh halted him. With another grunt of anger, he released Gabriel abruptly and hurled a punch into the stone wall that would have crushed the man's skull.

A sharp intake of breath had him glancing up to meet the gaze of a woman, her sunset eyes filled with shock and her countenance white as chalk.

Declan staggered back as fury turned to shame.

Unable to meet the condemnation on Evangeline's face, he warped.

EIGHTEEN

Carefree puffs of white skimmed the endless expanse of cerulean blue, completely at odds with Evangeline's dark and broody demeanor. The feathering streaks of orange swirling at the horizon in promise of a warm, sun-drenched day did little to cheer her, and even the birds' gay greeting of dawn sounded shrill to her ears. Annoying.

With a resigned sigh, Evangeline lowered herself to the ground. Shut her eyes. Peace. Drawing in a deep breath, she attempted to calm her mind and open her senses. *All* her senses.

Magic was the essence of nature, and some might say, the lifeblood of Ozenn, the god of chaos, himself. Flowing through every sentient being and found in every element of nature, it was a mystical energy readily accessible to all Ozenn's offspring —the fae.

Now she knew what to look for, Evangeline felt it, saw it, tasted it everywhere. It was an intricate web that linked every creature back to nature, and it tingled against her skin. Threads so fine they glistened like spiderwebs under the sun.

Flavors so subtle they tasted of snowmelt on sun-warmed stone.

Evangeline inhaled another breath and pushed her senses further. Deeper, until she sensed the dormant slivers entrenched in the soil beneath her fingertips. A shiver of anticipation prickled beneath her skin. Magic. She recognized it as easily as she did her own face.

"Grow," she urged. "Grow."

She opened her eyes and sighed. Not even a blade of grass.

A hand on her shoulder.

Her perpetually silent companion frowned at her, worry glinting like copper coins.

"I can't do it." Evangeline hung her head. "I see it. I can feel it. I summon it, but it doesn't answer."

Shyaree made a motion that Evangeline had come to recognize as *Try with me*. With a weary sigh, Evangeline nodded and linked their fingers, bracing herself for the wild stampede that was Shyaree's magic.

While Ozenn gave his children the ability to wield magic, Thurin, the god of might, ensured his creation never lacked strength. Magic suffused every animati, allowing them to shift into creatures more powerful than their human forms.

But Shyaree never shifted. Magic brimmed in her blood, churned in her marrow. Every fiber of her strained such that Evangeline wondered how the woman could stand it.

Magic cascaded from Shyaree's skin. Evangeline jolted, her body still unaccustomed to the sudden influx of mystical energy, but it no longer hurt as badly. She grasped at the roiling waves, desperately trying to wrangle them into some form before lethargy sank in.

A shriek from the skies distracted them both.

Shyaree broke their contact to squint up.

Using a hand to shield her eyes, Evangeline followed the

shaman's line of sight. A hawk of reddish-brown plumage, striated with light and dark markings, winged toward them. As it arrowed down, Evangeline held out an arm in invitation. She had donned her leather gloves in anticipation of Gabriel's return. The hawk circled once before landing precisely on her outstretched forearm, talons curving around her gloved flesh as it cocked its head and peered at her quizzically.

Evangeline smiled. "Gabriel."

Inky tendrils leached from the hawk's nostrils, stretching to form the silhouette of a man before solidifying into the fae's lithe form.

"Good morning, Evie." He noticed her company, and the curve of his lips turned into an aggravating smirk. "Wildcat."

The shaman narrowed her eyes to slits and angled her head away in a silent snub. Evangeline coughed into her fist in an attempt to stifle the half sigh and half laugh climbing up her throat. No matter the days spent together, Gabriel never did redeem himself.

The freed hawk flapped its wings and hopped from Evangeline's forearm to settle on Gabriel's shoulders. He ran an affectionate finger over the bird's mane before it took off in a single swoop, angling up into the skies.

"It took you long enough to show up today," Evangeline commented.

"I had to take care of some guild business." Gabriel surveyed the sparring compound, head swiveling like a weathervane. "Bastard's still away?"

Evangeline gave a stiff nod.

With a derisive snort, Gabriel muttered something that would likely have him thrown into the dungeons if overheard by a guard.

"Have a care with your words," Evangeline chided. "He's still the archmage of Amereen." Though Gabriel's wounds had healed quickly enough, his burns superficial, Evangeline had no wish to witness a repeat of the scene from the hallway where her archmage had been so riled he'd been on the cusp of lethal violence.

Gabriel scoffed, still undaunted. "He'll turn up soon. The man's too obsessed with you to be gone for long."

If only. Declan had been gone for four days. Without a single missive informing her of his delay or when to expect his return. Evangeline pantomimed a smile, attempting to shroud her gloom.

Gabriel cleared his throat. "And how's practice faring? A rising tide?"

"I wish," she muttered with a rueful shake of her head.

Shyaree motioned, and Gabriel chuckled. "The sullen shaman thinks you've been working too hard. You need a break."

"No, I need more practice," Evangeline insisted, removing her gloves.

Gabriel folded his arms. "How about you try mimicking me today?"

"Mimic you?" Evangeline frowned. Dark fae wielded magic in a significantly different manner from Seeliekind.

"We're still two sides of the same coin, aren't we?" Without giving her a chance to respond, Gabriel searched the skies and whistled. A long and impressive treble that was answered by the same hawk. It circled back, a speck growing in the distance.

Gabriel held out his hand, inviting her touch. "Feel it," he said.

With a resigned sigh, she clasped his palm and shut her eyes. Once again, she sucked in a steadying breath, expanding her senses.

Gabriel's control of magic was as natural to him as breathing.

He pulled at the threads of magic flowing through the hawk's mind, calling to the creature. Instead of dominating it, Gabriel *surrendered* to it. He inhaled magic into himself, allowing the mystical energy to dissolve his physical body, rendering him an amorphous state quintessential and exclusive to the Unseelie. When the shadowy mist of Gabriel's form seeped into the hawk, she felt him exhale. A breath that sealed his possession of the creature, keeping it under his thrall.

Evangeline opened her eyes and exhaled with a rush of exhilaration, as though she had just possessed the bird herself. She released a shaky laugh and waved at the circling hawk in the sky. It swooped low with an encouraging screech.

Adrenaline still coursing through her body, Evangeline lowered herself back to the ground. She inhaled as she sought the threads of magic humming in the soil. She reached for them, brushed up against vibrant sparks—of *life*—only to draw back.

She didn't *trust* what she was doing enough to surrender to it the way Gabriel did.

She'd only ever used magic in a state of abject desperation. Somewhere, deep down, fear coiled like chains in her chest. How could she consciously surrender to something she had never truly learned to wield?

The first time she'd cast a portal, it had imploded, and she'd been trapped in the Abyss for four centuries.

She hadn't even been able to grow the right *flowers* to match Mama's roses.

Fear paralyzed her, repelling the magic.

What if magic sent her back into the Abyss?

Another screech from the hawk. Its call took her back to a shadowy forest, where fear nipped at her heels.

"Never use magic in fear, Freya," a woman's voice echoed in her mind. *"Promise me."*

A promise that had inadvertently crippled her.

A tear trickled down her cheek. Mama had never intended for her to be debilitated. Mama had shown her strength. Bravery. Sacrifice.

A sob leaked from Evangeline's throat. She trembled, consciously opening herself to the web of magic rippling against her. When welcomed, magic swarmed, a seemingly live entity pulsing for her touch. She drew threads into herself, allowing it to course through her veins.

"Grow," she whispered.

Mama's humming filled her ears, a haunting echo from a time so long ago, gentle and sweet. *"These reflect who you are, little one, and they are beautiful."*

Tears flowed, a flood of anguish and loss for a mother whose voice she would never again hear, whose touch she would never again feel. Felicity's laughter lit her mind, her sister's spectral features a glimmer she would never again see.

"Don't forget me, Frey. Don't forget who you are."

"Grow!" An anguished sob from her throat.

From above, the hawk released a lilting cry. Fabric rustled, the sound of Shyaree's startled movements. Fragrance permeated the air, saccharine and floral.

Evangeline opened her eyes and sucked in a breath. She staggered to her feet. A shaky laugh escaped her lips.

The sparring compound was no longer covered in trampled soil.

A riotous conflagration of wildflowers carpeted the entire surface. A patchwork of colors—dainty white freesias, blue foxgloves, bright poppies . . .

In the center of it all was a singular rose bush, regal and perfect, crowned by blooms. With trembling fingers, Evangeline reached to caress roses larger than her palm, every lush petal the shade of snow.

Shyaree's mouth was agape and her usually serious expression filled with wonder. The hawk landed a distance away. A shadow seeped from the bird to coalesce into a man whose triumphant laughter filled the compound.

Magic continued to surge from the ground, evanescent threads dancing around Evangeline as though in celebration. Tears continued to flow from her eyes, a deluge from a past she couldn't change but had finally reclaimed. She didn't try to fight either. With every thread of magic glancing off her skin and tear tracking her cheeks, she grew stronger.

NINETEEN

Declan warped into the colonnaded courtyard without warning and stormed past familiar hooded guards without slowing his stride. Two guardians hurried from the main alcove to intercept him. On realizing who he was, they bowed low.

"Lord Archmage, you honor us with your presence," said a thin and papery voice from beneath a hood. "What can we do to serve you?"

Declan detested those hoods.

They concealed the monsters wearing the skin of ancient men.

"Let me be," he said, and the guardians dispersed, leaving him alone to peruse the monumental foyer of stone and pillars. The last time he'd been here, he had just ascended. He'd made sure then that no guardian ever forgot who they'd raised, or what they'd raised him to become.

Declan strode past sparsely decorated halls, his footsteps echoing off the walls. So empty, the enclave appeared abandoned. Yet every surface was perfectly polished. Bricks gleamed like marble; grout lines shone clean, not a single speck of dust to be seen. The Thorne Enclave was secluded, hidden away in the highlands where magekind's most irrepressible were sent, and its guardians valued cleanliness above all else.

"Cleanliness is a chastity of the mind, the emblem of control," his guardian used to say. And control had been the mantra pounded into him and every resident of the enclave—be it by painstaking routine or an actual fist.

But now, Declan had never felt further removed from the word.

He was fighting a losing battle, and control slipped through his fingers like grains of sand.

He climbed a flight of stairs, turned left, ducked below a beam he'd long ago grown too tall for, and ascended another series of winding steps. Another left, and he was there. A section of the enclave that was well and truly abandoned.

Here, somber air filled with swirling dust motes greeted him. Cobwebs had begun to gather in corners, spiders the only tenants making merry. He strode past a corridor of plain and serviceable metal-hinged doors and halted by the seventh.

The door swung open with a creak on hinges unoiled for centuries.

Stepping within the four walls, he found the room exactly the way he remembered, yet subtly different. Smaller. As though time had magnified the space in his memories.

As a child, he had been made to scrub every surface, polish every mantle. Now the narrow cot at the farthest corner was bedded with dust and bookended by wooden chests. A rusty sink stood beside barren shelves, and tacks lined walls that had once displayed polished swords, finely tuned bows, and arrows.

The guardians had kept their word and shut this section of the tower since Declan's last visit. Good. In his current mood, he would have no qualms decimating the entire enclave should he find another child in residence.

He circled the room, absently running a finger over the dust-coated walls, and found himself inadvertently back at his favorite spot in the room: the window. Moonlight spilled through concave panes, showing off a remarkable view of the Lindenbough Forest. He'd spent most of his time huddled here, especially at dawn, when he could marvel at the sunrise. As a child, he'd fantasized often of levitating into the skies. Escaping the enclave, free of his mother. Flying into the sun where he would meet a fiery embrace that would purge the cold from his bones.

Completely illogical, of course.

No mage—not even an archmage—could levitate themselves long enough to take flight. But his fantasies hadn't changed much over the years.

Once, Declan went months without seeing sunrises, blind from a brutal beating. Yet he'd been content. Because that was when he'd met *her*. Freya, who'd made him feel all warm inside. A girl who had been his sun.

A harsh, humorless laugh escaped his throat.

Now she was finally back in his life, he'd unwittingly returned to this hellhole.

The irony of it.

"My son," Nathaniel had called to him at the conclusion of the Echelon's gathering. *"You'll bring that slip of a girl you call elorin to Zion's coronation?"* he had asked, as though Zion's crowning were a given and Evangeline's presence nothing more than icing on a cake.

Declan had kept his expression stony even though he wanted to hurl firebolts into Nathaniel's smirking face.

The three-day affair had resulted in a consensus that the Echelon would attend the Winter Court coronation—a result of much instigation by Nathaniel. The whole affair soured Declan's gut. He could not fathom the underlying reasons for Nathaniel's sudden interest in fae statecraft, but alas, his personal decision had been swayed by the image of Evangeline's furious gaze and her blatant need to see her sister's Soul Tree.

The mere thought of Evangeline in enemy territory made him want to draw bloody furrows into his skin.

Declan punched the stone wall, unsettling dust in a spray.

He'd been so disarrayed that he hadn't been able to bring himself to warp back to Evangeline, his sun. Instead, he'd come here. A place he'd tried to forget but could never seem to escape.

A woman's husky laugh echoed in the recesses of his mind, the ghost of her touch so smooth it was the glide of a serpent's scales. *"Ah, my little dragon, but this is where you belong,"* Corvina had said in the rare times she'd been gentle with him.

Another punch, dislodging more dust and debris.

Where he *belonged*. A small, dank prison cell with a window to ensure he'd always glimpse his greatest desire, but never be free to reach it.

His mother's mocking visage faded, replaced by the indignant expression of a bearded councilor with haughty eyes.

"A sham! She is manipulating you, sire! I have seen her perfidiousness in your absence. I have witnessed her discussing vulgarities with the Unseelie male you have so wrongly placed your trust—"

Another punch.

Gabriel's lips curled as his violet eyes narrowed with derision.

"If you paid her more attention, you'd realize she likely cried herself to sleep last night, you bastard!"

Something crunched, yet he continued to rail against the

wall, every crack of his knuckles a satisfying release of his pent-up control.

Control. He couldn't lose control.

Acerbic laughter bounced off the walls in concert to cracks.

He couldn't even make love to his own woman in his own bedchamber without risking annihilating the room! Evangeline didn't seem to understand that even without her fainting spells to deter him, Declan could *never* fully lose control. Not with her. Not with anything. He had never been an ordinary mage to begin with.

His ascension was as much his freedom as it was a curse.

"You're the devil's child, my son," Corvina had once said with a sneer after she'd taught him the most effective way to use a corded whip. A lesson practiced on him. *"Your body is a vessel for power you have done nothing to earn. Nothing but being the spawn of two archmages with powers that were never meant to co-exist."*

Fire and ice were never meant to live harmoniously. Yet they both existed within him—raging elements warring for dominance in his every fiber. Without strict control, they would destroy him and everything around him.

How he had despised Nathaniel for giving him life. For Corvina's *rape*.

He had grown so comfortable blaming Nathaniel for every taunt that had chipped away at his soul, blaming Nathaniel for every brutal lashing that had broken his skin and bones. But now . . .

"I once loved your mother. Did you know that?"

Declan drew in another shuddering breath. Could it be true? Could Nathaniel and Corvina really have been lovers to begin with? Nathaniel was an adept liar, yet the man's words unearthed a long-buried memory.

When Corvina had learned of Declan's ability to wield ice, she had demanded he show her the extent of his abilities.

Every so often, she would insist he fashion *ice spheres*. Of course, Declan had been punished every time for *"Not doing it right."*

He had never thought much of it.

Nothing he'd done was ever good enough for his mother, but now . . .

Had Corvina been hoping for Declan to fashion the same ice gems as his father? Could Nathaniel be telling the truth? Could Declan be the result of a torrid love affair?

It would mean every abuse Corvina had meted out hadn't been a result of a woman wronged, but of a woman spurned. And somehow, that made it all worse.

His existence, a cosmic joke.

He was as malformed as Byrne, only his deformity was on the inside. He was an abomination: conceived from depravity, birthed in hate, and bred in deceit.

How could he expect anyone, most of all a sweet, gentle soul like Evangeline, to love someone like him?

Another memory flashed.

"You've all but ripped her from her home. She must be terrified."

Worse, Evangeline's sunset eyes had filled with such *disappointment* when he'd admitted he would have taken the shaman one way or the other.

And how furious she had been with his decision on the Unseelie coronation.

Declan sucked in air as he slumped to the ground, weary to the bone. Dust swirled around him amid the scent of iron.

He'd made decisions on her behalf because that was what he knew how to do. His people, his council, the kingdom of Amereen trusted him to make decisions for their welfare and safety. He'd done it believing he was taking care of her. It had been his way of showing love.

But judging from her reaction, he'd grossly miscalculated.

Unilateral decisions were clearly frowned upon in intimate relationships. She'd only been his for less than one summer, and he had disappointed her again and again.

His gut twisted.

Evangeline had gazed up at *Gabriel* with such open trust and affection.

Declan shoved the memory violently from his mind. No, Evangeline *loved* him. She'd shared every part of herself with him. She was his.

A bark of laughter made its way from his throat. He'd made sure of that, hadn't he? He'd devised the employment contract, courted her, and would have killed any man who'd dared touch her. He'd left her with no other choices.

But now Freya was reawakening. She'd never had a chance to mature, had never been given a chance to meet other men. Men of her own kind.

A sly, sinuous voice whispered in the back of his head, vile and taunting. *Perhaps that's why you were not able to complete the bond. Evangeline might not know it yet, but Freya doesn't really want you.*

Declan slammed a fist to stone again. Windowpanes rattled, and the railing wheezed.

If fate hadn't brought them together during the Unseelie attack in Arns, Evangeline might never have come to remember her past. Freya would remain lost, and Evangeline would have remained mortal. But she would have led a safer life.

A happier life . . . without him.

Declan swallowed the grit scoring his throat.

She might have met a good man. A *better* man. Someone who could love and cherish her the way she deserved. Someone who could love her without the need to hide the darkest part of himself.

Declan shifted so he sat in the pool of moonlight, needing to escape the suffocating shadows. A butterfly fluttered from some dust-bitten crevice, settling its wings at the edge of the windowsill as though to bathe in the moonlight. In the pale glow, Declan realized it was a moth, its wings dull and gray.

All creatures of darkness craved the light. Especially, he mused, the ones best kept hidden in shadows, where moths could pretend to be butterflies and abominations like him could pretend to be knights in shining armor.

He glanced down at the pulpy mess of his knuckles. Bloodied flesh, cracked bones, yet it hurt less than the pounding in his head.

Hurt less than the fear corroding his chest.

Freya. Evangeline. His little fire. He loved her more than his own life, needed her more than his next breath. But did he deserve her? He, a man unloved by even his own mother.

TWENTY

I f there was one thing Evangeline detested about living in Castle Amereen, it was that she was unable to leave the premises on her own. Wedged between Torgerson Range and the Jachuanuan Seas, the castle was a fortress not easily accessible by physical roads. Without Declan or a battlemage to teleport her, she was literally confined within the castle's walls.

She could ride, of course, but she was no seasoned rider. No stablemaster would allow her on anything but the gentlest mares, which were only good for cantering on even ground. Even if she managed to procure a gelding trained to navigate the steep slopes to the nearest settlement, no soldier would allow her past the drawbridge without her guard. And even then, there was no way she could pass the wards without her archmage sensing her departure.

No way, unless she exited via the portal of an Unseelie who had free access to the castle grounds.

Walking through the swirling shadows of Gabriel's portal, Evangeline stepped into an alleyway compacted between grime-worn walls capped by lichen-kissed gables. The faint but pervasive scent of decaying food and rancid oil suggested they were in the rear of taverns and dining houses. Shyaree gave a silent gag and pinched her nose, yet she regarded everything from the emptied ale barrels and overflowing trash buckets to the grease-stained gutters with wide eyes.

"Could you not have opened your portal somewhere more palatable, Blacksage?" Alexander muttered. "I believe the Quarter is still two streets away."

Gabriel rolled his eyes, which were currently the shade of the ocean. At Evangeline's insistence, he'd humanized his appearance. "With the autumn bazaar in session, the Quarter is more crowded than a jail cell after a marshal raid. Every merchant willing to travel the distance will already be here, vying to make a last rush of coin before the winter drought."

Alexander laughed. "Your portal would cause the crowds no major alarm. One look at that ugly, bloodthirsty countenance of yours would cause people to run screaming."

Not the least offended, Gabriel shot the councilor a grin that would have flashed fangs had he not veiled them, too. "I wasn't worried about causing unnecessary alarm. I was more worried for the women you'll leave swooning with that pretty face of yours, golden boy."

Alexander aimed a rude gesture at the fae. "I'll take swooning women over screaming ones any day."

Gabriel chuckled. "Oh, but I do enjoy screamers. Especially when they're beneath me."

"Well, no sane woman is coming close to *either* of you if you don't watch where you're headed," Evangeline quipped. Amid their good-natured bicker, both men had attempted elbowing past the other, trampling into indeterminate foul-smelling puddles in the process.

Evangeline exchanged a smirk with Shyaree. Once, neither

of these men would have exchanged such bawdy banter in her presence. The fact that they did now without fear of offending her sensibilities pleased her immensely.

The end of the alleyway revealed a busy street with shopfronts of brightly painted signs and polished glass windows. A harried mother sprinted after two towheaded children, who giggled and darted toward a street performer juggling small curios.

Evangeline flipped up the hood of her furred cloak. Not only did it keep her warm, but it hung large and low enough to shroud her eyes. She'd also taken care to clasp the cloak high over her neck, thoroughly obscuring Declan's mark upon her skin.

Unlike Gabriel, she was still unable to veil her appearance, and she had no wish for anyone to realize the elorin of Amereen was meandering through the capital, exploring the papermakers.

A young man ambling by—likely a scholar judging from the scrolls tucked beneath his arms and his blue robes—shot a rather licentious gaze at an oblivious Shyaree. The shaman had ambled onto the street, drawn by the fanfare of the street juggler, seemingly as awed as the children. Then the scholar caught sight of Gabriel's glower and immediately crossed the street. The young man dropped a couple of scrolls and hastily picked them up before moving to the far side of the footpath.

"What did I tell you?" Alexander sniggered as he nudged Evangeline with his elbow.

Evangeline couldn't help the chuckle escaping her lips. She had never found Gabriel intimidating. But then again, Declan had likely desensitized her to the subtle danger certain men exuded. Whatever menace Gabriel inspired, the double blades he wore strapped to his back undoubtedly enhanced it.

Gabriel folded his arms, sneering at wary passersby. "Will you tell me now the reason for this little excursion?"

"Nothing to worry yourself with, Blacksage," Alexander responded smoothly. "Relax. Go find something to amuse yourselves for a few hours. Evie and I will meet you back here before dusk falls," he added with a dismissive wave.

Gabriel's gaze bored a hole into her temple.

Evangeline shot him an apologetic smile. "Would it truly be such hardship to while a few hours away in the capital?"

She would have preferred the privacy of Alexander's company—he remained the only person privy to the threats—as she investigated the papermakers. But Shyaree had grown so attuned to her daily routine that it had been impossible for Evangeline to leave without explaining her absence to the shaman, and by default, Gabriel.

The Unseelie had, in turn, insisted on accompanying her. Though Evangeline hadn't tried hard to discourage him. Gabriel's portal did allow her to slip out of the castle without an entourage of guards. While Alexander could teleport her out, he couldn't do so without alerting Declan to their departure.

"What are you two up to?" Gabriel asked with a suspicious scowl.

When it became clear he wasn't getting any answers, he jerked his thumb at the wide-eyed shaman, who remained awestruck by the vibrance of the busy street. "Fine. Keep your secrets. But what am I supposed to do with the churlish cat?"

Shyaree appeared anything but churlish. She had ambled over to the nearest shopfront, her nose almost pressing against the glass as she gawped at the display of intricate clocks.

Alexander's gaze roamed down the shaman's form, and his lips curved. "Oh, I can think of quite a number of things if you need some ideas, Blacksage."

Evangeline narrowed her eyes, no longer too innocent to notice Alexander's appreciative gaze. "Railea's sake, Lex!" She shook her head even as Gabriel sneered and said, "Not even if I were blind."

Alexander shrugged. "You may as well be."

They parted ways in pairs, with Gabriel markedly reluctant and the shaman too fascinated by her surroundings to express much complaint. Alexander led Evangeline down the other side of the street, leaving the assassin and the shaman to meander through the crowds.

The last time Evangeline had walked these streets, Declan had been by her side. People had watched from a polite distance, wearing curious but wary smiles. No one had dared venture too close, and all had been quick to genuflect. Her archmage was a man feared as much as he was revered.

Walking through the street with Alexander was a markedly different experience. True to Gabriel's earlier remark, maidens blushed and whispered as he passed. People called out at the sight of him, waving to catch his eye. Children skipped close, and merchants offered free wares. He was the golden prince of Amereen, born with enough charm to blight the stars and clearly adored by his people.

"Why did I even bother with a hood?" Evangeline asked wryly as Alexander shot another one of his devil-may-care smiles at a passing girl and her mother. Both giggled like schoolgirls. "No one will likely notice me with you here."

"Ah, jealous, are we?" Alexander waggled his brows.

Evangeline attempted a scowl of mock offense but ended up grinning instead. She was more than delighted to walk through the capital where no one batted an eyelash at her. For once, the weight of her new title seemed to disappear.

Their first stop was a spiffy-looking shop sporting the sign of a scroll and quill painted beside the words *Toru Brothers*

Papers. They were quick to discount the cordial brothers who manufactured parchment using hemlock pulp, which yielded distinctly textured papers. Nothing like the ones she'd received. They were about to turn down the street leading to another papermaker when a distraught voice reached their ears. "Lord Councilor Alvah! Lord Councilor, a moment of your time, please!"

A woman shoved through the milling crowd, waving her arms desperately. Wearing a stained apron over a tattered dress that had clearly seen better days, the woman caught up to them with a rattling gasp. "Lord Councilor, you must help me."

"Calm down, woman," Alexander ordered, but not unkindly. "Where's the fire?"

"My husband has fled." She wheezed a little whimpering sob. "But his debtors care only for what they are owed. They have taken my daughter to the pleasure district, to be auctioned to the highest bidder!"

Evangeline's eyes widened as Alexander's hardened.

"Have you approached the Circle?" he asked.

The woman fidgeted but refused to falter. "I understand this isn't a matter in your purview, Lord Councilor, but . . . " She choked. "By the time I got an audience with the Circle, even a high mage couldn't return my daughter's innocence. Please, there is *no* time. Andreda is barely a hundred summers!"

Evangeline blanched. A hundred. The mage child would be no older than a human girl of thirteen years. The woman's story was unfortunately not unique, but it was tragic all the same.

"Lex, we must help her."

Alexander's gaze darted between Evangeline and the sobbing woman, conflict clear in his eyes. "I can't warp three of us. And I can't leave you unattended."

Evangeline narrowed her eyes at him even though he couldn't see them from beneath her hood. "Nonsense! I'll be fine on my own." She reached out to give him a gentle nudge, knowing he needed little to sway his decision. "The girl is just a child. You *must* go."

Just as she expected, Alexander gave a decided nod, not at all reluctant. "Return to the bazaar," he said, gesturing back up to the crowded street. "I will look for you there."

Evangeline didn't argue.

The woman was still murmuring her gratitude when Alexander teleported with her. Evangeline heaved a breath, praying hard to Railea that Alexander would arrive in time to stop whatever horror the girl might face. What would Andreda's fate be if Alexander could not intervene?

A breeze waffled by, and Evangeline's thoughts inadvertently wandered to her archmage. A pang struck her chest, but she shoved it aside with steely resolve. Even now, she could sense the threads of magic dancing in the air, trundling in the ground beneath her feet. Surely, Declan would have less of a need to treat her like a fragile bloom once he noticed her returning abilities.

Their senseless estrangement, petty disagreements, his growing distance—she would find a way to address them all when he returned.

One way or another, she would make things *right* between them.

"Please, come home soon, Archmage," she said with a sigh into the breeze.

Fresh determination lifting her chin, Evangeline glanced toward the busy bazaar, then turned back to face the quiet lane down to *Quills and Wills, Paper and Parchment*. Long branches of the willow trees lining the street swayed, seeming to beckon her.

Perhaps she *should* save time, venture in on her own.

Evangeline was only halfway down the lane when a blush of darkness kissed the air. A portal. She sighed but was not the least surprised. She should have known Gabriel and Shyaree couldn't stand each other's company enough to last the afternoon.

"Can't the two of you at least try getting along for just one day?" she asked.

The exasperated smile slipped from her face when a horse bolted through the growing shadows. Its rider, shrouded from head to toe in hostile black, was most definitely *not* Gabriel.

TWENTY-ONE

A startled cry leaked from Evangeline's throat.

Horseback riders emerged, clad in uniform black leather, with swords strapped to their backs and faces completely obscured by leather masks. They whooped as their mounts sailed from the portal. The fifth rider, distinctly smaller than the rest, cantered almost leisurely through it before the chasm ebbed and closed.

A quick glance around told Evangeline the street remained deserted. No movement from behind shop windows. No one had witnessed the abrupt invasion of the fae brigade.

"Ozenn smiles upon us," the first rider said, with the unmistakable musical lilt of the fae. "Didn't think it would be this easy, but here she is! The archmage's whore, all alone and ripe for picking."

Lewd laughter erupted. Clearly, they had no doubt of her identity despite the hood shrouding half her face.

"Forgot your guard dogs, milady?" quipped his comrade.

"Was looking forward to bloodin' my blades, but guess we're just playing pick up today," another said with a chuckle.

Evangeline glared up at them, more outraged than afraid. Until she noticed the tattoo inked at one rider's throat. A howling wolf. A symbol linked to the slave-trade cartel, and by default, the mad king who had sanctioned it.

Her pulse ratcheted.

Again and again, history repeated itself.

Evangeline scrambled backward until her feet hit the sidewalk. They laughed and urged their mounts forward, maintaining a taunting distance. Evangeline had the distinct impression they would only enjoy it all the more if she attempted to flee. A clowder of cats eager for a game of chase the mouse.

"Who sent you?" Evangeline demanded. "Is Zephyr still alive?"

More guffaws.

The smallest of the five spurred his mount forward and held out a gloved hand as though in gallant invitation. Cold blue eyes bored into Evangeline's through the narrow slit in his mask.

"There now, little lady," called his companion with the tattoo, words laced with an evident sneer. "There's no need for airs. Come quietly, and we'll make it painless."

Evangeline let out an incredulous laugh. There must have been something in her gaze that surprised the rider into withdrawing his proffered hand. History might repeat itself, but she was no longer a scared child. Nor was she utterly defenseless.

"Grow," she whispered.

Magic stirred the air. The horses whinnied, and their hooves clopped nervously over *cobblestone*. The tattooed rider smirked. "Pathetic! No wonder your kind has gone extinct. You're helpless the moment you run out of dirt!"

He snickered, accompanied by the heckling laughter of his comrades.

A weeping branch slashed into his face without warning.

"I wouldn't exactly say helpless," Evangeline said with a smirk of her own. Not when the sidewalk was lined with weeping willows.

More branches lashed out like leafy whips, startling the rider's horse into bucking, and he went sailing from his saddle. Evangeline didn't linger to enjoy the show. She sprinted up the sidewalk, dashing for the crowded street.

Shouts and curses filled the air. Thundering hoofbeats alerted her to their pursuit. She risked a look over her shoulder and stumbled as her feet caught on uneven pavement. The riders had unsheathed their swords, and whipping branches didn't hold against slashing steel.

She pushed off her knees and lurched into the busy street. A sea of faces blurred as she shouted for help. Then she remembered that the Amereen militia conducted regular patrols in the capital.

"Guards!" she cried without slowing. "Where are the guards?"

All she attracted were curious murmurs and startled glances as she careened down the street. She must have appeared a madwoman.

She flung off the hood of her cloak that was still obscuring her face and nearly collided with a cartful of cabbages.

A potbellied merchant, too infirm to be a mage, glared. "Railea's skies, where do ye think yer . . . " His eyes widened as recognition lit his expression. "Lady Barre!"

"Help me!" she cried. "I need—"

Pounding hooves. A chorus of startled shouts. The masked riders were plowing down the street without a care for casualties.

The old man shoved her forward. "Go, my lady! Run! Run!"

Evangeline didn't hesitate. She sprinted until alarmed cries turned to screams.

She turned back in time to see an arc of crimson spraying across the street. A rider had slashed the back of a woman too slow to move.

The merchant shoved his cart outward to obstruct the horses. Cabbages tumbled out to scatter over the street.

The blue-eyed rider, discernible by his smaller size, leaned from his saddle to seize the defiant merchant by his shirtfront. A near-impossible maneuver given the old man's considerable girth and the rider's galloping mount. Yet the rider hefted the man off the sidewalk with one arm in a show of brute strength.

Piercing blue eyes lifted and met Evangeline's for one terrifying moment. Enjoying her helplessness.

Then the rider thrust his blade into writhing flesh.

Evangeline screamed till her vision blurred.

She had led death and destruction directly into the path of innocents.

"*Mordida sipa!*" she screamed, a curse from a tongue she hadn't spoken in centuries. "If you want me, then come get me!"

She turned and darted left into one of the many alleys leading from the main street. Away from the crowd. Her pulse soared, and her breaths grew short. But the beating hooves grew louder with her every breath. *Run, run, run!*

She dislodged boxes of litter, empty barrels, and anything her hands could reach as she sprinted past. Horses whinnied, stymied by the barrels trundling down their path.

"*Rutta!*" yelled one of her pursuers. The proximity of his voice made her heart rabbit and her legs pump faster.

Her feet splashed into a grimy puddle, and she nearly skidded off balance. *Don't stop! Don't stop!* Her lungs threatened to explode. Stacks of water-stained crates lay ahead, but she spied a narrow opening, large enough for her to slip through.

Hope flared in her chest.

Just a pace away, the crates toppled as though shoved by an unseen hand to obscure her path.

"No!" She came to an abrupt halt, and her breath hitched.

Heckling shouts and encroaching footfalls. She glanced up in sheer desperation to see sagging gables and tired railings that were too far to climb.

Then she sensed it. A constellation of magic writhing just within her reach—a cluster of potted plants on a worn-out balcony just overhead.

Dehydrated tomato plants that cried for water.

The vines reached out for her just as the riders neared. Her barrels had caused them to dismount.

"What do you think you're doing?" The rider brandished a blood-soaked blade with a sneer at the vines creeping in Evangeline's direction. "They're nothing but weeds!"

Vines thickened into branches, tightening over her forearms like bracers. Tendrils coiled circles around her midsection. Lethargy spread in her muscles as she compacted years of growth into mere seconds. There was only so much life she could summon in so little time, and she prayed to Railea it would be enough.

"Rise," she commanded.

The vines stiffened and gave a rustling groan, lifting her from the ground.

Her would-be captors cursed their shock, but Evangeline was already clambering halfway up the crates. The branches acted as her anchor as she scaled the stack, relinquishing their hold the moment she was up. The crates shuddered.

Her pursuers were attempting to topple them from the bottom.

She jumped.

Her vines were too far stretched to lower her to the ground, but they served to slow her fall. Still, she landed with a painful thud, the wind knocked from her lungs, and a jarring impact to her knees.

She clambered to get up, her fingers clawing into dirt. Loose soil.

Magic for the reaping.

Evangeline forced herself to her feet. She didn't turn back, fleeing even as she commanded life.

Thorny vines speared from the ground, brambles sprouting from her every step, weaving obstruction in her wake.

From behind her came a groaning creak and a shuddering crash! Her pursuers cussed.

Evangeline didn't slow to see.

She ran until brine-laced winds whipped at her face. The pier was just up ahead and the shore just beyond. Her feet sank into sun-warmed sand, and she realized her folly.

She had run into open ground. Nowhere to hide. The sand impeded her pace while fatigue slowed her muscles. She risked a glance to see the alleyway yawning wide, the crates scattered as though dislodged by a huge force. Her pursuers hurtled at her, blurs of black with their blades glinting sunlight.

Her heart ratcheted. Fear spurred her legs.

Evangeline sprinted over the dunes patched with scraggly grass, taking care to avoid the smooth sand that would inevitably slow her further. Crashing tides came into view, an endless stretch of golden sand against glimmering blue. A couple loitered in the distance.

A tall man with ash-white hair and a willowy woman whose hair gleamed copper under the sun. The *sea*.

Gabriel had taken Shyaree to view the sea.

Evangeline waved her arms wildly over her head without slowing her stride.

"Gabriel!" The wind swallowed her scream.

"Gabriel!"

Something snagged at her foot. Evangeline hurtled face-first into the ground. A sharp pain screamed up her ankle. She rolled to her knees, trying to scrub the sand from her eyes.

Agony jolted up her leg, sending her back to the ground.

Pounding footsteps were near soundless in the sand.

A large hand clamped over her forearm and dragged her up.

"Got her!" shouted one of her pursuers. A jeering laugh. "Aw, did the little mouse break her ankle?"

His comrades crowded them, laughing like baying hounds.

"What a great hunt!" crowed another, utter exhilaration in his voice. "We shouldn't be late. He'll be expecting you."

Shadows split the air before Evangeline's eyes, a dark chasm widening into a doorway that could only lead to hell.

Her canines sharpened. "Railea take you!"

She raised her arm, fingers clawed as she aimed for his eyes exposed by the slits in his mask, but he shifted too quickly. Her nails scraped against leather, inciting another wave of delirious laughter.

The flash of a blade was the only thing she saw before a spray of scarlet stained the air. Laughter ceased. Her captor's head tilted at a grotesque tangent before tumbling off his shoulders to the sand.

Relief had her sinking to the ground in time with the headless corpse. Evangeline had witnessed Gabriel in combat before—he wasn't someone one wanted to face in battle. Even though they were outnumbered now, the oppressive fear in her chest ebbed. Gabriel moved faster than the eye could follow.

A barest whisper of a blade and another one of the masked men sank to his knees, his hands clamped over his abdomen as though trying to hold in the pulpy mass spewing from his belly.

The rest of her pursuers recovered from their shock, and the third managed to parry Gabriel's slashing onslaught, while the fourth delivered a blow that sent Gabriel rolling back into a defensive crouch.

"Who the fuck are you?" Gabriel snarled. "How dare you hunt a princess of the Summer Court!"

"Traitor!" The tattooed rider circled them. "It's Seelie sympathizers like you who've ruined our nation!"

"You're more stupid than you look if you think the Guild has anything to do with the sorry state of the fae realm," Gabriel said before he lunged forward, twin blades flashing.

Gabriel went hurtling back as though punched by a phantom fist. Evangeline had suspected a mage with telekinetic ability had been among her pursuers, but now she knew it.

An invisible force pinned Gabriel to the ground as he strained and spat imprecations.

The smallest of the five stepped up to grab Evangeline.

"Unhand me, you snake-swiving scum!" Roots speared from the sand and wrapped gnarled fingers around her legs to keep her grounded. She was *not* about to be abducted. Not again. *Never* again. With her free hand, Evangeline ripped at the mask shrouding the man's face. He slammed his fist into her jaw just as she tore the edge of the leather mask.

Blond ends curled at his nape. Blue eyes narrowed.

A bird shrieked.

Her blond attacker glanced up at the same time Gabriel's body turned amorphous, breaking from the telepathic chains. Shadows slithered into the sky—Gabriel reaching for the spiraling hawk.

Evangeline slammed her own fist into her distracted

captor's throat. He staggered back only to draw a deadly-looking shiv from his belt. The roots receded from Evangeline's silent command and she rolled, narrowly avoiding what would have been an incapacitating stab when a flash of copper pounced onto her attacker.

Shyaree tackled the man to the ground.

He swiveled, swift as a snake, to thrust the shiv into the shaman's gut. Shyaree's scream was soundless.

"Shya!" Evangeline lurched forward despite her throbbing ankle.

"Cease and desist!" came a furious roar. A flare of flames burst at the periphery of her vision, and a masked assailant shrieked.

Alexander had found them.

Unlike his brother who mastered fire the way he did a blade, Alexander wielded fire like a corded whip. It lashed from his hand again, and the man screamed in a fiery death.

The hawk landed. Shadows coalesced into a man.

Outnumbered, her blond captor *twisted* his shiv before tearing it from Shyaree's shuddering body. He retreated into the swirling chasm, with his last standing comrade fleeing after him.

Evangeline crawled to the shaman's side.

"No, no, no . . . " Blood seeped from the wound. Evangeline glanced up at Alexander, whose eyes were wide and face was pale.

"Get Mailin," Evangeline cried. "Now!"

Alexander blinked once then warped from sight.

Gabriel's breathing was ragged when he crouched beside them and pressed his palm over the shaman's wound. "Hang in there, now, wildcat. You'll be all right."

Crimson continued to seep through his fingers as Shyaree gasped for breath. Inky blood trickled from her nostrils and leaked from her lips. Gabriel murmured a string of reassurances, his voice a strangled babble.

Evangeline choked out a sob. This was all her fault. Even Mailin couldn't heal fatal wounds. No one could. Unless . . .

Evangeline blinked back her tears. *She* was Seelie. Her kind were the forefathers of supernatural healers. She pushed Gabriel's hand away, covering the shaman's gaping wound with her own. Shut her eyes.

"Mend," she whispered, willing broken flesh to knit.

Magic was everywhere. In the sand, the salt-laced air, and the crashing waves. It answered, the threads seeping into her skin, coiling beneath her palms.

Blood continued to weep.

With a shuddering exhale, she commanded, "*Heal!*"

Light coalesced beneath her palms, a bright spark. Luminescence seeped into Shyaree's wound. The shaman's shuddering body was the last thing Evangeline felt before her vision dimmed and darkened.

TWENTY-TWO

Something was amiss.

Strain prickled through his half bond, the subtle tension rousing Declan from the last vestiges of slumber. He rolled his shoulders, trying to work out the knot in his muscles. He'd fallen asleep by the window, finally lulled by the streaks of gold painting the skies and soothed by the warmth of the rising sun.

The strain was faint, like a gentle ripple on still water, but it must have been caused by a great impact, for he felt it despite the enormous distance separating the Thorne Enclave and Amereen Castle.

Evangeline. Was she in pain?

The notion woke him fully.

Declan returned to his castle, materializing in the Great Hall. The startled and fearful glances from the servants were to be expected. He was slicked in grime and smeared in his own blood, his fists a battered mangle. But the fabricated smile on his steward's face and the milling ministers' constipated expressions confirmed that something was *terribly* amiss.

Without a word to his blathering steward, Declan located Evangeline's mind and found himself in one of the wards of the infirmary.

Blood drained from his face.

Instead of caring for the convalescent, Evangeline was tucked up in one of those beds, her body curled against Shyaree. Surrounded by bloodied sheets.

A chorus of *Sire's* resounded, but he couldn't look at anything else. If not for her bluish pallor or the scarlet-stained bedding, Evangeline would appear to be taking a nap. As did the shaman beside her.

He crouched by the bedside to brush a trembling finger over Evangeline's cheek. He could see no major wounds on her. Nor on Shyaree. But Evangeline's jawbone held a purple tinge that spoke of a blooming bruise.

Declan brushed against her mind and found her psyche stable but dormant. *Again.*

He lifted his gaze to meet that of his lead healer. "What happened?"

Mailin blinked and swallowed, as though she'd misplaced her tongue. "They were attacked, sire," she managed. Her hands wrapped around her rounded belly. "Shyaree was injured, and Evie . . . healed her."

"Attacked?" Declan rose from the side of the bed, and Mailin, a woman who had a tongue sharper than a rapier and a sword's worth of steel in her spine, shrank from him.

Killian sidled up to place a protective arm over her shoulder, clearly reading the fractures in Declan's self-control.

"Horseback riders pursued Lady Evangeline through the capital streets," the commander recounted without preamble. Killian relayed the reports he'd received from civilian witnesses with the stolidity of a soldier.

"None of it would have happened if I had kept closer

watch on Shyaree and Lady Evangeline," Killian added once he concluded. "I take full responsibility for the incident."

Declan stared at his commander, not trusting himself to speak before he tried to make sense of the information. Incredulity howled in his mind like a savage beast.

What had Evangeline been *doing* in the capital, unprotected, in the first place? He had an entire contingent of soldiers, had established an elite guard, just for her protection. How could this have happened?

His fists clenched. Something dark slithered in his blood, restoking the pent-up emotions he'd barely banked from the previous night.

"Brother," Alexander muttered, his tone suspiciously meek and stance unusually discomposed. "There's something else you need to know."

Alexander had entered the ward in the middle of Killian's account, and Gabriel lurked by the doorjamb. The Unseelie had clearly been involved in the tussle—smatterings of dried blood still covered his face and clothes. Alexander, however, was implicated by his expression. Self-recrimination slouched his shoulders and dipped his chin, reminiscent of the time Declan had caught him as a child riding the geldings without a saddle.

By the time Alexander completed his account, a glacial rage solidified Declan's face. But in his chest flowed sheer molten fury.

"All this time, you *knew* someone had been threatening Evangeline," Declan repeated slowly. "Yet you kept it from me?"

Alexander's throat bobbed, but he nodded.

Declan advanced so he stood toe to toe with the man he'd regarded as his only kin. "Not only have you encouraged her foolhardy plans, but you've knowingly disobeyed my decree and allowed her out of the castle without her guard."

Alexander's gaze fell to the ground in silent affirmation.

"Why?" Declan whispered.

He'd forgiven Alexander for every egregious blunder and every fatuous mistake. Forgiven even all the attempts made on his life when he'd first assumed control of Amereen. Never would he begrudge a boy who sought vengeance for his mother, but Declan did not so easily find forgiveness for a man who would openly endanger his heart.

Tawny eyes met his, filled with shame. "I thought I could protect her," Alexander responded, his voice a rough whisper. "I thought . . . I'm sorry, brother."

Declan's fist connected with Alexander's jaw before he could stop himself. "You fool!"

Too enraged to use anything but his knuckles, Declan hauled Alexander to his feet and hurled another punch. Alexander went sprawling into a workbench, spilling an array of glass jars and pitchers.

"Evangeline could have been taken! She could have died!"

Declan was about to throw another punch when someone restrained him. Killian. The battlemage held him back with an iron grip. "Sire, stop! Lex was trying to save a girl from the whorehouse!"

Caring nothing for excuses, Declan headbutted Killian. A crack of bone. Killian grunted, releasing him to cover his nose. Red spurted through his fingers, dribbled down his chin.

"Restrain me again, and I'll have your hands!"

"Sire, please!" Killian protested, his voice garbled. "You must calm yourself."

How could he calm himself when *everyone* had conspired to disobey him? With an enraged snarl, Declan let his fists fly.

Killian slammed into the wall before he slumped into an unconscious heap on the ground. Declan didn't stop until Mailin launched herself over Killian's insensible form as if to shield him.

Declan staggered back, drawing in sharp breaths. Alexander lumbered toward him like a drunken man, his jaw hanging at an odd angle.

Brother, I never meant for this to happen. Alexander's telepathic voice only served to reignite his fury.

Declan seized Alexander's shirtfront.

"Shut up! Your foolishness could have cost me my mate. I should tear your scalp from—"

"Enough!" Someone hurled a punch to his cheek, knocking Declan to his knees.

Violet eyes filled with disgust stared down at him. "Have you ever thought to blame *yourself* for this?"

Declan slammed a hand to the ground. "Insolent fae! How dare you turn this on me!"

"Turn this on you? Because of you, Shyaree nearly died!" Gabriel balled his hands. "If you'd acted less of an overbearing ass, maybe Evie would have *trusted* you with her secrets. Maybe she wouldn't have felt a need to sneak from the castle!"

Declan blinked up at the fae, the remnants of rationality in his brain finally functioning. "*You* took her out with a portal?"

Gabriel hadn't just been complicit in the lies; he'd been the bloody *key*. The one who enabled this calamity. Bitterness was a nail at his chest and betrayal was the pounding hammer. He had trusted Gabriel. Trusted the man enough to give him free access through his wards.

"Yes, because you made Evie feel like a prisoner in her own home!"

Declan flinched.

Gabriel sneered. "Truth hurts, doesn't it?"

Declan clenched his fists, uncaring for his shattered

knuckles and the fresh blood welling from torn scabs. He was numb everywhere but for the mindless rage scorching his vision and the resentment lacerating his chest.

"Want more?" Gabriel taunted, lifting his fists. "Come on, then!"

With a guttural roar, Declan leapt to his feet and charged.

The scent of briar roses and death permeated the air. Evangeline sucked in an involuntary breath, nauseated by the blend of saccharine blooms, smoke, and blood.

Honeysuckle vines curled thick around ivory pillars, and the roses remained plush, oblivious to the bedlam that had befallen the Courtyard of Song. The palatial steps, usually gleaming from the warm rays of the sun, now glistened in patches of crimson, littered with slain servants and fallen soldiers.

Chaos crowed from every corner as the living mourned the dead. Some worried over the wounded, some keened their anguish, and some simply wore the vacant stares of one overwhelmed by grief.

Bewildered and barefoot, Evangeline wandered down the ash-licked steps, charred in places where Unseelie blackfire had scorched stone, taking care to avoid the blood and bodies. The steps led to the Orchard of Solace that was filled with trees of gnarled branches and tawny leaves.

The trees called to her.

She needed to get to them, yet she didn't want to.

She didn't want to relive this, yet she must.

She stepped past mourners, her limbs sluggish yet her pace measured, but none gave any indication of having noticed her.

She was nothing more than a specter, sifting through the stairs like a shadow.

As she ventured into the orchard, her feet sunk into the cool grass, thick and smooth as a pelt. More people gathered here. Silver-armored soldiers bearing the Summer Court crest trampled the grass, arranging corpses in rows while the priestesses of Ozenn flitted over them, reciting verses of *Roschim bel Jorim*, the prayers for the dead.

Preparing the bodies for their final resting place.

She approached two grieving girls. Sisters. The elder one had slumped to her knees, her tearstained face twisted with grief as inarticulate sobs leaked from her throat. The younger merely stared, her eyes glazed with heartbreak that echoed in her chest.

How strange it was to see herself and not be seen.

To relive a sorrow she had thought long forgotten.

"Papa . . . " Felicity sobbed, reaching for the grieving soldier huddled on his knees. He cradled a woman's bloodied and broken body. The General of the Summer Court, fresh from battle and still in full regalia, rocked the body back and forth, back and forth.

"Ildara . . . ," he moaned. "Ildara."

The woman's hair, once the color of the wheat fields in Rivven, was now tangled and matted with blood. Her neck was mangled, covered in dried gore, her eyes eternally shut.

Something in Evangeline's chest constricted so tightly that nausea churned in her belly and bile rushed up her throat. Her eyes burned, but they remained dry, and her lips remained sealed. Her presence remained unnoticed.

After what seemed like an eternity, the general laid the woman back onto the grass. With jerky motions, as though each one pained him, he pressed a kiss on the woman's bruised temple before he drew back and murmured, "Sleep now, Ildara.

I'll come to you when our daughters are safe, when our people are free."

Vines whispered from the ground, breaking through the carpet of soft grass to twine green tendrils around the woman's body. They curled and coiled, lifting her up in an almost loving embrace, until a mass of rippling green encased her body.

Tendrils thickened into stem, and stem hardened into wood. Budding leaves from the branches unfurled in the shade of blood. The tree seemed to moan, the bark groaning, the branches whispering unrest through the mass of startling red leaves.

"Peace," the general whispered. Tears trickled down his cheeks as he gazed up at the branches. He flattened his palms against the bark that had turned black as a starless night.

"Be at peace, my love. I will send our daughters to a realm where Zephyr will not find them."

The tree continued to radiate distress. Evangeline felt it as keenly as she felt the General's pain, heard it as clearly as she heard Felicity's sobs.

"I will do everything to keep them safe, I promise you, *min ria*."

Slowly, almost reluctantly, sooty bark lightened into dark oak; the crimson leaves sighed and turned a golden shade to match the hue of the summer sun.

"Ankara roshim, my *min ria,"* he whispered.

Into the next life, my dearest love.

TWENTY-THREE

Evangeline opened her eyes to see a filigree of light filtered through stained glass windows. She blinked furiously to stymie the threatening deluge of tears.

Reliving Mama's burial had reopened scars she'd thought long healed.

Recalling her father's grief with such startling clarity felt like knives stabbing against her chest with every breath.

She had been shelving Freya's memories in the deepest recesses of her mind. Unwilling to dwell in the past. Too scared to scrutinize a history filled with loss.

Only her past seemed unwilling to let her go.

Felicie. Mama . . .

Her eyes burned.

Papa.

A yearning yawned wide in her chest for a man she had so adored. A man who'd always had a pocket filled with sweets and a secret greeting shared just with her. He'd called her his starflower. Evangeline could almost feel his strong arms hoisting her up upon his broad shoulders, and how she'd laughed when he'd swung her round and round in the air. And yet that was her last recollection of him—a man broken by grief.

Soft murmurs nudged her from the past back to reality.

A warm body lay beside her, and for a moment she thought it was her archmage. Only the bed was too narrow, and the body felt much too small.

Shyaree!

Evangeline shoved up from the bed, every movement an assault of prickly needles. Her head pounded, jarred from one moment in time to the next—both instances equally harrowing. But Shyaree appeared merely asleep, her torn and bloodied dress replaced with a fresh shift.

"Lady Barre," someone said in a hushed tone.

Evangeline twisted around. One of the castle maids, dustpan in hand, surrounded by a sea of broken glass, was hunched beside . . . Evangeline frowned. An upended cabinet?

Mailin bustled into view.

The pregnant healer appeared unnaturally aggrieved, her nose pink and eyes red rimmed. "Evie . . . " She drew her into a hug. Evangeline returned the healer's embrace readily, startled by Mailin's discomposure.

"Shyaree . . . "

"She's fine," Mailin whispered. "You did it. You healed her."

The burst of elation in her heart was stalled by the sudden awareness of her surroundings. Evangeline lay in one of the larger wards of the infirmary lined with four makeshift beds. On the bed just beside hers perched a golden-haired man, his usually perfect profile marred by such terrible swelling that he couldn't seem to keep his mouth closed.

"Railea's tears, Lex." Evangeline pulled away from Mailin's embrace. "What happened?" Alexander had been unharmed when she'd sent him to retrieve Mailin . . . hadn't he?

"Evaugghie," Alexander managed, with one hand cupped over his battered jaw. The evidence of his pain caused the knives in her heart to slice just a little deeper.

Alexander uttered another inarticulate mumble before Mailin huffed. "You really ought to stop speaking. I've only just managed to get the swelling under control."

Alexander dutifully shut his mouth, only he couldn't seem to do so without a significant overbite. Evangeline gasped. "Your jaw is *dislocated?*"

"Broken," Mailin amended.

"How . . . ?"

Alexander gave her a woeful look and reverted to telepathy. *Don't worry, little sister. A week or so and I'll be good as new.* He attempted a nonchalant shrug, but it came out pained. *Hey, at least I'm conscious . . .*

She followed his line of sight to the two beds on the other side of the room. Evangeline sucked in a sharp breath. The man occupying one bed was utterly unrecognizable save his mop of ash-white hair.

"It looks worse than it is," Mailin said quickly. "The sire used only his fists."

Sickness churned in her gut. *"Declan* did this?"

As though in a trance, she walked up to Gabriel's bedside. His nose was distorted, shattered at multiple points. His eyes were swollen, and his left cheekbone appeared concave.

Crushed.

As though someone had taken a hammer to his cheek. Every patch of his face was so bruised that his complexion was blotchy hues of purple and black.

His breathing whistled.

She yanked the sheet off his chest, and her legs threatened to buckle. His jerkin and leather vest had been removed, and it was clear Gabriel had suffered the same blows on his torso. Some of his ribs . . . sunken.

Evangeline pushed away from Mailin's steadying hand. Sickness fouled the back of her mouth.

"Declan did this?" she repeated, a shrillness in her voice she could not control.

"All because *someone* thought to have a little excursion into the capital," muttered the maid, who was sweeping shards into her dustpan.

Evangeline flinched.

Mailin shot the maid a pointed glare before shaking her head. "Never have I witnessed the sire so angry."

"Where is he?" Evangeline demanded.

Mailin shook her head. "I think it's best to leave him alone—"

"Where is he?"

Mailin's lips tightened, and Alexander remained equally silent. The maid who had followed their entire exchange only curled her lips in open contempt when Evangeline stared in mute question.

Evangeline stormed through the door only to be halted by Killian. The battlemage's crooked nose and split lip did not escape her. His bruise appeared older, ugly purple faded to a mild, patchy yellow. That only meant Mailin had gotten to healing him first.

"He did that, too?"

At the taut line of Killian's lips, Evangeline shook her head in disbelief.

"My lady." Killian pinched the bridge of his nose with a sigh. "I wouldn't go in search of the sire now. He's . . . not himself."

"Killian, if you've ever regarded me as the elorin of Amereen, you will tell me where he is. Now."

Evangeline pushed through the double doors of the bedchamber. The air was chilled, as though winter had come prematurely and whispered through the room. The droplets of blood on the carpet stopped her in her tracks. A miasma of conflicting emotions rushed through her. She sucked in a steadying breath and darted past the sitting room into the bedchamber.

She found him on the ground, leaning against the bedframe on her side of the bed, next to her open dresser. Parchment notes lay scattered around him like windblown leaves. His head was thrown back, eyes closed as though he was asleep.

"Declan." Her voice came out threadbare.

He still wore incriminating blood on his skin. But he appeared to suffer no open wounds or broken bones. His nose still straight, his cheekbones just as sharp. But the extent of dried blood and the yellowing bruises told a different story. As an archmage, Declan healed far quicker than any mage, and mages certainly healed faster than the fae.

His eyelids parted, but one eye seemed unable to open beyond a slit.

Clearly, her archmage hadn't been the only one using his fists.

She took another hesitant step forward, and then she was in his arms, wrapped in blood, grime, and something so intrinsically Declan that her rage dulled momentarily.

"You're awake," he muttered roughly. "You're awake."

She remained in his arms because she needed his embrace as much as he seemed to need to hold her.

"What have you done?" she whispered, tracking fingers lightly over the deepest bruise that colored the corner of his slitted eye. Broken skin had knitted back together, but its echoes were kohl-colored patches across his face. Her vision watered without warning. She simply couldn't *stand* the thought of him hurt in any way, regardless of the cause.

Especially when it was her fault. All of it. She should never have persuaded Alexander to be involved. Should never have asked Gabriel to cast that portal. How she despised herself at this moment, and yet . . .

"How could you?" Her lips trembled. "How could you have hurt them?"

Evangeline knew of the atrocities done to him as a child, knew his capability of committing the same atrocities against others. She had thought she understood him. She had believed she wasn't ignorant of the man she'd fallen for—but truth was an ugly thing.

It stared back at her with flat, remorseless eyes.

A tear slid down her cheek.

"How could I?" He gave a small, humorless laugh. He shifted back. Shut his eyes. Then he jabbed a finger at the parchment littering the ground.

"How could *you* have kept this from me? How could you have thought to leave the castle without your guard, knowing Zephyr might still be alive?" His tone remained soft, but a vein pulsed at the side of his neck. "How could you have been so reckless?"

Evangeline blanched, shame rising to flame her cheeks. She hadn't been merely reckless. She had been foolish to have brought such risk upon herself and everyone that went with her. At Shyaree's expense.

He fisted his hands as though he wanted to punch something, and to her shock, she realized his knuckles were raw and no longer aligned.

Sickness caused her to stumble back.

He mistook it for fear and quickly unclenched his fists.

"I won't hurt you, Evangeline." He growled the words. "I will *never* hurt you. I would sooner tear off my limbs, carve out my heart than lay a finger on you."

An agonized sob leaked from her throat. Something cleaved deep in her chest because she didn't need his reassurance—she knew it down to every fiber of her being. He had always been so gentle with her that she had never imagined he would behave so brutally with the people who had come to be her friends. The people she knew *he* loved.

"No," she agreed. "You won't hurt me. But you would blame your own brother, hurt your own friends for *my* mistakes?"

Declan stared for a moment, but a bark of harsh laughter escaped his throat. He loomed over her with curled lips. Every bit the arrogant king.

"Alexander may share my blood, but he is no more special to me than any other councilor. Killian is a battlemage, useful for nothing but his skill with the sword. And Gabriel?" He sneered. "That bloody fae is nothing but hired help."

Her vision clouded, and for a moment, he existed as a silhouette of blurred colors.

"Liar," she whispered.

He seemed not to hear. He rose to his feet and stepped forward to seize her shoulders. "And you," he said. "You belong to *me*. Mine." As though she were nothing more than an object. "You will not leave the castle without your guard and without my knowledge ever again. And you are never to keep secrets from me. Do you understand?"

Evangeline stared up into eyes of emerald ice. She opened her lips to voice her apology, confess her folly. To plead reason.

She snapped her mouth shut.

Somehow, she understood that this one moment would define the rest of their life together. Her response would set the tone for the dynamic of their relationship. He would cow as much as coddle her.

One day she might even come to resent him.

She shoved hard against his breastbone. He must be wounded there because he stumbled, back bowed as he coughed and gasped for breath.

It tore at her to have caused him further pain, but she stifled her instincts and defied remorse. "I thought we'd been through this before," she murmured, straightening her back so she could meet his gaze with her head held high.

"Perhaps you've forgotten. Allow me to remind you once more, Archmage. I may have shared with you my body, given you my heart"—she swiped at her eyes because there was no hiding her tears, but she found the strength to inject steel into her tone—"but I am not a dog to be led on a leash, or a puppet jerked around by strings."

Pain flashed over his face before his veneer of inscrutability fell into place.

"Now the question is," she said, forcing herself to meet emotionless eyes with an unflinching gaze. "Do *you* understand me?"

TWENTY-FOUR

She'd left him.

According to Killian, Evangeline had stormed up to him and demanded—no, *commanded*—he warp her from the castle. And she'd left a field of withered wildflowers in her wake.

Declan stared at the sparring compound, rendered mute by a strange combination of awe and desolation.

"It appeared far more impressive before they wilted," Mailin said, a snub evident in her voice. She had corralled him from his chambers three days after Evangeline's departure. The halfbreed healer was the only one who'd dared venture inside.

She had not only barged in; she had threatened to *manhandle* him.

"The soldiers were so awed that no one sparred over it for days. Your men wanted to keep the field pristine as a surprise for *you*, sire. To share the beauty their lady had created." Mailin sighed. "Of course, that doesn't matter now, does it?"

The stalks were browned, petals shriveled. The very ground seemed to mourn Evangeline's departure.

"Why didn't anyone tell me she'd recovered her magic?" Declan asked dumbly. Mailin folded her arms, and he could almost feel her scorn as daggers over his skin. Funny how the tiny healer no longer feared him.

"Because you were too busy plowing your fists into your men, *sire*."

She seemed ready to roll her eyes but stopped herself with a huff. "Evie used magic to defend herself in the capital, too, which you'd know if you'd bothered to read Killian's report. And she healed the shaman. Remarkable, if you ask me."

Mailin started to turn away, but then she halted. "With utmost respect, sire, my mate's broken nose has healed, and the bruises on his skin have faded. Unfortunately, I'm not sure the same can be said for your mate's heart."

With that, the pregnant healer executed an exaggerated curtsy that was more insult than deference and left him standing in a field of withered flowers.

Declan spent the next two days plotting the demise of the author of the threats. Then he deluded himself into believing that Evangeline's departure was a good thing. He had demonstrated himself dangerous. Out of control. She was right to leave him. She was safer away from him. Then he spent the next three days wishing she would return, throw her arms around him, and declare her undying love despite his many faults.

It was on the ninth day that Declan accepted his heart as an organ he'd ignored for too long and decided his pride worth nothing if he couldn't draw breath without hurting.

The Barre Cottage seemed to mock him with its pale stone face dressed in lichen and moss. Inhaling deep, Declan rapped on the door. He was about to rap again when the ironwork of the peephole lifted and gray eyes peered out at him. The metal flapped down almost immediately.

He could warp inside, but he would be damned if he offended yet another person Evangeline cared about. Painstaking minutes ticked by before the deadbolt slid and the door opened.

"Agnes," he said with a nod of greeting. "Is Evangeline here?"

Agnes's arched brow tore through his flimsy query.

"I'd have thought your men would have told you, my liege."

Of course, he *knew* she was in residence. Not only could he sense her presence telepathically, but Declan had stationed her entire guard and more around the cottage and the village Arns.

He cleared his throat. "May I come in?"

Agnes narrowed her eyes but bobbed a facetious curtsy and disappeared into the house, leaving the door open as a response. Declan trailed in after her, eagerly scanning the couches covered in colorful plaid, only to find them empty. A quick sweep of the small kitchen showed no sign of his little fire.

"She's still asleep," Agnes said, clearly reading his disappointment. "She's been sleeping in quite a bit these days."

Declan frowned. "Is she unwell?"

"No," was all Agnes said. He gazed up the narrow stairs to the alcove where the small door stood between him and his mate.

Agnes shook her head. "I wouldn't warp into her room unannounced if I were you."

Declan swallowed his disconcertion. His shattered control

hadn't quite mended, and it seemed harder and harder to wear his mask of impassiveness.

Agnes sniffed, then left him for the kitchen.

"If it weren't for the army you have stationed around my home, I would have assumed you'd tired of my daughter, my liege."

The symbols on his skin ignited involuntarily. Must *everyone* assume this of him and, by implication, insult Evangeline?

"She means more to me than you'll ever comprehend." He struggled to keep the bite from his tone. Evangeline was his life. But the flare of his markings was quickly doused by the woman's open smirk.

His ire had *pleased* her, which annoyed him even more.

Did she think to test his intentions, when he'd already declared his commitment to the world by making Evangeline his elorin de ana? By giving her his mark? What more did he need to do to prove his feelings?

Agnes gestured at the chair at the head of the dining table. "Perhaps you'd like to take a seat here, my liege?"

"Declan," he corrected before drawing in a deep breath to mellow his agitation. "I've given you my name and wish for you to use it."

Agnes curtsied once more. "As you wish."

Irritation was gnats on his skin, but he sat. "If you have something to say, I would hear it." Better to allow the woman to say her piece than to be treated like an unwelcome lord in her home.

Another raise of her brows. "Would you rather I treat you as a son than as my liege, then?"

A *son*? He hadn't expected anything of the sort. He wanted Agnes to treat him as she would Evangeline's elorin de han. But how would that be, if not as a son? Uneasiness roiled in his stomach. He'd been many things, but never a son. Not a real one. But to have the woman Evangeline regarded as mother treat him as one . . . was not as unappealing as it was unsettling.

Slowly, he nodded.

A small curve tugged the edges of her lips, and her eyes gleamed. As though she had accepted a challenge. "Have you breakfasted yet, Declan?"

He shook his head.

"Good." Her smile broadened. "Neither have your men."

The implication didn't quite sink in until Agnes heaved a large portion of flour onto the table to form a small, white mountain. Then she made a depression at the center, where she cracked in raw eggs.

"You're baking for my soldiers?" he asked, incredulous.

"Of course. They need to eat, don't they?"

"You're not required to feed them. They are more than capable of feeding themselves."

She nodded. "But they only eat when their shift has ended, and the ones who still stand guard at this early hour have been standing guard through the night—despite the increasing chill of the season."

"It is their duty," Declan said. His men required no pampering for merely carrying out their tasks.

"That it may be," Agnes agreed. "But this is my pleasure."

Declan frowned at her. A woman who rose at the crack of dawn to serve soldiers stationed to serve her. No wonder Evangeline had grown to be a creature of such compassion, with such a bighearted woman as her mother.

Agnes beckoned him forward.

Declan rose from his seat, assuming she wanted help starting the fire in her oven. It wasn't until amusement lit her expectant eyes that he realized what she intended for him.

"Kneading enough dough for six hungry men can be quite a task," she said. "And you've got such large, strong hands. A son would make himself useful. Don't you think?"

He stared down at the mound of unmixed batter.

Agnes cocked her head at his hesitance. "Never prepared dough, Declan?"

He shook his head. At the enclave, he'd been taught to sow and harvest, to tend to mares and to clean. Never had he been taught to prepare food in any form or fashion. He met the laughing gleam in Agnes's eyes, and his resolve hardened. If the woman thought she'd make him balk, then she was mistaken. How hard could kneading dough be?

He rolled up his sleeves.

She tutted. "Wash your hands before you begin, please."

Gritting his teeth, he did as she'd bid. Then he melded the contents to create a sticky mess.

At his inquiring gaze, Agnes nodded. "Go on. You're doing a fine job," she said before leaving him to the task as she puttered about the kitchen. It wasn't until his dough folded into a tight ball that Declan deemed it ready. Agnes made a judgmental sound but popped it into the oven. They spent another length of time in awkward silence as he scrubbed his hands clean of dough and she plied him with tea. Declan sat and stared up at the stairs, where his heart remained abed.

Worry wormed in his chest. It was close to midmorning. How could Evangeline still be asleep? The sun shone bright through the curtains by the time they removed the loaf from the oven.

Declan frowned as he bit into a slice. "What did I do wrong?"

Dense and hard, it tasted more like biscuit than bread.

"You used too much force. Overkneaded the dough."

"You could have told me when to stop."

"Yes, but where's the fun in that?" she asked, eyes twinkling.

Irritation whipped him. "There is no fun in wasting time and effort for a poor outcome."

Agnes shook her head. "Ah, when you've lived to be as old as I, you find fun in every endeavor. Did you not enjoy pounding your fists into the dough? I believe you have a penchant for fisticuffs."

Declan's brow furrowed. The fact that he *had* found the process oddly satisfying further annoyed him. Agnes's chuckle sprinkled the air like a pall of flour, and hot shame raised his hackles.

"Is that why you had me knead?" he asked bitterly. "To punish the use of my fists?"

Before Agnes could respond, Evangeline padded into the kitchen, soft footed as a cat. She froze at the sight of him.

"Sweetheart, good morning," Agnes said. "Care to join us for breakfast?"

Declan swallowed hard as he rose to his feet. The simple sight of her evaporated every word of his carefully practiced speech.

"I . . . I-I-" Was he fucking *stuttering*? He cleared his throat.

"I want you to come home," he said finally, with the tact and sophistication of a schoolboy.

Her eyes narrowed; her pink lips pinched. She redirected her gaze to the kettle as though it was more deserving of her attention than he. Declan swallowed again. He was making a mess of things before she'd even had breakfast . . . not that she had much to eat given his ruined loaf. He racked his brain for the right words, but all he could seem to do was track her movements around the kitchen. When it was clear she had no intention of joining the table, he began to panic.

"Little fire . . . ," he pleaded, almost afraid to utter anything lest he inadvertently set her on edge.

"I *am* home." Quiet words before she afforded Agnes a small smile. "I'll see you at the apothecary, Mother."

The front door closed with a hollow thud. He heard her boots on cobblestone, her voice, filled with a false cheeriness as she greeted his men by name with familiar ease. Declan stared down at the plate holding the slice of his hardened bread, suddenly nauseated as though he'd been punched in the gut. Her three tiny words packed more punch than any blow he'd ever had to endure.

Agnes sighed and patted his forearm. "I'd better bake a fresh loaf. Perhaps you should stay and watch." She gave him an unexpected smile, soft and motherly. "As you've just learned, kneading dough right can be tricky business. When force is overused, it will only harden the outcome."

TWENTY-FIVE

"How are the Hanesworths?" Agnes asked.

Evangeline looked up from the letter in her hands with a genuine smile. "Stefan found work in a small fishing village." She gave her mother a quick summary of the letter's pleasing contents, her heart lighter than it had been since she'd returned. She pulled out a quill and spare parchment and searched the escritoire drawers for an inkwell.

Agnes cocked her head. "Does Declan know the two of you are exchanging letters?"

Evangeline frowned. "He wouldn't stop me from writing to a friend."

"A friend who once thought to betray you."

Evangeline sighed. "You know why he did it."

A raised brow. "Do Stefan's reasons make his actions right, then?"

"I didn't say that." Evangeline toyed with the quill in her hands. "Nor do I agree with the choices he made . . . but I do *understand* his reasons. And because I do, I can find forgiveness in my heart."

Agnes released a musing hum. "So you would forgive a man who would have bartered you into the slave trade but not an overprotective man who lost his temper?"

Evangeline scowled as she unscrewed the top of an inkwell. "It's not like that. He didn't just lose his temper. He . . . " Evangeline exhaled, weary. Mother made the situation sound so straightforward. Simple, even. But Declan had hurt people she had come to care for—worse, he'd hurt the people *he* cared about. Punished them for *her* mistakes. How could she forgive him, when she couldn't forgive *herself* for her own foolishness?

"Is it not? Railea's sake, how long would you have me torture the poor man?"

Evangeline folded her arms. Annoyance pursed her lips. How had Agnes completely changed her tune where Evangeline's archmage was concerned?

"And how is feeding him freshly baked goods from your oven torture?"

She had woken every morning over the past week to find Declan at her mother's table, his plate piled with whatever Agnes had baked. Every day, Declan had attempted to speak to her, which she'd largely ignored in hopes of discouraging his advances. She simply needed time away from him.

He didn't stop showing up, but he did keep his silence.

And despite herself, she'd begun rising earlier each morning in anticipation of glimpsing him at the breakfast table.

A sly gleam lit Agnes's gaze. "Only because I enjoy the way he looks at you every morning." A chuckle. "Isn't every day you see an archmage looking like a lost pup. One who behaves as though he's been kicked in the rump every time you leave the house."

"Mother!" Evangeline exclaimed, affronted by the comparison. She huffed. "You really shouldn't keep letting him in. You're only encouraging him when all I need is space."

Agnes lifted a shoulder. "Are you sure?"

"*Yes.*"

"Very well. But I should also mention that no one else is feeding that lost pup of yours."

"What?"

"Haven't you noticed your entourage of guards has dwindled down to *none* around our cottage?"

"The guard still escorts me out daily," Evangeline pointed out. Admittedly, she hadn't thought about where her guard went whenever she returned to the cottage.

"Precisely. Your archmage has taken on the task of safeguarding the cottage himself. Shooed his own men away." Another chuckle. "Probably doesn't want more eyes to witness his humiliation as he plays sentry day and night."

"*What?*"

Agnes's eyes danced. "Mmm. He's been guarding the cottage for four days now. Railea must find it entertaining, too, because she made it rain in the last two. Can't say I feel sorry for him, though. Any man who makes my baby cry deserves a little rain."

Evangeline dropped the quill, causing a large blot of ink to stain the parchment. "You mean he's . . . *outside*? Has been this whole time?"

"Oh, yes. He typically sits out in the backyard, just beneath your bedroom window."

Evangeline glanced through the square glass panes of her mother's window. The moon hung like an oversized pearl in the sky, its buttermilk complexion marred by a flurry of fattened clouds. She itched to reach out with her mind, project her thoughts to see if an archmage did reside beneath her window . . . but what then?

Mother sighed, and all mischief leached from her face. "Honestly, sweetheart, why are you still here?"

Evangeline picked up the quill and fidgeted with the feathered tip. "I . . . I need time. To think."

Mother rolled her eyes. "Of *what*? Railea's tears, you're just as miserable as he is! I'm tired of watching the two of you moon about like a pair of depressed songbirds."

Evangeline glared but couldn't quite muster up enough annoyance to maintain her stance. Instead, she slumped into her seat and drew in a deep inhale. "I don't know if I can do it," she admitted. "I don't know if I can bear the responsibility that comes from being his elorin de ana. I've recovered my memories. Regained my magic. Yet I am still haunted by the past."

It had become clear that so long as he lived, Zephyr would *never* stop hunting her. And so would any other who learned of her Jilintree identity. She would live the rest of her life as a target. A target who would be forever shunned by Declan's people for her weaknesses.

Evangeline shook her head, recalling the maid's disdain in the infirmary. "No matter how far I come, I'll never be good enough in Declan's court. His people will always see me as their archmage's weakness. But how can I blame them?" Evangeline's shoulders curled. "If I stay with him, Declan will forever be saddled with a woman who needs protection at every turn."

And a woman who brought out the worst in him. Sudden warmth burned at the edges of her eyes, blurring her vision. "I don't know if I'm right for him."

Agnes harrumphed, throwing her arms in the air. "Gods, help me! I've always hoped to have done your real mother justice. Now I know I haven't."

Evangeline blinked and sputtered, "How could you say such a thing? You've been a fine mother."

"Railea's tears, your real mother was royalty. You are the

daughter of a Seelie princess. A *princess!* But all I've raised is a woman scared of her own shadow!"

Evangeline gaped, but Mother didn't give her a chance to speak.

"When you first brought your archmage into the house, I wondered if you'd lost your mind in the shadow realm. But now I see what you must have seen back then. Beneath all that power, he's just a man, Evie."

Evangeline released an indelicate snort. Declan was not *just* an anything.

"A man who would likely swallow broken glass if you demanded it." Agnes sighed when Evangeline's lips remained a sealed seam. "Sweetheart, listen to me." She waited until Evangeline met her solemn gaze. "My own mate *chose* to walk away from me. For centuries, I have existed with a part of my heart missing. It is not a pain I would wish on anyone, especially you."

Evangeline swallowed the lump in her throat, for she knew the pain Agnes had carried over the years. A sudden sickness lined her gut. Was she prepared to subject Declan to the same?

She scrubbed hands over her eyes and blew out a frustrated breath. "I've only stayed in the castle for a little over six months, and already I've done nothing but sow discord in his court, raise contention between Declan and his people."

"Stop seeing yourself the way you *used* to be! You are no longer the child Freya once was, nor are you the woman Evangeline was before she learned of her past." Agnes reached over to clasp her hands. "Your past may be an accumulation of grievances, but you are also stronger for it. If you haven't realized that yet, then perhaps your archmage hasn't realized it, either."

Agnes tipped up Evangeline's chin to gift her a wistful smile. "I never met the woman you call Mama, but I know deep in my heart that she would agree with me on this. Do not allow fears from the past to eclipse your future."

Railea must be in a devious mood, for she made it rain. Again.

Evangeline pressed her palm to the window as she stared out into the darkness of the backyard. Shadowed trees and bushes shivered beneath a smirking moon and the grumbling rain clouds.

"Sounds like the start of a storm," Agnes mused from her spot beneath the bedspread. Her gaze remained affixed to the pages of her book. Evangeline pulled away from the window and returned to the escritoire where she was penning her response to Stefan.

"Just a drizzle," she muttered. Declan was a grown man. More, he was an archmage who could create shields to bar the elements.

The pitter patter of rain had never felt quite so offensive. She looked up from the letter to glare at the window. The wind whistled and spat, distorting the glass with heavy rivulets.

She exhaled. Declan didn't feel the cold, she assured herself. Oh, but how she *detested* the thought of him out in the dark. Alone.

"Isn't this relaxing?" Agnes asked in an aggravatingly cheery tone. "I've always enjoyed a good storm."

Evangeline ignored her and scribbled a few more lines of well-wishes.

A merciless gust of wind rattled the windowpanes.

Thunder boomed.

Evangeline signed the letter with a hasty scrawl, then slapped down her quill.

"Don't worry. I'll make sure to send your correspondence with the next mail envoy," Agnes said with a knowing smirk. "Oh, and next time you come for dinner, do bring that arch-mage of yours."

Evangeline flattened her lips. "I'm *not* leaving."

She bounded from Agnes's room as her mother's chortle bounced from the walls. Evangeline's legs carried her down the short stretch of the hallway into her own little room, where she parted her curtains and threw open the window.

Rain billowed into her face.

"Archmage?" she called into the darkness, but the roar of the downpour was all she heard. For a moment she wondered if Agnes had been mistaken and Declan wasn't here at all. Then, a familiar silhouette emerged from the comfrey bushes directly beneath her window.

She swallowed. He was truly here. In the dark and the cold. Soaked to the bone.

"What are you doing in the rain?" she yelled over the howling wind.

Go back inside, and shut the window! He telepathed with his usual bossiness. *You're getting wet!*

She slammed the window shut. Never had she met anyone who roused such conflicting emotions within her. Grinding her teeth, she stomped down the stairs and made her way into the kitchen. She flung open the back door and marched out into the pouring rain.

TWENTY-SIX

Evangeline slammed the window with a force that left no misconceptions as to her ire. Declan sighed and shut his eyes with his face still angled to the sky, allowing Railea's tears to wash over him. Cool and crisp. Cleansing.

"What do you think you're doing?"

A mirage, conjured from his fanciful imaginings, glowered at him just three short steps away. Definitely a fantasy, for she was clad in a thin, provocative linen shift. One growing sheerer by the second due to Railea's merciless—*merciful?*—deluge.

Strands of unbound hair clung to the graceful arch of her neck. Droplets of rain kissed the delectable column of her throat. She folded her arms, drawing his attention to the heaving of her small, pert breasts. Her nipples, deliciously hardened, were outlined by the sodden material clinging to her flushed skin. Chill-bumped skin.

Declan blinked. Then gave himself a mental slap.

As he was ogling her breasts, she was standing in the rain.

He conjured a shield in his next breath, wrapping them both in a telekinetic bubble that kept the rain out.

"Why did you come out here?" he groused half-heartedly. Hope beat like a flurry of wings in his chest. This was the first time she'd acknowledged his presence in days. He wanted to reach out and take her into his arms, but her narrowed eyes gave him pause.

Instead, he said, "It's too cold for you. Go back inside."

A flash of lightning flared in sunset eyes. "Do not order me about, Archmage. This is my home, and you're trespassing."

"In my village," he reminded her. "On my lands."

"Of course." She sniffed. "And dare I ask what the lord archmage Thorne is doing in my humble backyard on such a fine night?"

Declan swallowed, unaccustomed to taking the brunt of her scorn.

"Just performing my duty," he muttered.

"Duty?" She scoffed. "When has it been an archmage's duty to stand as a common guard?"

"It is when he's guarding his own heart."

Her lips parted and shut, as though she were at a loss for words. Then her eyes narrowed once more. "That's not fair."

He frowned, confounded by the simultaneous softening of her tone and the hardening of her gaze. "What?"

"You don't get to come here and . . . and say these things." She laid her hands on her hips, and for all that was divine, gave him a perfect view of her damp shift clinging to every tantalizing curve. "It is when he's guarding his own heart," she mimicked in an absurdly gruff voice. She pointed an accusing finger at him. "I know what you're doing, Archmage, and I'm not falling for it."

Declan blinked at her implication. He had been known to

manipulate his opponents with calculated words. But with Evangeline, he could sometimes barely string coherent sentences together without stumbling over his own tongue—or rousing her ire. Resentment wrapped a fist over his heart. Perhaps that was why she was constantly vexed with him. She did not trust him enough to hear him even when he spoke the truth.

"Do you wish for me to leave you alone and unprotected?" Agitation tensed his muscles and sharpened his words. "Because that is *not* happening."

"Of course not," she retorted with a huff. "Even if Zephyr were dead, I am not fool enough to forget what an easy target I've become."

So she wasn't annoyed with her guard performing the duty. Just him.

"Then you should have known better than to leave the castle unprotected."

Her anger seemed to deflate, the hard edges of her mouth shifting into a downward turn. "I wasn't unprotected. I had Lex by my side . . . " She swallowed. "The ambush wasn't something I could have anticipated. I'm not sure how those bandits knew exactly where to find me." She wrung her hands, and her gaze dipped to her bare feet. "I'm sorry, Declan. I should never have left the castle."

Her apology only served to terrify him. He had come so close to losing her to the clutches of the Unseelie, all because he'd been too steeped in his own insecurities to see to her safety. "Precisely why I am never letting you out of my sight again."

She dipped her chin like a chastened child. "It was my mistake. I promise I'll never leave without my guard again. I—"

"You're never going anywhere without *me*." His words came

out with more bite than he intended, and her meekness dissipated as quickly as it had come.

A strangled sound escaped her throat. "Is this always to be the way with you? Dictating my every move?"

"If you don't want to be dictated to, then perhaps you shouldn't sneak about behind my back."

"I only snuck out of the castle because I knew you'd never have given me a chance to solve my own problems!"

"Your *own* problems?" Declan gave an incredulous shout of laughter. "Someone is threatening you. You! *My* elorin de ana. It is as much your problem as it is mine. And it isn't a problem to be resolved, but a danger to be nullified. If you'd told me earlier, I would have long since had the perpetrator's head on a spike."

"And that is exactly why I didn't tell you! Bloodshed is not the answer to everything."

"No," he agreed with a thin smile. "But violence remains the most effective way to curb unnecessary dissension in a world of bloodthirsty immortals. You are no longer human, Evangeline." Declan stepped forward until they were a smidgeon apart, but she shifted back to glare up at him. Standing barefoot, she only reached his chest. He swallowed.

She was truly his *little fire*, a burning flame that could be snuffed out far too easily. "Mortal rules do not apply in my court, Evangeline. Any transgression against you is a transgression against *me*. And because you have kept it from me, you have encouraged their daring. You have allowed this to escalate when it could have easily been dealt with. I cannot afford to show any vulnerability if I am to rule."

"And I am exactly that," she said, her shoulders sagging. "A vulnerability that needs to be compensated for with violence."

Declan frowned at the resentment in her tone. Why did she make him seem the villain? He was only trying to keep her safe. "Would you blame a sword for drawing blood? A shield for blocking an arrow?"

Her gaze flew up to meet his. "You are not a sword, nor are you a shield!"

"No," he snapped. "I am an archmage. One who might as well be worthless if I can't even protect a single woman."

"I am not completely defenseless anymore, Archmage." Her frustration was obvious from the sharpening of her ears into delicate points.

"No?" A muscle in his cheek ticced. "Yet if it weren't for Lex and Gabriel, you would have been taken from me."

Something jerked at his ankle abruptly, startling him to a stagger. A vine had sprung from the ground and latched over his leg like a live snake.

Declan stared down at the tightening vines. Awe tempered his anger. The vines coiled along his calf, almost lovingly, before stretching up to wrap tender shoots around his knee. "Mailin told me you healed Shyaree from a fatal wound."

"Yes," she said, seeming to respond to the huskiness in his tone with a gentling of her own. "Thank Railea I found enough strength, but I can't seem to push beyond a certain threshold . . . or I'll risk unconsciousness. It seems I'll always be weak."

"You've healed a fatal wound *and* summoned an entire field of wildflowers in the two short months since Shyaree's arrival." Uncontrollable pride colored his voice. "How could you still believe yourself weak?"

She blinked. "I didn't think you noticed the sparring ground."

"Mailin brought it to my attention even though *you* didn't think it pertinent to inform me."

"You didn't give me a chance to say anything," she protested.

"*Would* you have told me given the chance?"

"Of course I would have!" She swept both her hands up into the air as though in utter exasperation. "I've only kept the threats from you. And only because I thought to handle it on my own."

"*Only* the threats?" Declan ground his molars. "I never took you for a liar, Evangeline. But you kept your proposal from me, too." It was small of him, but he couldn't quite keep the bitterness from his voice as he added, "I had to learn of it along with the rest of the council . . . through my own brother!"

She blinked at him. "You thought I kept the proposal from you on purpose?" When he failed to respond, she added, "Why would you even think that?"

"Because you don't trust me!" The words burst from him, startling them both with their vehemence. She reached for him, but he couldn't seem to stop the next words from tumbling from his mouth. "You don't trust me to protect you. Don't trust me to take care of you. You don't—"

Declan choked his next accusation back and dragged a frustrated hand through his rain-slicked hair as he paced the length within his shield. He would not blame her lack of trust for their incomplete mating. He turned to stare at the rain lashing against the translucent outline of his shield, seeking to regain some semblance of control.

"Declan . . . "

He shook his head. "Enough of this. Go back inside and get out of those wet things before you catch a cold."

She hissed. "Stop ordering me about, you boor! Now, look at me."

When he didn't turn quickly enough, more vines speared from the ground to rope around his leg. "Evangeline, you will cease this childishness at once!"

"*My* childishness?"

More vines speared from the earth to twine themselves up his other leg, crawling up his knee, wending over his thighs. He could easily sever or burn them, but Declan would never harm the life that came from her.

"Stop it." He tried to shake them loose. Five flaming hells, he was growing *aroused* from the feel of her vines alone.

"Then turn around and face me."

Expelling a breath, he did. And his heart slammed into his rib cage. In this instant, she resembled nothing of the sweet innocent who had once been Freya. Nor did she appear the beguiling, tenderhearted woman who was Evangeline.

No, the fierceness she radiated roused a strange fluttering in his stomach, as though her vines had somehow perforated his gut and were taking root in his innards. With her rain-kissed skin and flashing eyes, she was glorious. Breathtaking.

An angry *queen* ready to smite him.

She breached the distance between them in three purposeful steps.

Capturing his face between her hands, she hauled him down and kissed him.

TWENTY-SEVEN

Evangeline kissed him *hard.*

"You silly, impossible man," she said between angry kisses. "How could you believe for a moment I didn't trust you?"

She had trusted him with her body, her heart, her soul. What else did he want from her? She gave him another punishing nip, not caring that her canines drew blood. The low groan rumbling from his throat shot liquid heat between her legs.

What was I to think? he telepathed, his lips occupied. *Even Gabriel was privy to your actions, but not me.*

Evangeline pulled back and sighed at the sulkiness in his tone.

"Oh, Declan," she whispered. "Ever since we came back from the shadow realm, so much of everything has been new to me. Sometimes, I feel . . . overwhelmed. Suffocated. Do you understand?"

His brows furrowed, but he remained quiet, waiting for her to continue.

Evangeline swallowed. "I've regained my memories"—her voice cracked—"only to relive the loss of my family. I've found you again . . . only to realize how poorly matched we are."

The firm line of his lips lacerated her heart, for it served as a silent affirmation of her claim. Even he couldn't refute their inaptness.

"I don't know *how* to be the elorin of Amereen, Declan. I don't know how to be a mate worthy of you . . . but I want so badly to be."

He started to speak, but she shushed him with a finger.

"I truly had no mind to keep the proposal a secret from you . . . It just happened. First, it was because you appeared so busy with your council. Then, I believed I was helping to ease your burden by completing it on my own and surprising you with it." Her lips formed an unhappy curve. "It was rather silly of me, wasn't it? But I wanted to show you that I could do the things expected of the elorin of Amereen. That I was capable."

His only response was the bobbing of his throat.

"I was such a fool for keeping those threats from you," she added in a rush. "I wanted so badly to prove to you, to your council, and most of all to *myself*"—she shook her head ruefully —"that I am capable of defending me." Evangeline dipped her chin. "And not only have I caused such trouble because of it, but I have also hurt you. I am sorry."

"You needed space to grow." He said the words slowly, as though he was turning them over in his mind. "But I gave you no room for it. Instead of helping, I was . . . suffocating you."

"Declan." She sighed, hating his self-recriminatory tone. She had intended for him to hear her reasons and her apology. Not to lay blame at his feet.

"Is that why you didn't tell me when you were hurting during Shyaree's sessions?" he prompted. "Why you allowed Gabriel to soothe your pain instead of me?"

"I haven't allowed Gabriel anything."

At his deepened frown, she arched her brows. "Jealous again, Archmage?"

"Of course not."

Evangeline smirked. The words had tumbled from him too quickly to be anything but false denial. He huffed. Then he tugged her close, laying his forehead against hers so their breaths mingled.

I admit I had . . . worried you'd find Gabriel a more attractive choice as a mate.

Her eyes widened. "How could you *possibly* think that?"

"Because I've seen the way he looks at you." The column of his throat worked. "And I saw the way you looked at him."

Incredulous laughter sprung from her throat before she could check it. "Yes, I've grown to love Gabriel . . . in a way one would a friend."

She grinned at the wary slash of his brows. "Have you noticed the way I look at *you?*"

His jaw tightened, and he gave a solemn nod. "With open censure in your eyes."

Evangeline's lips parted.

Where she'd struggled with her weaknesses, she had unwittingly fed his doubts. She curved her arms over his shoulders, eager to set things right.

"Take us to the clifftop," she whispered. "Let me remind you how I've always looked at you."

His breath hitched, and yet he said, "I won't risk you again, Evangeline."

"You may be the archmage of Amereen, but you forget. I *am* a princess."

He swallowed as he held her gaze for a drowning moment. "You have always been and always will be my princess. My *queen.* I will give you everything I have and everything I am, but not when it hurts you. Never when it hurts you."

"Trust me," she whispered, pressing kisses to his lips. Her headaches and bouts of lethargy had all but disappeared of late. She had recovered her ability to wield magic. Healed an otherwise fatal wound. Surely she would not fall into unconsciousness after the act of loving her archmage?

"The clifftop," she urged as her kisses grew more urgent. "Now."

The air evinced no change, but Evangeline was beyond caring. She was eager to show him exactly what he meant to her, and she would do so in her backyard with no compunction. Agnes would gift them privacy.

She clawed at his sodden shirt, seeking muscled flesh until she realized he had obeyed, for the walls of Barre Cottage were replaced by the wide expanse of darkness that could only come high above Torgerson Valley. Declan's shield remained steadfast, buffering them from the swirling storm that echoed the raging desire in her heart.

"*Evangeline*," he pleaded, voice tortured. "Slow down. I-I can't control myself."

She paid him no heed.

She went to her knees and undid the laces of his pants with frantic dexterity. She didn't want his control. She wanted to see him lose himself, as he had their very first night together.

She flashed him a reassuring smile. "I'll be fine. Trust me." Without waiting for his response, she took the blunt tip of him into her mouth.

His body jerked as though he'd been flogged.

Hot, hard silk upon her tongue. Another tortured groan escaped his lips, and his fingers tunneled into her hair. She worked at him until she tasted a bead of his seed. She lapped at it hungrily, half tempted to wring him dry with her lips alone. But she wanted so badly for him to be inside her.

When she tried to pull away, his hand fisted in her hair, holding her in place. She smirked. She would happily swallow every delicious drop of him if he wished. Then he drew in a shuddering breath and allowed her to rise. She stood only long enough to peel off her own wet shift and undergarments.

He watched her with rapt eyes. The glyphs on his skin swirled brighter with every passing second. She gave his chest a gentle shove, and he complied readily, lowering himself to the ground. Evangeline pressed another kiss at his defiant member as it jutted proudly, still glistening from her lips. She straddled him.

"Evangeline," he groaned. "You're not ready."

Silly man. She was *so* ready that her undergarment had been wetter than her rain-soaked shift. She shushed him with a nipping kiss, then eased over him with a moan.

So hard he was, filling and stretching her deep—the same way he filled every part of her heart, of her soul.

She began rocking her hips, relishing every moan from his lips.

Then he rose up to one elbow to clamp his mouth over her breast, and she nearly screamed from the pleasure. He shifted beneath her, parting her legs wider as he bucked his hips with a mastery that made her head roll back and her eyes shut. She clutched fistfuls of his hair to anchor herself against the tiny tremors already racking her body.

His lips curved against her breast, clearly sensing the subtle change in power between them. Soon he would have her writhing mindlessly beneath him.

But she did not intend to be ridden this time.

Vines speared from the grass, sinewy tendrils of gentle

green unfurling from the earth to loop around his wrists and tug him back to the ground.

Declan's eyes widened as the vines held his arms down like leafy manacles.

Evangeline's husky laughter drew his gaze. She straddled him like a pagan queen, wearing nothing but a wide, wicked grin.

Declan enjoyed chains in bed as much as the next man, but never had he attempted to bind her, knowing the horrors of her past. Since he cared little for being the one *in* chains, he'd never introduced bindings to their bed play.

But this wasn't a quick tryst with another faceless courtesan.

This was *Evangeline* who had him bound and clamped between her thighs. The excitement in her eyes alone was enough to make him spill prematurely. She could have him trussed up like fowl ready for the roast, and he'd happily help her light the fire in the oven.

He lay back and devoured the sight of her every move as she used him for her pleasure. Every glide of her skin against his sent a spark of power dancing through his sinew, as though she were flint and he were tinder. Actual fire threatened to spill from his veins.

Control.

She clenched over his shaft like a slippery fist, wrenching a groan from his throat. Power surged and simmered in his blood. Declan shut his eyes and diverted his powers into their surroundings, causing rocks to split from the cliff face.

Control.

She traced the symbols on his body with sultry eyes and appreciative fingers.

"I thought you were the most beautiful boy I'd ever seen. I loved you, even though I couldn't see your eyes," she whispered as she ground herself against him, her sheath tight, hot, and unbearably slick.

Declan heard the sweet shyness in her voice, recognized the child that she'd once been through her eyes.

"Even though I couldn't see you, you were my light," he said on a rasp. "My little fire."

Her smile deepened into the smirk of a woman who knew full well her power over him. She rocked her hips and took him so deep that his eyes rolled back in his head and a moan tore from his throat.

"My beautiful love, my precious heart," she said as though she could read his mind, hear his desperation, and sense his yearning. "There is no one else I'll ever crave, no other I'll ever need, no other man I'll ever want. Just you."

She hastened her movements until his breath came in ragged pants.

"Only ever you," she said between gasping breaths, causing a hot joy to explode in his chest. "Only you."

He was at the edge of spending when he saw it. Saw *her*.

On the psychic plane, pale tendrils of light spread from her mind like ethereal vines.

Her mating bond.

"Evangeline," he gasped, bucking desperately beneath her as the luminescent threads reached out to entwine with his bond of ice and fire.

She came with a spasming scream, his name flung high into the stormy skies as she crumpled onto his chest. His own euphoria blanked his mind. He knew not how long it took for his heart to regulate, but when he finally found a semblance of clarity, he realized rain cascaded over them like a fine mist. He had been in such ecstasy that his shield had barely held.

Sudden panic clutched him until he realized her fingers were caressing his chest, her body still trembling from the aftershocks of pleasure.

A grin split his face. She was *awake*.

His cheeks ached from smugness, his chest so full it threatened to explode. But his happiness only lasted for a fleeting moment before he heard the sniffle, felt the dampness on his chest. Not the coolness of the rain, but the heat of tears.

"I'm so sorry, Declan," she whispered.

He glanced down at his chest and realized she traced the spot over his heart where he should be wearing her brand.

But apart from the glyphs of his ascension, his skin remained unmarked.

TWENTY-EIGHT

Disbelief was a brick wall that battered his heart. Declan was certain he'd seen her bond manifest, felt the warmth of her light complete their mating. Yet when he receded to the mental plane, his half bond remained unchanged. Incomplete.

"I can't," she said with a bleak sob.

Panic rose again, punching holes through his chest.

"What do you mean, you *can't?*"

She shook her head. "I-I can't do it. I want so desperately to claim you . . . " She choked on a sob. "But my bond couldn't hold."

Declan shuddered with *relief*.

Gently, he tugged at the vines still holding him captive. They loosened almost reluctantly to rescind into the ground. Free, he wrapped arms over her trembling body. A body that had ridden him with such ferocity and was yet so fragile. He pushed up so he sat with her still straddling his hips. He tipped up her chin to smile into stark eyes.

"It doesn't matter, little fire."

Her brows knotted. "How can you say that? I want to, so badly. I *want* you."

A laugh escaped his throat in tandem with the bubbly sensation in his chest.

He touched his forehead to hers. "That's all that matters."

He had wanted nothing more than to complete their mating bond. He'd yearned for it. Obsessed over it. But now, he realized he didn't really need it. What he truly needed was to believe she'd chosen him—that she would always choose him—and *keep* him.

"You want me," he repeated softly. "Despite who I am, despite all the things I've done, you still want me."

She frowned. "Of course I do. I've wanted you for centuries, Declan. I'll never stop wanting you. You're irreplaceable to me." With a single breathy whisper, she reached deep into his soul and slayed all remnants of his crippling insecurities. "Precious."

The bubbly feeling in his chest overflowed to fizz in his blood.

"Foolish girl," he chided, curling his arms tighter around her. "Only you would see a moth and think it a butterfly. Mistake a monster for a man."

She glared at him, indignant. "I've met true monsters, Declan Thorne. You're not one." She kissed him with a tenderness that caused the fizzy sensation to flood his brain.

"Besides," she murmured, "moth, man, or monster—it doesn't matter to me what you are. I just want you to be mine."

She wrapped her limbs around him, curled her arms around his back, coiled her legs tight over his hips. Attaching herself to him like a human vine, making him the luckiest bastard in all the five realms. For the first time in months, he drew in an easy breath.

"I've been yours since the day you found me by the glade," he declared.

Her face crumpled. "Then why can't I claim you? I've rediscovered my use of magic, but why doesn't my bond hold against yours?"

The depth of devastation in her voice only deepened his grin.

"Mailin has a theory. She believes your recovered abilities may be those of an immortal child because they are picking up where Freya's were. She warned me you may need time to mature and grow into your powers before you're able to mate."

Declan beamed like a fool. However long it took for her abilities to *mature*, he would wait. He had all the patience in the world when he knew her choice.

She must not share his patience, for her frown deepened.

"We have time, little fire," he murmured, a reminder to her as well as himself. Never again would he stifle her. "Give yourself a chance to grow."

Gathering her tight into his arms, he warped them back to their bedchamber. He settled her on the middle of the bed and climbed over her with an eager grin. Loving her within the confines of his castle walls meant he had to be very, *very* careful to keep his powers in check or risk annihilating the room. But he had a sore need to slake, and he would be damned if he rutted her into the hard ground.

She embraced him with equal eagerness, her sigh of satisfaction the warmest of welcomes as he delved deep into her. He shuddered against the desperate want to shed the reins of control, but he pulled hard at the instinct to plunder.

Instead, he set a slow, gentle pace and kept his urges on a tight leash. He might never make love to her with true abandon, but self-control was a small price to pay. Especially when she gazed up at him with such love in her eyes. Despite all his flaws, she thought him irreplaceable.

Precious, even.

Happiness—he was drowning in it.

She leaned up on one elbow so she could better admire his sleeping form. Lying on his side, Declan rested one possessive arm over her hip, with his fingers tucked intimately between her thighs. She stroked his ruffled hair and smiled.

He didn't even stir.

Evangeline shifted and stifled a moan as her tender muscles twinged. Though Declan had been heartrendingly gentle, he'd seemed intent on making up for lost time in a single night. It wasn't until dawn breached the night sky that he allowed her sleep.

But how could she sleep when she was racked with such worry?

Her gaze landed on his chest, where her mating mark should have manifested.

Her archmage had been buoyant, clinging to Mailin's theory. He harbored hope that she would one day *mature* enough to mate. But Evangeline knew otherwise. Had she been a true immortal child, she would never have been able to summon her own urge to complete their bond. For once, Mailin was wrong.

Declan's half bond of frost and fire was simply *inimical* to the softness of her light. He was too powerful, and she, too weak. They could wait another millennium, and still she wouldn't be able to complete their bond.

They were incompatible.

Her heart twisted. The gods had made it clear that they were not meant to be, for her every attempt throughout the night had been thwarted.

An involuntary hiss escaped her lips.

She would not fall into the trap of her own insecurities. Not when Declan had made it clear he cared nothing for the bond, so long as she loved him.

Never would she doubt her claim over him. Never would she allow herself to feel unentitled. He belonged to *her*. No one else.

She curled closer to his sleeping frame, listening to the steady rhythm of his breathing, and her need to claim him heightened abruptly.

She sighed. Had she finally shed her mortal skin and slipped back into her Seelie self? Was that why she now felt the intense urge to complete their bond? She wanted him so much it resulted in a near-physical ache.

Evangeline stroked the air above the chiseled line of his jaw, careful not to disturb her lover's slumber. A lover who called her his little fire, his source of light.

Yet *he* was *her* light. Her beacon. Even in the Abyss, she'd clung desperately to her promise to return to him. Memories of him had kept her sane in that gray and amorphous prison. Her one promise of warmth.

She may be his little fire, but he was her winter sun.

Evangeline gave in to temptation and leaned close to kiss the hollow above his collarbone when she heard a loud, scandalized "Oh!"

A maidservant stood by the doorway, eyes filled with surprise and hands filled with linen sheets. "My deepest apologies, sire . . . Lady Barre. I didn't realize you were still abed."

Roused by the maid's exclamation, Declan lifted a sleepy head.

"Get out," he mumbled before burrowing his face into the curve of Evangeline's neck. The maid stammered a string of incoherent apologies, bowed jerkily, and disappeared through the doorway.

Half distracted by Declan's nuzzling, Evangeline frowned.

"Who was that?" she asked.

"Ginley," he muttered into her hair as his hand roved up her belly to fondle her breasts.

"What happened to Tessa?"

"Who?" His hand roamed back down to caress her rear.

"Tessa. The girl who cleans our bedchamber every morning."

He gave a drowsy grunt in response. "Who cares?"

Evangeline sighed and wriggled out of his grasp. "Sleep," she said, and his thick eyelashes closed to form crescent fans. "But I wish to speak to the maid."

There was something rather dubious about Ginley. Maids knew better than to enter their archmage's chambers so boldly. At the very least, Tessa had always knocked before bustling in.

Declan's protest was another grunt as his hands reached for her, but she pressed a firm kiss to his cheek. "I'll be back to join you in a few minutes," she promised.

He relented with a rare pout that had her laughing and leaning in for another kiss before she slipped from their bed. Pulling on the nearest silken robe, she hurried out the door.

The hallway was not crowded, but far from deserted. A couple of maids dawdled, gossiping between tasks, an errand boy darted past, and a scribe laden with scrolls made his way to the library. Evangeline ignored them all and searched for the dark-haired maidservant. She caught the flash of a blue kirtle at the end of the lengthy corridor.

"Ginley, wait!" Evangeline called, loud enough to draw the

attention of every person in the vast hallway. "May I have a word?"

She hurried down the corridor. At the woman's austere frown, Evangeline blinked in recognition. This was the same maid who had swept up broken glasses in the infirmary—the one who hadn't been shy with her censure.

"*Madam* Ginley, my lady," the maid retorted in a sullen tone. "I am the head chamberlain of the castle."

"Madam Ginley," Evangeline repeated with an apologetic nod. "I was wondering about Tessa. She is usually the one who freshens our bedchamber."

"Begging your pardon, Lady Barre," Ginley said with a prim sniff. "Before you moved into the sire's rooms, *I* was the one he trusted to clean his quarters. Tessa had replaced me because she'd been designated as your handmaid. Since you left . . . " A tart look. "I thought it fitting to resume my duties."

Evangeline blinked. "I see."

"Shall I send Tessa to help with your needs, then?"

"No, thank you." Evangeline retreated a step. "That won't be necessary."

Ginley's lips flattened to a line as she gave Evangeline an assessing glance, lips curling at her bare feet. "Perhaps it's more necessary than you believe, my lady. Your presentation reflects upon the sire, after all." The chamberlain sniffed. "Of course, it's not your fault. If you'd been trained at the Keep, you'd know these things."

Evangeline stiffened. "And what education did you have prior to becoming head chamberlain, Madam Ginley?"

The woman's chest puffed. "I need no education. I've worked in this castle for eight centuries. I became the head chamberlain purely on the merits of my hard work."

Evangeline straightened her spine, yet she was still a

handspan shy of meeting the haughty chamberlain's eyes. She tilted her chin for extra height.

"The Keep is meant for ayaris. I am no ayari, but your liege's elorin de ana. I need no education to love him. I am the elorin of Amereen because I hold his heart."

Evangeline turned on her heel and cast the madam a sidelong glance. "Next time I see you in the hallway, I expect you to greet me accordingly."

TWENTY-NINE

"What's this?" Evangeline glanced up from the pile of threats she'd been thumbing through in attempt to identify more reason from the rhyme of malice.

Declan sat down on the settee beside her with a black velvet box in his hands.

The last time he'd presented her with a similar box, it'd had the symbol of their first night spent in his chambers. Since then, he'd made a habit of draping precious stones over her body on a whim.

"I'll soon need a treasure chest for all the jewelry you've given me," Evangeline exclaimed, only half jesting.

Declan tapped her nose with a gentle finger. "You're meant to wear them, not keep them buried in a chest."

"But I do." Evangeline fingered the golden elder tree tipped with emerald leaves hanging around her throat. It was by far her favorite piece and one she kept tucked beneath her clothes—but she wore few others. "Jewelry often gets in the way when one is working in the infirmary."

Declan shook his head. His lips curved in quiet amusement before he handed her the velvet box. "Well, I hope you'll find this more useful."

She opened it with a small smile, then she blinked. "A . . . glove of some kind?"

Declan's chuckle was a delicious rumble in her ear as he leaned close to remove his gift from the box. "A spyblade," he murmured. "I had it specially made for you."

Only when he held it up did she realize the spyblade was designed to be worn like a bracer over her forearm. The actual blade was concealed within the finest leather. A series of miniature cogs responsible for deploying the blade was attached to a delicate chain with a gold hoop.

Declan pushed up the billowing fabric of her bell-shaped sleeves and helped her with the thin leather straps. He fiddled with the fastenings and examined her forearm with his brow knotted in concentration. When he finally seemed satisfied, he slipped the hoop over her middle finger, as though it were nothing more than an innocuous ring.

"Tilt your wrist upward as far as you can, then tug at the gold chain with your thumb."

Evangeline followed his instructions and her breath hitched.

A steel knife slid from its sheath, its deadly point reminiscent of a sharpened fang.

"It's too fine to kill, but certainly enough to debilitate." He clicked a small button near her wrist that wound the knife back into place. "The blade is short, so you must ensure you know exactly where to aim." He guided her hand toward a place beneath his pectorals. "Position your hand here, and the blade will slide right through the rib cage and nick the heart."

Then he tugged her hand up to the hollow of his neck. "Here, pressed deep, will be enough to puncture a throat."

Evangeline pulled her hand away. The mere thought of aiming it at him caused a sickness in her gut. She studied the spyblade with a frown. "Why are you giving me this?"

He had given her flowers and fripperies, jewels and trinkets. But since the last time he'd allowed her to handle the *draga sul* in the shadow realm, he hadn't gifted her a weapon.

Declan shrugged, his gaze flicking over to the pile of threats strewn on the settee. "It eases my mind to know you'll have something more than your wit or magic to defend yourself . . . should you ever feel the need to venture from the castle and find yourself without your guard."

Evangeline blinked up at him. Her heart swelled. It was a seemingly small gesture, but a great leap from his compulsive need to wrap her in cotton wool.

She caught him by the collar. By the time she pulled back in favor of breath, his eyes were glazed.

"Lex was wrong," Declan muttered, as though to himself. "Women clearly fancy weapons far more than jewelry."

Evangeline snickered and leaned back against him to better admire her new adornment. As she deployed and retracted the spyblade again and again, Declan busied himself with her stack of threats, studying each one with a furrowed brow.

"I do not believe my councilors wrote these," he murmured after a long moment. "I have read their reports for years, and I am familiar with their penmanship. But this,"—he shook his head—"is not familiar to me."

Evangeline bit her lower lip, then blurted, "Would you be familiar with your head chamberlain's handwriting?"

Never again would she keep her thoughts from her archmage.

"Ginley?" Declan's head cocked.

"I'm not saying it was her. But . . . " Evangeline began recounting Ginley's censure from their previous encounters.

"Also, it would be all too easy for her to slip in and out of our chamber without raising any suspicion . . . Declan? What's wrong?"

Tension had stiffened his muscles. "First Reyas, and now *Ginley?*" His lips thinned. "Tell me, little fire, who else has spoken to you with such audacity?"

Evangeline's eyes widened at the grimness in his tone, and she quickly shook her head.

Declan pinned her with a look.

"No one else," she insisted. At his continued scrutiny, she sighed and shrugged. "Though I am certain many in your employ share Ginley and Reyas's beliefs . . . even if they do keep their thoughts to themselves."

"I will have the name of every person who has dared make you feel this way."

Evangeline sighed. "Declan . . . "

"Disrespect toward you is *not* an option, little fire."

She shook her head, exasperation and adoration welling simultaneously in her chest for this man. "And what do you intend to do with these people?"

He eased back with a faint smile that was more alarming than assuring. "Only to remind them of who you are, and what you mean to me. And on the chance that they are involved in threatening you"—a dangerous flash crossed his eyes—"they will be dealt with accordingly."

A soft knock at the door interrupted their conversation. Declan tucked the threats behind his back while Evangeline jerked her bell sleeve down to cover her newest *plaything* before calling, "Come in!"

There was something intimate about the weapon. It was a secret she didn't want to share with anyone else.

Tessa pushed a trolley laden with food into the antechamber. Her face lit up as she viewed Evangeline, though her eyes shied from Declan's chest exposed by his unbuttoned shirt.

"Sire." Tessa bobbed a curtsy and shot Evangeline a delighted smile. "My lady, it is so wonderful to see you home."

Declan waited until Tessa disappeared through the door before he said, "Ginley may have the means, but there is clearly another possibility you have not considered."

Evangeline arched her brow, incredulous. "Tessa?"

He settled her on the settee before moving to uncover the plates on the trolley. "The maid has the same access as Ginley. She has worked in the castle for a handful of years as opposed to Ginley's centuries. Her loyalty to me has not been tested against time. In fact, she knows your daily movements and your habits better than any other staff member. Who better than her?"

Evangeline shook her head. "Tessa would *never*."

Declan's continued gaze spurred her on.

"Tessa's not just a handmaid. She's my friend . . . " Evangeline bit her lower lip.

It wouldn't be the first time she'd been betrayed by someone she considered a friend.

It was Declan's turn to sigh as he placed two plates and levitated another two onto the table before tipping up her chin to peer into her eyes.

"Your heart is too trusting, my little fire. Sometimes it blinds you to the things you do not wish to see."

Evangeline swallowed. "Ginley clearly thinks me inadequate for you. It makes sense that she would want to see me go. But Tessa has been nothing but nice to me from the very beginning—what could her motives be?" She blew out a frustrated sigh. "And we could be completely mistaken. Really, *anyone* could have snuck into our chambers."

"It is simple enough to find out," Declan said as he selected a roll stuffed with sliced meats and cheese. It disappeared in three bites before he picked up another. At her questioning glance, he levitated a pastry into her hand.

"I'll just have her mind scoured. If she is found innocent, I'll move down our list of suspects until we find the perpetrator."

"Scoured?" Evangeline blinked. "What? Like . . . prying into her mind?"

Declan nodded. "Not a pleasant process. Every mind is resistant to forced telepathy." A flippant shrug. "But it does no more than give mages a headache, maybe some nausea. Fortunately Tessa is not human. They tend to go insane from the process."

Evangeline parted her lips in shock while Declan wolfed down his second roll and reached for a bowl of scrambled eggs, utterly oblivious to her horror.

"That's a violation."

Declan chuckled, but the mirth in his eyes quickly dissipated when he met hers. He swallowed. "That may be so, but forced telepathy *is* indisputably the fastest and the most effective way."

"The most effective way?" Evangeline shook her head. "It's . . . rape, Declan. Mind rape."

Declan coughed as he choked between bites.

"I won't have Tessa, Madam Ginley, or anyone else for that matter, subjected to such a violation based on nothing more than speculation."

Declan frowned down into his half-eaten roll. "I never thought of it that way before," he mumbled. "But I suppose you're right."

Evangeline stared at him with sick suspicion. "Has anyone *scoured* your mind in the past?"

A slow moment ticked by, and Declan nodded without

lifting his gaze. "Corvina used to do it when I couldn't explain myself quickly enough."

Anger constricted her throat. The she-devil. Though Evangeline found a small measure of comfort in knowing Declan was now free from his miserable excuse for a mother, she drew him close to pepper him with kisses—to calm herself. When she was suitably soothed, she settled back against the settee and turned her attention to the pastry in her hand.

A little breathless from her attentions, Declan said, "I'll find a less intrusive method."

Evangeline grinned and swallowed a bite before saying, "Well, I am not exactly against your *methods* employed on the guilty. I just want to be absolutely certain of our suspect before subjecting them to forced telepathy. That's all."

"And how do you propose to be absolutely certain?"

Evangeline smirked. "Have you ever set a mousetrap, Archmage?"

Declan strode down the hallway to the infirmary with determination in his steps and a lightness in his chest. If he was to be worthy of Evangeline, some changes had to be made. He mulled over the right words, but before he made it to his destination, a couple exited from a patient ward into the hallway.

Laughter and lighthearted banter quieted as they sighted him.

"Sire," Killian said with a curt bow. Mailin echoed her mate's greeting but remained uncharacteristically silent. They continued past him, and Declan said, "I've brought Evangeline home."

Killian nodded. "We know. She was in the ward with Gabriel earlier this morning."

Of course. Evangeline had told him as much.

The commander shuffled his feet, then met Declan's gaze, a genuine smile on his face. "Sire, we are pleased to see you and Lady Barre . . . reconciled."

The healer, however, flattened her lips. "Evie has the heart of a newborn lamb. That girl would likely forgive anything in time."

Declan averted his gaze, chastised by the truth behind Mailin's scorn. Then he cleared his throat. "I was looking for Gabriel."

Mailin raised her brows. "Gabriel? He's long gone. Departed the moment Evie had him healed enough to get up from bed."

Declan's lips parted. *That* he had not known. He'd woken from the most satisfying sleep to Evangeline's excited mental chatter informing him that she had managed to *fix* Gabriel's collapsed lung. Where Declan had long since recovered from the scrapes from the altercation, Gabriel had remained convalescent. Faekind might be immortal, but their regenerative abilities could hardly compare to those of an archmage.

With another one or two sessions, I'm certain Gabriel will be fully healed, Evangeline had announced brightly through the mental plane. For a soul as compassionate as hers, regaining the ability to heal was akin to a rambunctious child receiving a play sword. He hadn't seen her the whole day, as she'd scampered from ward to ward, eagerly seeking fresh wounds in need of healing.

Her effervescence, however, only dredged up an acute sense of guilt and a hefty dose of shame in Declan. He had consciously shelved his thoughts where Gabriel was concerned. Now the fae wasn't even at the castle for his intended amends.

Mailin bobbed another one of her stiff-backed curtsies, one hand over the rounded bump of her belly, breaking his sheepish thoughts. "If there is nothing else you require of us, sire, we will be on our way."

"I appreciate it," Declan said to their retreating backs.

Killian turned to regard him with a questioning frown. "Sire?"

Stifling the urge to warp, Declan tucked his hands into his pockets and forced the words from his throat. "I appreciate all the years you've both stood by me. And more recently, for your willingness to intervene. I . . . have behaved poorly. For that, I would apologize." Declan bowed his head. "And express my gratitude."

His lead battlemage blinked, utterly bemused, and Mailin's wide-eyed expression made Declan shift his feet, eager to be on his way.

"Sire," Mailin called after him, delaying his escape. "Not once have Killian and I regretted our decision to make our home here or to serve you. Never have we regretted our choice of allegiance."

Instead of giving one of her recent stiff curtsies, Mailin offered him an easy smile, lifting the awkwardness from the air until the curve of her lips turned into a haughty smirk. "I must admit, I already knew Evie was back even before I saw her in the infirmary this morning. In fact, I'm sure the whole castle knows by now."

Declan frowned.

Mailin's eyes twinkled. "Anyone who has ventured past the gardens near your quarters could easily have guessed."

Follugowing Mailin's cryptic comment, Declan warped into the gardens abutting his private quarters, expecting to find destruction. Though he had no recollection of redirecting his powers. He had been so careful . . .

His jaw hung.

Evangeline couldn't blame him for her humiliation this time.

A climbing rose bush had infiltrated the gardens overnight. Slim branches now scaled the sandstone wall, as though the plant attempted to scale to the balcony of his bedchamber. Blooms dripped in spectacular clusters of white, contributing to the saccharine fragrance of the gardens. Wildflowers had also sprung up to sprinkle the perfectly manicured lawn with spots of color. Tiny daisies, pink freesias, and bright orange poppies waved their cheery heads at him. Even the recently replanted alder sapling had grown at least a foot taller.

Declan sniggered, perversely pleased.

His little fire would be mortified to discover her pleasure and passion so clearly etched onto the castle grounds. Out of sheer curiosity, Declan trailed the garden path by foot. How far did her magic extend?

Everywhere he ventured, blooms appeared larger, grass greener, and colors somehow more vibrant. Wonderment filled his chest. How could Evangeline's magic have such far-reaching effects? Soon he ventured into a section of the gardens that displayed a group of marble statues. The curve on his lips flattened.

Alexander sat beside the sculpture of a drakghi frozen in fierce animation with wings stretched in flight, jaws snarling at prey no one else saw.

Alexander shot to his feet. "Brother?" His physical bruises

had long since dissapeared, but the glumness on his face indicated deeper, festering wounds.

Declan made his way over. "It's come to my attention that you were responsible for terminating a ring of usurers involved in the trade of children."

Alexander nodded.

"That was good work, Lex."

Faint surprise colored tawny eyes, but Alexander kept his chin dipped. "Only at the expense of Evie's safety."

"Evangeline would have found a way to help the woman had you refused." Declan released a soft exhale before saying, "I should not have reacted the way I did, Lex. I have shamed myself."

Alexander's gaze widened. "It is I who should bear the shame. I have failed you, brother. I should have handled the whole situation differently." Alexander rubbed a hand at the back of his neck and shook his head. "I know what she means to you, yet I have not been careful with protecting what you hold most dear."

"Evangeline can be rather persuasive if she wants to be." Declan shot his brother a wry smile.

Alexander's throat worked. "Still, I am sorry for the damage I've caused. I never meant to betray your trust."

The sincere regret in Alexander's tone caused Declan to meet his gaze. Declan frowned, suddenly aware of how much Lex had grown. An odd ache pinched his chest. "And I should have listened before I reacted," Declan murmured.

Alexander was his younger *brother*. One he'd inadvertently raised over the centuries to be a man he trusted with more than his own life. "If there is anyone I trust to keep Evangeline safe in my absence, it is you."

A long moment passed while Alexander simply stared.

Then the wily blackguard ambushed him so rapidly Declan didn't have time to warp.

"I won't disappoint you again, brother," Alexander said, his voice muffled as he held Declan in a stifling embrace. Lex had always been the tactile sort.

Stiffly, Declan issued an awkward pat to his brother's back. "How would you like to prove yourself?"

THIRTY

Evangeline shoved open the wrought-iron doors and stormed into the taphouse. It was a crowded night. *Perfect.* Women draped themselves over lounges or the laps of their next pleasure, some already indulging themselves in darkened corners. But all eyes widened as they noted her presence and quickly slunk out of her way.

Evangeline's gaze narrowed at one of the curved nooks in the recesses of the room that held a small crowd. Alexander sat amid laughter and fawning courtesans, raising his glass to three other men Evie recognized as councilors. But her eyes were drawn to the cluster of women gathered on the plush maroon divan, cooing over a single man.

A courtesan served as his recliner, her arms and legs wrapped sinuously around him as she hugged him from the back. Another appeared to be nibbling at his earlobe while a third kneaded his shoulders. The same shoulders Evangeline had lavished with kisses the night prior as he'd pounded her into their bed.

A rash of true anger heated her blood, and her fingers curled.

Declan hadn't yet noticed her, for he was distracted by the fourth courtesan straddling his lap. The brunette had already shed half her clothes, revealing undergarments of glittering scraps. Her hands were roving over muscles that weren't hers to touch, her mouth kissing lips that weren't hers to taste.

A ragged sob surged up Evangeline's throat, quieting the hum of conversation and laughter around her. Before she knew it, she had a fistful of the woman's hair and was jerking the whore from his lap.

"How *could* you?" Evangeline hissed.

The courtesans took one look at her face and scattered like larder mice before a cat, but Declan only met her gaze with unabashed boldness. His eyes were hooded, his hair disheveled, and his lips bruised. A slow curve tugged at the side of his lips.

In that moment, the illusion was so real that Evangeline had the urge to screech and scratch. She gritted her teeth, trying to bank the fire blazing in her belly. Not real, she reminded herself. Just a charade. Yet her heart pounded, and the tips of her ears and canines lengthened without effort.

"Little fire," he crooned and patted his vacated lap. "Come. Join us."

"I don't think that's a good idea," Alexander said hastily as he rose by way of intervention. "Evie, let me walk you back to your chambers."

Evangeline silenced him with a withering glare.

Declan chuckled as he rose from his seat to loom over her, playing his role to perfection. "Worry not, Lex. My elorin de ana can join us if she so pleases."

"How dare you call me elorin while you consort with

these . . . " Evangeline bared her fangs and hissed at the still-staring courtesans.

The curve of his lips deepened into a grin. "Jealousy is rather unbecoming on you."

He hauled her close, handling her with a rare roughness that had her gasping. Another woman's perfume wafted between them, cloyed by the scent of hard liquor.

Evangeline batted at him, but he only gave a crude laugh.

"I'd be happy to fuck you first, if you prefer."

Evangeline gaped. He was *truly* foxed.

With a fist in her hair, he jerked her head back to expose her throat. Then he leaned close and licked the length of her neck, sending an involuntary frisson of lust dancing down her spine. Evangeline shoved hard at him, but he barely budged.

"You're disgusting!" She slapped at his hands.

Annoyance flickered over his face, then his lips curled in contempt. "Isn't this what *you* wanted? Did you not think me overbearing? Desire more space?" He threw a smirk over his shoulder and corralled a bout of uncertain laughter from his wary councilors, clearly thrown by their archmage's uncharacteristic behavior.

"Unlike you," Declan said, his voice slightly slurred, "other women covet my attentions."

"Bastard!" She shoved at his chest. "Cheating bastard!"

His grip firmed. "Do not forget to whom you speak. I have the right to every female in my lands. I can take whom I want, when I want."

As if to demonstrate, he seized her by her chin, his grip hard and unyielding. He forced her lips to his, one hand groping at her hips as though to lift her skirts. Her primal instincts rose to the fore, and her hand cracked against his cheek.

The harsh slap echoed in the now-silent room of shocked spectators.

Declan turned slowly to regard her with hard eyes. His cheek bore the imprint of her hand. The markings on his skin flared an otherworldly gold, and the crowd skittered back.

He released an acerbic laugh. "Was that supposed to hurt?"

Her lips trembled. This was yet another side of him she'd never glimpsed—one capable of crass cruelty. She blinked, willing herself to stay in the moment.

She stifled a sob. "Fuck you!"

The onlookers released a collective gasp, and Evangeline felt a hysterical urge to laugh. She'd overdone it. No one insulted an archmage so blatantly and walked away unscathed.

His eyes narrowed to slits.

Invisible hands wrenched her up into the air without warning, so she dangled by her wrists. She writhed and kicked. No one came to her aid. No one dared.

"Let me go! Bastard!"

Declan only levitated her higher, invisible bonds holding her hands over her head. It reminded her far too much of the time monsters had once chained her in a dilapidated cabin. She peeled back her lips in a hiss and hurled another imprecation. In the next instant, the binds at her wrists loosened and she went crashing to the ground with a shocked yelp.

Declan's eyes widened, and in that fleeting moment, his facade fractured.

Evangeline grabbed a glass from the table and launched it at him. It cracked against his chest as though he were truly fashioned of stone, and the shards splintered on the ground.

"Don't you *ever* touch me again."

With another imperious curl of his lips, he scoffed. "While you reside on my lands, you will be mine to have when and where I please."

Evangeline picked herself up from the floor and fled.

"That must have been quite a nasty fall you took." Mailin tutted with a disapproving shake of her head as she examined Evangeline's sprained wrist.

Declan stiffened. His throat worked frenetically as if to tame a tempest raging in his chest. "I didn't mean to . . . I-I don't *know* what happened." He scrubbed a hand against his temple. "I shouldn't have drunk so much Mujarin."

The remorse in his tone had Evangeline pulling from Mailin's grasp to face him. "It doesn't hurt very much."

Mailin arched her brows. "It's going to swell."

"Even better." Evangeline conjured a wide grin for Declan's benefit. "And when you give me more bruises, it should make it even more compelling."

Alexander crossed his arms where he stood. "How will that even work?"

"Healing is the act of gifting energy," Evangeline said, attempting to simplify the convoluted theory in her head. "Seelie heal by drawing magic from the environment and channeling it into a wound. But as a halfbreed, Mailin also possesses some psychic abilities. In the way true telepathy enables two-way communication, Mailin should be able to *absorb* energy the same way she gifts it."

The halfbreed shot a worried glance at Evangeline. "But the act of absorbing is not something that comes naturally to me. I'm not sure if I can do it . . . or control it once I begin reversing my abilities."

Declan dragged a hand through the short strands of his hair with a harsh exhale. "I do not like this. Why must we go to such lengths? Wasn't our act sufficient?"

Evangeline released a considering hum. "One small argument is hardly going to convince people that I'll be driven from your protection."

"One small argument?" Declan scowled at her wrist. "You slapped me, and I . . . I *hurt* you." The latter of his words were hushed, spoken as though he'd committed the worst form of sacrilege.

Evangeline cringed and rose to her toes to press a pacifying kiss on his assaulted cheek. "I had to make it look convincing." Then she narrowed her eyes, body tensing from the recollection. "Although I didn't think you'd actually allow a woman to crawl down your throat."

Declan's scowl deepened. "Why do you think I consumed so much Mujarin? It was the most demeaning thing I've ever done."

Evangeline pinched her lips together. "Was it truly so terrible to have all those beautiful women touching you?"

His nod was grim. "It was easier when I imagined them to be you."

The courtesans he'd selected *did* resemble her in coloring and size. Her lips twitched, and she softened as Declan tugged her into his arms.

"You're the only one I'll ever want," he murmured, voice growing husky.

"Are you sure? From what I saw, you appeared quite engrossed."

"Because I convinced myself she was you." He pressed a tender kiss to her wrist, and Evangeline leaned into him with a breathy sigh.

Mailin snickered openly while Alexander masked a gag with a cough. "For all that's divine, the two of you are even worse than Mailin and Killian were when they first moved in."

Mailin rolled her eyes and patted her belly with a shake of her head. "Killian and I were never so lovestruck."

Alexander scoffed. "Is that so? Funny. I distinctly recall the both of you steaming up the air . . . " The pair continued ribbing at each other in the background.

Declan ignored them and frowned down at Evangeline's wrist, his thumb rubbing gently at the small bruising patch. "I really don't like this."

Evangeline sighed. "We'll need whoever it is who wants me to leave to believe that I am truly on my own. Do you think people will believe I would flee from you after a single disagreement?"

Alexander grinned. "I wholeheartedly agree, brother. Your performance was convincing, but most will assume your behavior borne of inebriation."

Declan scowled again.

Alexander only shrugged. "I did tell you not to drink overmuch."

Declan sighed and shot Mailin a begrudging nod. "Small bruises. And make sure they don't hurt."

Resignation filled Mailin's tone, and creases marred her forehead. "I'll try."

Evangeline offered her other hand, and Mailin clasped fingers over her forearm.

Nothing happened.

Mailin exhaled after another long pause. "I can't do it, Evie."

Evangeline bit down on her lower lip. She'd known the act wouldn't come easily to a healer. "Don't think of it as hurting someone, but as an act of helping."

Mailin shook her head and shut her eyes. Instead of the warmth of the healer's usual touch, a numbing cold spread at the contact. Evangeline shivered, and Mailin withdrew her hand. Declan's sharp intake of breath and Alexander's low whistle drowned out her own gasp.

She rubbed at the spot where Mailin's hands had been.

A twinge of soreness was all she felt, but no one would miss the patch blooming like a purple rose against her skin.

Evangeline grinned. "Perfect."

THIRTY-ONE

"Thank you, Tessa," Evangeline murmured after she took a sip from the steaming mug. Tessa's kovi teas always soothed her nerves.

Tessa acknowledged with a smile that didn't quite reach her eyes—the maid's gaze still lingered on the bruise decorating Evangeline's neck.

Evangeline licked her lips nervously, returned her gaze to the gilded mirror on her dressing table, and resumed the silent task of brushing her hair. Tessa might be her designated handmaid, but Evangeline had long since dismissed the maid's desire to help her in daily grooming. No matter who she had been or who she had become, she would always be Evangeline Barre, daughter of a bighearted apothecarist from a simple village.

"Evie, I may be overstepping my boundaries, but are you all right?" Tessa asked after a taut pause.

Evangeline ducked her head, afraid Tessa would see the deception in her eyes.

"Declan has been . . . " She faltered. *Obsessively kissing my fake bruises every night. Making love to me as though his life depended on it.* Evangeline bit down on her lip and choked out, "Rather displeased with me."

"The *sire* left all those bruises on you?"

Over the last two weeks, Evangeline had been careful to perpetuate their farce, making a point to shoo Declan from their bed well before Tessa arrived in the mornings. Evangeline rarely left the bedchamber and when she did, was careful to don the dejected expression of a scorned lover whenever she came into the presence of councilors and chambermaids alike. The hardest part of the farce, however, was ensuring the maid caught glimpses of her fake bruises by *accident*.

Evangeline set the brush down on her dresser and gave a sullen nod while guilt perforated her gut. Tessa's expression held nothing but disbelief and concern. Evangeline swallowed her discomfort, reminding herself that the plan would as easily prove Tessa's innocence as it would her guilt.

"He scares me," Evangeline added, injecting a waver in her voice. "I've made a terrible mistake . . . and now there's no way for me to leave."

"You mean to *leave* the sire?"

Evangeline kept her eyes averted as she murmured, "If only," hoping her evasive gaze would be perceived as grief. After a long pause, Tessa lowered her voice and whispered, "I can help you."

Evangeline's heart thudded. "How will you help me flee an archmage?"

"An archmage may rule supreme in their lands, but they have no say outside their borders."

"Gabriel was the only person who could help me slip past Declan's wards unnoticed," Evangeline said. "Now he's gone, I can never hope to go past the wards or stray from the guards. I will never see Amereen's borders."

"The guards are of little consequence," Tessa said with a confidence unexpected from a maidservant. "But the wards are your true barrier, for they are linked to the sire's consciousness." A sly smile trailed unease down Evangeline's spine. "But even an archmage needs sleep."

"**D**id you add the whole vial to his drink like I told you?" Tessa's voice was a low whisper, even though there was no one about the moonlit pavilion to hear them.

Evangeline nodded as she adjusted her hood, not trusting herself to speak in case her tone revealed her resentment.

"Good." Tessa secured her travel sack to her sand-colored gelding.

Evangeline stroked the glossy black mane of the smaller mare Tessa intended for her. The horse flicked its tail and whickered, nudging at Evangeline's palm, rooting for treats.

"Let's go," Tessa said. "No amount of sedative will keep an archmage down for long."

The powdered substance was no mere sedative. Evangeline bit down on her lower lip, trying to tamp down the urge to hiss. "Are you sure about this?" she whispered instead. "There's no returning to the castle. And if we get caught . . . "

Already mounted, Tessa stared down at her intently. "Did you use the entire vial?"

At Evangeline's nod, the maid further prodded, "Did he consume it all?"

Evangeline gave another silent nod, and Tessa shook her head, clearly impatient. "Railea's breath, if so, we have nothing to fear. The sire won't be conscious, not for hours to come . . . Don't tell me you're changing your mind now?"

Evangeline met Tessa's eyes, and guilt coursed through her. Ending the farce now would do nothing but prove Tessa to be a handmaid with questionable connections. Connections that gave her access to substances a normal citizen of Amereen should never have.

"That girl is more dangerous than I thought," Declan had snarled the night prior. *"If she had means to acquire such poisons, what could she have done to you?"*

Though Evangeline had been livid when she'd realized the sort of poison Tessa had intended for her archmage, she was not eager to condemn the maid. Not if Tessa believed she was helping her. And if Tessa proved innocent of the threats . . . Evangeline would still protect her from Declan's wrath.

No, her ploy must continue.

"I'm worried about the guards. That's all." Evangeline was no seasoned rider, but she could ride astride well enough. Using the bench in place of a mounting block, she climbed onto the mare with little difficulty.

"Just keep your hood up and your head down. Leave all the talking to me."

Following Tessa's lead, Evangeline guided her mount through the castle grounds until they arrived at the heavily guarded entrance.

"Halt right there! What's your destination and purpose?" A guard moved close enough that Evangeline glimpsed boots and black metal greaves in her periphery.

"Philip." Tessa's voice took on a sultry quality Evangeline had never heard before. "It's me."

"Tessa?" The guard sounded surprised. "Where are you headed at this late hour?"

"To the village Arns," Tessa replied. "And we cannot be

stalled. Lady Barre's mother is suffering from red fever." A debilitating illness that afflicted magekind, which lasted for months.

"*Red* fever? You'll be away for a while, then?"

"Likely. As you can imagine, Lady Barre is aggrieved and has sent us to her mother's aid for as long as she ails."

Philip took another step closer. "Will Lady Barre not return to care for her mother herself?"

"The sire won't allow it," Tessa said with her voice discreetly lowered. "Which is precisely why Lady Barre has sent Eloisa and me in her stead. You understand . . . "

By now, everyone in the castle had heard of Evangeline's tiff with Declan in the lounge. Including Mailin's well-fanned whispers of the conspicuous bruises marring their new lady's skin.

The guard shifted as though in consideration, then he moved close to Evangeline's horse. Evangeline tightened her fingers over the reins. Before the guard could peer beneath her hood, Tessa murmured, "Eloisa has a skin condition. Afford the girl some privacy, won't you?"

Philip seemed to hesitate, but he must have relented because his boots moved from her sight. The portcullis lifted with a heavy groan. Wordlessly, the women spurred their mares through the wrought-iron gates. Soon they came to the golden line that bisected the field several yards from their exit. The castle wards. When they passed without consequence, a wide, conspiratorial grin lit Tessa's face.

Tessa guided Evangeline from the twisty main road that led to the harbor and the capital, opting for a beaten-down trail into the woods. When the castle was nothing but a speck in the horizon behind them, Evangeline slowed her mare to a canter to glance behind her shoulder. The only thing buoying her spirits was the knowledge of her archmage's ability to warp and retrieve her no matter their distance.

Tessa misread her longing. "Is he awake? Looking for you?"

Evangeline shook her head.

Obvious relief crossed Tessa's features. "If he wakes prematurely and seeks you, feed him an excuse as to why you are not in his bed. All we need is to stall him till dawn. By then, we'll be too far from the castle for him to track you easily. If it all goes to plan, we'll be at the Yarveric border by midday."

"What will *you* do in Yarveric?"

"Help you disappear. What else?"

Evangeline frowned at Tessa's matter-of-fact response. Could the other woman truly be a devoted friend intent on helping her escape? Evangeline had wholeheartedly believed Tessa's sincerity, otherwise she would never have devised such an elaborate ruse to keep Tessa from having her mind reaped. Yet the moment Tessa had handed her the vial . . .

"How did you come by the sedative?"

"I told you I got it from a shady apothecary in the capital."

The lie was so outlandish that Evangeline felt a rash of anger. "No apothecarist in Amereen has the means to acquire grootworm venom."

A venom from a snake indigenous only to the far-off lands of Batuhan. A substance so rare that it was strictly regulated and never allowed beyond the kingdom's borders. The only reason Evangeline recognized it was because Agnes had once served as an apothecarist in Batuhan, long before she'd met her mate and followed him to Amereen.

"A thimbleful is enough to paralyze a human man."

And Tessa had given her enough to fell a horse.

"Grootworm?" Tessa's laugh took on a high-pitched quality. "I don't even know what that is. Surely you're mistaken."

"My mother hailed from Batuhan. She used to tame snakes and other poisonous creatures for her brews. I know groot-worm venom when I see it." Evangeline slowed her horse to a halt. Now that they were out of the castle, she would have the truth. There would be little sense in riding halfway across the kingdom for a ruse she was no longer certain protected the right person.

Tessa slowed her mount and canted her head back. Defiance darkened her expression. "Even if it is, no amount of poison can kill an archmage."

"No, but archmages feel pain like everyone else. Given that amount, Declan would be paralyzed for hours while his veins constrict and his blood coagulates."

The vehemence in her tone caused Tessa to narrow her eyes. "You're upset to cause him a little pain? What about all the times he's hurt you?"

Evangeline jerked up her hood as her chest heaved. "Tessa—"

"Railea's tears, are you *still* in love with him?" At Evangeline's expression, the maid threw up her hands. "Impossible! What is it with women and that man? I fail to see his appeal!"

Tessa dismounted with an angry curse, pacing toward the closest tree, where her boot connected with a loud thud. Another kick. Then the little maid pulled at her curls and paced, hurling maledictions alongside Declan's name.

Unsettled by Tessa's reaction, Evangeline blurted, "Do you have anything to do with the threats in my dresser?"

Tessa's sharp intake of breath was admission enough. Disappointment weighed on her chest like a brick, but a promise was a promise. With a heavy sigh, Evangeline projected her thoughts. *You were right, Archmage . . .*

Declan's response was immediate. Quiet fury laced every word. *She will be punished.*

Wait, she said. *I wish to understand her reason.*

What is there to understand? Exasperation brimmed in Declan's tone. *When I scour her mind, we will know everything we need to know.*

Evangeline swallowed. The thought of Declan *scouring* anyone's mind made her innards feel greasy.

"Did you write them?" Evangeline dismounted from her own mare. "I need the truth, Tessa. Otherwise I can no more spare you from Declan's wrath than I can shield you from the light of the moon."

"You . . . this is a trap?" Tessa's eyes widened, and her mouth twisted as though she'd drunk a glassful of bitterberries. "But the sire drinking each night . . . Those bruises on your skin . . . "

"The truth, Tessa. I need you to tell me the truth."

"I didn't write them." Tessa punctuated the statement with another kick to the tree. "I knew it was a bad idea from the start. I never wanted to do it. I just wanted things to go back to the way they were . . . "

What is happening? Declan sounded harried, and Evangeline knew he was likely pacing wherever he was. *I do not like this, little fire. Let me come to you now.*

"I believe you," Evangeline said aloud even as she gave Declan a mollifying caress with her mind. *Allow me more time, Archmage.*

Tessa was at the cusp of crumbling, and she was certain Declan's presence would only spook the little maid.

Evangeline—

Trust me, she pleaded. *Just a few more minutes.*

Pinning her gaze on Tessa, she ventured, "Who was it? Who wrote those threats?"

Tessa lifted a hand to her throat. Shook her head. "You

should never have come to the castle. Don't you see? You've ruined everything!"

"What have I ruined?"

"You chased away the *one* person who mattered most to me. Why did you have to come?" Tessa kicked the tree again. "And why do you have to be so damned . . . *kind?*"

Evangeline frowned. "Please, Tessa. Tell me what happened. Who did you lose? I can help you."

Tessa swallowed as tears formed in her eyes. "I didn't know they would harm innocents in the capital, Evie. I didn't know they would hurt the shaman. You must believe me."

The words struck her like a slap. "*You* told them I was in the capital? How did you even know I was there in the first place?" She had taken such care to tell no one but her companions that day. Not even Mailin had been privy to her plans.

Tessa dipped her chin. "It was a coincidence. I was in the capital when I caught sight of Councilor Alexander and the woman beside him. Even with the hood, I recognized you."

"But how . . . how did you . . . " Evangeline couldn't seem to form the right words. The maid hadn't only delivered the threats to her dresser. Tessa had also been the reason for the attack in the capital. The reason Shyaree had nearly died. The reason for the death of the poor cabbage merchant who had tried to help her.

On the psychic plane, Declan only compounded her riotous emotions with his incessant demands. Evangeline rubbed her temples, trying to calm her thoughts. She had nothing to fear from Tessa. Declan could track her and warp to her at any minute, and would have already if it weren't for her insistence for more time. Yet . . .

"You're not a telepath. How could you have summoned the Unseelie riders?" Evangeline's mouth went dry. "The person you're communicating with is a *mage.*"

A powerful telepathic mage who could receive distant thought projections the same way Declan received her thoughts. Evangeline could only think of a handful of battlemages with that ability . . . and Alexander.

"I really wanted to help you, Evie. I would have brought you to Yarveric and found a place where they wouldn't find you. But now . . . " Tessa shook her head with a sad shake. "I have no choice but to tell her the truth."

Her? Them? Evangeline shook her head in confusion. "Who are they?"

"I didn't want to do this, Evie, but you've left me with no choice."

"Wait," Evangeline cried, her mind whirling. "Let's talk about this. There has to be another way."

"Your archmage will burn me at the stake for my deceit!"

Evangeline shook her head. "I won't let him. You just need to tell me the truth. Who put you up to this?"

Tessa appeared torn, her brows furrowed. "You would protect me? Even though I've betrayed you?"

"I will do everything I can to help you, if you'll just tell me why."

Tessa opened her mouth at the same time the air shimmered, and Declan materialized unbidden. Tessa released a little scream at his sudden appearance while Evangeline released an exhale of exasperation. Clearly a little patience was too much to ask.

As Declan's gaze raked Evangeline from head to toe, Tessa fled as though the world were already afire. She scrambled onto her horse and spurred her mount into a gallop.

Declan muttered a low oath. He shot Evangeline another sharp glance before breaking off into a loping run after Tessa's galloping horse. His long legs blurred before he leapt into the air. Midlunge, he warped. In the next heartbeat he rematerialized behind Tessa on the mare, trapping the little maid as he yanked the reins from her hands to halt the horse. Then he dismounted and plucked Tessa off the saddle.

Too distracted by Tessa's shrieking, Evangeline hadn't noticed the shadows coalescing in the dark until it was too late.

Riders galloped through the portal, with black leather masks concealing their faces. The only difference from before was that this time they came heavily armed, swords strapped to their backs, bows in hands.

Evangeline was glad for her riding breeches because skirts would have hampered her escape. She ran in Declan's direction, but her archmage warped to meet her halfway, materializing close with one hand still holding Tessa by the forearm.

The riders surrounded them in a semicircle, arrows notched, bows drawn.

"You've got a lot of gall trespassing on my lands," Declan said, and Evangeline was satisfied that a visible ripple of nervousness passed through the riders.

"Help me," Tessa whimpered, still struggling against Declan's hold.

"We only seek what rightfully belongs to us," a rider said, his voice muffled by the mask. "Relinquish our women, and we will leave in peace."

"Your women?" Declan murmured with a raised brow. The symbols on his skin flared, liquid gold warning of death and destruction.

Stay within my shield, little fire. His telepathic voice brooked no argument, and Evangeline wasn't about to contest him. She had no doubt Declan could easily overpower five Unseelie warriors—any interruption from her would only distract him.

He gave her hand a squeeze before he said, "These women

belong to *me*, and the only peace you'll find is when Ozenn receives you back into the earth."

Evangeline hadn't expected the riders to shoot. Not when Tessa stood vulnerable before them like a sacrificial lamb. But arrows flew.

"No!" Evangeline cried.

Bolts of fire and ice lashed out, decimating arrows to ash and spooking the horses into a disarray. Amid the chaos, Tessa squirmed from Declan's grip and fled, but Evangeline's arch-mage made no move to pursue her. Moonlight gleamed as the staverek materialized in his grip. Fire lapped up his arm to light his sword while frost crawled along the ground, throwing the frenzied horses off balance.

"Tessa, stop!" Evangeline made no move beyond the shimmer of protective gold, but there was no way she could let the maid escape. Vines erupted through the grass like a snare, and Tessa stumbled to the ground.

There were questions Evangeline needed answers to.

A rider crept through the fray, his bow notched and aimed —at Tessa. A quick glance told Evangeline the rest of the riders were either dead or dying a grueling death by frost and fire.

Without hesitation, Evangeline drew and expelled another surge of magic. Roots trundled up from the soil to throw the rider askew. His arrow flew off course, striking Tessa in the shoulder, and the maid's scream echoed through the woods.

The rider scrambled up. Turned, and charged right for *Evangeline*.

The rider lunged and, to her shock, bypassed Declan's shield.

Evangeline! Declan's telepathic voice bellowed in her head even as he yelled, "Get away from her!"

Evangeline knocked the bow from the rider's hands. Her eyes met the cold blue ones of the rider who had nearly cost Shyaree her life. Evangeline bared her teeth in a hiss, and they grappled for one instant before the world grew mottled into a medley of colors.

THIRTY-TWO

Evangeline gasped and kneed her aggressor in the groin. He released a soft grunt and rolled off her. Pinpricks of white and patches of black obscured her sight. Whenever she had been warped, she had always felt a hint of disorientation. This time the sensation was magnified tenfold.

The brisk night air had turned humid. The stench of decaying flesh filled her nose as though she'd been shoved face first into a pit of corpses. She gagged and caught sight of a darkened row of trees before a sharp crack and a jolt of pain exploded at the side of her skull. Everything dimmed.

The next time she lifted her lashes, nausea flooded up her throat to accompany the pounding in her head. Blood. The ironlike tang was unmistakable despite the overpowering smell of rotting meat. Where in Railea's world was she? Evangeline groaned, gingerly touching her throbbing temple. Her hair was matted on that side. The blood was dry. How long had she been out?

She shuffled to her knees. Bits of gravel bit into her palms.

Fear shallowed her breaths as a sickening realization seized her.

The rider had been no Unseelie, but a mage. One powerful enough to teleport.

A low, menacing growl drew her from her disorientation.

Evangeline blinked, looking up to come face to face with a snarling muzzle. Her breath hitched even as she froze in place. Wolf.

A very, very large wolf stared back at her with eerily intelligent eyes. Then it bared its teeth to emit another snarl, revealing spittle-laced canines.

"Shhh," crooned a surprisingly feminine voice. "Calm down. I won't let her hurt you." Amid the dimness of their surroundings, the rider moved into view to crouch beside the animal and run a loving hand through its gray pelt. The movements were oddly familiar, echoing the way a woman had once stroked a ferret at a dinner party.

"Vera?"

Blue eyes met Evangeline's gaze for a moment before the rider yanked off the black leather mask to reveal a blond crown of tightly coiled braids.

She smirked. "Took you long enough."

"You . . . " Evangeline released a breath, trying to exhale the wave of disbelief overwhelming her chest. Then, comprehension lit through her confusion like a fog lamp.

"You wrote those threats?"

Ignoring her, Vera ran fingers into her crown, unraveling her braids so silken strands of gold coiled about her delicate features. "Now he knows . . . He knows, and he'll never forgive me."

The wolf remained by Vera's side, seemingly sedate as it lowered its rump to the ground, as though to comfort the woman.

Evangeline cast a quick gaze about the gloomy cavern, and her eyes landed on the odd cluster of oversized blooms growing in the crevices. Small, hairy-looking flowers with a dusky tinge. Dread filled her.

Carrion blooms. Their petals exuded a scent that mimicked that of rotting flesh, and they were native only to the central lands of the realm. *Far* from Amereen.

Evangeline whirled to the other woman. "Take me back. Declan—"

"Knows!" Vera's shriek bounced off the walls of the shallow cavern. "He touched my mind, and now he knows *who* I am. I had no choice but to bring us here!"

Evangeline blinked, then shook her head. Her archmage's final warning—*"Get away from her!"*—suddenly took on new meaning.

It wasn't a warning directed at the rider, but at Evangeline.

"Why are you doing this?" Evangeline dragged in a breath of foul air and tried not to heave. Perspiration began beading on her forehead and over her upper lip. Wherever they were, they had to be close to the tropical region of the realm. The air was moist. Sweltering. Her woolen surcoat far too thick.

The floor was pure granite and utterly barren of magic. She couldn't feel a single thread of Ozenn's essence in the ground, in the air, or within the rocky walls. Even the cluster of carrion flowers seemed as dead as their scent. No magic. When she reached out for Declan on the telepathic plane, she was met with a chilling hollowness. No matter their geographical distance, Evangeline had always sensed his presence in the periphery of her mind. But now, the mental plane was utterly silent.

"Now he knows. He knows." Vera had risen to pace the cavern, as though she'd forgotten Evangeline's presence. "He'll never forgive me now." She ran hands across the wolf's gray

pelt, and the wolf released a low, rumbling huff with its predatory eyes latched on Evangeline's every move.

"How did you get Tessa to betray me?"

Vera snapped up her head. Her eyes narrowed. "So entitled.
Did you simply assume Tessa had no prior loyalties before you
swanned into the castle?"

Vera stroked the wolf with the languidness of a woman
touching her lover. "Years ago, I came across a girl who was
forced to trade her body for coin. She was pretty enough, so I
brought her to the lounge. But Tessa never did enjoy men . . . "
Vera lifted her gaze with a sultry smile. "And I was an ayari who
was never used. Yet I would be scorned and stripped of my
title should I admit another man into my bed. Do you know
how lonely the years can be?"

Evangeline parted her lips. "You just tried to kill her."

Vera's blue eyes darkened into a storm. "Did you think I
wanted to? She *lied* to me! She asked for grootworm, promising
to deliver *you* in a state of paralysis, but clearly, she hadn't tried
to! Declan was never supposed to know of my involvement, yet
she called for me, when she knew my disguise would never fool
him. She set those soldiers up for death. She set *me* up."

"Set you up? Tessa called for you because she was in fear for
her life!" The pieces finally clicked, falling together to form a
convoluted puzzle of malice . . . and sheer stupidity.

"Did you think you could run me from the castle and . . .
what? Take *my* place? Did you think Declan could have so
easily replaced me?"

"I am worth a hundred of you!" Vera curled her fingers
into fists. Her body vibrated with a silent rancor that roused
Evangeline's own hackles. "I am the sole heir of Sebastian
Khan, archmage of Batuhan. I have manifested powers far
beyond your dreams. Yet I demeaned myself in the Keep.
Subjected myself to ten years of pain, blood, and tears just so I

could one day share Declan's bed and bring him pleasure." She scraped fingers into her hair again, tugging at the wispy threads in open agitation. "All I wanted was to be his ayari, but never once did he show me interest. Never once did he show me an ounce of tenderness, which he showers upon you!"

Vera's cheeks flushed to mirror the redness at the edges of her eyes. "Because of you, he sent me packing without so much as a second thought."

Sariel's words echoed in Evangeline's memory. *"As a mageling, Vera used to follow on his heels like a devoted lamb."*

Evangeline expelled a soft sigh. "You can't force love, Vera."

"Love?" Vera's voice dropped to a whisper. "I've never been fool enough to expect his love, but I had hoped to share his . . . affections."

She laughed, the bitter melody of a spurned soul. "But I *am* a fool, aren't I? I've waited years for a man who would never spare me a second glance . . . especially not when you're around."

Evangeline's shoulders sagged. Her animosity vanished like the flame of a snuffed candle. She couldn't fathom the agony of unrequited love, but she had witnessed Agnes's pining for her lost mate through the years. It had been painful to watch, much less to endure. Evangeline met Vera's gaze, and the woman's lips twisted with disgust.

"I don't need your pity! You're nothing but a whore who isn't fit to lick his boots!"

Evangeline couldn't find it in herself to summon resentment. Instead, all she felt was a hollow sadness: for Vera's pining and plotting, for Tessa's blind devotion. But her lack of anger only served to infuriate the other woman.

"Don't you dare act like you're above me. You're not as chaste as you appear, are you? I know your dirty little secret."

A malicious smirk. "I know exactly what happened to you and your whore of a sister in that cabin, *Freya Jilintree*."

Evangeline reeled as though Vera had slapped her. "How do you know who I am?"

Vera's smile widened. She leaned down to rub her cheek over the wolf's fur before pressing a reverential kiss to its large head, raising bile in Evangeline's throat.

"Zephyr," Evangeline whispered.

The wolf chuffed, as though in laughter.

"At least she's not too stupid to recognize you this time, my king."

Evangeline scrambled back, only to stumble on loose gravel. Renewed sickness bloomed in her gut. Zephyr had been there from the start.

As the ferret draped over Vera's shoulders.

Vera chuckled as sinister delight lit her gaze. "If I had only wanted you out of the way, I could have easily convinced Tessa to murder you, don't you think? But doing that would only condemn Declan to a lifetime without a woman he'd chosen as his *mate*."

Vera pursed her lips and shook her head. "He should never have used his one choice for a mate on you. That will never do. No, what I wanted was for Zephyr to break Declan's half link with you before I ensured your death. I had it all planned out. Declan would be devastated by your . . . disappearance, but I'd wait, of course. Ten years. Twenty. A hundred, if he needed. And when he was ready, I would be there for him. But now . . . " Hatred hardened her gaze.

The wolf rose from its haunches, bared its muzzle to display fearsome teeth.

Evangeline reached instinctively for the starburst pattern over her breast as an involuntary shudder slithered down her spine. "No one can break the bond between a mated pair. Not even the goddess Railea, herself."

"Not a completed bond, no." Vera narrowed her eyes. "But you're not truly mated, are you? Tessa told me Declan doesn't yet wear your brand upon his skin."

How many times had Tessa ventured into their room when Declan had been shirtless?

How could Zephyr even attempt to remove Declan's mark on her skin?

The wolf advanced in slow, soundless steps, scattering her thoughts.

"How did you come here?" Evangeline directed the question to the wolf. Since regaining her abilities, she had never been in a place where she couldn't sense a single scrap of magic. It made her skin crawl. How could Zephyr stand to be in such an unnatural place?

Vera wrapped her arms in a near-amorous fashion over the wolf's flank. Her smile was almost proud.

"This is the only place across all the realms where he can rest. Heal, without the fear of being found." Vera chuckled as though she'd made a joke. "No one would think to look for a fae king where magic can't be used, now, would they?"

"*Where* are we?" Evangeline repeated, slowly edging herself toward the opening of the cavern. Vera released the wolf and rose to her feet with a wry tilt of her lips.

"The only place where the goddess's essence soaks the ground. Her energies are so overwhelming they mask all other powers. Even magic." A smirk. "Your tricksy vines won't grow here."

No wonder she couldn't sense Declan on the mental plane. They were in the province where none of the Echelon reigned. Mount Arksana. The fabled mountain where mages went for ascension . . . or never left again.

Evangeline edged to the lip of the rocky outcrop, close enough to peer beyond the cavern walls. The sky was dark and starless, yet the moon was full. So full it illuminated the strange sight beyond as clear as day. In the distance, a series of curved rocks stood stark against a clearing framed by a webbing of trees that hugged the horizon. Intricate, curling lines rippled in waves of iridescent gold and white across the ground that was as dark as soot and as flat as pavement. Evangeline sucked in a breath.

Not lines. *Glyphs.* The same arcane symbols that adorned her archmage's body were etched into the ground, growing thicker and more convoluted toward the center of the clearing, where the curved rocks formed a circle.

The whinny of a nearby horse broke her awe.

A mean-looking stallion was tethered to some dead, dried-out branches in a nearby outcropping. It clapped its hooves, seemingly impatient.

"Go ahead." Vera sneered, clearly reading Evangeline's intent. "Try it. The horse may have carted you up here, but one whistle from me and it will trample you to the ground."

Evangeline cast another frantic glance at the entrance to gauge the distance to the dense treeline.

Vera shook her head. "I must warn you, though. If you run, you'll only incite him to chase. He's been in this form for weeks now . . . Sometimes I think he's grown more wolf than man."

The wolf rumbled low while Vera unsheathed the slim sword strapped to her back. "And he hasn't fed for days." She drew the edge of the blade over her palm, slicing a thin line. Blood welled, and the wolf released a low, eager whine.

"Here now." Vera crouched down.

Evangeline stared as Vera offered her palm as though she were feeding a puppy a treat. The wolf lapped up her blood with an unnatural relish, and Evangeline swallowed, trying to stomach her nausea.

She finally understood the intimacy between them.

Literal bloodlust was a disease in fae kind. Vera was encouraging a codependency that allowed Zephyr to lengthen his possession of the creature. To survive in animal form for as long as she fed him her blood.

Evangeline willed her racing heart to calm. Running would only result in a hunt, and she was not confident commandeering Vera's mount. She needed to gather her wits and survive for as long as it took Declan to find her. Her archmage *would* find her or die trying. That, she knew without a doubt.

"How did you come to work with Zephyr?" Evangeline blurted the words, interrupting the wolf's nuzzling licks. "How did you come to command his soldiers?"

Vera narrowed her gaze. "Distracting me with questions won't work. You ruined my life with that double-crossing bitch."

Evangeline swallowed more disgust. "Your lover, who would have crossed an archmage for *you*."

Vera pulled her hand away from the wolf, who released a reluctant whine, to brandish her sword. "Tessa was merely a pawn who outgrew her use. Declan is the only one I ever wanted. If I can't have him, then I don't want anyone else having him either."

THIRTY-THREE

The little maid slumped to the dirt, cowering from him with her hands clutching her temples.

Declan hadn't wasted any time scouring her mind.

And the treachery he'd found sickened him.

He had meticulously handpicked soldiers for Evangeline's guard, but he had never thought to vet his own servants. Never would he have allowed the maid to come within speaking distance of his little fire had he known of her involvement with Vera. Yet he had inadvertently given his elorin de ana a snake for a handmaid.

The darkness within him rose, seething in tandem to the anger roiling in his chest. He curled his fingers around the slim column of Tessa's throat, but he stopped himself before he did something he would regret.

Squeezing the life from this traitorous cretin would be far too kind. "How does it feel to betray a woman who believed only the best of you?"

Tessa shook uncontrollably, pawing at the arrow jutting

from her shoulder. But the maid knew not to test his patience. He had seen all he needed in her mind.

"I only added a drop to her tea once every three days." Her words fractured between sobs. "It wouldn't have been enough to kill her."

No, the venom had not been enough to kill, but enough to debilitate. Evangeline's *afflictions* had never been symptoms of her returning immortality, rather, a chronic manifestation of Tessa's betrayal. Declan ground his molars. Had Evangeline not returned to Agnes during the length of their disagreement, she would have been continuously poisoned, while *he* had foolishly believed her bouts of unconsciousness signs of her *frailty*.

"Evangeline wanted so much to believe you blameless in the matter. She pleaded for me to play along so she could prove your innocence." Declan tightened his grip, her pulse thundering in the hollow of her neck. "She acted to save you even as your insidious lover would have seen you dead!"

Tessa sobbed harder, blubbering something incoherent. Declan lost his patience. He squeezed until she went limp. Still, satisfaction eluded him. He wanted nothing more than to burn her until she was ash in his hands. But a sliver of Evangeline's censure in his mind held him back.

He would deal with her *after* he found Evangeline. And Vera.

Grabbing her by the wrist, he warped back to his castle and deposited the unconscious maid into the arms of his startled commander.

"Who from the fae realm would have allied themselves with the likes of Vera?" Killian mused as two soldiers carted the still-senseless maid to the dungeons. Declan recounted the events, seeking both counsel from his lead commander and clarity in his own mind. The Unseelie riders Declan had left alive for questioning had all chosen to slit their own throats.

"Zion," Declan muttered. "That snake-swiving princeling must have discerned Evangeline's true identity."

"Surely you must sense Lady Evangeline enough to warp to her general location. No matter how far I go, I can always find my way back to Mailin."

Declan rammed both hands into his hair. Evangeline was not fully mated to him yet. Their bond was incomplete. "I can't sense her at all."

It was as though their half bond had been severed. Or perhaps Vera had somehow taken her through a fae portal, and they were no longer in this realm. Panic threatened to choke him. What if she was in the fae realm right now, at the mercy of her captors?

Killian must have come to the same conclusion, as he rose to his feet. "I will contact the guild, have Gabriel rally his men to search for her." He turned with a pensive frown. "Vera may have manipulated the maid, but it feels . . . unlikely she orchestrated the whole scheme without her father's knowledge."

Declan shook his head.

Sebastian Khan wouldn't—couldn't—be foolish enough to antagonize him by threatening his elorin de ana. It would only have led their kingdoms to war.

Declan blew out a breath to acknowledge a far darker possibility.

Could Vera be another pawn on the chessboard? One controlled by an Unseelie monarch who had feigned death? Had Zion's approach been a ploy to distract from his father's nefarious plans?

"Make it known that I am searching for Evangeline. Anyone harboring Vera Khan within their borders will be declaring war against me. Send the message to all kingdoms in the realm . . . but leave Batuhan to me. I will deliver the message personally."

Mastermind or pawn, Vera remained the prized princess of the Batuhan kingdom.

Evangeline ducked, narrowly missing the sharp point of the sword tip. It struck the wall, steel screeching against stone before Vera spun and rammed an elbow into the side of her head. The impact sent her reeling. She was gasping for breath when the end of Vera's sword found the hollow of her neck.

Evangeline stilled.

"Seeliekind can't heal themselves, can they?" Vera murmured, her eyes fixed intently on Evangeline's throat. Pain prickled and warmth dribbled.

Evangeline held up both hands, barely able to speak past the trepidation in her chest. "It doesn't have to be this way. You'll gain nothing if you kill me."

"Oh, I don't mean to end you." Vera stepped closer to the observing wolf without shifting her gaze. "Fortunately for you, your *king* wants you alive."

Evangeline's heart pounded in her ears.

Vera's gaze dropped for an instant as she shot the wolf an affectionate smile. "You don't mind if I bloody her up a little, do you, my sweet king? Seeing all the pain she's caused you . . . "

Evangeline did not hesitate. She shoved up with her bare hands, knocking the blade from her throat, lacerating her palms. Vera lunged so rapidly she had to pivot to avoid the sharp edge of the blade. Ignoring the pain biting her palms, she lashed out. She tugged on the golden chain at her wrist. The spyblade slid from its sheath, scoring a line of red against Vera's flawless cheek.

The sword clattered to the ground as she shrieked and clutched at her face. "You little bitch!"

Evangeline seized the fallen sword, but her palms were still stinging. She could hardly wield it without the heavy handle slipping in her grip.

"Stay away from me!" She brandished the sword, knowing full well her stance resembled that of a woodcutter with an axe. If she lived through this ordeal, she would strongarm her archmage into sword-fighting lessons.

Vera's eyes widened, focused on a sudden shadow looming over Evangeline's shoulder. Her breath shallowed; her muscles coiled. She sprang around just as a large hand clamped over her forearm.

"There now," said a gruff male voice. "You don't want to hurt yourself."

A hard shake and he wrenched the sword from her hand the way one might snatch a toy from a child.

"Dadyia!" Vera exclaimed. "What are you doing here?"

The archmage of Batuhan tossed the sword back to his daughter, who caught it with the deftness of a seasoned swordswoman. Sebastian turned his gaze to the wolf and acknowledged the creature with a regal nod. "Old friend."

Sickness speared her innards. The archmage of Batuhan clearly knew *who* the wolf was. The creature had settled by the side, tongue lolling as though it was enjoying a show.

Sebastian returned his gaze to his daughter. "I would ask you the same. Do you know who just stormed into my court, threatening to set the entire kingdom on fire? He is demanding your head!"

Vera paled.

"Have you ever stopped for one instant to think of the repercussions of your actions? Declan Thorne is not one to antagonize!" Sebastian's voice boomed, as hard and jagged as the granite walls. "I had to lie through my teeth to keep him from decimating the palace. You've jeopardized everything I've been working for with your impetuousness."

Evangeline struggled ineffectually against Sebastian's grip before grating, "You would betray the Echelon for the delusions of a mad king? Have you seen what Zephyr has done to the fae realm?"

"Betray the Echelon?" Sebastian scoffed. "A world such as ours would fall to savagery without the control of archmages. No, I would never betray the Echelon. I mean to repair it."

Evangeline stared up at the man, an incredulous laugh forming in her throat. "You can't repair something that is not broken."

"Not broken," Sebastian agreed grimly. "But it is languishing under poor guidance and ill influence. The Echelon was once an indomitable and revered force across all the five realms. The likes of fae or animati would never have dared cross our boundaries." A shake of his head. "Now the Echelon has been reduced to fawning over the machinations of a princeling hoping to usurp his father's crown, all under the hand of Nathaniel Strom. An archmage who thinks himself a god."

Evangeline gritted her teeth. "And yet *you* harbor Zephyr? King of the Winter Court! He's the one behind the slave-trade cartel!"

The wolf emitted an answering growl.

The narrowing of Sebastian's eyes chilled the blood in her veins. "The cartel was necessary to show the Echelon the folly of turning its back against its allies." At Evangeline's incredulous expression, Sebastian sneered. "Yes, allies! We were once allies with the fae courts . . . until Nathaniel Strom started the Winter War with his selfish seduction of the Unseelie queen."

Sebastian pulled her close, so close she could feel his hot

breath on her skin as he snarled. "But even that wasn't enough to satisfy Strom's depravity. His murder of Corvina cannot go unpunished. It's even more vile that she bore him a son from their torrid affair."

Evangeline's brows winged. Affair?

Sabastian smirked. "You didn't know? Of course not. So few do. Strom has set himself up as a god. Irreproachable. Untouchable. Yet he is nothing more than a feckless philanderer."

Evangeline tried to swallow the shock swelling in her throat. Declan and Alexander had both believed in Corvina's rape. Could they have been wrong?

Sebastian's grip on her tightened. "The Strom line isn't untouchable, girl. It's tainted by sin. And I will see that sin rooted out of the Echelon. Nathaniel's influence is an absurdity to be corrected before true order can be restored."

"You wish to restore order? And yet you consort with"—Evangeline curled her lips at the wolf—"this monster?" She sneered. "And here I thought archmages were all-powerful."

"Witless girl! I cannot hope to destroy Nathaniel Strom without the help of like-minded allies. Not while he holds the loyalty and respect of the Echelon. Especially not when he managed to breed a son from Corvina. A child he took years to mold in his own image. Brutality wrapped in charm and arrogance."

Indignance lifted her chin. "Declan doesn't rule according to Nathaniel's decree. He is his own master." In fact, her archmage could barely tolerate his father.

"Which only makes him all the more dangerous! No one knows where his true loyalties lie. Thorne is more ambiguous than a shifting fog. Why do you think I allowed my Vera, my only daughter, to serve as his ayari?" Sebastian snapped, his voice echoing off the cavern walls. "Why do you think I did *nothing* when he spurned her, as though she were nothing more than a common whore?"

Vera, who had turned meek from her father's presence, blanched as though she had been physically struck. Sebastian squeezed Evangeline's forearm, nearly crushing her to the bone. Bruises would bloom, but Evangeline refused to whimper or even lower her chin. She would not cower before a disillusioned madman.

Sebastian released her with a rough shove so she fell to the ground. "It is a real shame things had to pan out this way. Declan Thorne would have made a magnificent ally. But now I must do what Corvina should have done all those years ago."

Pushing up to her knees, Evangeline bared her teeth, her canines sharpened to points. The only thing that kept her from lunging for Sebastian's throat was knowing she could not draw blood before he would subdue her.

"You can't mean to kill him," Vera interjected with an unexpected quiver in her voice.

Sebastian narrowed his eyes at his stricken-faced daughter. "After you and your foolish schemes, what other choice do I have?"

"Dadyia, please," Vera protested. "Declan will serve our cause far better as an ally than dead. I'll run. I'll hide. I'll hide *her*. You can deny all knowledge of my involvement. We'll find another way—"

"And waste more years attempting to secure his loyalty?" Sebastian huffed, his next words nothing but a gruff snarl. "Foolish child, it's time you discarded those fanciful desires. If the lad possessed a whit of sense, he'd have long since bedded you."

Vera blanched and hung her head. A fresh trickle ran from her eyes.

"There, now, my fair jewel, do not despair," Sebastian said, tone softening. "The loss is most assuredly his. We will find you a better suitor."

Vera's soft sobs filled the cavern. "But there is no other like him."

Sebastian's sigh was heavy as he shook his head. "Indeed. Corvina once admitted the same." A muscle in his jaw ticced. "But I will not repeat her folly. If he cannot be our ally, then he is an aberrant force best eliminated."

Evangeline's heart thumped when Sebastian regarded her with a slow, calculative smile. "And how better to snare a beast than to lay out bait?"

THIRTY-FOUR

Sebastian had lied. Declan could tell from the other archmage's shifting gaze.

"There has to be some mistake," Sebastian had said with grim warning in his tone. *"Vera may be impulsive, but she couldn't possibly have dallied with a common maid. Nor would she have been foolish enough to abduct an archmage's elorin."*

The bullheaded archmage had adamantly denied all knowledge of Vera's whereabouts. Declan believed none of it, but ravaging the Batuhan Palace with frost and flame would have done nothing but ignite an immediate war. It would have done nothing to recover Evangeline. Sebastian *had* allowed him to scan the area telepathically, confirming wherever Vera had taken Evangeline, it hadn't been back to her father's palace.

Declan warped from the Batuhan Palace into Strom Castle, expending enough energy that he felt a faint ache in the scars left over from his battle with Zephyr.

He appeared in the middle of the hall of ice and mirrors, triggering Nathaniel's wards and terrifying the few courtiers and servants with his sudden appearance.

"Nathaniel," Declan demanded of no one in particular. "Inform him that the archmage of Amereen requires his time."

People scrambled, but he knew Nathaniel had sensed his presence the moment he'd warped within the castle walls. The other archmage materialized in the hall in the next breath, dressed in a green silk robe and an expression of ire. He made a gesture for the space to be emptied before showing Declan a semi-curious but scathing glare.

"You're always welcome in my court, son, but you would be wise not to barge in unannounced, demanding an audience. Even if you refuse to treat me like a father, you owe me the respect an archmage deserves."

At Declan's stony expression, he released an audible sigh. "What in the five hells are you doing here at this ungodly hour?"

"What dealings have you made with Zion?" Declan asked flatly.

Nathaniel's brows drew together. "Come, let us adjourn to a parlor." His gaze roamed the now empty hall, as though searching for a servitor. "I will have some wine brought—"

"No," Declan snapped. "I have no time for your ridiculous pomp and stifling customs. What dealings have you struck with the Unseelie princeling? You knew Evangeline to be Seelie. You knew I fought Zephyr tooth and nail for her. Why did you allow Zion's presence at the Reckoning when you knew Evangeline would be present? Why do you even care about who takes the Winter Court throne? What has that conniving little prince offered you in exchange?"

Nathaniel firmed his lips and crossed his arms. "Haven't we already discussed this? Helping Zion secure the throne is beneficial to us *all*. It is the Echelon's prerogative to rebuild our allies in the fae realm. Wasn't it *you* who began a taskforce for the sole purpose of retrieving slaves? Commissioned spies and assassins through the Red Guild? If the rumors are to be believed, you've even granted its notorious guildmaster direct access through your wards." Nathaniel shook his head by way of censure. "With Zion on the throne, you will no longer require the services of simple mercenaries. We will have the loyalties of a new king. Begin a fresh era of peace."

Declan ground his teeth before he throttled the other man and incited a backlash from guards. "Do not feed me lies." He had served Nathaniel's court for over eighty summers prior to his own ascension. He knew the man lost no sleep over the loss of his own citizens to the workings of the Unseelie cartel and cared nothing for lost slaves or broken allies.

Nathaniel's expression darkened. "Lies? I speak only the truth. I worry for you, son. You surround yourself with—"

"Evangeline is *missing.*" Declan swallowed to regain his composure before he revealed further vulnerability. "Vera Khan has her. That woman has been in league with Unseelie soldiers that could have only come from the Winter Court. Are you saying you knew nothing of this?"

Nathaniel blinked. "Vera? Sebastian's daughter? Why would the chit have anything to do with the Unseelie?" His lips curled. "Do you realize how preposterous your claims are? If you're not careful, you'll cause a civil war. This is precisely what I am worried about. Your devotion to that . . . " He scowled. "Seelie wench has turned into an unhealthy obsession."

Declan grabbed the man by the collar of his silk robes and slammed him to the wall, his patience frayed. "Why are you working with Zion? What has Zephyr's spawn offered you?"

Nathaniel's expression darkened. He struck out with a psychic shove that sent Declan staggering three steps back. "You will treat me with respect!" A heavy scoff. "And Zion is *not* Zephyr's spawn. If you must know, he is a halfling. Your brother."

Declan blinked, too startled to retaliate. "What?"

Nathaniel folded his arms. "You heard me. Zion is your brother. Your half brother, born of Seraphina. He is not of Zephyr's seed, but *mine*."

"Your . . . son?"

Declan released an incredulous bark of laughter. Nathaniel was not seeking to reestablish new allies; he was looking to elevate the position of an illegitimate son. "You impregnated Zephyr's queen and brought *another* bastard to the world?"

Nathaniel's lips flattened to a seam. "I can't help my virility any more than a river can keep from flowing. It is only an ironic turn of fate that none of my ayaris have borne me a child. No matter. A son is a son. My blood runs in Zion's veins as surely as it does in yours. I always held the suspicion even when he was a lad, but now I am certain. When he approached me with the truth, I had the healers check."

"And you don't think it odd your bastard thought now was timely for a reunion?"

Nathaniel waved a dismissive hand. "That is between us. Just know that Zion has my complete trust. And if your precious Seelie plaything has been stolen, it has nothing to do with Zion. Perhaps you should look at the Red Guild and its ill-reputed members. You'd be a fool to expect loyalty from those who kill for coin."

At Declan's incredulous stare, Nathaniel gave another imperious wave of his hand. "Believe me, son, Zion wants nothing but to reconnect with his family. He has even asked to be introduced to you as such, but I thought it wise to keep you in the dark. At least, until we've resolved matters in the Winter Court. Besides, Zion has no cause to harm a simple wench belonging to his brother. He has no vendetta against Seeliekind. And his halfling magic is extraordinary!" He scoffed. "What would Zion want with a Seelie girl with no magic?"

Declan exhaled a soft breath. *No magic.*

Nathaniel remained ignorant of Evangeline's identity.

But Vera had known. She had supplied Tessa with the information Declan had gleaned from scouring the maid's mind.

Someone had divulged Evangeline's identity as Freya Jilintree. Someone who had managed to evade Declan's scouts and Gabriel's spies . . . because he was never in the fae realm to begin with.

"**D**o you know the most effective way to kill an archmage?"

Sebastian dragged her toward the circle of stone pillars in the clearing. The instant she strode over a glyph on the moonlit dirt, an involuntary shudder racked her bones. The power emanating from the ground seemed to surge through her skin. Intense. Overwhelming. And utterly unnatural.

So much raw power in the ground, yet there was no magic available. It was like drowning in a river empty of water. Railea's power masked every supernatural gift, including the threads of Ozenn's magic.

Sebastian chuckled, clearly reading her expression. "These markings are called arksana. Railea's veins. Some say they hold the lifeblood of Railea herself."

They approached the stones, which loomed overhead like talons curved over a huge pit—a *crater*—in the ground. Sebastian shoved her forward with enough force that she pitched against one stone talon. It was no ordinary stone. The glyphs that marked the ground were etched into it. Up close, she could make out every symbol, and they were intimately familiar. She had spent countless hours tracing them across her lover's skin.

Evangeline's gaze landed on the yawning pit in the center, and she staggered back, trying to put as much distance between herself and the bottomless hole as she could. An otherness emanated from it. A feeling she vaguely recalled from when she'd first met Declan on the snowy plains in the shadow realm . . . only the sensation was now magnified a hundredfold.

Evangeline flattened her back against stone, seeking support for her trembling knees. While Vera and the wolf watched her every move, Sebastian paid no heed to her actions.

"And that is the Heart of Arksana. The Heart that fuels Railea's veins. Anyone who braves the Heart will be filled with the power of the goddess. If Railea finds you worthy, she will use your body as a vessel for her power . . . and you will ascend"—Sebastian gestured up toward the starless sky, his expression rapturous—"an archmage."

Sebastian shot her a flash of teeth. "Conversely, the goddess destroys all she deems unworthy. Many souls have been lost here . . . the brave, the foolish, the ambitious."

Evangeline sucked in a breath. The image of Declan flinging himself into the endless crater filled her mind and drew an involuntary shudder down her spine. Declan had not been brave, foolish, or ambitious. He had been suicidal.

"Life seemed meaningless in Nathaniel's court," Declan had said one night as he lay beside her, tracing idle lines over her navel as he spoke of his reasons for ascension. *"I was toying with the thought of eternal sleep by way of my sword when I remembered a promise I once made to you."* His lips had curved then. *"A girl who*

believed I should attempt ascension because no one could ever hurt an archmage."

Had she known what ascension entailed, she would never have wanted it for him. Evangeline shivered again as she pressed harder against the stone pillar, but she issued silent thanks to the goddess anyway. *Thank you for keeping him*, she thought, though she was no longer certain if Railea had ever heard her prayers since she was fae, and technically, a being of Ozenn's creation. *Thank you for keeping him so I could find him again.*

"Only archmages rise from Railea's Heart," Sebastian continued, eyeing the crater the way a licentious man might a whore. "And no archmage survives the Heart twice." Sebastian's gaze scoured over her, a greasy weight slick against her skin. "And it will only be a matter of time before your lover shows up. Do you think he loves you enough to brave Railea's Heart a second time?"

Evangeline narrowed her eyes but refused to give him the satisfaction of her response. She straightened her back, steeling her spine as a dark decision settled over her. She would sooner throw herself into the crater than be used as a device for Declan's downfall.

Sebastian raised a brow, clearly annoyed by her defiant silence. Then he smirked before addressing the wolf lurking around the edges. "Old friend, are you absolutely certain this chit is the last descendant of the fabled Jilintrees? She seems nothing more than an inert little creature."

Evangeline clenched her fists.

Vera seized her arm with an abruptness that had her hissing. Evangeline retaliated with a swipe of clawed fingers, but Sebastian intervened before she could draw blood.

Vera tore at Evangeline's sleeves, red-rimmed eyes brimming with hate as she uncovered the spyblade strapped to her forearm. "You and your treacherous little trinkets."

Sebastian's brows drew to a frown as he peered at the slash that had already begun to heal across his daughter's cheek. "Is that what she used to hurt you?"

At Vera's vehement nod, Sebastian tutted. Then he reached to his back and unsheathed a large, violent-looking axe. "Well, the chit doesn't need all her limbs to serve her purpose."

Vera stretched her arm against one of the stone pillars with a zealous glint in her eyes.

Evangeline fought the scream rising from her throat. "I will be useless to you dead."

The wolf released a low, warning growl, its fur bristling. It took Evangeline a moment to realize its discontent was aimed at Sebastian.

"Old friend," Sebastian said, brows stitched together as though in puzzlement. "Given the role she played in the mutilation of your real form, I can't see how you're against the removal of a single limb."

"If I bleed to death," Evangeline interjected as she struggled in vain against the hold of both father and daughter. "All of Seeliekind ends with me. The fae realm will *never* go back to how it used to be." With everyone she had ever loved now dead, she had no wish to return to the fae realm regardless— but Zephyr didn't need to know that.

The wolf's bristling intensified and its growls deepened.

"Don't listen to her, my king. She's nothing but a manipulative bitch!" Vera dug her nails deeper into Evangeline's forearm.

"Vera is right," Sebastian said. "The girl would never have found her way into an archmage's bed otherwise. You'd be wise to see her for what she is." He turned to pin his gaze on Evangeline as he brandished his axe. "Let this serve as a reminder to never challenge your betters."

Evangeline jerked frantically to free her arm, but Vera's grip was viselike, and Sebastian's hold on her other arm could well be iron bands.

The archmage raised his axe.

Evangeline screamed.

Sebastian's axe clattered to the ground. Astonishment colored his gaze as it fell to the sudden flare of brambles sprouting from the ground beneath Evangeline's feet. Vera's grip slackened as she backed away, and the brambles grew into a defensive wall of prickly thorns.

A violent shudder racked Evangeline to the bone.

Instead of reaching out for Ozenn's magic, she had drawn deep within herself, dredging up the birthright that made her Freya Katerina Jilintree.

Evangeline expelled more from deep within her core, plumbing her soul for all she was worth. The glimmering veins of color beneath her feet dimmed further, and the darkening patch widened in circumference until she stood upon nothing more spectacular than hard rock and dry land. The more the veins dimmed, the thicker her brambles grew.

"Impossible," Sebastian whispered with eyes wide. "No one draws directly from *arksana*."

Evangeline retreated, unable to form a coherent response while concentrating on her birthright. She wanted to tell him he was right. She wasn't drawing power from Railea's veins. No. She had *muted* it so she could access magic without interference from the goddess's roiling energy.

Sebastian's visage twisted in a mixture of awe and disgust as he picked up his fallen battle-axe. "You're no mere fae . . . You're a demoness."

In one hacking swipe, Sebastian cut through her brambles.

Evangeline jumped back with a yelp, her concentration withering alongside her brambles. Her birthright might have brought her the element of surprise, but a wall of brambles could not shield against an axe.

Or a bloodthirsty archmage.

THIRTY-FIVE

The scent of decay teased his nose.

Declan inhaled through his mouth as he hiked up the mountain, already regretting his leather cuirass. He had forgotten how unpleasant Mount Arksana could be with its sweltering heat and carrion flowers. It seemed a lifetime since the day he had first hiked up this mountain, with death on his mind. At the time, the stink of putrefying flesh had seemed macabrely fitting, but now he wondered if the goddess had filled her mountain with carrion blooms as a subtle deterrent to those not meant for ascension.

"Sire." Killian's features were beaded with sweat and scrunched from the stench. "How far off are we from the Heart?"

Killian did not feel the compulsion of Railea's power, not even when he trod over the faintly glimmering veins in the ground. Unlike his commander, Declan felt the pull of the Heart as keenly as the humidity dampening his skin, heard Railea's call as surely as the murmuring leaves of the forest.

"We are close."

He marched through the maze of trees and wildly growing roots, backed only by a handful of battlemages. He'd had little time to wait on the entirety of his army. Amereen rested on the southern border of the continent, and it would have taken his foot soldiers days to get here, even on horseback.

Declan had rallied only the teleport-capable, and together, they had warped to the base of Mount Arksana, as close as they could get to the power-stripping demarcation of the goddess's mountain. The moment they stepped past the threshold into the swirling lines of Railea's land, they were divested of all psychic abilities.

Including their ability to warp.

Declan and his men had been hiking for hours now, their ascent guided by his instinct, their path lit by the moon. He hastened his steps, setting a harsh pace. Zephyr was here. The blackguard had to be. Or Declan had just wasted at least a day's worth of time hiking up this damned mountain, in futile search of a fae king who should already be dead. A fae king who could well have taken his little fire. Sickness tore at his gut.

What if he was too late? What if—

"Commander." The urgency in Leif's tone snapped Declan back to reality. The battlemage was crouched on one knee, examining something on the leaf-strewn ground.

Leif was one of the best hunters, his tracking skills unmatched.

"What is it?" Killian made his way to the battlemage's side.

Normally, Declan would have gleaned the necessary information through telepathy, but now they relied solely on verbal communication, and it was proving grossly inefficient.

"Look." Leif gestured to the dirt.

Leaves had fallen to obscure the ground, but with a keener

look, Declan noted the battlemage's discovery. A subtle boot print in the dirt.

Declan frowned and followed the trajectory of the prints down the path.

A pallet lay on the ground, so artfully concealed by a mound of dried leaves and other forest detritus that it would have been unnoticeable without scrutiny. Declan gave a subtle nod, and Killian nudged the pallet sideways with the edge of his boot to reveal a hastily dug pit.

Declan moved close enough to take in the trap, inlaid with sharpened spikes.

He expelled an incredulous breath. *A bear trap?*

Mount Arksana belonged to no one but the goddess herself. No mage or human came here for anything other than to brave Railea's Heart for a baptism of power. What hunter . . .

There were no fucking bears in this part of the land.

The gravity in Killian's gaze told him the commander had derived the same conclusion just as the whizzing sound filled the air.

"Ambush!" Declan yelled, far too late.

He lunged at Leif, shoving his battlemage to the ground. The sudden hail of arrows would have knocked them both into the pit. Battle cries splintered the air, breaking the stillness of the night as axe-wielding soldiers swarmed into sight.

Declan unsheathed his sword in time to thwart a fully-armored soldier charging right at him. His blade glanced off a brass pauldron with a metallic shriek. The soldier growled before meting out another blow that would have relieved Declan of his forearm had he been slightly less agile. Instead, he grabbed the soldier's helmeted head and brought his knee up to his face. Pain jolted as his kneecap collided with corru-gated metal. Still, the soldier grunted and staggered back, shaking his head like a disconcerted dog. Declan tensed his muscles to ease the bone-jarring impact, preparing for his next move.

The soldier's next aim would be for his head.

His prediction proved true. The soldier shifted, his axe ripping through the air with the heavy-handedness of an adrenaline-frenzied warrior. Declan dipped at the last possible moment and slammed the staverek against the soldier's armored body with enough force to knock the man back. Without giving his opponent a chance to recover, he slammed an elbow into the man's temple. The soldier went sprawling, exposing a gap of the overlapping metal plates between his neck and shoulder.

The armor's weakest point.

An opportunistic thrust was all it took to drive his sword into the unprotected sliver, skewering the soldier in the neck. His opponent stilled and slumped to the ground, but Declan was still surrounded by moonlit chaos. Swords gleamed against axes as his men engaged in a near-choreographed dance of devastation. Killian was fending off two fighters, slender in stature with pointed ears.

Unseelie fighting alongside the armored soldiers of Batuhan?

Sebastian Khan had all the five gods to answer to.

There were too many to fend off, and Declan's men were at a severe disadvantage, protected only by lightweight leather cuirasses.

"Fall back!" Declan yelled as he slammed his pommel into the soldier attempting to lop off Leif's head. "Fall back!" With a grunt, he issued a well-aimed kick and sent an enemy soldier sailing face-first into the exposed pit.

Killian echoed his command. His men took on a herringbone formation and cut through the swarm of enemy soldiers until they reached an open clearing. Declan led the sprint through the trees, following nothing but an instinct to protect his men.

Here, on Railea's mountain, he was no more potent than a soldier grossly outnumbered on the battlefield. He needed to draw the soldiers out of Mount Arksana, where his powers would turn the tide on their numbers.

One of his battlemages slammed into the forest floor with a shout of pain. Bastion, with arrows embedded in his back. Declan cursed. He sent his sword sailing through the air in a fanning twist to smash a torrent of incoming arrows midair.

Now he was weaponless.

Enemy soldiers were too close to outrun. They closed in on them, archers with their bows poised and soldiers brandishing their axes.

Killian came to his side, poised to fight even as he bellowed, "Protect the sire!"

His men formed a protective barrier before him, but Declan wasn't about to hide behind his own men.

"You dare attack the archmage of Amereen?" Declan flung his query at the soldier who appeared leader of the squadron.

The soldier took an uneasy step back, clearly ingrained by years of training to fear the Echelon above all else, even when Declan was now no more powerful than a well-trained soldier. "We cannot disobey the commands of our own liege, Lord Archmage. But all who enter the mountain pass must be eliminated."

Declan drew up Bastion's fallen sword and narrowed his eyes. "Then you'd better make sure I'm dead."

The soldier made it to a sword's length away only to crumple to the ground.

A silver star penetrated the eye slit of his helmet.

Declan whirled to see more men charging up the mountain

pass. His muscles locked, tension building in his veins until he caught the flashes of red.

Then his lips curved. Not soldiers. Mercenaries.

They hurtled up, some astride horses and others on foot, wearing red bands on their left arms. The Red Guild. Charging at the front of the pack on the back of a black stallion was its guildmaster, a blade in each hand.

"Seelie sympathizers!" someone yelled from the opponent's army sparking a bout of clamoring shouts.

Gabriel's men responded in a series of ululating taunts.

A large beast—one now familiar to Declan—charged forward, half running, half loping, one enormous bicep proudly displaying a crimson sash. With a ferocious snarl, Byrne grabbed hold of an enemy soldier and broke his neck like a matchstick before hurling the body into the pit of spikes.

Another flying star met its mark, felling another soldier before Declan could test his sword. Hoofbeats thundered close and came to a halt beside him.

Declan regarded the rider with a raised brow. "What in the five hells are you doing here?"

Gabriel scowled down at him from his black steed. "I've never been one to argue with coin." He flung another star from nimble fingers before adding, "Your brother sent for me." Gabriel veered to the side, leaning far on his saddle to sever the head of an opposing soldier unfortunate enough to have come within distance of his blades.

"*Lex?*"

Gabriel rolled his eyes. "How many brothers do you have?"

Given Nathaniel's self-proclaimed virility, Declan didn't want to contemplate the possibilities. "You thought it necessary to involve half your people?"

"Lex said you might be in need of cavalry. From where I sit, you sure look like you need it."

In truth, Declan had never been happier to see the man, but that was an admission he would just as soon take to his grave. "And you looked better when I rearranged your face," he replied without a hint of a smile.

Gabriel's lips flattened, yet a light danced in his eyes. "Arrogant, ungrateful sonofabitch. I'd wager Evie didn't think so."

Declan sunk his blade into a black-clad Unseelie wearing no red sash. He should put Gabriel in his place for his insolence, but strangely, the Unseelie's ribbing only eased a weight from his shoulders.

Gabriel might have claimed motivation from coin, but Declan knew the Red Guild never involved themselves in battle outside the fae realm.

Declan recognized a favor when he was gifted one. "Thank you."

The beginnings of a smirk played on the guildmaster's lips just before an enemy fighter lunged and dragged him clear off his saddle. The stallion reared, and Declan whirled out of the way before the spooked beast could trample him with its hooves. Muttering a low curse, Gabriel eviscerated his opponent and slayed two more soldiers with a blur of his blades.

"I'm not here for you," Gabriel said with a cavalier roll of his shoulder. "This is for Evie. The last hope of Seeliekind."

Declan shot the man a true smile. "Thank you. I am now in your debt," he shouted before he sprinted off.

He found his commander, wearing the blood of his opponents the way members of the Red Guild wore their banners. "Take command!"

Killian's assent was a roar as he thrust his sword through the neck of an armored soldier, decapitating the man in one brutal smash.

Declan darted up the path, away from the raging battle.

The Red Guild were legendary with their blades. His men

now had the upper hand.

Shouts sounded as two stray soldiers jumped at him with their battle-axes raised. "No one is to breach the Heart," one intoned.

Declan sidestepped the first attacker and slammed his knee into the second's groin before severing his throat. The first soldier roared as his comrade fell and charged like a metal-plated bull.

Gabriel burst from the trees and tackled the man into the dirt.

"Go! Get Evie!" the guildmaster yelled before the soldier threw him off.

"Fucking Seelie sympathizer!" The soldier's growl was loud from beneath his helmet. "I'm going to hang you up with your innards strung about your throat."

Gabriel's answering snarl was more animal than human.

Declan didn't wait to see the outcome. Gabriel could take care of himself.

He sprinted through the woods, following both instinct and the pull of Railea's powers to the place where her veins flowed deepest through the mountain. The Heart.

He ran hard, until his lungs emptied. As he neared the clearing, he slowed his steps in favor of stealth. But a distant shriek from a voice he knew intimately sent him barreling into the open.

He emerged in time to see the woman who was the other half of his soul a hair's breadth from being scalped by a battle-axe.

Sebastian.

The whoreson raised his axe again, and all semblance of rationality fled Declan's mind.

He tore through the clearing. Lunged. Declan's blade would have split Sebastian's skull when a blur slammed into him, knocking the wind from his chest. Growls filled his ears. Jaws snapped at his face. Wolf.

Declan slammed his pommel into the creature's neck, drawing forth a satisfying yelp. The wolf scrambled off, and Declan rolled into a defensive crouch. He'd made an egregious error by charging headfirst into the fray. Not only had he lost the element of surprise, but he'd failed to note the wolf and Vera skulking near one of the curved stone monoliths.

Sebastian, axe still wielded midair, sneered with no small amount of indignance. "You would have struck me down from the *back*?" An archmage of old, Sebastian held fast to a warrior's code.

"You dealt deceit, and yet you expect honor?" Declan kept the wolf in his sights as he shot Evangeline an assessing glance. She crouched behind an uncanny fence of brambles, her face stricken, but still she nodded at him, silently conveying she was unharmed. That was when he noticed that the brambles continued to grow about her feet. Fresh tendrils pushed from the ground, thick and fluid, like the tentacles of a kraken rising from the sea.

Declan stared.

"That's right, Thorne." Sebastian huffed. "Take a good, long look at what you've been keeping in your bed."

Declan couldn't contain his wonderment. "Magnificent, isn't she?"

Disgust filled Sebastian's face. "You'd rather swive this *creature* than bed my daughter?"

Vera. He had never viewed her as anything more than a callow girl. And underestimating her was his mistake. The viper would soon pay for her devious schemes.

"*Zephyr*," Evangeline mouthed, her eyes darting to the wolf.

Declan had already guessed as much, but the obvious fear in Evangeline's eyes tightened his grip on his sword.

"So this is how you've evaded detection all this time?" Declan made a show of his distaste with a slow sneer. "By hiding in the body of an animal and associating with a traitor?"

The wolf growled low, spittle dripping from its bared fangs.

"Traitor?" Sebastian's indignation was a scowl. "I seek only to revive our alliances."

"Alliance?" Declan spat the word. "Is this how you broker an alliance? You just tried to kill my elorin. You're in league with an enemy of the realm. You'll have the gods to answer to when the Echelon learns of your treachery."

"Zephyr is not our enemy," Sebastian insisted. "You were young when this all started . . . but can you not see that all the blame lays at the feet of one man? *Nathaniel* dishonored our alliance by making a cuckold of Zephyr! He is the true cause of the Winter War. The blackguard killed your mother!"

Sebastian was a fool to think Declan cared anything for Corvina. When Nathaniel ended her life, Declan had felt nothing but a twisted sense of relief. It was the same twisted sense that had spurred him to serve Nathaniel for a near century before he concluded life to be hollow and meaningless. He stole a quick glance at Evangeline.

Until now.

Now he wanted to live.

Declan turned his gaze to the bristling wolf, infusing his tone with empathy. "If someone ever made a cuckold of me, I would tear him limb from limb." He lowered his sword and catalogued his distance to the wolf. And the distance it would take for Sebastian to intervene.

"Then I would reduce him to ash in the wind." Not a lie. "Nathaniel may have contributed to my birth, but his actions are not mine. I never took his name because I want nothing of his legacy."

Sebastian grunted his approval. "Indeed. I've always hoped

you saw beyond the blinding magnitude of his power. Hoped you would one day avenge your mother. That is what she intended for you. Your purpose was to be Nathaniel's downfall."

The wolf continued to pace warily, but tension seemed to leave Sebastian's shoulders. Fool.

"My only purpose is to protect what is mine." Declan went for the weakest link.

The wolf. Zephyr was an impediment that must be nullified before he could deal with the deadlier threat that was Sebastian.

The wolf met him head on.

Evangeline's terrified cry rang in his ears as he wrestled the oversized beast, trying to avoid the creature's slicing claws and snapping jaws. Before Sebastian could intervene, Declan slashed his sword into the wolf's soft underbelly.

The wolf scrambled off, too quick for him to inflict more damage. Declan threw himself upon the creature and thrust his sword into the wolf's side, eliciting another agonized howl. Before he could drive it in to the hilt, he was forced to withdraw, narrowly avoiding the sharp edge of Sebastian's battle-axe.

"Impertinent fool! Corvina should never have let you live!"

A violent clang rent the air as they came to blows. Steel scraped against steel. Declan rolled to the ground and scissored his legs to swipe Sebastian from his feet. The other man swerved just in time to evade the stab of his sword.

Feminine shouts pealed. Declan glanced up to see Vera hacking at the brambles—

A staggering impact slammed into his back. Sharp claws tore through his cuirass, digging into flesh. His knees buckled, and his vision muddied as the wolf clamped its jaws over the back of his neck, choking him in a miasma of pain and blood.

Sebastian's boots came into view. He kicked the sword from Declan's grip. Stomped down hard enough that his fingers broke.

"Finish him off," Sebastian said with a sneer. "He has proven worthless to our cause. You deserve the honor, my friend."

In the blurring haze of his consciousness, Declan heard his own gasping breaths and Evangeline's frantic cries. If he died here, Evangeline would never be free of Zephyr. Worse, she would be in the hands of *another* megalomaniac.

One who was now striding over to aid his daughter.

Declan dug for the wolf's injured flank. The whoreson hadn't broken all his fingers. The wolf loosened its jaws, growling in pain. Declan bucked and shoved back, using his weight to topple the creature onto its wounded side. He dove for his sword. Sliced the sharp edge against the wolf's neck. Crimson seeped over gray fur as the wolf's whines slowly faded.

Before the other archmage even realized what had happened, Declan charged headfirst, using his body like a battering ram. They grappled for one short moment before Sebastian had him pinned to the ground, bringing his axe over Declan's head.

"Foolish boy! I was fighting wars before you were even born!" The axe descended a notch closer to Declan's neck. The only thing that kept the axe from decapitating him was the length of his own sword, bearing the brunt of Sebastian's weight.

"You've made a fatal mistake, Thorne. You should never have spurned my daughter. Spurned this opportunity." Sebastian grunted as he bore down harder.

Declan kneed the other man in the groin.

A move Sebastian would never think to guard against

because he would never expect such a dishonorable act. But honor meant nothing when Evangeline was under threat.

Sebastian grunted in surprise. It was all Declan needed to maneuver his neck out of the way. With an enraged growl, Sebastian slammed his axe down. Declan didn't resist this time. He couldn't afford another battle of strength. Not in his current condition.

Sebastian's axe plunged into his chest.

It was by far the least vulnerable part of him, protected by his cuirass. Still, the thick blade tore through the leathers and the thin film of steel, severing muscle and snapping bones. The searing impact tore a cry from his throat and threatened his consciousness, but Sebastian's widened eyes kept him tethered to his senses.

The other archmage noticed, far too late, that the tip of Declan's sword had penetrated his stomach. Sebastian tried to pull away, but Declan reared up, causing the axe to rend deeper in favor of plunging his sword through.

Sebastian's breath shallowed. "Y-you're . . . mad!"

Declan released a gurgling laugh of triumph, the taste of iron thick in the back of his mouth. "My mother made certain of it."

With the final reserves of his strength, he shoved Sebastian backward, where Railea's Heart gaped like a carnivorous plant awaiting an unsuspecting insect. The shocked expression never left Sebastian's face as he teetered precariously over the edge, arms windmilling for balance.

Declan swayed on his feet, staggering close enough for Sebastian to catch the handle of his axe. He ripped it free. The impact sent Declan pitching forward.

Evangeline's cry was the only sound in his ears as he crashed into Sebastian and they both fell into the Heart.

THIRTY-SIX

E vangeline screamed at the same time Vera ceased fighting, her sword clattering to the ground.

They had both witnessed the moment two archmages tumbled over the edge into the crater. The dark chasm illuminated with a blinding blaze, as though shooting stars from the night of the Reckoning exploded within the pit. All sliver of light from the veins in the ground ebbed abruptly, as though emptied into the Heart.

Evangeline scrambled to the edge.

Both archmages clung precariously to the rocky cliff face by their fingertips. Declan was farther down from the precipice, Sebastian closer to the ledge. Their bodies spasmed as streaks of light flowed through the rocks, rushing into their bodies, radiating their skin. So bright that Evangeline's eyes watered. Light crackled as it sparked into the void, flowing into the depths of the crater and fogging the air in wisps of iridescent color.

A fog that scalded where it touched skin.

Evangeline pushed forward anyway, trying to reach her

archmage despite the blistering haze of crackling light and raw power. If she could only reach his wrist . . . A desperate sob escaped her throat when she met his gaze. Death was in his eyes. The flowing light withered the brilliant green of his gaze until his írises were almost black.

"Hang on," she cried. "Don't let go!"

Evangeline withdrew her hand and pressed bleeding palms into the gravelly surface, digging her fingers deep.

"*Grow!*"

Tender shoots began growing from her palms, long and sinewy. Perhaps it was her desperation, or perhaps Railea had heard her prayers and had chosen to give her grace, but her vines grew faster than they ever had. Tendrils threaded together, coiling over the edge like a live rope.

"V-Vera!" Sebastian screamed, his voice juddering like his quaking body. "Hel-p me!" Vera seemed to snap out of her shock. She reached for her father, then retracted her hand, gasping as the fog stung her skin.

Vera hesitated for another moment, but it was a moment too late. A stray spark of light shot Sebastian directly between the eyes. With a cry, he lost his grip.

"Dadyia!" Vera's shout echoed into the chasm, but it was nothing compared to Sebastian's tortured screams as his body disappeared into the depths. There was a blinding flash of light, followed by a haunting silence.

Tears clouded Evangeline's eyes. Not from fear, but horror.

A jerk of her vines had her lurching forward with relief.

Her vines had wrapped over Declan's body, coiling around him where she could not, keeping him tethered. Railea's power continued to gush through the crater, and Evangeline's vines withered even as new ones took their place. She couldn't keep this up.

"Climb, Declan! Climb up!"

He obeyed. His movements were labored, but he crept up, scraping his way with one arm. Without the vines anchoring him, he would have been lost. Evangeline made no movement lest her concentration falter, but the moment he came within reach, she dove for him, shaking with relief as she grasped his hand.

But her fingers, wet with her own blood, began slipping from Declan's wrist. The shuddering of his body only caused her grip to waver. *No, no, no . . .*

"Declan," Evangeline moaned, even as her fingers slid another smidgeon. "Just a little more, my love."

Evangeline let out a strained whimper as she desperately lunged farther, using both hands to haul him up. Declan grunted from effort; his knuckles strained white as he scrambled for grip.

Boots appeared in her periphery. Scuffed and bloodstained.

Evangeline looked up to find Vera looming, her eyes flat, sword in hand.

"*No.*" Declan's voice was that of a desolate man. "Vera, please!"

"The indomitable Archmage Thorne, who submits to no one, has been reduced to a man begging *me* for mercy." Vera's lips formed a bitter line. "For *her*. All for her. What wouldn't you do for her?"

Evangeline choked back a sob and returned her gaze to Declan. Should Vera swing her sword, she wanted her last sight to be his face. Declan's eyes implored her to let go. To run.

"If you truly love him," Evangeline dared whisper, "then help me."

A long and terrifying moment passed before Vera's sword clattered to the ground with a hollow clang. Evangeline released a shuddering breath of relief as Vera went to her knees beside her and grabbed onto Declan's other arm, lending her strength as they worked to haul him up.

Declan lay in a convulsing heap, body still aglow. An uncontrollable moan escaped Evangeline as she saw the back of his mangled neck and the gaping wound on his upper torso. White bone jutted from torn muscles and raw flesh.

How was he even conscious?

Evangeline gingerly flexed an open hand over his wounds. Then she pushed all she had to mute Railea's veins that were still shimmering bright where Declan lay. Whatever little she had left, she poured it into his body, healing what she could.

The wounds inflicted by the wolf's jaws closed over to form scabs, and scabs peeled to reveal smooth, pinkened skin.

She could seal flesh and knit bones, but she couldn't do it when splinters of fragmented bone mangled the wound. She didn't have the tools to remove the broken pieces. They would need a healer's surgical skills before she could attempt to mend his wounded shoulder.

A gasp from Vera broke her concentration.

Evangeline's brows furrowed as she followed the woman's line of sight. What was she *seeing*?

Darkness slithered from the body of the *slain* wolf. Shadows coalesced into the figure of a tall, slender man. Barely corporeal, he was like a phantom sifting through the air. Immaterial. Malicious.

Vera's face paled. "My king?" she said, uneasiness making her voice brittle.

She shook her head as the shadow encroached, wafting over the ground toward them like a mellow breeze.

Evangeline whimpered, and her magic suspended. Fear gripped her, choking her magic—her long ago promise to Mama returning to haunt her.

Declan stirred, sluggish in his movements.

The shadowy fog emitted a whisper. A rasping laugh.

Vera sprang for her sword, swinging it ineffectually against the immaterial cloud of shadows. "No," Vera cried as the shadow engulfed her. "No! Please!"

Evangeline could only stare in mute horror as the shadows sifted, fingerlike, into Vera's nostrils, slinking into her mouth, seeping into the corners of her eyes. Vera thrashed as though Railea's veins speared through her body.

Then she crumpled to the ground.

"V-Vera?" Evangeline whispered, knowing all too well that the Unseelie could only possess animals. But Vera might have been feeding her blood to Zephyr for *months,* instigating his bloodlust, allowing an unnatural bond to form between them.

Vera's eyes sprung open, her expression blank.

She sat up in one sweeping motion. Her head turned, eerily slow and disturbingly twitchy, until their gazes collided and every hair on Evangeline's body stood on end.

"Hello, my little Jilintree."

THIRTY-SEVEN

"Hello, my little Jilintree."

Declan sucked in a labored breath. *Not possible.* He reached instinctively for Evangeline, who stared at Vera's possessed form with the wide eyes of a doe sighting a hunter.

Vera's lips spread wide into a maniacal grin. Her blue eyes appeared glazed, filled with an unnatural presence. She began to stand, her movements jerky and puppetlike. The puppet opened her lips, and Vera's feminine voice flowed out in a sickening singsong tone. "I should punish you for such misbehavior, little Jilintree. Oh, but to have witnessed such *glorious* power . . ."

Evangeline whimpered. Her fingers dug into Declan's forearm. He struggled to push himself upright, drawing Vera's gaze. Her grin stretched wider.

"Tell me, Thorne. Are you ready to face your goddess?"

Vera's insidious chuckle seemed to snap something within Evangeline. She sprang to her feet and grabbed hold of Vera's abandoned sword.

"Don't you dare touch him!"

Declan struggled to his knees, forcing himself to stand. His body felt akin to a furnace, and his blood flowed like sludge in his veins.

Vera took a swaying step forward.

Evangeline snarled, and her ears flattened in warning as she handled the sword in an unpracticed maneuver. "Come any closer, and I'll run you through!"

Vera cocked her head, still wearing a macabre grin. "Put that down, sweet Jilintree. We both know you're no killer."

Declan gripped Evangeline's shoulder to steady himself. "But I am."

Vera tittered. "If you can keep yourself upright." She ran a lascivious hand down her own body, slowing at the chest to fondle her breasts in an utterly disturbing fashion. "This is a surprisingly strong body. Supple, too."

"Stop it, you sick lunatic." Evangeline hissed, and her small canines lengthened. "Get *out* of her."

Hoofbeats and shouts rang out from afar.

Vera released a quintessentially fae snarl before she turned and fled. The moment Vera disappeared into a copse of trees, Declan slumped heavily against Evangeline.

"Sire! My lady!" Killian bolted to the fore, riding astride a brown gelding with Gabriel and two other battlemages close behind. "Is Sebastian dead? His battlemages fell at once." Killian's eyes widened when he saw Declan's wounds. "Sire!"

"Vera is under Zephyr's possession," Declan said, struggling to straighten himself while Evangeline propped him up. "She ran into the woods. Find and kill her."

"That *mordida sipa* still lives?" Gabriel swung from his saddle. The loathing in his expression shifted to bewilderment. "Did you say he possessed a *woman*?"

"Bloodlust," Evangeline said, her voice was shaky, but her

hands were firm around him. "Zephyr is in bloodlust, and Vera shared her blood."

Disgust filled Gabriel's eyes.

Unlike the fae, the commander appeared more concerned with Declan's injuries.

"Sire, you're hurt. We must get you back to Mailin immediately." Killian was a warrior to the bone and rarely protested his directives. Declan must truly appear at death's door for his steadfast commander to refute his orders.

"Hunt her down," Declan insisted. "Zephyr must be eliminated once and for all."

"Be careful, Killian. I think Zephyr only survived here all this time because he's been feeding off Vera," Evangeline added, distress thinning her voice. "And now that he's possessed her . . . "

"He has a corporeal body under his command," Gabriel concluded.

When Killian continued to hesitate, clearly hampered by his liege and lady's injuries, Gabriel added, "I'll go. I've got a bone to pick with that whoreson."

"No," Killian said. "The sire is right. I'll go with my men. You take them back to the camp, Blacksage." He re-mounted his horse and called to his men, "With me!" before riding in the direction Vera had fled.

Though he appeared disgruntled, Gabriel offered no objection. They made their way down the mountain with Declan riding astride while Gabriel walked alongside the mount with the reins. Evangeline, not wanting to overtire the horse, opted to walk on its other flank. It severely stung Declan's pride, but he didn't protest. He could barely keep his feet in the stirrups, let alone walk. Getting Evangeline off Mount Arksana, back to the safety of his castle, was his priority.

An archmage's death could always be inferred from the fall

of his battlemages. And some of Sebastian's army might have fled the battle, carrying the knowledge back to Batuhan. A larger army might be arriving at any moment to avenge their fallen leader. Declan was in no position to battle, and Evangeline wouldn't be safe until she was back in his lands.

When they finally reached the base of the mountain, Declan insisted on dismounting before they crossed the border that separated Mount Arksana from common ground.

The symbols on his skin felt feverish. His body trembled, not merely from his injuries, but from the sheer *power* coursing in his blood. He ached down to his bones, as though Railea herself had seeped through his skin and into his marrow.

Declan gripped Gabriel's forearm before the other man could back away and held his gaze. How he wished for telepathy so he could say these words without Evangeline listening—but he could not risk crossing the threshold. Not yet.

"Do I still have your loyalty, Gabriel?"

He received a wry gaze. "If you didn't, would I have trudged all the way down this damned mountain while you sat on *my* horse?"

"Would you pledge the same loyalty to my elorin de ana?"

Evangeline's brow furrowed as she came to his side with wary eyes. "What are you asking, Declan?"

Declan stroked a hand down her back but did not take his gaze from Gabriel's face. The Unseelie sniffed. "You know Evie has my loyalty regardless. She is the last heir of the Summer Court."

"And what if she chooses to remain in Amereen?" Declan pressed. "Will you still give her your protection?"

Evangeline drew in a sharp breath. Her grip tightened around his arm. Declan couldn't bring himself to look at her, to see the fear he must be inflicting with his words, so he kept his gaze trained on Gabriel—who scowled.

"She's *your* woman." Gabriel leaned back as though to distance himself from Declan's words. "Yours to bloody protect!"

"It will take Lex another century or two before he will be ready to consider ascension. Should he not succeed . . . ," Declan shook his head. Then his brother would be dead, and another archmage would eventually rise. Where would Evangeline go then? Only a man like Gabriel could continue to keep her safe.

"Your answer, Gabriel."

The guildmaster's scowl deepened, but his voice was one of grim understanding. "I told you I would serve you and yours until Ozenn draws me back to the sand."

Satisfied, Declan nodded and clasped the man on his shoulder. "I will repay the debt. If not in this life, then in the next."

"Don't say that," Evangeline interjected, her voice breaking, her gaze beseeching. "You'll be fine. We just need to get you home. Once Mailin removes those fragmented bones, I'll be able to heal you completely . . . I *can* do it, love."

Declan met her glistening gaze.

He dipped his head and brought their foreheads together in the way that made him feel so connected to her. Intimate, even though they were not kissing. Through the rays of the sun reflected in her eyes, he could see himself framed in her irises.

He wanted to stay there forever.

"I can heal you," she repeated, hands cradling his face, desperation darkening her eyes.

To ease her, Declan forced a smile. "I don't doubt you can heal my wounds."

Her lips quivered. "Then why are you speaking like you'll be gone?"

He had never lied to her, and he never would. "No one survives Arksana twice."

"What are you saying? You already made it out!"

Declan shut his eyes. "Not without taking in more power." *Too much.* "The moment I step from this threshold, everything inside me is mine to bear."

Declan leaned further onto her, drawing more comfort. He grazed his busted knuckles along the delicate line of her jaw and ran another palm down the arch of her back. He could never touch enough of her, could never have enough of her.

He pressed his lips against hers, desperate for a taste. She was blessedly cool against his feverish lips. He sipped deeper, losing himself in sheer sweetness . . . until he tasted tears.

Declan drew back with a shuddering breath.

Longing and loss whipped him simultaneously, but he mustered a fake smile and gave her the truth. "I need to know you'll be safe no matter what happens. And I don't know what is going to happen when I step out of Railea's land."

The roiling sensations beneath his skin . . . scared him.

Her lips trembled, yet she nodded, understanding him wordlessly. He kissed away the wetness on her cheeks, then he tipped her chin up for one more kiss before he forced himself to release her. He clenched his fists as he said, "Now, go on over to Gabriel"—who had crossed the threshold and wandered a short distance away to give them privacy. "I want to make sure you're a safe distance away before I step over."

She gave him a fierce kiss. "Everything will be alright. You'll see." She spoke as though she were the goddess of light herself. Declan didn't really believe her, but he nodded anyway, because she might not be Railea, but she was *his* goddess.

Watching her walk from him, toward another man, galled

him, but he shot her an encouraging smile every time she turned back to look at him. When she reached Gabriel's side, the fae gave him a firm nod, his expression grim.

Declan drew in a shuddering breath, then took a step over the border.

His powers returned instantly, filling him in a way that relieved the ache in his bones. Another heartbeat passed, and nothing extraordinary happened. Hope bloomed in his chest, and he dared meet Evangeline's gaze with a tentative smile. The only pain he felt radiated from his wounds. Perhaps Evangeline was right. Perhaps he would be the first person to brave *Arksana* twice and live to tell the tale. Perhaps he—

Violent power surged deep within him, emptying his lungs and knocking him to his knees. Declan glanced down to his hands. *Something* seeped from the glowing glyphs on his skin. Too viscous to be blood, too red to be anything else.

Scalding trails on his face told him it was leaking from his nose. Heat stung his gaze. He clawed at his eyes. His vision had turned to a haze of blood. "Evangeline!" he howled but heard nothing but the roar in his ears.

Power raged within him, a screaming maelstrom trying to rip through his skin. Raw, unfettered, and utterly terrifying in its urge to consume the world.

THIRTY-EIGHT

"N o!" Blinding heat made her eyes water, thinned the air, and stole her breath.

Her beautiful lover was bleeding . . . molten *fire*.

Where his blood dripped, the soil went aflame.

Declan writhed on the ground. His telepathic screams pounded in her head. A man who *never* permitted another to hear his pain unless it was truly beyond his control . . . it near slayed her to hear his unending screams.

Strong arms held her back. Gabriel had grabbed her to keep her from running into the blaze. To Declan. His screams were incoherent. Inconsolable. The tortured sound of a man pleading for death, only to be denied.

And in the space of her next sob, he simply vanished, leaving a circular field of crackling flames in his wake.

"Declan!" she shrieked into the haze of raging fire. But he was gone, and the blaze ebbed until all that remained were plumes of smoke rising from blackened ground.

A crippling chill ravaged her.

Had the fire consumed him, the same way Railea's light had

disintegrated Sebastian's body? She swayed on her feet. Pinpricks of black dotted her vision; a rash of heart-wrenching images flitted across her mind. Each one of her archmage and the things they'd done together . . . and the things they'd yet to do.

Sudden realization razed her like wildfire.

Evangeline tore at the ties on the front of her dress, desperate to see his claim. The starburst pattern glowed against her skin. Not the mark of a dead man.

Driven by sheer impulse, she whirled to Gabriel, who wore more shock than she'd ever seen on his face.

"I need you to take me to the beach near Torgerson Falls."

She couldn't explain the inexplicable pull to the place. The peak of Torgerson Falls overlooking the Amereenian ocean had been Declan's refuge of solitude before it became their love nest. And somehow she *knew* her archmage had warped there.

If Gabriel had any misgivings, he didn't voice them.

Evangeline stepped from swirling shadows into sand . . . and shock.

Gabriel coughed violently.

Astringent fumes of burnt sulfur assailed her senses, making her gag as fresh tears watered her eyes. Blinking rapidly, she tried to make sense of the staggering sight before her.

"Fuck me." Gabriel's whisper was barely audible over the whipping winds and crashing tides.

What should have been placid waves lapping over golden sand dunes was now fire. Waves and waves of fire, washing up on the beach. Sizzling seafoam blistered the shoreline as far as the eye could see. A fog had risen over the waters like a thick pall, obscuring the horizon, yet Evangeline made out the silhouette of a man she knew as intimately as she knew herself.

A man thrashing and howling *in* the sea of fire.

She started to move, but Gabriel caught her by the forearms. "Are you crazy?"

She jerked against his grip.

"Stop it!" he hissed. "What are you doing?"

Evangeline attempted an ill-aimed kick to his shins. Tears distorted her vision so badly she could barely see. "*LET.ME.GO!*"

"You'll burn!"

Declan's distant howls reached her ears, distorted by the conflagrant waves yet no less harrowing.

"Please." She wept. "I need to go to him."

"I promised him I'd keep you safe!"

"He won't hurt me."

"He can't control himself!"

"I won't *let* him." She met Gabriel's stricken gaze before the vines snared his feet. Startled, he loosened his grip for an instant, and that was all she needed to dart from his grasp.

"Evangeline! No!"

She paid him no heed. She ran to the edge of the beach, the sand scalding beneath her feet. She stepped closer still, till vapors of dancing salt and spume singed the hem of her skirts and the fabric started to burn. With a gasp, she hopped back onto dry sand and batted smoldering embers from her dress. She tore it from her body with a curse.

Squaring her shoulders, she closed her eyes in an attempt to shut out her fear.

Never use your powers in fear, Freya . . .

Declan had broken the bonds of fear and set her free. Her archmage with eyes of brilliant green, who always looked at her as though she was the only candle in a windowless room.

She dipped her feet into liquid flame.

Fire licked her skin. She didn't know if she screamed, but she refused to yield.

She forced her thoughts back to Declan.

She thought of the serious set of his lips and the way his tiny smiles tripped her heart every single time. She thought of his rumbly out-of-practice laughs and of his secret enjoyment in being stroked and petted like an overgrown cat. Of his unfailing tendency to care even though he preferred to believe himself immune.

Scorching heat mellowed, replaced by the warmth of lapping water.

Evangeline dared open her eyes. Fire continued to blaze the waters as though the ocean were filled with oil . . . yet she remained unscathed. She stretched out her arms slowly, testing her boundaries. Flames receded, a miniature radius stretching around her.

From afar, Declan had appeared like a man drowning. But now she was closer, she realized he was tearing at his skin, as though he was trying to scrub himself clean.

The water had risen to her collarbone, so she swam toward him.

"Declan." She gasped when she was close enough to touch, but shock kept her treading water. His skin was slick with molten blood that seeped from his glyphs, melded with gold and licked by fire. It made her sick. The arcane symbols were no longer glorious to behold but savage to her eyes. As though the gods had taken a knife and mutilated his skin.

With a sob, she reached for him. Her flesh seared where it touched blood, but she didn't withdraw.

"Don't touch me!" he roared, deafening her both audibly and on the mental plane. A careless swing of his hand knocked her beneath the water. Evangeline resurfaced with a gasp, coughing up seawater. She swam closer and threw herself at him—wrapping her legs around his hips—touching him everywhere she could.

"EVANGELINE!"

She clung to him. *Calm, my love.* She projected her thoughts, hoping to better penetrate his frenzy. She caressed where she could find flesh.

Calm. I am here. All will be well.

She didn't know where her confidence came from—only knew with unequivocal certainty that she would nullify the powers leaching from his skin. She *must.* Or it would be the death of her mate. And she would never let that happen.

Get away! Get away from me!

While the water barely reached his chest, she struggled to stay afloat in the choppy waves as Declan pushed against her, trying to shove her away.

She only tightened her grip, clinging to him like a sea star as she shushed and stroked, channeling her magic wherever she touched, giving as much of herself as she could. His usually smooth skin felt riddled with scars, the symbols inflamed and bumpy to her touch. But where her fingers grazed, light dwindled from the markings and blood seemed to abate. He howled louder when she grazed his partially healed collarbone, still mangled from the axe.

"Do you remember the time you dropped me in the taphouse?" She whispered the words into his ear. When he didn't respond, she added, "What about during the altercation in the woods? Did you wonder how Vera managed to get past your shield?"

His thrashing slowed, as though he was listening.

"You didn't drop me in the taphouse because you were inebriated. Nor did your shield falter in the woods." She leaned close and kissed his neck, using her lips to trace the bloodied symbols as she traced down his back.

"You dropped me because I had muted your power unknowingly. And Vera passed through your shield because I had muted it accidentally."

Declan leaned into her, groaning against her touch.

"Let me help you, love," she whispered. "Let me *in*." Into his mind.

Hurts . . . Evangeline, it hurts. His telepathic voice was a thready whimper in her head she wasn't sure he meant to share. He seemed to have retreated to a time long ago, when she had once found him broken and bloodied in the glade. *Evangeline . . .*

"I'm here, love. All will be well." Never had her birthright been so important. "All will be well," she repeated, a mantra whispered for the both of them. Where her fingers traced, his symbols ceased bleeding.

Instinctively, she lifted her lips to his. His ragged breath whistled into her mouth as she kissed him with a fervent need from her soul, from the endless well of her love for him.

A low moan escaped his throat as his arms tightened around her body to hold her closer. Evangeline pressed every part of herself against him, wanting to touch as much of him as possible with her own skin. To nullify every fiber of him over-charged by Railea's Heart, to heal every offending symbol still seeping blood.

He shuddered against her, in pain or lust, she couldn't tell. But her own kisses grew less gentle, more manic. She continued to trace the glyphs over his skin while desire rippled through her, amplifying her own magic.

Groaning, Declan broke their kiss.

"My blood . . . " His voice was roughened, yet she still heard his awe as he held a hand up from the water. He stared at the markings, no longer illuminated.

"The fire. How are you unharmed?" He wore a dumbstruck

expression, eyes wide with wonder. Vulnerable, even, with his face streaked with blood and his lips agape, staring at her like a lost wanderer discovering his lodestar.

His vulnerability only roused her desire.

She drew his face down again to press her forehead against his in the manner that made her feel like the only woman in the world, infinitely cherished.

"I muted everything within my vicinity." She couldn't bank the flames still ravaging the waters, but everything that was important was here, safe, within the circle of her arms.

Their breaths mingled, and in that moment she cared not that they were in the middle of a burning ocean. Nor did she care that he was wounded and bleeding. The only thought in her mind was: *mine*. An uncontrollable surge of magic rose in her own blood, primitive and possessive, drawing a cry of shock from his lips.

Declan's breath left his lungs as her magic shot through his body like a bolt of lightning. She had physically embraced him, but on the mental plane she had wrapped him in her light, too.

Her skin took on a luminescent sheen as though the sun rose within her body. Bright, warm, incandescent. Everything he imagined love to be and more.

Her magic coursed through him, gentle but insistent. It coiled around him, a chain of light coaxing his surrender. Declan shuddered against her, welcoming her claim that wound through to his soul.

When she finally pulled away, he gaped. His chest was still slick with blood, and the water barely up to his pectorals. But what kept him thunderstruck was the new mark etched over his heart.

A delicate curve, feathered like a fern with thicker tendrils curling over his chest, glowed in iridescent white.

"Well," she said with a wobbly smile that was no less dazzling in its perfection. "Even Railea herself can't take you from me now."

Shock kept him mute. He could only stare as the waters around them calmed to mirror his emotions. Or perhaps it was because he no longer affected the waters. Wrapped in the radius of her magic, he barely felt a whisper of power in his veins—she had *muted* all his powers. Never had he felt so . . . free. Not only that, he was claimed.

Finally.

Like a man in a thrall, he bent forward, needing a blissful taste.

"Hoy there!" The faraway voice penetrated his trance and startled Evangeline enough that she tightened her arms over his half-healed collarbone, causing him to wince.

Gabriel waved wildly from the beach. "Glad you lovebirds are not burnt crisps, but can you stop the heat? It's fucking burning up the beach!"

It took Declan a moment to realize Gabriel meant it literally. Sure enough, fire was slowly catching on the shoreline. Soon it would reach the brushes and cause a wildfire. Sand did not easily burn. Declan could only guess at the extremity of his fire to have vitrified the sand and formed fulgurite clumps on the beach.

Evangeline parted her lips, and he saw the wary question in her eyes.

Would he be able to control his powers if she ceased nullifying them?

Declan didn't know. But now that they were bound by her

mating bond, he wouldn't risk his own life for anything—risk killing her.

"Can you try loosening your hold? But not too much," Declan said with no little astonishment as he realized he couldn't even speak to her telepathically. She had well and truly rendered him powerless, as though he were still standing on the sacred grounds of Mount Arksana. She screwed her brows and nodded. Cautious, but confident.

A fraction of power welled up within him, heady and raw, but not debilitating in its force. With a soft exhale, he turned flame to frost. Ice floated around them in fractured pieces, and condensation in the air thickened to snow.

Evangeline turned her head up to the sky with a gasp at the clearing fog.

"Have you ever seen anything like this?" Snowflakes dusted her lashes. Relief and awe filled her tone. Declan shook his head, equally awestruck.

Never in his life had he encountered a being as resplendent as she.

THIRTY-NINE

Declan lay quiescent. He did not even flinch as Mailin plucked a sliver of fractured bone from his mangled shoulder, but Evangeline whimpered on his behalf.

"I'm sorry, Evie," Mailin said with a grimace, as though it were her flesh she was prying apart with a pair of bloodied tweezers.

Alexander, who had been speaking quietly with Gabriel in the corner of the room wandered over with a frown on his face. "Is the color of his blood *normal?*"

"Oh, quit worrying, the lot of you," Gabriel said in a dry tone. "If he didn't die in that fiery ocean, he's unlikely to kick the bucket now."

Declan was inclined to agree with the insolent fae, but Evangeline's deepening frown distracted him. She stroked his hair and squeezed his hand, her sweet concern more effective than any sedative.

"Won't you just take the sleeping draft?" Evangeline asked, imploring him further with her eyes.

Declan shook his head.

Evangeline sighed with exasperation while Mailin clucked her tongue. But with Sebastian dead and Vera-Zephyr still on the run, he couldn't risk losing consciousness. Knowing the other archmages would inevitably catch word of Sebastian's death sooner rather than later, Declan had dispatched envoys to the other six kingdoms, requesting a formal gathering of the Echelon.

Besides, having Mailin pick and prod at his wound was almost welcome. Pain served as a reminder that he was still alive. He didn't realize he'd uttered the sentiment aloud until Mailin stared down at him, utterly bemused.

"I believe the sire is still in shock," she declared.

"All that power must have addled his brain," Gabriel mused.

"It won't have a long-term effect, will it?" Alexander asked, tone anxious.

Evangeline's sunset eyes filled his vision. "Declan . . . ?"

He reached up to wipe the offending creases from her forehead with his thumb, seeking to reassure her. A woman who had waded through a sea of fire for *him*.

Emotion constricted his throat.

I love you. Words seemed to pale against the enormity of what he felt in his chest, but he needed desperately to express himself in some small way. Her response was a soft, tremulous smile as she leaned close to whisper the same into his ear.

"Just a few more shards and you can work your magic." Mailin eyed them with a little chuckle.

Another jolt of pain. Declan found Evangeline's hand, interlaced their fingers, and shut his eyes. He couldn't stop himself from dipping into the mental plane, admiring the beauty of their completed bond. A bond of frost and flame threaded with a sleek and slender vine of opaline white.

"What are these?" Evangeline asked, worrying his cheek with a washcloth.

The hitch in her voice had him opening his eyes. But her question was directed to no one in particular, and as a result, Declan found three curious pairs of eyes staring down at him.

Mailin paused in her ministrations. A wrinkle marred her forehead. "Railea has marked him . . . again?"

"But ascension symbols are never on the face," Alexander protested.

Declan drew his own brows together.

"I'd thought these were cuts, but you seem to have grown more symbols, Archmage." Evangeline trailed feather-soft fingers over his collarbone, traced a jagged line up his neck to curve over his cheekbones. The lines of concern bracketing her lips made him swallow.

"Does it look bad?" It wasn't a question borne of vanity, but from the sudden fear that he was now less desirable to her.

"It will take some time getting used to, that's all. It makes you look . . . " She bit her lower lip as pink stained her cheeks.

"Formidable," Mailin supplied.

"Fierce," Alexander agreed.

Gabriel's snort drew everyone's attention. "Fucking *scary*, if you ask me."

Evangeline glared. Her pointed ears angled in protective annoyance before she glanced down at him. "Striking," she said, her fingers caressing the symbols on the side of his face as though she was already trying to commit them to memory. "I would say they make you look more striking, Archmage. Even more . . . beautiful."

The truth of her thoughts rippled through their newly completed bond in the form of fierce desire. Declan grinned.

The color on Evangeline's cheeks deepened when the

healer, councilor, and assassin all stared before they burst into a series of infantile sniggers.

Flattening her lips, Evangeline ignored them with a regal ease. "They're glowing. Are they hurting you?"

"No." Perhaps they did, but everything paled in comparison to the excruciating pain he'd just endured. "Is it hurting *you?*" Declan wasn't asking if witnessing his pain had hurt her. He knew it had. He was more concerned with what it cost her to ameliorate it, for even *now*, she was holding his powers in check, allowing only a fraction to flow through him at a time.

Her lips pursed. "I know it sounds impossible, but somehow, I feel more energized than ever. I feel . . . strong."

Her response rendered him more than a little breathless. No wonder Zephyr had gone to such lengths to possess her. She could subdue even a goddess's powers. She truly did possess the ability to make or break kingdoms.

I can't believe you came for me, little fire.

Gentle fingers stroked his cheek. Her love was a silent kiss through their bond. *I'll always come for you, Declan. Just like you'll always come for me.*

Declan grinned wider. He truly was the luckiest bastard in the five realms.

"There. That should be the last of it," Mailin declared cheerily. "Do you want to seal the wound, Evie?" The healer was wiping her bloodied hands on a washcloth when Declan's commander entered the room. The usual smile Mailin reserved solely for her mate froze on her face. Evangeline gasped as they all stared at the bloody rucksack in Killian's grip.

"Sire."

"Fruitful hunt, commander?" Gabriel nodded with a wry smile.

"Is Zephyr dead?" Declan asked.

If Killian noticed any difference in Declan's appearance, he showed no indication. Instead, he dipped his shoulders as though in shame. Mailin hurried over to his side.

"We pursued Vera to the edge of the woods. Leif had her in his grip, but the witch *bit* him in the neck. Then she commandeered his sword and steed."

Alexander's brows reached for his hairline. "Are you saying she escaped *three* of Amereen's finest?"

Declan echoed his brother's disbelief. Vera might be under Zephyr's thrall, but three battlemages were more than equipped to overpower one female mage. "If not her head, then what do you have in the bag?"

Lips in a grim line, Killian reached into the rucksack and drew out a slender forearm that ended in a bloody stump where an elbow should be. "This."

There was a beat of silence before Mailin's bewildered exclamation, "Vera cut off her own hand?"

"*Zephyr.*" Evangeline corrected. Her pointed ears flattened like an irate cat's. "That monster clearly cares nothing for what he does to her body. But he—she—couldn't have ridden far if she's so severely wounded."

"She didn't. The moment she crossed the threshold, she warped." Killian dropped the severed arm back into the rucksack. "But due to a stroke of luck, I know exactly where she . . . *he* went."

Declan cocked his head in question.

"The envoy you sent to Flen is outside the ward, waiting to see you. Apparently, his audience with the lord archmage Strom was cut short when a woman warped forcibly into the court. A woman missing half a limb."

Never would Declan have considered bringing Evangeline into the stronghold of another archmage without an invitation, but then, he hadn't ever been a mated man before.

"I'm going with you, or you're not going at all," she had said with challenge in her eyes as she sealed the wound in his shoulder. *"We don't know if your powers will surge again, so you're not going anywhere without me."*

He had found it impossible to argue with her insistence pulsing in the bond between them. Besides, her argument was sound.

He would be a fool to think himself free from the maelstrom of raw power that had nearly torn him apart. While Evangeline continued to mute the excess and claimed she felt no hardship, he was not convinced she could do so indefinitely without repercussion.

They needed a sustainable way to keep his powers manageable, but until they found a solution, she was his only salvation.

Declan kept a shield around her as they materialized in the Flenian Castle. Not wanting to waste time, he had warped them directly to Nathaniel's exact location, that turned out to be an airy, sun-drenched solar. It was a room the other archmage often used when he intended to impress. With one half of the walls a series of full-length glass windows, the solar had a remarkable view of a pavilion of frost-riddled trees and the harsh glaciers beyond.

Since he'd been forewarned by his envoy, Vera's presence did not come as a surprise, but the second man in the room made Evangeline stiffen and Declan snarl, *"You."*

The Unseelie prince jolted up from his seat, knocking his gold-winged chair to the ground. Vera, who had been nursing some form of drink in her hand, dropped the mug with a shriek before scuttling to the farthest corner of the room.

"Calm, my son. It may come as a surprise to you, but Zion enjoys my company, almost as much as you seem to loathe it." Nathaniel remained seated at the head of the oval table, appearing more concerned by Declan's countenance than his sudden presence.

"It's true, then," Nathaniel added, staring at the new markings on his face. "Vera spoke the truth. You and Sebastian both fell into *Arksana* . . . but *you* rose." Pride suffused Nathaniel's laugh. "Legends were made on lesser tales, my son."

Declan ignored the fool. He had survived solely by the grace of the small and seemingly meek woman by his side. A woman who clung to the crook of his arm as though *he* were the protector, when *she* dictated the amount of power currently flowing in his veins. A woman Nathaniel barely spared a second glance.

"If my survival had been in any way within my control, then I would have taken care to wipe this creature from the face of the realm and saved us all this confrontation." Declan fought the urge to turn Vera into a live bonfire right here in the solar, but Evangeline had insisted on first freeing the bitch from the wolf. *"Vera spared me—us—when we were at our most vulnerable,"* she had argued. *"She helped me pull you up from Railea's Heart."*

As far as Declan was concerned, Vera had caused the problem. She *was* a problem.

The shrew deserved no mercy.

Nor would he allow Zephyr another chance for escape. He spun a translucent web around Evangeline, encasing her in his shield before he warped across the room and cornered Vera against the wall before wrapping hands over her neck. The manipulative creature shrieked and writhed as though his touch were a firebrand. He could almost be convinced she was nothing but a hapless female recently relieved of a limb. Almost.

Declan held her firmly in place and gave her a little shake. "Show the truth, you conniving little snake, or I'll have no qualms in burning this new body of yours, too."

Zion lurched to his feet, his sharp features twisted in disgust. "Stop! *You* condone this, Lady Barre? The mutilation and manhandling of an innocent woman?"

"Innocent?" Evangeline exclaimed. "You have no idea what she is!"

Vera cradled the bandaged stump of her arm with abject fear masterfully plastered over her face as she whimpered, "P-please, my lords, don't let them h-hurt me."

"Liar," Evangeline cried, revealing sharp fangs with uncharacteristic aggression. "Release her, and show your true self!"

Zion frowned. "What in Ozenn's name are you talking about?"

"This innocent is under Zephyr's possession," Declan said flatly. "Or perhaps you already knew that."

The lines of confusion deepened on the prince's face, morphing to show near-comical shock as he stared at Vera as though she'd grown two heads and a glider tail. "Zephyr's *possession?* How is that even possible? He is . . . dead."

Declan huffed out a laugh at the man's theatrics. "Dead? That was what you would have had us believe, wasn't it? That's why you're here, isn't it? To solidify your father's farce?"

"Zephyr is *not* my father," Zion grated, hands fisting with such intensity his knuckles whitened.

Tiny twitches rippled through Vera's body even as her body tensed. Trying hard to contain herself.

"Enough!" Nathaniel barked, rising to his feet. "I don't know what delusions you're suffering"—a pointed look at Evangeline—"but these preposterous claims must cease.

Zephyr is *dead*. The Winter Court wouldn't be looking to crown a new king otherwise."

Nathaniel, oblivious to the impact of his revelation, continued, "Really, I had hoped for a better way of introducing you to your brother, but it seems—"

Vera bit into Declan's arm with the aggression of a rabid dog, belying her appearance of a weak and wounded creature.

"Sonofabitch!" Declan raised a smattering of frost, but Vera was already darting away. Not for escape. It seemed Zephyr had only one motive here. A glinting flash in Vera's good arm alerted Declan to a concealed weapon.

He released a pulse of telekinesis meant to shove Nathaniel from harm's way. Only the other archmage was already moving. Nathaniel darted to the side before Vera's knife could meet its mark.

Declan's psychic punch hit Vera squarely in the chest. She hurtled back, crashing through the windows in a tinkling hail of shattered glass.

"Pathetic fae bastard!" Nathaniel snarled, kicking shards of broken glass hanging like sharp fangs on the doorframe as he stalked toward Vera's crumpled form. "Did you truly think you could deceive me? That you could best me?"

Declan reined in the fire in his veins and raised a brow.

Interesting. Clearly, he had given the other archmage less credit than he deserved.

Vera's body convulsed as though she was suffering a seizure. Her head snapped up, and her body spasmed as she grated out between roughened breaths, "I'll see you burn in the five hells for what you did to Seraphina! You're the reason she's dead!"

"Me?" Nathaniel roared, the markings on his skin sparking. "*You* killed her!"

Frost cemented Vera's remaining limbs to the ground.

Declan returned to Evangeline's side, keeping his arm and

psychic shield around her while he kept the Unseelie prince within his sights. Zion picked up Vera's discarded knife from the ground, and then he *warped*, showcasing the mage blood in his veins, before reappearing in the frost-lined pavilion.

Without a word, he plunged the knife into Vera's chest.

She couldn't seem to scream. She choked up a mouthful of blood, her eyes wide with shock before Zion drove the knife in a second time. With the dispassionate demeanor of a butcher in a slaughterhouse, the prince wrenched and thrust the knife in again and again. Vera's twitching body stilled, but the prince continued.

Declan had both lived and dealt enough violence to numb his senses, but Evangeline's shock reverberated through their bond. He cupped the back of her head and turned her face firmly into his chest. The extent of her horror distressed him. She was not built for brutality, and he was not used to sensing the breadth of her emotions so clearly.

Vera's chest was nothing but a gore-drenched cavity when Zion slowed, his breathing ragged as though he'd run for miles, yet he still kept *stabbing*. The man was unhinged.

"That's enough. He is dead." Declan needed the man to cease the mindless carnage. Every wet plunge of the knife only served to compound Evangeline's horror. But Zion couldn't seem to hear him.

Stab . . . Wrench . . . Stab . . .

"Zion!"

Zion paused, knife quivering midair. The prince frowned down at Vera's mutilated chest, staring at the corpse as though he didn't know who she was or how she got there. He blinked and scrubbed his face, smearing a grisly streak of blood from chin to cheek before a laugh spewed from his throat.

"Raw meat," he muttered between fits of hysterical laughter. "Mother looked just like *this* when Zephyr was done with her. Raw meat."

Declan stared. The man wasn't merely unhinged. He was well and truly mad.

"Zion," Nathaniel said, his voice unusually gentle. "My son, it is *done*. He is gone. Give me the knife."

Zion's laughter ebbed. The knife slipped from his hand and clattered to the ground with a clang.

Declan returned his attention to Evangeline, needing to distance his mate from the raving lunatic. *Let's go home.* There was no longer a reason for them to be here.

He tilted her chin up for a quick, reassuring kiss, so he didn't notice the dark ribbons snaking from the bloody cavity that had been the corpse's chest. He didn't see black tendrils leaking through its nostrils and its mouth until he heard Nathaniel's startled shout.

FORTY

Evangeline parted her lips in shock. One moment Declan was soothing her with a kiss, and the next . . . chill bumps crawled over her skin. Fury seeped through their bond, a frigid and frightening sensation, foreign in its intensity.

"How can the motherfucking whoreson still live?" Declan shoved her behind him as though to shield her from the source of his rage.

Evangeline pushed past his shoulder, and her knees threatened to buckle.

Her greatest nightmare had come back to life. Not in the form of shadow, but flesh.

No longer was Zephyr the arresting king with hair of silver white, but a shell of an unrecognizable man. Every part of his skin appeared stippled, made worse by lesions gaping across his face and hands. His lower lip had been completely burned away, revealing a row of pearlescent teeth adhering to singed gums. He lifted his head, and Evangeline caught sight of the sleek ivory of his collarbone, visible beneath sinew and blackened flesh.

Zephyr had never recovered from the injuries sustained during his battle with Declan. He laughed, his voice withered and whispery and *wrong*. "You fools! Nothing can kill the Deathless, and I've long cleaved my soul so I could see this *sipa* to his grave."

That was when she realized Nathaniel had fallen to his knees. His hands clawed at his neck. The blade that had hollowed Vera's chest was now lodged to the hilt—in Nathaniel's throat. Declan must have noticed it at the same time, for his shock echoed her own.

"That's impossible . . . You're dead. You're supposed to stay dead." Zion had retreated to the far wall, his eyes as glassy as the shattered windowpanes beneath his boots.

Zephyr's nightmarish face twisted into what must be a sneer, but with a missing lip, it was a gruesome perversion of one. "What's more impossible is your traitorous heart . . . to think I raised you like my own." Like a monster crawling out from under a child's bed, Zephyr stalked the prince, his motions stiff and rickety.

Evangeline took the opportunity and darted to Nathaniel's side.

Declan didn't try to stop her. Instead, sudden heat punched through the air. Her archmage was never a man of many words.

The thing that was Zephyr erupted in flames.

Ignoring the smoke and screams, Evangeline focused on Nathaniel, who was now choking on his own blood and bile.

"I'm sorry," she whispered, not knowing if Nathaniel could even hear her. "But this is going to hurt." Evangeline clamped her fingers over the hilt of the blade still slick from Vera's blood and wrenched it free.

Nathaniel gurgled as his body went limp.

Heat flared at her back, and the screams turned to shrieks, but Evangeline drew magic from the ground and poured it into Nathaniel's neck. Flesh knitted and skin smoothed. When she was certain the archmage was no longer fatally wounded, she pulled back.

The stench of blood infused with burnt flesh made her gag.

Declan had moved so he loomed before her, protective in his stance, but the look on his face told her Zephyr wasn't quite dead.

The pavilion was scorched, Vera's body nothing but fine ash, yet the shell of a man remained standing amid the flame. When the flames receded, the walking corpse of bone and blackened skin that was Zephyr cackled his mirth.

"Foolish mageling, don't you understand? You may kill my vessels, but you *can't* kill me. Not with steel, fire, or ice." Its voice was a hollow echo, its expression twisted into a macabre smile. "But I can hurt you. And I will keep coming back until you are dead."

With a growl, Declan stepped forward. The air around him pulsed with barely leashed flame. "I'd like to see you try."

Evangeline barred him with a hand to his chest. *Trust me, Archmage,* she projected.

Declan snapped his gaze to meet hers, indecision warring in his eyes. A muscle ticced at his temple, but he seemed to concede, for he stilled.

Her own rage churned through their bond, so hot and stark it overwhelmed even the intensity of her archmage's cold fury. No way would she permit Zephyr to hurt another person she loved. Not if she could help it.

"Ah, my little Jilintree, have you even found a way to leash an archmage? Do you finally see your worth? Your destiny?"

Her destiny. "Yes."

A vine, tipped with a thorn sharp as a talon, punched

through Zephyr's blackened chest in one fluid jab. The pavilion might be paved with slabs of smooth stone, but her archmage's flames had caused fissures. That was all she'd needed to draw life from the earth, coax it from the fine crevices, widen the cracks until thicker vines took root.

Shock flared in Zephyr's lidless eyes as he glanced down at his chest where the vine protruded. More speared from the ground, tendrils of green that coiled and sprung up to latch over his legs. The sinewy stems grew thicker with every breath she took and sprouted thorns like the scales on a snake. Zephyr kicked and ripped, wrenching the vines apart.

Beside her, Declan vibrated with restless energy. His lust for Zephyr's blood pumped through their bond, but he didn't act. His inaction emboldened her.

He trusted her to do what she wanted for herself.

Unable to escape her vines, Zephyr turned amorphous, necrotic flesh melting into shadows.

Evangeline shook her head. She released a pulse of her birthright to nullify his efforts, and shadows coalesced into flesh.

"You can't kill me!" Zephyr screeched. "You can't kill one of the Deathless!"

Evangeline lifted her arms, feeding more life into her shoots. Maybe he couldn't be killed, but he *could* be entombed.

And her kind had been preserving bodies in Soul Trees for centuries.

"You're the cause of all the rot in this realm," she murmured.

"The weight of the crown never comes without bloodshed, little Jilintree," Zephyr said through harsh gasps. "You are not so different from me."

Evangeline slackened her vines.

Zephyr cackled and coughed, blood-laced spittle leaking

from his lips. "You are weak, just like your mother. Too weak to rule."

Mention of Mama caused renewed rage within her breast, and her vines thickened with alarming intensity, coiling around Zephyr's legs like a mass of writhing pythons. They hardened into rough bark to keep him firmly rooted.

"My mother never wanted the crown." Evangeline blinked back tears. "You're right. I may never rule." More vines coiled over Zephyr's arms. Her heart pounded in her ears, a deafening rhyme to the rhythm of her roots that dug deep into the ground. "But neither will you. Never again."

Zephyr's scream echoed across the pavilion as her vines covered his face and enveloped his head. Tiny branches speared from his skull like a crown, shifting and stretching as the branches hardened. Leaves sprouted from the branches, bloodred against black.

Evangeline didn't move until she felt Declan's arms around her and his lips against her temple. He held her, his presence filling her with steady strength, until the shuddering tree stilled.

"Will it hold him?"

Evangeline nodded with a confidence she rarely felt. "Zephyr may not die, but he can't leave unless someone releases him."

The lips still pressed against her temple curved into a smile.

"Then you've left him in the perfect place. Nathaniel will ensure it remains . . . guarded."

Evangeline turned to bury her face in his chest, glad for the strength of his frame and the gentleness of his touch. Declan turned her toward where Zion stood beside a still-sprawled Nathaniel, both men in seemingly stunned silence. In that fleeting moment, Evangeline caught an eerie whisper of Declan—of *Nathaniel*—in the set of Zion's features.

"You healed me," Nathaniel said, his tone more curious than grateful. "Why?"

Evangeline held the other archmage's gaze, so eerily similar to her archmage's that her breath caught in her throat.

"Because you were hurt." Evangeline had never needed more cause to heal a person than the urge to ease their pain. But if she were truly honest, she hadn't healed Nathaniel for so simple a reason. Declan had felt a sense of loss when he'd witnessed the knife lodged in Nathaniel's throat. A sort of pain. And Evangeline would do everything she could to alleviate *all* his hurts.

When Zion stepped forward, Declan curved a protective hand around her waist and raised another in warning.

"I would never seek to harm my future queen." The prince went down to one knee like a soldier waiting to be knighted.

Evangeline blinked at the prince. "What did you say?"

"You have defeated the *king* of the Winter Court." Zion gazed up at her with a sort of reverential awe. "You've every right to his throne."

The breath whooshed from her lungs, and she struggled for words. Zion however, seemed to have enough to fill the silence.

"The fae realm has been dying, *is* dying, without Seeliekind. Come back with me, and I will do everything I can to see you on the throne. Even Zenaidus won't contest a descendant of the Summer Court, especially not one with Jilintree blood."

Beside her, Declan had turned to granite.

Evangeline glanced up at her archmage, whose expression had gone indecipherable. But she was now fully bonded to him; he could no longer hide behind his quiet reserve. She sensed his possessiveness as much as the underlying prickle of fear that had stiffened the thew of his arms.

"You honor me, my prince. The fae realm is more a husk of broken memories than a home. I have no wish to return. And besides . . . " Gazing into emerald eyes that were her forever, she murmured, "I already *am* a queen."

Declan's rumbling chuckle shot liquid heat through her veins.

"Take us home, Archmage."

His answering smile was godlike in its beauty. "As you wish, my queen."

FORTY-ONE

Seedlings sprang from where she caressed the ground. Evangeline hummed absently, coaxing the sprout with a lullaby from a long, long time ago.

The stem lengthened and hardened; the slender twigs bore tiny green buds that unfurled into luscious white roses. A bittersweet smile slid across her lips.

If only Mama could see her now . . .

"Lady Barre," said a deep, male voice.

Evangeline whirled around, hand at her throat.

Councilor Reyas stood by the terrace with his mouth slashed in its usual disapproving line.

"Lord Councilor." Evangeline exhaled.

"Apologies, my lady. I did not mean to startle, but I found these two miscreants spying on you." Reyas bowed deeply before moving aside to reveal two guilty-faced charges.

Evangeline chuckled and beckoned them over. "Surin. Chito. What are you doing out here?"

Surin, whose dark hair had grown long and glossy to match

the healthy sheen of her rounded cheeks, darted forward to embrace Evangeline at the waist, which earned her a harrumph from the observing councilor.

"Child, get your grubby paws off the elorin! Has no one taught you manners?"

Evangeline wrapped her arms around the girl with a laugh. "It is quite all right. Thank you for bringing them to my attention."

When Reyas lingered, Evangeline raised a questioning brow. "Anything else I can do for you, Lord Councilor?"

Spine stiff as a broomstick, the councilor bowed again. Ever since she'd healed his frostbitten legs, Reyas had made a habit of genuflecting to her at every opportunity, but Evangeline had an inkling the man had never bowed to a woman other than Declan's mother—and Evangeline was a far cry from the ruler Corvina had been.

"No, my lady. The gods know you've done enough." The words could be perceived as sarcastic, but Evangeline heard genuine gratitude in his tone and saw respect in his eyes. Maybe even a little warmth.

Evangeline shot him a parting smile before returning her attention to the little girls. "And what can I do for you two?"

Surin clung to her skirts, while Chito kept her head bowed and hands wringing, seemingly unable to meet her gaze. Evangeline didn't push for contact. Chito had only been brought to the survivor's ward a few short months ago—the child would open up when she was ready.

"Can I have flowers?" Surin blurted the moment Councilor Reyas moved from earshot. "Mama and I are living in staff quarters now. I want to . . . pretty the room."

Evangeline beamed. Surin was still learning the common tongue, but now she enunciated well—great improvement from the speechless girl she had once been.

"Of course." Evangeline was already reaching for the clippers in her workbasket. "Which ones would you like?"

"The pink bells," Surin said decisively, pointing at the lily patch. "They make Mama happy. And I like pink."

Evangeline chuckled. "Yes, of course." Evangeline glanced at the other child. "What about you, Chito? Would you like some lilies, too?"

Chito's gaze darted longingly to the white blooms before returning to her sandaled feet. She shook her head.

"My lady," called yet another somber voice from the terrace. Chito froze like a startled rabbit, and Evangeline cringed internally.

"Yes, Ginley?"

The austere chamberlain approached them, a wrapped package in hand. "I'm sorry to interrupt, my lady, but a *courtesan* asked to see you." Ginley gave an incredulous huff. "I sent the lightskirt away, of course, but she insisted, and quite rudely, I might add, that you were expecting this."

She held the soft-wrapped package by its edge as though it harbored a contagious disease.

Evangeline pinched the bridge of her nose and stifled a laugh.

With Tessa gone, Evangeline had been fresh out of handmaidens. Her archmage had meted out a sentence on the treacherous maid, and Evangeline hadn't asked for the details. There were instances where she would sway Declan's decisions, and instances where she understood she could not.

In this instance, Tessa had been living on borrowed time from the moment she served Evangeline her first cup of doctored tea.

Offers to fill the role had occurred swiftly after the fast-circulating news of Amereen's elorin braving an ocean of fire for her archmage. Amereenians had lapped up the tale, which had since—to her and Declan's unending amusement—been dramatized by playwrights and even spun into songs. But somehow, the head chamberlain had seen fit to assume the role of handmaid herself.

"I assure you, my lady, no one is more qualified than I to see to your needs," Madam Ginley had said with a prim sniff. While her archmage had made it clear the position was only for as long as it took Evangeline to select another maid of her liking, Madam Ginley seemed intent on making her role a permanent one.

Evangeline had never thought a handmaid was necessary, but if it would release Madam Ginley from her self-appointed position? She had never been more eager.

Evangeline eyed the package in the chamberlain's hand. "Was her name Ilana, by any chance?"

"I wouldn't know. No matter, my lady. You really shouldn't be associating with women of such ill repute."

Evangeline stifled the urge to roll her eyes. She would pay Ilana a visit later. Taking the prosaic-looking package from the chamberlain, Evangeline gave it a little squeeze. Soft. She would have squealed with excitement if not for the impropriety of it.

Instead, she plastered a neutral expression on her face and said, "Thank you, Ginley, but next time, please consult me before turning callers away. Courtesans included."

Madam Ginley frowned down the length of her nose but conceded with a sigh. "As you wish, my lady."

Evangeline rattled off a stream of instructions and a list of items, which caused furrows in the chamberlain's forehead.

Turning back to the girls, Evangeline clasped her hands together with a grin. "Now, could you be a couple of dears and run an errand for me?"

Declan drummed fingers on the hardwood table as he considered the disgruntled assassin leaning against the wall of his study. "You would have me void a deal?"

The lines bracketing the fae's mouth deepened. "The *draga sul* doesn't belong in the hands of a brute like Reiken."

"A deal is a deal, Gabriel." As far as Declan was concerned, the soul catcher rightfully belonged to the primus. Shyaree had fulfilled the terms of their deal. The shaman deserved to be returned to her clan with the unending gratitude of an archmage—expressed through enough gold and riches to make her the wealthiest woman in the animati realm.

"And if Reiken attempts necromancy? Raises the dead?"

Declan returned his gaze to the grain of the hardwood table as he considered the possibility. Highly unlikely. "The soul catcher doesn't work without the soul cleaver. Even so, Reiken must first have access to a seer. The last one died in the Winter War."

"Then how did Zephyr do it? Turn himself Deathless?"

Declan flattened his lips. "I am not convinced Zephyr *is* Deathless. He couldn't have achieved true immortality without the soul catcher." The *draga sul* had been in Declan's possession the whole time.

The guildmaster prowled the length of his study like a restless leopard. Declan was not entirely at ease himself. Despite his rationale, Zephyr had attained *some* form of immortality.

"The only way to be certain is to retrieve the soul cleaver. The *draga morli*," Declan murmured. If Zephyr had cleaved his soul without the soul catcher to preserve it, parts of it might still be within the *draga morli*.

"Zephyr could have hidden it any-fucking-where in the five realms."

"Unlikely. If Zion is to be believed, then Zephyr must have kept it close. If you leave now, you'll have the best chance of infiltrating the Winter Court before the next Unseelie king is crowned."

Gabriel paused, and his next words were entirely unexpected. "Who will take the wildcat home if not me?"

Declan lifted a glass of Mujarin to his lips and took a slow sip as he regarded the other man over the rim.

"Evangeline wants Shyaree present for our Promise Ceremony, so I've decided the shaman will remain with us until after." Declan noted the subtle loosening of Gabriel's shoulders.

Curious.

The fae resumed his pacing. "If I go talisman hunting, I won't be around to cater to your every whim."

"A *minor* inconvenience." Declan allowed his amusement to show by way of a smirk. "One I'm certain I'll survive."

Gabriel's scowl deepened, and he muttered a string of ill-advised profanities that Declan pretended not to hear as he downed his drink.

"Evangeline expects *you* at the ceremony, too." In truth, Declan himself wanted the fae there, for reasons he did not care to examine too closely. He was no sentimental soul. That was his little fire's forte. "So whatever you do, make sure you show up."

When he received a grumbling nod, he was quick to dismiss the conversation before Gabriel could finagle more of his time.

Declan was eager for his mate.

He had quickly discovered more uses for Evangeline's Jilintree abilities. While in bed, he had taken to coaxing her into muting not just the excess of his powers, but *all* of them.

Declan hadn't dreamed of taking a woman with such wild abandon since the day he'd ascended. If it weren't for the added demands on the Echelon due to Sebastian's death, he would have kept her sequestered in their chamber for a full week. Even so, he was determined to seduce and keep her in bed for as many hours of every evening as was physically possible . . .

Two unlikely minds outside drew his curiosity.

Declan opened the door. If he hadn't detected them lurking about, he would have stepped right onto the sprig of foxgloves laying innocuously on the ground.

He picked up the stalk of purple bells and twirled it in his fingers. "Strange."

Gabriel chuckled. "Found yourself some new admirers, have you?"

Declan followed Gabriel's line of sight and found two adorable little faces—one familiar to him and one not—peeking from around the corner. The moment they met his gaze, their eyes widened and they scurried off. Not without leaving another sprig on the ground.

"Never thought I'd see the day I'd catch you smiling down at flowers and children. Ah, how the mighty have fallen."

Declan frowned at the irksome fae. "Do you not have a guild to run? Assassins to train?"

Gabriel nodded with a smirk, taking his cue. "And marks to kill."

As the fae disappeared through the swirling depths of his portal, Declan rounded the corner to retrieve the second sprig.

A fluffy red clover.

Amused, he followed the trail of wildflowers like a mouse

with breadcrumbs. When he finally came upon the shaded courtyard, he had a colorful bouquet in his hand. The girls were long out of sight, and there were no further stray blooms to lead his way. He could reach out telepathically and scan the area, but he didn't want to. He was quite certain this was a game, one he very much wanted to play.

Excited whispers rose from the gardens.

Declan followed the sound to see the little perpetrators cooing over two large baskets of freshly cut flowers. The baskets were almost too large for them to carry, but the girls clutched at them eagerly, two tiny pirates and their bounty.

"Where is she, little one?"

Surin grinned up from her basket of lilies. "She said you'd know." With that, she darted off with her comrade, who carried a basketful of white roses.

Alone, Declan drew in a deep breath, enjoying the heady fragrance of wildflowers that had always been her scent. He'd know, would he?

Then he chuckled. Of course. Now that she had him baited into her element, she no longer needed her tiny henchmen to lay out her lures.

A string of colored wildflowers lined the perfectly manicured grass, dictating his path. The bright, velvety trail led him deep into the castle grounds, cutting past the hedge mazes, through the orchard, and past the fountains where the rolling hills were peppered by ancient trees.

His trail ended with a bright orange poppy beneath a wide-limbed tree overlooking the horizon. Declan grinned as anticipation hummed in his blood.

A blanket lay on the ground, complete with a picnic basket and a small pile of logs clearly set up for a cozy campfire. He glanced around eagerly, feeling like a treasure hunter who'd accurately deciphered his map. But where was his bounty?

A soft giggle and the rustling of leaves gave her away.

Declan looked up, and his blood heated.

Seated on a large tree branch overhead, feet bare and shapely legs swinging, was his gorgeous little woodland nymph in all her glory. Moss and tiny flowers patterned the bark where she sat, as though life itself revered her every touch.

He crooked his finger. "Come down, little fire."

A coy smile kissed her lips, one she donned only for him. "Come up, Archmage."

Declan raised his brows. It had just occurred to him he had never climbed a tree in his life. He had never seen reason to do so. He took in the seductive opening of her cloak that flashed bare skin. Now he saw great reason.

After laying down the bouquet of wildflowers and shrugging off his coat, he scaled the tree in a heartbeat.

He tested the branch to make sure it was strong enough to hold both their weight, then he crept over to his queen. Evangeline practically purred in his arms. Her back bowed like a cat inveigling a scratch.

He indulged her with a tongue-melding kiss. When he attempted to slip a hand beneath the heavy wool of her cloak, she pulled away.

"Uh-uh." She shook her head.

He gave her a mock scowl.

"My game, my rules." An impish grin. "Besides, you're just in time. Look." She turned her face toward the setting sun that painted the horizon a brilliant blend of deepening azure lashed by streaks of oranges and pinks. He returned his gaze to her.

He knew what he much preferred to watch.

Before the sun truly dipped, Declan couldn't resist any further. He leaned over to undo her cloak so he could treat himself to more of her skin.

She batted his hands away. "You'll ruin my surprise."

More surprises? His blood heated even more as his head suddenly filled with a slew of branch-shaking fantasies. It would require some balancing, but with the help of telekinesis . . .

He had to know.

"Are you naked under there?"

She giggled again, sliding close to part her cloak, allowing him a glimpse of bare, creamy flesh.

Railea, mother of the realm . . .

She slid over to straddle him on the branch. "Of course . . . *not,*" she whispered into his ear, her breath warming more than his skin before she scuttled past him with unexpected dexterity and descended the tree.

"Little minx." He warped to the ground before she reached it. He couldn't possibly climb down a tree when he was this hard.

"Wait," she protested, but he was already hauling her up into his arms.

"I'm hungry," he declared, laying her over the blanket like a sumptuous feast. He crawled over her eagerly. "Feed me, little fire."

To his bemusement, she rolled out from under him. Then she pulled him up to his feet and drew him from the blanket back to the spot beneath the heavy branches. He cocked his head. Did she want to be taken against a tree?

Oh, yes, he was happy to indulge her.

"No," she said with a laugh, clearly reading his intentions. "Stay where you are, Archmage. Don't move."

Declan frowned as she released his hands and stepped away from him.

She reached up to undo the clasp of her cloak.

He hardened even more in anticipation. *Oh, yes.*

She licked her lips tentatively and released a wrung-out chuckle.

Declan frowned at her shyness.

His little fire hadn't been sexually nervous around him for a long time. Had he overdone it these last few days? Scared her in some way? But the glimmer of mischief dancing in her eyes assured him otherwise.

"Are you ready, Archmage?"

Declan raised a brow as he glanced pointedly down to his straining member. For her, he was *always* ready. She smiled, visibly relaxing. She undid her cloak, her movements near bashful as the garment crumpled around her feet.

Declan's mouth went dry. He swallowed convulsively.

"Wha . . . what are you wearing?"

His reaction must have pleased her because her grin deepened. She sashayed closer and did a tantalizingly slow turn so he could fully appreciate her *surprise*.

White lace with floral motifs cupped her breasts and adorned her hips. A semi-transparent garter encircled each slender leg. Tiny silk ribbons tethered to eyelets crisscrossed over her navel and twined all over her lace-encased torso as though she were a gift for his unwrapping. A gift that screamed *fuck me*.

Every fiber of him gravitated toward her.

"Uh-uh," she said again with a shake of her head.

Then she turned and bent, giving him a mind-blanking view of her lace-kissed rear before reaching for a tiny vial hidden in her cloak. She uncorked it.

A heady scent wafted up his nose. He frowned as he leaned forward and sniffed. "Ozenn's seed," she murmured before taking a small sip. She lifted it to his lips with a nervous smile. "It's just oil from crushed vitalis seeds . . . "

She could have given him poison, and he would have drunk it without compunction.

Seemingly satisfied with his sip, she emptied the rest of the vial into her mouth. She licked her lips and tossed it aside. "I know our Promise Ceremony is only days away . . . " Without taking her eyes off him, she released the braid of her hair, letting it fall loose before running her hands down her inciting outfit, touching herself in a way that wrenched a groan from his throat. She smirked. "But I would really like it if we could do a Choosing."

"A Choosing?" Declan echoed dumbly.

"Mmm . . . you see, where I come from, the women choose their men." She ran a finger down the front of his shirt, and her touch might as well have been liquid fire. Her hands skimmed back up to undo his buttons. "And I'd like for us to *mate* . . . in the fae sense."

She tossed his shirt, purring with desire as she stroked her brand over her chest. She began to circle him. Declan shifted, turning his body, wanting to keep his eyes on her as she moved around him.

Wildflowers sprung with her every step, caressing her ankles as though they, too, needed to touch her. She kept a hand on his body while she swayed to the beat of rustling leaves and sighing winds, her movements slow and erotic.

"I don't recall ever witnessing a Choosing," she murmured, her voice growing huskier. "But Gabriel was pretty descriptive."

Declan's eyes, which had grown progressively hooded, popped open. "*Gabriel?*"

She giggled, this time in sultry delight. She leaned teasingly close to give him a playful, nipping kiss. "Well, he didn't exactly prescribe such an outfit." And proving that she under-stood his concerns down to her core, she added, "I certainly haven't practiced any of this with *anyone* . . . so you don't need to kill him yet." She puckered her lips. "Which also means I may be a little awkward."

Railea's tears, if she got any more suave, he might not last her ceremony with his ego intact.

She doled out another kiss, this one so long and lingering Declan wanted to fall to his knees and worship her.

She held his gaze, enthralling him with eyes more striking than any sunset. "With the sun as my witness and the moon as my guide, I choose you."

She trailed slow, languid hands down his bare chest.

"As the roots delve into the earth and branches worship the skies, I choose you."

She took a sensual dip, hands caressing down his hips and legs before leisurely rising to cup his face as though he were the only star in the sky that she could see.

"For as long as the sky embraces the sea, I will rise where you rise, lay where you lay."

She swept around him in another bewitching circle where she paused behind him to press tiny kisses from his neck down his spine.

"My love for you will never falter, and my devotion will not fray. You are the keeper of my heart, the protector of my soul."

She paused, and her eyes brimmed with so much love he could hardly breathe.

"You will be the man I follow."

She stepped into her own circle of wildflowers to press her body close, pliant and perfect in the way she fit against him. "Will you accept my choosing?"

Did he need air to breathe?

"Yes," he whispered roughly. "By all that is holy, *yes*."

Then it occurred to him that she might require something

more eloquent from him. He racked his brain for something more expressive.

"I-I . . . I . . . " He couldn't seem to think. Not when she fixed those large, beautiful eyes on him, so he uttered the words oozing from his soul. "I love you, Evangeline. I love you. I love—"

With a soft, knowing chuckle, she saved him from the conundrum of his tangled tongue by treating him to her lips.

EPILOGUE

Dusk followed hard on her heels.

The last rays of the sun dimmed just as Freya darted into the palace walls. Felicity would soon be seeking her, and she didn't want her sister to worry. But Freya had spent every one of her sunlit hours in the Orchard of Solitude, huddled beneath the dappled shade offered by Mama's Soul Tree. No one could draw her away.

As the light drained from the sky, eerie shadows danced across the crenelated walls. Freya meandered along the hallway into the Courtyard of Song, where she knew Queen Katerina —Aunt Kati—had sequestered herself ever since Mama had passed. Ever since Papa had become obsessed with his war plans with the Winter Court.

The Courtyard of Song appeared different in the night. Darkness tended to shroud everything in gloom, yet there was something beautiful about the quiet stillness of shadows . . . and Freya couldn't help but wonder if it ever got lonely. Just like her.

"Aunt Kati?" Freya called hesitantly. Sure enough, a silhouette moved in the distance. The queen sat hunched in the middle of the courtyard, outlined by the glimmer of a moon not quite risen. Her profile was so much like Mama's that it made Freya's heart squeeze. She hurried to the queen's side.

"Aunt Kati?"

Her aunt glanced down at her as though startled from a daydream. Then she smiled a faraway smile that spoke of a broken heart Freya should have been too young to comprehend, yet she did.

"Why are you sitting here in the dark? Where is everyone else?" Freya couldn't remember the last time she'd seen her aunt without her entourage of ladies-in-waiting, bodyguards, and councilmen.

"Everyone is at war, my little starflower."

Freya frowned. "Even the servants?"

Aunt Kati drew in a trembling breath and wiped a hand over her eyes. "I've . . . just sent all the servants and the courtiers away."

Freya widened her eyes in alarm. "Even Felicity?"

Aunt Kati shook her head. "There is a different place for you and your sister. Quentin and his men have found an obscure village in Railea's realm he believes to be free from Zephyr's influence."

Railea's realm. Freya frowned. "The realm of mages?"

Aunt Kati nodded. "Once the Winter War is over, we will come for you."

Freya did not want to leave her home, but still, she nodded, not wanting to further upset her aunt. It mattered little where she went, so long as Felicie was by her side.

"But where did you send the servants and the courtiers?"

Aunt Kati ran gentle fingers across her hair and spoke words so soft Freya had to lean forward to glean them. "The mortal realm."

"The human world? Why wouldn't you send Felicie and me along with the rest of them?" Though it mattered not to her where she went, it didn't make sense for her to be separated from their people.

"Listen, my little starflower. The seer believes our people are doomed, but she has foreseen a small chance . . . ," The queen trailed her fingers down Freya's hair. "A possibility"—she gave Freya's nose a gentle tap—"that just might help our survival. Just as she believes our people have the greatest chance in the mortal realm."

Freya frowned up at her aunt.

What possibility could be had in the mage world? Mama had told her stories of mages. They manipulated things with their *minds*. She didn't like that. It defied all principles of magic.

The queen smiled that sad, faraway smile again. "It is for the best, child. Should your father and my generals fail, then it is best our people remain hidden among mortals. Zephyr is not one to relent."

Tears welled in Freya's eyes. She didn't want to think of Papa failing.

Aunt Kati sighed and drew her into a fierce embrace. "I am sorry, my dearest niece. Sometimes I forget you are only a little girl. But I can promise you this . . . should the Summer Court survive the Winter War, even by a single *seed*, our people will all come home."

THE END

... Or is it?
Blood Song (Warriors of the Five Realms Book 3)

Gabriel's story ;)
Coming November 2022. Show me some author love and
preorder here.

ACKNOWLEDGMENTS

What can I say? 2021 has been one hell of a year. The year I ticked off an item on my bucket list. The year I overcame my fears and put pieces of my heart out on public display.

The year I became a published author.

But 2021 wasn't just about publishing. It was a tumultuous year in many respects. Taxing. Exhausting. A year that challenged me like I'd never been before. So it isn't a stretch to say that without these legends, my books would never have seen the light of day.

Kelley Luna

Has it only been three years since we met? It feels like we've known each other forever. Thank you for holding my hand every step of the way. *Lullaby Scars. Little Fire.* And now *Winter Sun.* These books could never be what they are without you and your big heart. And I'm not talking about the editing, Kels. Thank you for keeping me upright.

Denali Day

Where would I be without you? Not self-publishing, that's for sure! Thank you for showing up for me where it counts, and for the incredible lengths you go to to ensure I don't drive myself into a ditch. You really are a powerhouse. One that keeps me charged with confidence. Thank you for helping me stand tall.

Tina Emmerich, Alyssa Morgan, Courtney Kelly and Aimee Moore

Your collective feedback helped shape Winter Sun into its final form. It's not easy trekking through over 100,000(unedited) words, but you did it with enthusiasm to boot. A thousand thank-yous. This baby author is forever grateful.

To my amazing ARC readers

I've said it before, but I'll say it again because I want it in print. There are too many of you for me to list by name, but I know who you are, and I treasure each and every one of you. I had no idea what to expect from an ARC team, but I think you've spoilt me. Thank you for making my debut such an incredible one. And thank you for coming back for Winter Sun.

2021 has been one hell of a year.

Thank you for being my bright spot amid the rough patches. :)

ALSO BY HOLLEE MANDS

LULLABY SCARS

(Warriors of the Five Realms Prequel)

Want a full-length, standalone freebie? Sign up for my newsletter to claim your gift. Lullaby Scars' e-book is exclusive for my newsletter subscribers!

He's the only man she's ever wanted. She's everything he can never have.

Killian's scars are all people see, but with his wretched past, he doesn't want them to look closer. He has long since resigned himself to live as an indentured slave to a powerful and capricious high mage —until a chance meeting with a temptress outside a brothel teaches him to *want*...

If only he hadn't asked her price for the night.

Lady Mailin's escape from her tyrannical father is so close she can taste it. All she has to do is to fake her magical prowess long enough for the high mage to sign a marriage contract and whisk her away. Then she'll lose him and start a new life. The last thing she needs is a tortured bondsman mistaking her for a woman who works on her back...

If only she could forget his gentle, callused touch.

When a stormy sea strands them together on Prison Island, Mailin and Killian's illicit desires may prove deadlier than the convicts out for blood. Or, worse.

They've spent their lives yearning for freedom. Can they survive long enough to make it last?

Little Fire

(Warriors of the Five Realms Book 1)

She's broken from a past she can't remember. He's scarred from a past he can't forget.

Declan can kill with a blink of his eye. Jaded and cold, he rules his kingdom the same way he does his heart—with ruthless pragmatism. So why does he risk all to protect a little mortal during a slave-trade uprising? Now stranded in the demon realm, the loss of his powers is the least of his troubles. The woman may have a frustratingly tender heart, but she has enough fire in her soul to thaw the ice in his veins.

He could take her by right, but he wants more than acceptance. He wants her willing surrender...

Evangeline is chained by a past she can't remember. Her fractured memories keep her shy and single. When she is thrust into a savage world in the arms of a deadly archmage, he becomes her only chance of survival. But soon she realizes her unnerving protector may not be as callous as he appears, and her heart may be as much at risk as her life.

His desire for her is no secret, but she wants more than scalding lust. She wants his icy heart...

Can they survive the nightmarish realm long enough to break down each other's walls?

ABOUT THE AUTHOR

Hollee Mands used to be that kid who sat at the back of the class, scribbling stories and doodling in dreary math workbooks. Much older and still unrepentant, she's now determined to bring her imaginations to life through the keyboard. When she isn't squirrelling away time to write, read, or sketch, she is a communications consultant, wife, and proud mom to a tiny dictator who has the speech patterns (and physical energy) to rival a steam train.

She currently resides in fickle-weathered Melbourne and is a proud member of Romance Writers Australia.

Connect with Hollee
www.holleemands.com
@holleemands

Made in United States
North Haven, CT
19 December 2022